**"ENJOY Y****ING WITH ROUTIER?"**
Michael asked coolly.

"I tolerated it," Abbey replied, noticing that he seemed perturbed. She found this highly amusing, given that he had just been dancing with his former lover. "And did you enjoy yours?" she asked.

"I would not even call it tolerable," he muttered. Michael frowned slightly and then pulled her onto the balcony, pushing her toward a dark corner.

"Is something wrong?" Abbey asked.

"Yes, something is wrong, Abbey. I have not kissed you all damned evening," he said, pulling her to him and claiming her mouth in a bruising kiss.

*"Michael,"* Abbey scolded, then smiled seductively.

He groaned and brought her hand to his lips. "Will there ever come a time when I don't want you?" he whispered.

"Bloody hell, I hope not."

Michael laughed and led her farther into the shadows.

# DELL BOOKS BY JULIA LONDON

*The Devil's Love*
*Wicked Angel*

The Rogues of Regent Street series:
*The Dangerous Gentleman*
*The Ruthless Charmer*
*The Beautiful Stranger*
*The Secret Lover*

# The Devil's Love

## JULIA LONDON

A Dell Book

THE DEVIL'S LOVE
A Dell Book

PUBLISHING HISTORY

Dell mass market edition published December 1998
Dell mass market reissue / September 2008

Published by
Bantam Dell
A Division of Random House, Inc.
New York, New York

This is a work of fiction. Names, characters, places, and incidents
either are the product of the author's imagination or are used
fictitiously. Any resemblance to actual persons, living or dead,
events, or locales is entirely coincidental.

Dell is a registered trademark of Random House, Inc., and the
colophon is a trademark of Random House, Inc.

ISBN 978-0-440-22631-4

Printed in the United States of America
Published simultaneously in Canada

www.bantamdell.com

OPM   16 15 14 13 12 11 10 9

To Nancy. for making me do it;
Jim, for giving me the time and space;
and to Meredith and Christine,
for believing I could do it

# The Devil's Love

# *Prologue*

The day dawned bright in brilliant contrast to the previous night's raging storm, which had all but sunk the merchant vessel. An exhausted young man lay sprawled against the hull of the ship, still a little green from his first battle waged against nature's wrath on the high seas. With his eyes closed and his body protesting against the slightest movement, he mused that it had been no less exacting than any battle he had ever fought on the continent.

A commotion above forced him to open one eye. Michael Ingram groaned when he spotted a little girl, dressed as a pirate, scampering about the quarterdeck. A scarf was tied about her dark curls, and her skinny legs were sticking out of a pair of men's pantaloons cut below her knees and belted at her tiny waist. She was barefoot and looked as if she had not seen the inside of a tub in weeks. She also was waving a wooden sword about, the very same wooden sword she had driven into his stomach two days before when she had leapt from behind a barrel yelling "*En garde*." On this beautiful, clear morning, she was shouting at something beyond the ship—no doubt at whitecaps, as she was fond of doing—and yelling about pirates.

"Good God, look at her," Michael muttered. Amid a pile of wood shavings, the man sitting next to him squinted up at the little girl. "Did you see her last night? In the worst of it, she was up there with the captain, waving that thing around as if she were fighting her make-believe pirates," Michael complained.

The older man shrugged. "She be a little girl, Ingram. You pay her too much heed," he responded in a typically gruff manner. Michael smiled. A bear of a man with fists that looked like hams, the giant had taken to the seas when the estate at which he had gardened most of his adult life was lost in an all-night gaming spree.

When Michael joined the crew, at first he had been very wary of the man. The rough crew outwardly resented the fact that he had been born to privilege. But circumstances—his father's oppressive debt, to be precise—had brought him to Carrington, a minor baron his family had known some years ago and a man with a solid reputation for having mastered the seas. He had struck a bargain with Captain Carrington that made the crew his bedfellows, and Withers the most frightening of them all. Yet it was Withers who had saved him from certain bodily injury—if not death—by grabbing the scruff of his neck and yanking him from a scrap with three other men. From that moment forward, Withers had been a staunch ally and protector of the young man.

The little girl spied the two men and waved furiously to them. Neither moved.

"Do not encourage her, whatever you do," Michael grumbled.

Withers grunted and turned his attention back to his whittling. "She ain't interested in me, lad. It's you she admires; that's why she torments you so."

Michael groaned again as the girl stooped to retrieve her doll before climbing down from the quarterdeck. Dragging the wooden sword behind her, she began to make her way through the storm debris on deck.

"She is a terror, that one. A bloody hellion. A menace to every man on this ship," Michael avowed. "Captain Carrington has no shame letting her run amok like that. I don't think the little beastie even owns a frock."

Withers glanced up as she began to run toward them. "She's a spirited thing, all right. Reckon that's why the captain brought her along when her mama died a few years ago. There'll be plenty of time for frocks and ribbons," he muttered as the girl skid to a stop in front of them.

"Did you not hear me? Land ahoy!" she announced breathlessly, then wiped her runny nose with the back of her hand.

Michael glanced at her scabby knees and the dirt caked on her bare limbs. He shielded his eyes from the sun and looked up at the little hellion's face. "There is no land, Abigail," he said with the strained patience of a weary parent.

The girl fisted her hands against her hips and scowled at him. "There *is* land, and I saw it first! It's a *pirate's* cove, and we are going to attack and steal their treasure!" she announced triumphantly, lifting her doll high above her head. "All men are to lend a hand to turn the ship about! That's the rule!"

"We are hundreds of miles from land," Withers said impassively.

Ignoring the big bear, Abigail thrust her doll in Michael's face. "*She* saw land too! Get to your feet, Michael Ingram, or my papa will have you flogged!"

"Abigail, run along," Michael said, waving his hand at her as if she were a gnat. With a swiftness that momentarily stunned him, Abigail dropped her doll and slammed her wooden sword down on his foot.

"*Ouch!*" Michael yelped, grabbing for the injured appendage. Abigail laughed loudly and raised her sword.

Michael scrambled to his feet and glared down at the little girl before she could do it again. She jutted out her chin, squared her shoulders, and glared right back. That is when Michael did the unthinkable. He grabbed the doll out of her hand and angrily wrenched the head from its socket.

"She *cannot possibly* see land without her head," he said, and thrust the mangled doll in her face. Abigail's fierce look crumbled into one of horror as she gaped at the maimed doll.

"Good God," Withers muttered to himself as the little girl's mouth twisted into a blood-curdling scream.

Dropping her sword, she whirled about, racing for the captain's cabin and screaming for her papa with each step. Her horrific screams brought half the sailors running toward the main deck looking as if they honestly expected to find pirates.

Withers pushed himself to his feet and clamped a large hand on Michael's shoulder. "Get below, lad. I ain't losing a perfectly good mate over this." He shoved Michael with all his might toward the door leading to the lower decks.

Without argument, Michael quickly disappeared below-decks with the broken doll, making his way through the darkened bowels until he reached his bunk. There he searched for a place to hide the incriminating doll parts. Finally, in desperation, he opened his trunk and buried them beneath his few personal belongings.

"That little beastie will be the death of me yet," he muttered as he threw himself on his bunk and slung an arm over his eyes.

Several days later Michael had a change of heart after seeing the despondent little girl search the deck for her doll. He was not so hard-hearted that the poignant face did not stir him at least a little. Deciding she had paid sufficiently for her crime, he determined he would repair the damage as best he could and return the doll. With some twine, he managed to secure the head to the body, but in the process, he ripped the doll's soiled dress. With a frustrated sigh, he held up the doll and studied it in the dim light of the lantern that swung above his bunk. An idea struck him, and well after midnight, he held up his creation for his bunkmates Withers, Bailey, and Hans to see. He had fashioned a pirate scarf out of the dress and had used a stick to make a peg leg where a cloth leg had once been. He had ripped the hem from the doll's bloomers and fashioned short pants like Abigail wore. With a square of dark cloth cut from his own coat, he had made an eye patch. The doll was transformed into a miniature version of Abigail the pirate.

"Perfect," Hans drawled. "A miniature hellion to haunt my sleep."

Michael laughed and tossed the doll into his trunk. But he never got the opportunity to return the doll to little Abigail. The next morning when the ship weighed anchor off the coast of Italy, Captain Carrington put Abigail on a small skiff to shore. To the collective astonishment of all hands, the little monster was dressed in a fashionable frock with satin ribbons and a lace collar. Rumor belowdecks was that she was too much for even the captain to handle, so accompanied by Carrington's solicitor, she was being hauled off to school, where a host of nuns would try to tame her. Mildly amused, Michael watched from the main deck, the doll dangling at his side. The little beastie stood defiantly in the middle of the small boat, ranting at her papa for sending her away. As the boat made for shore, she shouted at Captain Carrington that she would return with a *hundred* pirates, stabbing the air with her fist for emphasis.

Captain Carrington laughed and waved. "I look forward to the challenge, sweetheart!" he cheerfully called after her. Michael watched as the beastie accidentally knocked a sailor's cap into the water. The small boat circled round several times before they were able to retrieve it, Abigail screaming at Carrington the entire time. The men on deck laughed uproariously at the comedy below them, but Michael could only shake his head. *Good riddance,* he thought impassively.

# Chapter 1

Abbey Carrington stood at the bow of the luxury passenger ship with her hands stuffed into a muff. For the last hour she had watched intently as the coast of southern England grew increasingly larger, as had her excitement. She had anticipated this day well over half her lifetime.

She could not suppress a faint smile that curled her lips as she recalled the things her father had told her about her betrothed. Since she was a girl, Captain Carrington had told her Michael Ingram loved her dearly and could not wait for the day she would be old enough to be his wife. Although Abbey had not seen Michael since she was a child, her papa had seen him often and swore his esteem of her was steadfast.

His assurances had been constant and had begun when, at the age of nine, she had been sent to her first school in Rome. Her father, during a visit the following summer, had gleefully told her of the betrothal, laughing gaily when he told her how fervent Michael was in his desire to marry her one day. Abbey had, of course, been surprised by that, since Michael had grimaced painfully every time she came near him on board the *Dancing Maiden*. Her father had next come at Christmas, bearing a gift from Michael—a violin. Suspicious, Abbey questioned why her betrothed had not written. Captain Carrington assured her that Michael wanted a well-educated wife. He preferred she concentrate on her studies and not be distracted with letters. At the ripe age of eleven, Abbey had accepted that explanation without question.

Two years later her papa had removed her from the school in Rome, complaining it was too rigid. It was his considerable opinion that a girl needed to experience life, a sentiment that Abbey wholeheartedly shared. But apparently a girl did not need to experience life so much as to warrant sailing all the way to India, and her papa had placed her in the care of an old Egyptian friend while he continued east. Depositing her in Cairo, he had ruefully told her that Michael was greatly disappointed he was detained in Spain and could not visit her as he had planned. In her adolescent fervor, Abbey was quite touched by Michael's bitter disappointment; she had felt it rather keenly herself.

When she was older and had studied deportment and elocution in Paris until she could improve no further, she had been allowed to sail to the Orient with her papa. She remembered her father's sad sigh when he informed her they had missed her betrothed by just a sennight, but he had waited as long as he could for just a glimpse of his heart's love. He had left a message for her that she should continue her classical training on the violin and that he hoped she was enjoying the study of history, a subject he loved dearly. When she had voiced her doubts several months later, her father had chastized her for her faithlessness. Michael, he had reiterated, was quite steadfast in his esteem of her. It wasn't very long after they returned to Europe that Captain Carrington cheerfully reported a conversation he had had with Michael in Amsterdam, during which the young man had professed undying love and impatience for the day he would be reunited with Abbey.

Abbey pulled her cloak tightly about her and peered up through the masts at the dull gray sky. At last deemed old enough to marry, she was now only hours away from seeing the man she had dreamed of and admired since she could remember. Her father's constant compliments of Michael's military career, the enormous shipping trade he had built, and the fact that he was now the very important Marquis of Darfield kept him constantly in Abbey's consciousness. The captain delighted in relating stories of Michael's courage in a world of ruthless shipping magnates and pirates, of fair business practices for which he was exalted among his peers, and of his relentless chase of unsavory pirates, racketeers, and injustice in general.

Her papa had been so admiring of Michael Ingram for the last twelve years that Abbey could not imagine another man who could possibly compare to him. That he wanted her as a wife thrilled her. That she might not measure up mortified her. But her occasional doubts were easily erased with a new letter from her father. The fact that Michael had never written her *directly* or that she had not actually *seen* him in all that time did not daunt her. He had been too busy building a fortune, her papa had said, so that Abbey would never want for anything. And naturally the responsibilities of his very important title did not leave him time for leisurely correspondence.

Three years ago her father's consumption had taken a turn for the worse, and he had sent her to live in America with her aunt Nan. She had been waiting patiently since then, believing the captain's letters explicitly when he told her Michael would soon send for her and their days would be filled with love, laughter, and strong, healthy children. She believed everything Captain Carrington told her about the man who was to be her husband.

Fortunately, in Virginia, it had been easy to wait for Michael. Abbey loved living on her aunt Nan's farm with her cousins, Virginia and Victoria. She loved working in the fields by day and tending her small garden in the evening. With no men about the house—except for a few freed men and occasional gentleman callers—life on the farm had been idyllic. At night, while her cousins sewed and Aunt Nan painted, Abbey would play her violin. Or they would sit and talk. And when they grew tired of talking about the farm, the people in town, and the various men that called for them, they would talk of Michael.

In truth, they *all* dreamed of Michael. They would take turns imagining him standing at the stern of his ship, his open shirt blowing in the breeze, his long, dark hair tousled by the wind. They imagined him, his crew incapacitated, fighting off wave after wave of pirates by himself, and boasted to one another that his skill with the sword was the greatest in all of Europe. They imagined him spurning the attentions of dozens of beautiful women with the excuse that his heart's true love was in Virginia. That particular daydream always had Victoria swooning.

Abbey dragged her gaze from the sky and looked at the coastline where Portsmouth was beginning to take shape. It wasn't until her father's solicitor sent word of his death that Abbey had her first pangs of serious doubt. The solicitor, Mr. Strait, was adamant that Abbey leave for England right away, as the will demanded she settle her father's estate by marriage. Heartsick by the news of her father's death and privately uneasy that she had not heard anything about Michael in more than eighteen months, almost immediately Abbey had begun to fight waves of doubt. What if he had changed his mind and her papa had not had opportunity to tell her?

She pulled her cloak tightly about her as she recalled the day she had pleaded with her aunt to let her remain in Virginia.

*"Nonsense,"* Aunt Nan had said. *"Are you going to leave that poor man standing on the dock in Portsmouth waiting for you, his arms laden with two dozen roses?"*

*"Yes!"* Virginia had cried, *"he'll have his best coach, at least the size of Mama's parlor, with four grays waiting to take you away!"*

Aunt Nan had added he would probably sweep her to the altar that very day, for he would not be willing to wait for her one more moment. Abbey had paled at that remark. Aunt Nan had read her expression and cuffed her on the shoulder, sternly reminding her it was *every* woman's duty to follow their husband to the marriage bed, *without complaint*, and lie there patiently while he did *that*. Virginia and Victoria had snickered behind their hands as Abbey's expression had turned to horror, but Aunt Nan had insisted, *"You are not the first and you certainly won't be the last woman to make do with it."*

Otherwise oblivious to the bitter cold, Abbey unthinkingly pulled her hood up over her dark head as a steady rain began to fall, and recalled how her emotions had warred during the voyage. Part of her doubted that Michael esteemed her as her father had claimed. But then again, her papa would never lie to her, so it had to be true on some level. Part of her doubted he was the heroic figure she had dreamed about. After all, how many pirates could one man fell? But her papa had said he was that and more. Perhaps the stories had been embellished, but surely they were grounded in truth.

She sighed quietly as she absently counted the masts bobbing in the port ahead. The part of her that had seen Michael through her father's eyes all these years had finally won out over the doubts. She had nothing to fear. Michael Evan Ingram, Marquis of Darfield and Viscount Amberlay, loved her with all his heart and even now, was standing on the dock, waiting for her with two dozen roses in his arms.

She abruptly turned on her heel and marched back to her cabin. She was not going to meet the love of her life in anything less than her best traveling clothes.

Michael Evan Ingram did not meet her on the docks of Portsmouth' instead she was met by a severe-looking woman with coarse gray hair and brows knit into a permanent frown.

Despite the jostling crowd of passengers and stevedores that crowded the dock, Abbey found the woman. Had it not been for the wooden sign the woman carried with the words "Abigail Carrington" crudely painted, Abbey would have missed her.

"I'm Abigail Carrington," Abbey said uncertainly as she bobbed a quick curtsey. The woman's mouth puckered as she eyed her from the top of her head to the tips of her toes.

"Show your trunks to Mannheim there, and he'll load 'em," she said curtly. She then turned abruptly on her heel and, tossing the sign to the gutter, stalked toward a sleek black coach emblazoned with a coat of arms bearing the name Darfield. Abbey glanced nervously to the man she had indicated, who was every bit as bedraggled as the woman.

She refused to dwell on the fact that these people were the *last* thing she had expected. For some reason Michael had sent them, and therefore, there had to be more than met the eye. For the moment, she would not allow herself to wonder why he had not met her himself.

"Git in the coach. Too cold out here for a young lass," Mannheim said through a gaping smile as he struggled with her trunks. Abbey hesitated only briefly, the cold and thickening snowfall propelling her toward the coach. There were no coachmen—only a driver who did not even acknowledge her. Abbey timidly opened the door of the coach and peered inside.

"Git in, git in!" the woman barked, and shivered violently to make her point. Abbey hauled herself up, promptly tripping over her skirts onto a seat across from the woman.

"Mrs. Petty's the name. I been hired on to see you to Blessing Park," the woman growled.

"It's a pleasure to meet you, Mrs. Petty," Abbey replied, relieved the woman had finally spoken and eager to believe she had misjudged the old crone. "I, of course, am Abigail Carrington. Well, actually, I'm Abbey."

"I know who you are," the dour woman snapped.

Abbey ignored her nasty demeanor and smiled bravely. If there was one thing she had learned in a life of travel, a sincere smile was welcome in all ports. For all she knew, Blessing Park was halfway across the country, and she faced the distinct possibility that she could be in the company of this sourpuss for some time.

"Are you a relative of Lord Darfield?" she asked in an effort to make polite conversation.

The woman's red-rimmed eyes narrowed. "Certainly not!" she snapped.

Confused, Abbey bit her lower lip. "Is Lord Darfield at Blessing Park?" she asked in a tight voice, wondering just how far *exactly* she would have to travel with this woman.

"Don't know. Just hired on to escort you, not to fill a book on his whereabouts," she snarled.

Abbey nodded, mouthed the words "I see," and slid her gaze to the window. The snow was beginning to thicken, which did not help in the least to temper the feeling of pure dread that was beginning to build in her. The coach rocked as her trunks were loaded. Suddenly, the coach lurched forward.

"How far to Blessing Park?" Abbey asked cautiously once she had secured herself again.

Mrs. Petty bestowed a disdainful gaze on her. "Two hours on a good day. Slower in the snow."

Abbey smiled politely and wondered if her wait of twelve years for Michael Ingram was about to be eclipsed by a more interminable wait of two hours with Mrs. Petty.

They rode in tense silence for what seemed like hours to Abbey. The uncommunicative Mrs. Petty sat rigidly in her seat, staring vacantly out the window. Abbey was dying to ply her with questions but she wisely kept silent and allowed her thoughts to wander to excuses for why Michael had not met her.

Obviously something very important must have kept him, or he would have been there. She further deduced that Michael had been forced to hire an escort, and seeing how this appeared to be a very rural area, he obviously did not have many suitable candidates from which to choose. She guessed that he was now impatiently pacing in front of his hearth, having realized the snowfall would delay her arrival. He was undoubtedly very worried and was probably, at this very moment, calling for a mount, determined to search for her himself . . .

A jarring of the coach jolted Abbey from her daydream; it took her a moment to gather her bearings. She had sunk down against luxurious squabs. Slowly she pushed herself upright, stealing a glance at Mrs. Petty, who was sneering openly at her. Outside, the world was a blinding white; the thick snow obscured any remarkable feature in the landscape.

"Where are we?" Abbey asked.

"Pemberheath," Mrs. Petty grunted, then leaned forward to peer outside.

"Pemberheath?" Abbey did not expect her to answer, and not one to disappoint, Mrs. Petty did not. The coach of the door was suddenly thrown open, and the toothless Mannheim shoved his head inside.

"Message says to stay here overnight. Roads are bad," he said with a grunt.

*"Overnight?"* Mrs. Petty fairly shrieked.

Mannheim shrugged indifferently. "He left some coin and arranged for two rooms." With that his head disappeared and the coach door slammed shut.

Mrs. Petty turned a murderous gaze to Abbey as if she had caused the foul weather. "I ain't no nursemaid, miss. You got to fend for yourself," she snapped.

Abbey raised one finely sculpted dark brow and, biting back the stinging rebuke that she had never been waited on in her life and certainly wasn't going to start with the likes of her, answered coolly, "I am quite capable of fending for myself, Mrs. Petty."

Mrs. Petty mumbled something under her breath before flinging the coach door open. Without a word to Abbey, she climbed out and began to stalk away, taking giant steps in the deep snow. Finally she turned and glanced over her shoulder.

"Well? Come on, then!" she snapped, and disappeared into the white haze.

Abbey sighed wearily, pulled her hood up and climbed down from the coach. She certainly hoped Michael would show himself *soon.*

Despite the heavy snowfall, the common room of the small inn was very crowded. A group of boisterous men was gathered around the dart board, while smaller groups of men and a few women were scattered about rough-hewn tables. The stench of ale permeated Abbey's senses, as did the uncomfortable notion that heads swiveled toward her and lips curled at the sight of her.

Mrs. Petty had stopped to talk to a rotund man with a red, rubbery nose and a dirty apron stretched across his ample belly. He bent his head forward, listening, then motioned toward the stairs with the three empty tankards he held in one hand. Without looking back, Mrs. Petty began to make her way up a rickety staircase. Abbey supposed she should follow, and lifting her chin, she marched past the ogling men at the dart board, wended her way through the crush of tables, and up the stairs.

The room in which she found Mrs. Petty was small and sparsely furnished. A single bed was shoved up against one wall, just a few feet from a charcoal brazier that provided the only heat in the room. A mound of dirty blankets was stacked next to the single chair. The only other furnishings were an old basin and a small, tarnished mirror. Abbey glanced at Mrs. Petty, who was standing in the middle of the room with her feet spread apart and her hands on her hips.

She returned a sidelong look at Abbey. "Can't sleep on the floor. Got a bad back," she announced, and tossed her cloak on the bed. The woman was beginning to grate on her nerves. Whoever this old goat was, Abbey suspected she had been paid well enough to see her to her destination and could at least be expected to be civil.

"I will sleep on the floor provided you tell me how far to Blessing Park," Abbey said defiantly.

Mrs. Petty lifted her arms to remove her bonnet and shrugged. "Five miles, not more." She tossed her bonnet onto the chair before stooping to stir the coals in the brazier.

"Is Lord Darfield there?" Abbey asked as she removed her cloak and draped it across the back of the chair.

"I told you, I don't know. His *secretary* hired me on."

Abbey turned to the little window and rubbed the stiffness in her neck. Why on earth was it was too much to ask where her fiancé was and when he would come for her? *Calm down*, she told herself. She had waited all these years; surely one more night would not kill her. At least she certainly hoped it wouldn't.

"Is he going to meet us here?" she asked hopefully.

"You ask a lot of questions, missy," Mrs. Petty replied rudely.

Abbey groaned with exasperation, picked up the crone's bonnet, and tossed it on the bed. With a frustrated sigh, she sank into the chair, righting herself when it swayed precariously with her weight. Mrs. Petty was busy with the brazier, and Abbey watched as she fidgeted with the thing, noticing how rough the woman's hands were. She shifted her gaze to her feet, which were covered by a pair of old, cracked leather boots that looked as if they were as old as the woman herself. She felt a sudden, unwelcome pang of pity and could almost hear Aunt Nan urging her to be charitable. She was stuck with this woman at least for one night, and it would be to her advantage to befriend her.

"I'm rather hungry. Do you suppose they'd send up a tray?"

Mrs. Petty snorted derisively. "This ain't no fancy inn. You got to go downstairs if you're hungry."

"Will you join me? I would rather imagine you are hungry, too."

"It takes coin to eat at an inn," Mrs. Petty mumbled.

"I have coin," Abbey insisted.

Mrs. Petty peered suspiciously over her shoulder at Abbey. "Don't want your charity."

"It's not charity. Consider it my thanks for seeing me through a rather trying day," she said brightly, trying to make her expression as sincere as she could.

Mrs. Petty considered her another moment. "I ain't no duenna," she cautioned.

To Abbey, that suggestion was nearly as absurd as their present situation. "I really did not think you were, Mrs. Petty," she replied. "Come on then, I'm famished. And do you know, I think I would like an ale. Do you like ale?" Abbey started to move toward the door, and from the corner of her eye she saw Mrs. Petty stand and smooth her plain brown skirt.

"It ain't proper for a young miss to drink ale," she muttered disapprovingly as she patted her thin gray hair.

"Why, Mrs. Petty, that sounded positively like a duenna." Abbey laughed as she opened the door, and when Mrs. Petty passed, she mocked a curtsey fit for a queen behind the sour woman's back.


They were shown to one of two private rooms in the back of the inn. As they waited for the innkeeper to clear the table, Abbey noticed a man seated in the room next to theirs. He was sitting alone, his long, muscular legs stretched in front of him and crossed at the ankles. He had one hand on a tankard, the other shoved in the top of his buff trousers. He was much better dressed than the other patrons, with a neckcloth tied simply at his throat and a brown brocade waistcoat beneath a tan riding coat. He still wore his hat, and since he was sitting in the shadows, she could not see his face. The only thing she noticed was the red glow of the cigar that was clenched between his teeth. Suddenly conscious she was staring, Abbey nodded politely, then crowded behind Mrs. Petty into the other room.

Abbey ordered two ales and two pies, and as they waited, she perched her chin atop her fist and eyed the very stoic Mrs. Petty. They sat in complete silence until the innkeeper brought the food. Only then did Mrs. Petty make a guttural sound and attack the food with a gusto that suggested she had not eaten in some time.

And the meat pie was awful. Abbey picked at it while she sipped her ale, choosing to rearrange the carrots to one side instead of eating them. When Mrs. Petty wiped her wooden bowl clean, she eyed Abbey's expectantly until the young woman pushed it across the table to her. "Really, I am not hungry," she said, but it was plain Mrs. Petty did not care if she was or not.

"I was expecting Lord Darfield to meet me," Abbey prompted as she watched the woman dig into her second pie.

"That's a laugh," Mrs. Petty said with a mouthful of food.

Surprised, Abbey asked, "Why is that?"

"Well, to begin with, he's a marquis, and a marquis don't go to the docks to meet his visitor. The visitor comes to him." Mrs. Petty spoke as if she were talking to an ignorant child.

"I see your point"—Abbey nodded politely—"except that I am not really a visitor."

Mrs. Petty stopped her chewing and glanced up. "What are you then?"

"Why, I am his betrothed!" Abbey said with some astonishment. Surely Mrs. Petty knew *whom* she was escorting, but she stared at Abbey as if she had just announced she was the Queen of England and burst into laughter, revealing half-chewed food.

Abbey's brows rose. "May I ask what you find so amusing?"

Mrs. Petty managed to stop long enough to swallow her food in one big gulp. "Ain't every day a fine lass marries a rake," she said sarcastically. "Then again, maybe you *ain't* such a fine lass."

Abbey sat back as if Mrs. Petty had just slapped her, but she hardly noticed the slur directed at herself. She was mortified Mrs. Petty would defame Michael.

"A *rake*? How could you possibly say such a thing?"

Mrs. Petty sneered contemptuously as she propped her elbows on the table, a knife in one hand and a fork in the other. "Let me tell you about your *marquis*. The Devil of Darfield is an outcast. He never leaves Blessing Park cause he ain't allowed in any *reputable* establishment. . . . Why, he probably ain't even allowed in *here*."

Abbey started to tell the stupid woman that she had clearly confused Michael Ingram with someone else, but Mrs. Petty shook a fork at her and continued. "The whole town knows his father ruined the family name with all his gambling and drinking. Drank himself to death, he did. They say the devil set those debts to right by *pirating*—"

"Mrs. Petty! You are mistaken—"

"I ain't mistaken about a bloody thing, you stupid gel! He *stole* his wealth, he did! Oh, that family lived in a high and mighty style to be sure, but in shame! He didn't care. He kept right on pirating!"

"*Mrs. Petty!*" Abbey gasped with outrage. "How could you say such a vile thing!"

"Then his no-good sister got with child by some scoundrel and ran off with him, and his mama, she was so distraught she *hanged* herself out there at Blessing Park. And what did he do? Took to the seas and pirated some more, till he couldn't go nowhere. He's an outcast all right! I'm surprised he ain't been dragged off to Newgate by now." Mrs. Petty stabbed a piece of potato and thrust it in her mouth and eyed Abbey with a look that dared her to disagree.

Abbey's initial shock quickly gave way to fury. How dare this woman remark so bitterly on the most generous man in the world? She leaned slowly toward Mrs. Petty, who had gleefully resumed eating her pie. "You are very sorely mistaken. The marquis is an honest man, a gentleman, and a noble soul. The good deeds he performs in a single year would put both our lives to shame!"

Mrs. Petty snorted contemptuously and reached for her ale.

Abbey grabbed the tankard before her fingertips could touch it and pulled it toward her until she had the woman's full attention. "I know how such awful rumors start. I think people naturally become a little envious when a man of such character and ability lives modestly among them. It's almost as if one perceives their own inadequacies to be somehow pointed up by the unique qualities of someone such as Lord Darfield. But I assure you, he is not deserving of your malicious gossip. He is more of a man than the sum of those in the common room, and I will not allow you to defame him!"

Mrs. Petty growled and lunged for her ale. "Well, ain't you a Miss Know-All? Look at you, fresh off the boat from America with those pretty eyes and that pretty hair, thinking you know all there is to know about the scoundrel! You are naive if you think your *noble* marquis is going to marry you. He don't believe in legitimate bonds! If he got you here by telling you he was going to *marry* you . . . well, then you're a bigger fool than I took you for, and you'll soon be on a ship bound for America in ruin, mark my words!'' With that Mrs. Petty drained her tankard and slammed it down on the table for emphasis.

Abbey angrily gripped the side of the table and glared at the woman. "If you think so ill of him, Mrs. Petty, then I can only imagine you are escorting me out of the generosity of your own spirit, for *surely* you would not have accepted payment for services from such a scoundrel!''

The remark obviously hit home and brought Mrs. Petty up short; her mouth puckered as if she were eating a lemon. She slowly leaned across the table so that her face was only inches from Abbey. "Why, you miserable, no good little American *chit*! You'll get what you deserve with that no-account scoundrel!''

Suddenly sickened by the sight of the woman, Abbey pushed away from the table and stood. "If you are *quite* through . . . '' She was so furious she could not continue. She drew a ragged breath as she reached for her reticule and began to root frantically within it until she pulled out some coins, tossed them carelessly on the table, and leveled a reproachful gaze at her companion.

"You may say what you will of me, Mrs. Petty, but I dearly hope I *never* hear you defame Lord Darfield again, for I am quite certain I will cause you bodily injury. Now, I am going to retrieve my satchel from the coach and go to bed. Please have *another* pie and more ale. I would not want you to spread your vicious lies on an empty stomach,'' she said, and turned abruptly from the table.

She was so livid she marched right into the middle of the common room without so much as a glance about and, with her hands on her hips, searched for Mannheim. Finally she spotted him across the crowded room, sitting at a table with the driver behind several empty tankards. He saw her at the same time and stood uncertainly, grasping the table for support.

"Something wrong, miss?" he asked when she had finally pushed her way through the crowd and to his table.

"Mr. Mannheim, if you would be so kind, I require a small green satchel I left in the coach," she said stiffly.

The man slid his bloodshot gaze to the driver, who had yet to look at Abbey, and then back to her. He swallowed an ale-soaked belch as he seemed to consider her request and slowly let go his grip on the table.

"Yes, mum," he muttered, and pushed past her toward the door. Abbey stood firmly rooted to her spot, her hands on her hips, and her chest heaving with each furious breath, oblivious to the chaos around her. Good *God*, she hoped Michael would come for her in the morning; her return to England was *not* getting off to a very good start.

As her temper began to cool, she gradually became aware that the din had lessened and had the awful feeling that all eyes were upon her. She turned slowly to look over her shoulder, her eyes widening slightly at the sight that greeted her. Several men at the dart board had stopped their play and were sheepishly staring at her behind the broad back of a very large, very ugly man. He was looking at her with a leer on his lips that made her want to poke out both his eyes. She turned to face him and folded her arms across her middle. The fingers of one hand drummed her arm as she angrily stared right back.

The men did not intimidate her. She had been in plenty of inns such as this with her father and had seen much worse in different corners of the world. In Virginia she and her aunt and cousins often had been in situations in which they were the only females.

She was about to ask the men to kindly stop ogling her when Mannheim shoved through the door, shaking the snow from his threadbare coat and clutching her satchel. His glazed eyes grew wide with fear when he realized the men were engaged in something of a silent standoff with Abbey. He hurriedly made his way through them and hastily thrust the satchel at her.

"Best git upstairs, miss," he mumbled, and surreptitiously eyed the men from the corner of his eye.

"Thank you, I believe I will do just that," she snapped. She had taken two steps toward the stairs when the big, ugly man stepped deliberately in her path. Abbey stared at his barrel chest, then squared her shoulders and looked up at him.

"Please excuse me, sir," she said coolly. He grinned; she recoiled at the stench of his breath.

"Eh, Danny. The lass wants you to egg-*scuse* her," someone called, and they all snickered. That made Abbey angry. Men could be so childish!

"Me and the lads want you to join us for a game," Danny said, brazenly shifting his gaze to her bodice.

Abbey stiffened; she *hated* the lewd look in his eye. Why did men always have to look at her so? Unbeknownst to her, the well-dressed man from the private dining room had moved to the common area, and watched her from the shadows beneath the stairs. When Danny stepped in front of her, he took a step forward.

"I am really very tired," she said, and stepped sideways, intent on going around him. Danny matched her movement and blocked her path again. Behind him, the men snickered disparaging comments to one another.

"Leave her be. She belongs to the marquis, she does," Mannheim said.

Danny slid little black eyes to Mannheim. "You the marquis's man?"

Mannheim shifted uncomfortably. "No," he answered truthfully.

"Then stay out of it. Possession is the law, and the marquis ain't here to defend what's his," Danny said with a growl. A hush fell over the room as patrons stopped their conversations and turned expectantly to watch the exchange between them.

Abbey glared up at the man. "Really, you make it sound as if I am a milk cow. No one possesses me, and no one tells me I must play darts."

"I'm telling you, lass. You *will* play." His tiny eyes shifted to her mouth, the leer touching his lips again.

"Your insistence is quite rude," she said almost casually. Danny laughed nastily and glanced over his shoulder. "She thinks me rude, lads. I reckon this pretty little thing don't know what rude is.'' From the corner of the room, the tall man took another step forward and slipped his hand into his pocket.

"Be a good lass and play darts,'' Danny said mockingly.

Abbey sighed and cocked her head to one side while she considered him, knowing full well she was going to have to throw a dart in order to leave the room. "And if I refuse?''

"Don't matter to me. I'll hold you so's you play, or you can play of your own accord.''

With a sigh of exasperation, Abbey slammed her satchel down onto a chair next to her. "Very well then, give me the blasted darts! If I throw and hit the king's eye, then I shall retire to my room. *Alone,*'' she added with a nod of her head. "If I throw and *miss* the king's eye, then I shall treat you to a tankard of ale, agreed?'' she asked as she motioned impatiently for the darts.

"If you miss the king's eye, you are mine,'' the man replied, then licked his lips as his gaze shamelessly swept her feminine figure. His companions hooted their encouragement.

"I shall treat you to an ale, but I am most definitely *not* yours.''

A lopsided smile curved on Danny's lips. "Whatever you say, lass,'' he said patronizingly, and stepped aside.

"As if this day could be more absurd,'' Abbey muttered to herself, and stepped up to the line that had been drawn across the floor. Without hesitation, she drew her arm back and hurled a dart, landing it squarely in the king's eye. A collective gasp went up from the common room, followed by startled silence. The men stood, slack-jawed, as they stared at the dart protruding from the king's eye. They were in such a state of shock that Abbey had to nudge a man standing next to her to take the remaining darts from her hand.

"Good night, sir,'' she said simply, and while the men stared with disbelief at the board, Abbey grabbed her satchel and fairly flew across the room.

Danny turned abruptly and made a move to come after her.

But his gaze shifted to the tall man standing just below the stairs, and with a final glance at Abbey's retreating back, he slowly stepped back and turned away. The tall man stepped back into the shadows, withdrew a cheroot, and settled his shoulder against a post underneath the stairs to stand vigil.

# Chapter 2

Abbey slept fitfully on the mound of dirty blankets, fighting the nagging thought that something was not quite right and waiting for Mrs. Petty to return. When the first gray rays of light filtered in through the small window, she rose, washed as best she could in the ice-cold water at the basin, then donned a plum wool traveling gown.

Surely Michael would come for her this morning. Surely he had been detained by the weather and would have come for her last evening if he had been able. *Surely* he *never* intended her to stay with Mrs. Petty or at this inn this long. Refusing to let herself think there was any other explanation, she forcibly buried any doubt. She clasped her hands tightly together and pressed them against her stomach, unsure if the queasy pangs she felt were hunger or nerves. Then she crossed to the small window and looked out at the village. The storm had passed, and the streets and thatch-covered roofs were blanketed in a thick layer of pristine snow. She mumbled a quick prayer that the roads would be passable and she could soon leave this awful place.

*          *          *

In the small courtyard below, Lord Samuel Hunt oversaw the preparations for the trip to Blessing Park. In addition to the driver and Mannheim, he had two outriders with him for the last leg of Miss Carrington's journey. It was a precaution he had taken himself; Michael had seemed unconcerned for her safety when he had summoned him and asked him to fetch his fiancée. He frowned as he tested the ropes that held her trunks to the back of the coach. What could Michael have been thinking when he had hired Mrs. Petty? Sam had dismissed her abruptly last evening after hearing her outrageous lies. He knew wild rumors circulated about Michael, but personally he had never heard such venom from anyone. His frown melted into a quiet smile as he recalled Miss Carrington's response to the accusations. She was nothing as Michael had described, nothing at all.

In the first place, she was not homely.

Far from it, Sam mused. Her dark mahogany curls were offset by flawless, porcelain skin and full lips the color of roses. She was a classic beauty, with high cheekbones and a small, straight nose. And her eyes—good Lord, they were magnificent. A peculiar and remarkable shade of violet, framed by thick, dark lashes.

Even more remarkable than her exquisite looks was the way she had stared that ruffian down and then hit her target with the dart. Sam chuckled to himself as he returned to the inn. He had never seen anything like it, and he could hardly contain his glee as he anticipated Michael's reaction to a woman he had described as a savage little hellion.

Outside her room, Sam sent away the outrider who had guarded her door through the night with instructions that they would leave within the hour. Then Sam rapped lightly on Miss Carrington's door. When she did not answer, he rapped again, a little more insistently. After a pause, he heard the bolt sliding, and then the door was yanked open.

Miss Carrington stood before him in a gown that accentuated her remarkable eyes, which at that particular moment were narrowed with suspicion. She studied him for a moment before her finely shaped brows snapped into a frown.

"*You* are not Michael Ingram!" she said angrily, and before Sam could respond, she whipped a small pistol from behind the deep folds of her skirt and pointed it straight at his chest. "I am no more interested in playing games this morning than I was last evening, sir. If you value your life, you will retreat down those stairs and not bother me again. Do not think for one moment I will not use this if I must," she said in a calm voice that belied the small tremor in her hand.

Sam slowly raised his hands, took a step backward, and bowed gallantly. "I have no intention of forcing you into a game of darts, Miss Carrington. I am Lord Hunt, a personal friend of the marquis, and I have come to see you to Blessing Park."

Abbey cocked her head to one side and considered that but did not lower her gun. "If you will pardon me, sir, I have had quite enough *escorting*. Certainly I would not get into a coach with a strange man."

Mildly amused, Sam arched a brow. "I applaud your caution. However, the Marquis of Darfield has asked me to escort you, posthaste, to Blessing Park," he said, steeling himself for the possibility he might have to carry her down the stairs and put her in the coach.

Abbey dropped the gun to her side. "*Really?*" she asked softly, suddenly looking very vulnerable. It occurred to Sam that she had traveled thousands of miles to marry a man she had not seen or heard from since she was a child. Coupled with her experience thus far in England, it was undoubtedly all very overwhelming.

"Indeed he did. The weather, of course—"

"I *knew* it!" she exclaimed happily, waving the gun carelessly. "I *knew* he would have come for me had it not been for the snow!" In a sudden whirl of plum, she flew across the room to her satchel. Sam had been about to say that the weather prevented him from escorting her last evening, but seeing the gloriously happy look on her lovely face, he did not dare contradict her. Abbey stuffed her pistol into the satchel, donned her cloak, grabbed her muff, reticule, and satchel, and started for the door, then stopped abruptly.

"I can't go until I know what has befallen Mrs. Petty. She did not return from supper last evening."

"Mrs. Petty is well enough, I can assure you, but she has been discharged from her duties. I will ask the innkeeper to see that her things are returned," Sam said, and motioned toward the corridor.

Abbey glanced skeptically at the woman's articles of clothing.

"On my honor, Mrs. Petty is quite all right," Sam said again.

Abbey lifted her gaze, studying him, then cautiously preceded him down the stairs. In the common room, she declined Sam's suggestion that she eat something and headed straight for the coach. She could not get away from Pemberheath fast enough to suit her. Clearly, her doubts about Michael, colored by the malicious accusations of Mrs. Petty, had been wrong. With a fat smile, she settled back against the high cushion and tucked the lap rug about her. The fears that had plagued her since she had disembarked in Portsmouth seemed laughable now. She had been nervous and unfamiliar with the ways of the English, nothing more. It was the snow, that was all. He could not come because of the snow.

Everything was going to be fine, just fine.

Sam appeared after settling with the innkeeper and climbed in, taking a seat across from her. He smiled as he signaled for the driver to proceed, then settled back against the squabs, stretching his long legs across the coach.

Abbey smiled brightly as they lurched forward. "Is it very far to Blessing Park?"

"Five miles or so. May take some time because of the snow."

"Is Lord Darfield there?"

"Of course."

Abbey sighed with obvious relief. "He must be very impatient," she remarked with a smile, then shifted her gaze to the window. "He has been waiting such a very long time to marry."

Sam was startled by her apparent assumption that Michael somehow *wanted* this preposterous marriage. "Do you remember him?" he asked uncertainly, to which Abbey looked surprised.

"Of course!"

"Lord Darfield told me it was quite some years ago when last he saw you. You could not have been more than a child," Sam explained.

Abbey's laugh was gentle, lilting. "You are quite right, of course . . . Lord Hunt, isn't it? I was only a child when I last saw him in the flesh, but my father had sketches made of him over the years—"

"Sketches?" Sam interjected incredulously.

"Oh yes, several sketches! You see, Lord Darfield could not come to visit me—we were forever in different ports—so when Papa had occasion to see him over the years, he had sketches made of him. He had one crewman who was particularly talented with a piece of charcoal and would send the sketches to me so I would not forget what he looked like. And, of course, he would send sketches of me to Lord Darfield, as he was always badgering Papa for a glimpse of me."

Sam seriously doubted that Michael had seen any of those sketches, or else he would not have described her so falsely to him. He also seriously doubted that Michael had ever badgered Captain Carrington for *anything*, with the possible exception of being released from the absurd agreement. "Your papa sounds like a kind man."

Abbey smiled, her full lips stretching across a row of straight, white teeth. "He was *very* kind, and very good to me," she said, a distant look clouding her eyes for a moment. "But, I think, not as good as Lord Darfield has been to me," she added softly.

Sam managed to hide his great surprise behind a cough. *"Lord Darfield?"*

"From the time I left the ship, apparently I was never far

from his thoughts," she said wistfully, and looked out the window. "My first year at school in Rome, he sent me a violin. He is a great lover of music, you know, and thought it would be very nice of me to learn to play."

Stunned, Sam was almost afraid to ask. "Did you?"

"Certainly! And the times when I despaired of ever mastering the silly thing, Papa would tell me that Michael . . . Lord Darfield . . . was so looking forward to hearing me play, I would try even harder. And he would send little trinkets, too," she said, flicking one of the amethyst earrings dangling from her earlobes. "He sent *these* on my sixteenth birthday. When I was bound for Egypt, he sent me a history book on the Egyptian culture, so I would know what to expect. I am particularly grateful to him for that, for certainly I would *never* have expected what I found there!"

"Lord Darfield sent you those things," Sam stated doubtfully.

Abbey seemed oblivious to his surprise and smiled warmly. "He's quite thoughtful, isn't he?"

Sam frowned. "But you never saw him."

"Well, not in *person*. But he kept in constant contact with my father."

In disbelief, Sam stared at the foolish young romantic, who was quite oblivious to his astonishment. Surely she could not be so naive. Something was terribly wrong. Sam had known Michael Ingram since they were young men. Never once had Michael mentioned a word of Abigail Carrington, until a few days ago, when he had requested Sam's presence at Blessing Park to assist him in an "indelicate matter."

That matter, as it had turned out, was an accursed *agreement*, which Michael had been forced into at the age of nineteen so that he might borrow money and pay the debts his father had amassed. Michael had turned to Captain Carrington, seeking out the very wealthy captain in a desperate bid to save his family from complete ruin.

The captain had been more than happy to oblige. The agreement they reached stipulated that if Michael had not repaid his debts in full by the time Captain Carrington died, he would take Abigail Carrington to wife. What at one time had seemed a rather innocuous arrangement to care for an only child had turned into a nightmare for Michael. At the time he signed the agreement, he had been unaware of the importance of a simple clause that stipulated any other debts incurred by Michael or his family against Carrington were subject to the same terms until all debts were paid in full. Michael did not know, until two months ago when the papers arrived, that his father had borrowed repeatedly from Carrington. As Michael explained it to Sam, he could no more extract himself from the agreement than he could remove his own skin.

"The agreement is explicit, Sam. My solicitors have reviewed the documentation and advise me it fully supports the claim that our debts were never repaid in full, despite the fact that I could have given the captain double what was owed. It would seem that my father gambled and drank away the entire family fortune not once but twice," Michael had explained bitterly, "and neither he nor the captain ever saw fit to tell me. I would expect as much from Father, but not Carrington. He never told me of the accumulating debt."

"But surely there is a way out! Are there no male relatives?"

"A son of a cousin somewhere, but it hardly matters. In the most legal sense of the word, the agreement is rather tight. Carrington was very artful in crafting the settlement of his estate to depend upon its execution. The captain tied so many other financial transactions to this marriage that I would have several creditors after my assets were I to try to remove myself."

"What are you saying, there is nothing you can do?" Sam asked incredulously.

Michael sighed and shook his head. "I'm afraid it's worse than that. I had thought that I could delay the marriage indefinitely, but the captain made sure other debts will go unpaid until a wedding occurs. My family stands to lose everything, as do several of the captain's business associates." He paled visibly as he spoke and turned away from Sam to stare blankly at the portrait of some ancient ancestor.

"He was a determined man, Sam. He made sure she and her family would not balk. Not only did he stipulate a rather large sum to his sister for relinquishing the little hellion to England, but his will entails all of her funds in this marriage." Michael sat up abruptly and perched his elbows on the desk so he could rub his temples.

"Meaning?"

"Meaning that Carrington's daughter has no access to money and loses it irretrievably if she does not marry me. The choice is solely hers; legally, only she may end it. But in that event, all of her dowry, save a small annuity, will go to pay his creditors."

"*What?*"

"Everything will be lost if I do not marry her," Michael said evenly. "My sister, my uncle's widow, my cousins as well, and at least three of Captain Carrington's business associates of whom I am aware. The will outlines the actions to be taken to collect on my outstanding debts as well as Carrington's."

Sam's indignation for his friend had mounted at a rapid pace. "Can't you pay the debts? You are a very wealthy man!"

"I need almost a million pounds—cash—today. I am a wealthy man, true, but it would take a considerable amount of time to liquidate my investments or access my funds on the continent to raise that amount."

Michael got up and crossed to a sideboard, poured himself a whiskey, downed that, and poured another. Sam followed helplessly behind him and helped himself to a brandy.

"In your assessment, there is no hope, no way out?" Sam asked again. Michael nodded slowly. A silence fell between the two men until Sam asked cautiously, "Is she so bad?"

Michael shrugged indifferently. "I remember a savage little hellion, dirtier than a pigsty and more mean-spirited than any man I have ever met. And in addition to that distant nightmare, for some reason, I balk at being forced into marriage. For the life of me, I cannot determine why Carrington heaped this upon me. Whatever his scheme was, it was worth enough to bestow a dowry of almost five hundred thousand pounds on her.''

"Five hundred thousand pounds!" Sam exclaimed.

"Rather a large dowry, wouldn't you agree?" Michael quipped.

Large? It was unheard of, Sam thought as he watched Michael resume his seat behind his desk, rub the back of his neck, and stare blindly at a stack of papers. Sam pitied his friend; he had suffered so much in his life. First, there had been the way the *ton* had turned their back on the family when his father amassed debts reaching unspeakable sums. They were pariahs, treated as if they did not exist when in town, and were forced to retreat to Blessing Park and live in solitude. From what he could gather, Michael's younger sister, Mariah, had been his only true friend growing up in the shadow of a drunken, cruel father. When Michael took to the seas with Carrington, his sister had suffered greatly from the ill treatment. She was shunned by the *ton,* and after a very disappointing debut, was courted by Malcolm Routier, an unsavory character with a dark reputation. Michael, acting in his incapacitated father's stead, had refused Routier's offer for Mariah's hand. That had caused Mariah much grief, and for a period of time she refused even to talk Michael. But time passed, and she had, at last, married a Scot and moved to the remote Highland regions where Michael had said she was happier than she had been all her life.

Mariah's departure had been difficult for him, particularly since her leaving was followed quickly by the untimely and accidental death of his mother. During a walk around the park one day, she had tripped and fallen over a ledge. In a freak mishap, her scarf had caught between some rocks and hanged her. Of course, the family's scandalous reputation only heightened the rumors that she hanged herself and, in some circles, that she had been hanged, with a suspicious eye cast in Michael's direction. It was not long afterward that Michael's father had at last succumbed to the liver ailments that had been brought about by years of overindulgence.

Michael had worked hard to restore the family name, but

after each scandal he had retreated further and further into himself, shunning legitimate relationships and dallying with loose women. He rarely went to London, and when business required it, he typically arrived late at night and left the same way.

Michael understandably despised the *ton,* but his elusive behavior had worked to make him all the more interesting to Polite Society. After a few years had passed between his father's death, *everyone* wanted to meet the Marquis of Darfield or, at the very least, get a glimpse of him. Michael resented that, and rarely left Blessing Park except to go to sea.

Until last year. That was when he had met Rebecca Davenport, a pretty, young widow. An attachment had developed between them that drew Michael out of his self-imposed banishment. Sam had been happy to see Michael appear in London during the last Season, if only for a fortnight. The *ton* had exalted in the presence of the elusive marquis. The same people who had once turned their backs suddenly showered him with invitations. Women threw themselves in his path, and men tried desperately to get him to sit at their tables in their exclusive clubs. Michael had endured it for Rebecca's sake for as long as he could but had finally retreated to Blessing Park. He confided to Sam he despised the *ton* more than ever, and not even Rebecca could persuade him to stay in London. Their liaison had almost ended over Rebecca's need to be seen and Michael's need to be left alone.

Now this. Sam felt an unwanted pang of sorrow. If word were to get out that he was forced to marry because of debt, a fresh scandal would erupt, vaulting Michael to the status of blackguard once again. It was grossly unfair.

"How can I help you, Michael?" Sam finally asked. Michael had shrugged and dragged his gaze to his closest friend.

"If you would, go and get the little hellion. I suppose there will be a wedding in a day or two," he had replied, obviously resigned to his fate.

# Chapter 3

After a long, grueling trip through the snow, the coach finally pulled up outside the pink sandstone Georgian mansion. Abbey guessed the house to be three stories; it was at least as large as the grandest state house she had ever seen. But at the moment, it held much less interest for her than the prospect of seeing Michael. After all these years, excitement, anticipation, and a bad case of nerves descended on her as she waited impatiently for Lord Hunt to help her down from the coach.

She was disappointed when the front door opened and a middle-age man hastened out into the snow. Behind him another, slightly older man waited at the door, twisting his white-gloved hands nervously together. The younger man glanced at Abbey without really seeing her, then back to Sam.

"Lord Hunt, don't *tell* me you could not locate her!" he said sharply.

"Don't be an idiot, Sebastian. *This* is Miss Carrington," Sam said gruffly.

Sebastian jerked his gaze to Abbey and stared in astonishment. "M-Miss Carrington?" he stammered. Then recovering quickly, he bowed and swept his arm toward the manor. "Miss Carrington, if you please," he murmured.

Abbey laughed tautly. "Should I conclude from your reaction that you were expecting a woman with two heads?"

"Certainly not!" Sebastian blustered, and motioned again toward the door.

Abbey dashed lightly across the snow to the foyer. Inside, the gentleman in black bowed deeply.

"Welcome to Blessing Park, Miss Carrington," he intoned. "I am Jones, the butler. May I take your cloak?"

"Is Lord Darfield here?" Abbey asked as she shed her coat, blithely ignoring the stunned look on the butler's face while she smoothed the wrinkles from her skirt.

"The marquis is here and awaits you in his private study."

She had understood when he had not come to Portsmouth for her, but she thought he could at least greet her at the door. Jones and the man named Sebastian stood watching her warily, as if they expected her to do something odd, such as flee. The thought did cross her mind, but she took a deep breath instead to dispell any doubts.

"Which way to the study, then?" she asked no one in particular. Sebastian stepped forward, gestured off to the right, and began to walk briskly down a long corridor of rich blue carpet and walls covered in silk.

"The marquis is waiting, Miss Carrington. We expected you an hour ago," he said. Sebastian turned down another long corridor, his walk becoming even more brisk until he came to a set of double walnut doors and stopped. He glanced at her briefly before swinging the doors wide open. He nodded to someone inside; Abbey's nerves surged to her throat. Aghast, she realized her knees were suddenly shaking. She looked frantically to Sebastian.

"Is he in there?" she whispered, ashamed that her voice shook.

"Yes, ma'am," he said, and stepped aside.

Abbey stood stricken, staring at the door. After all these years, she was happy to be reunited, of course she was, but the ugly thought that he might not find her to his taste, or find her unaccomplished, or even *vapid* began to tumble in her brain. She looked helplessly to Sebastian, then to Sam.

"I—don't think . . ." she started. Sam stepped forward immediately and offered her his arm and a sympathetic smile.

"I'm a bit flustered, I suppose. It has been a very long journey . . . one might argue a journey of a lifetime, and I . . ." She was unaware that she was fiercely clutching his arm.

Sam pulled her fingers from their death grip of his arm. "It is quite natural to be a little anxious," he said calmly.

Perhaps he was right, and perhaps she could stand outside the open door all day until her nerves had settled. What foolishness. Michael had waited long enough, and so had she. Smiling bravely, Abbey took a deep breath and lifted her chin high. With all the bravado she could muster, she swept through the doors of the study, with Sebastian, Sam, and Jones crowding in the doorway behind her.

He was leaning against a massive writing table, his weight settled on one hip, his arms folded across his flat stomach as he eyed her. His inky black hair was wavy and thick, and brushed past his collar. His breeches hugged his muscular thighs until they reached his polished Hessians. His gray eyes narrowed as he perused her, and unthinking, Abbey gasped with sheer joy. She had, of course, recognized him immediately. Perhaps he was a little taller and a little fuller, and his skin bronzed by the sun, but he looked *exactly* like the Michael she remembered.

Only more handsome. Impossibly handsome.

She was propelled by an unseen force toward him, her gaze locked with his fierce one. "Michael!" she exclaimed as she approached him, appalled by the nervous pitch in her voice and forgetting her manners.

He raised a brow. *"Michael?"* he repeated incredulously.

Abbey walked slowly, taking in every detail of him, from the way his brows burrowed into a frown, to his full lips set in an implacable line, to his strong jaw clenched tightly shut.

He was magnificent.

And he was not happy to see her.

Abbey stopped and peered into his stoic face. No, perturbed was more accurate. Surely she was misreading him. Perhaps *his* nerves were frazzled, too. Her laugh was softly nervous. "Were you expecting someone else?" she joked, immediately wishing she had not, and smiled expectantly.

Michael did not answer right away but blatantly studied her, his frown deepening all the while. She flushed under his intense scrutiny and attempted to dissuade him by smiling, but to no avail. The man who stood in front of her now looked angry and a little disappointed.

"I daresay I was," he finally answered with a coolness that Abbey immediately took for indifference. Her worst fear, that he would not find her to his liking, seemed to be becoming a reality.

"You were?" she asked with some confusion. The small seed of doubt she had so admirably quashed was now growing wildly out of control. He was supposed to be telling her of his great esteem and how interminable his wait had been. Instead it seemed he did not want her, did not even like her in fact!

"Is—is something wrong?" she forced herself to ask, despite the blasted tremble in her voice.

"I'm rather taken aback. You do not look like the Abigail Carrington I recall," he said bluntly.

Abbey's violet eyes grew wide as it dawned on her that he must not remember her. The fact that *he* might not remember *her* had not once crossed her mind. She laughed with great relief. "Oh, dear, I thought certainly you knew me as I did you! Perhaps my sketch artist was not as skilled as yours."

"I beg your pardon?" he asked coolly.

"It's been quite a long time, has it not? I know the waiting must have been unbearable for you; it certainly was for me," she said, and smiled broadly, like a simpleton, she thought, as she desperately looked for some sign of warmth from him.

Coolly dismissing the others, Michael pushed slowly from his perch, and walked around the writing table to take a seat. She remained rooted to her spot, looking at him as if she had seen an apparition. Very reluctantly, he silently acknowledged that she was even lovelier than he had fist thought when she had crossed the threshold. In fact, he thought, she was remarkably beautiful, which served only to increase his agitation. He could see a resemblance to the little hellion, but the transformation from the image in his mind's eye to the woman before him was more than his brain could comprehend. Gone was the look of stunned confusion, and in its place, an expression so benign that the only hint of anxiety came from her fist clutching at the skirt of her gown. *Don't be a fool,* he told himself. *This woman is the same hellion.*

"You may help yourself to some tea," he decreed curtly, and motioned impatiently toward the silver service.

Abbey frowned slightly and warily took a seat on the edge of the settee. She seemed to be unsure about the tea, and eyed the silver service suspiciously before finally pouring a cup. As she added two cubes of sugar, Michael cleared his throat.

"Abigail—"

"Abbey," she interjected softly as she reached for more sugar.

Michael snapped a cool gaze to her. "I beg your pardon?"

"Abbey. I am called Abbey," she said, and dropped two more cubes of sugar in the cup.

"That's quite enough." At Abbey's look of surprise, he gestured toward her teacup and clarified, "Quite enough sugar." He no earthly idea what made him say that; he certainly could not care less how much sugar she put in her tea.

She paused for a moment, then shrugged, and he averted his gaze to the window while she stirred her tea. He listened to her dainty sips before speaking again.

"We have much to discuss." When she did not respond, he continued without so much as looking at her.

"First, may I say I hope your voyage was uneventful," he began with smooth, practiced politeness. He looked at her from the corner of his eye; she was staring blankly at him.

"As for our . . . *predicament*—"

"Predicament?"

"Our *predicament,*" he repeated, spitting out the word as if it were acid, "the terms of your father's will dictate I act with some haste." He paused, momentarily unsure how to proceed.

Abbey was uncertain as to what was happening. He seemed exceedingly resentful, and the brusque tone of his voice was making her stomach churn. This was quickly turning into her worst nightmare. Nothing was as she had envisioned. Where was the armful of roses they had been so certain he would give her? The reminders of how long he had waited? For goodness' sake, why was he so disagreeable? She glanced at the sideboard where several crystal decanters of brown liquors were kept. She did not think she had ever tasted whiskey in her life—despite the fact that Aunt Nan was quite enamored of the stuff—but it suddenly seemed appropriate.

"May I?" she asked, nodding toward the sideboard. His cool gray eyes flicked to her, then to the crystal decanters, and he impatiently nodded his assent. She practically jumped from her seat and sprinted for the spirits, pouring a drink from the nearest decanter. Michael gave her full glass a doubtful look when she turned to face him but said nothing.

Abbey quickly returned to her seat before her shaking knees betrayed her. He was watching her, his piercing gray gaze following her every move. She carefully lifted the glass to her lips and sipped, and was immediately overcome by a spasm of coughing as the liquid burned down her throat. He stood slowly and came around the desk to take the glass from her trembling hand. She heard him go to the sideboard as she tried to regain her composure.

"I think," he said as he handed her a glass with a sip or two of the liquor heavily diluted with water, "you will enjoy it more if you just wet your lips."

"Thank you," she rasped. Very unexpectedly, he smiled. It was a gorgeous smile, full of brilliant white teeth, and Abbey found herself staring at his mouth and incredibly full, soft lips. She quickly averted her eyes when a blush began to creep into her cheeks.

"I must say you caught me by surprise," he said, his tone less clipped. He sat down in a chair across from her and casually balanced an ankle upon his knee. Behind the cover of her glass, Abbey gazed at his muscular legs straining against the fabric of his buckskins. "When I think of the little hell . . . girl I knew twelve years ago, I can hardly believe you are one in the same," he abruptly admitted.

"I am a bit surprised by that," she replied hoarsely, still recovering from the firewater. "You do not look so different now than you did then. A little fuller, perhaps, and a little darker, but all in all, you rather closely resemble yourself."

Michael's chuckle was low and deep. "I should rather hope I do." His smile was brief and thin. "I was nineteen when I sailed with your father. You were, what, eight or nine?"

"Ummm, nine, I think."

"Nine. A nine-year-old girl with scabby knees and the grime of several weeks on her neck is a far cry from a grown woman of one and twenty."

She made an effort to laugh lightly, but she thought she sounded like the hyenas of the Egyptian desert. "I most certainly was not covered with grime, Michael."

He looked almost surprised but quickly recovered his stern look. "You most certainly were. And your hair was always bound up in that pirate scarf. Do you recall? You were forever shouting and carrying on as if you were constantly beset by your imaginary pirates."

Abbey lifted her chin. "What I recall is being terrorized by an older boy, who, incidentally, decapitated the *one* doll I had as a child!"

"Ah, yes, that was a rather unfortunate incident," he agreed indifferently.

"I have thought it rather callous of you in hindsight, but I buried my grudge long ago."

Michael cocked his head to one side and considered her. "Excellent, for I, too, have buried the grudge for the torture I endured at the tip of that wooden sword you carried about."

She recalled the sword; a rush of memories invaded her that were close but not quite what he was telling her, and she blushed. "I am sure I do not know what you mean," she muttered. "I rather prefer not to reminisce about that summer. Clearly I was mistaken in my belief that you would remember me as well as I remember you," she said in an attempt to turn the subject from her childish behavior.

"My apologies, but as I said, you look nothing like the little girl who terrorized the quarterdeck."

Abbey hesitated. Suddenly she thought she understood him. He was apologizing. Of course! This absurd conversation they were having was his attempt to apologize for his abominable behavior thus far. He was trying to tell her that he had been surprised and therefore had reacted badly. What else could explain his strange demeanor? She flashed a cheerful smile to convey her understanding. A strange look glanced his features, but he was quickly stoic again.

"Well," he said, clearing his throat. "Twelve years ago I signed a paper pledging to take you to wife if my debts were not repaid in full upon your father's death. Although I believed those debts to have been paid, I have recently learned there is some dispute as to that fact. Therefore, we find ourselves bound by the original agreement today."

Abbey, having no idea what he was talking about, looked at him as if he were speaking Chinese. Hadn't Lord Hunt asked her about some agreement, as well?

"Allow me to speak frankly. This *agreement* does not please me in the least, for a variety of reasons. I am rather curious to know if *you* are desirous of this marriage."

She was flabbergasted. That was a perfectly ridiculous question, seeing as how she had desired this marriage since she was little girl. He *knew* that she wanted this marriage.

"I do not take your meaning," she said simply.

"I am saying that I have no desire to force you into a marriage against your will."

With a smile, Abbey exhaled a small sigh of relief. She had to stop jumping to conclusions. He was being a gentleman, that was all. He was afraid she did not care for him any longer and was nobly offering her a way to say it. It was a selfless gesture she had to admire.

"Oh, no, Michael," she assured him. "I am quite desirous of it!"

He blinked. Twice.

"Then allow me to go to the heart of the matter. I had hoped, perhaps foolishly, that you would desire the freedom of choosing a mate, even if it meant losing a fortune. Since the fortune seems to be of higher importance to you, let me say that I have no desire for a wife at this stage in my life. Nevertheless, I am a man of my word. I believe you will agree to some basic tenets that will allow us to live comfortably."

Abbey's admiration sank like a rock in water.

"I am willing to abide by my part of the agreement, given you agree to a few terms," he continued, as if they were discussing some boring business arrangement.

"Terms." She choked.

"Yes, terms." He smirked. His eyes flicked to her bosom, and he regarded her with what she could only interpret as disgust.

Disappointment shattered her, and a small kernel of betrayal and anger began to take root. She carefully placed the crystal glass on the table and folded her hands in her lap. "Pray, continue," she said coolly. If he noticed the change in her tone, he was careful not to show it.

"My responsibility extends to you only, not some bevy of relatives or favorites. Do you understand?"

"Do I understand?" she asked with rifling indignation. "I assure you, my relatives have no need to press you for favors!" Abbey's pulse was beginning to pound in her ears. She could not believe this! Her anger was eclipsed only by the outrageous hurt that began to constrict her breathing.

"Very good. Now, as to the matter of the marriage, there are certain terms I demand. I have determined that you will reside at Blessing Park and I will reside in Brighton," he announced.

"Are you suggesting we live apart?" she asked incredulously.

"You will be perfectly happy in Southampton, I assure you. I, on the other hand, will be much more comfortable near my business affairs. I see no reason for you to be there."

"I will not be sequestered away!" Abbey responded heatedly.

Michael repressed a smile. If the glint of anger in her pretty violet eyes was any indication, he would have no trouble achieving completely separate lives. In fact, he might be doing well enough to achieve his ultimate goal of making her cry off.

"I expect complete obedience from you. If you are to be my wife, I will determine what is best for your welfare, and I expect you to obey my judgment in all things. Is that clear?"

Wildly affronted, Abbey gasped. *"You* think you will know what is best for *me* from your superior position in Brighton? Oh, your arrogance is truly astounding, sir!" She breathed furiously.

"As for household expenses, I will see to it that your needs are met. Discretionary purchases, such as your clothing, will be made only with my prior approval," he continued. Judging from the way her delicate fingers dug into the cushion on either side of her knees, it looked as if she were having to physically restrain herself from lunging for his throat. He was beginning to enjoy his little charade, particularly since the angry flush of her cheeks made her extremely alluring.

"Michael Ingram, may I remind you that I come to this . . . this *marriage* with a substantial fortune of my own!"

Michael chuckled with an arrogance she found suffocating. "Your *fortune* now belongs to me," he said with a self-satisfied smile that made her want to claw his eyes out and, at the same time, sparked something deep inside her. Slowly she leaned back against the embroidered cushions of the settee.

She could see what was happening. He was bullying her into some ridiculous arrangement, for reasons that completely eluded her. Her fingers drummed loudly on the arm of the settee as she contemplated his motive. Perhaps he did not love her anymore. It was certainly possible. As she glared daggers into that handsome face, she thought he should have politely explained to her that he no longer loved her and even perhaps that he loved someone else. She was not so childish that she would not understand. She was not some foolish chit who thought grown men did not have intimate liaisons, nor was she incapable of grasping that his affections for her may have changed.

He should have politely explained, but no, he was determined to humiliate her so that *she* would cry off. But then why didn't he just say so? she wondered helplessly, until it struck her. It was her money. What was it Aunt Nan had said? If she refused him, she would lose her dowry. They had all laughed about it at the time, because it had seemed so patently absurd. But here the monster sat, wanting her money and not her. With sick regret and fury like she had never known, Abbey seethed. *Oh, no, Michael Ingram, you will not be released so quickly.* No, she would make him suffer before she would even entertain the idea. She smiled sweetly at him and hoped to high heaven he did not notice the trembling in her limbs.

"So that we are very clear, let me say that I do not relish the thought of being married under such ridiculous terms," she said. Her rage threatened to escape in a shrill scream when he looked inordinately pleased. "Do not misunderstand me," she continued softly. "I will not release you from this marriage if my own father begged it of me, which, of course, he cannot do as he is interred somewhere in the West Indies." She grinned when his smug smile faded. "That's right, Michael. You may keep me in Southampton or keep me in a cage, but I will not release you!"

Michael blanched at the unexpected turn of his game. Her eyes sparkled like rare gems as she smiled triumphantly at him.

"Abigail, I am giving you fair warning. I will make your life miserable—"

"I don't care."

"I am not a man given to the whims of women. I have no patience for games. You will do as I say, when I say, and how I say. It is well within my right to demand such from you, do you understand?"

Abbey laughed at him. "I understand clearly. I just don't give a deuce about your terms and conditions!"

Michael's face darkened and he leaned forward, glaring at her with eyes of cold stone. "Pay attention to me, *Miss Carrington*, for I mean every word I say. You will know no pleasure, none at all," he said in a low, threatening voice.

She leaned forward, so that their faces were only inches apart, with an equally scathing gaze.

"As *I* mean every word, Darfield!" she whispered heatedly.

Michael stared at her. Good God, but she was openly challenging him. In some small measure, he grudgingly respected her feisty spirit. He stood and walked slowly to the fireplace eyeing her like prey. She blithely pretended to be examining the sleeve of her gown. Despite his anger, he could not help appreciating that she was really quite stunning.

Alarmed at what he was thinking, he forced himself to stop his perusal. He decided to make his terms more onerous. "I am not quite finished," he said smoothly. She smiled sweetly.

"I will want an heir as soon as is reasonably possible," he said as he carelessly placed an arm on the mantel.

Abbey giggled irreverently. "And what would you consider reasonable?"

"You know precisely what I mean. I expect you to conceive quickly." It was an outrageous statement designed to send her running.

But Abbey only laughed. "I believe you have the upper hand in that, do you not? Shall I lift my skirts now? Or perhaps you intend to wait until we are actually married? Is that reasonable? Would you consider that quick enough?"

Michael fought the urge to smile at her equally outrageous remark, especially when delivered with such an enticingly sweet smile. He forced himself to glower at her.

"I do not appreciate such inappropriate talk," he said gruffly.

"I was only responding to your demand. Obedience in all things, is that not what you implied?"

With feigned indifference, Michael looked down at the toes of his boots. Bloody hell, she was gaining on him. He was loath to admit that he had miscalculated where the little hellion was concerned, but he had one other trick up his sleeve, one that would stir irrevocable hatred in most women he knew. He made a great show of looking at his pocket watch.

"I really must wrap this up quickly. I have several things to do before I am expected at the home of my dear friend, Lady Davenport, this weekend,'' he said matter-of-factly, then glanced surreptitiously at her through his long lashes.

Abbey, who thought that had to be the most perfectly ridiculous and transparent ploy she could have imagined, worked to keep from laughing.

He hesitated, waiting for her reaction. When he got none, he continued. ''While you are in the country, I insist you do nothing to sully my honor or your good reputation—I am, of course, *assuming* it is a good reputation.''

Abbey managed to maintain her serene expression, but her hand tightened into a fist in her lap. Michael turned his face slightly so she would not see his thin smile. If he could have patted himself on the back for the last word, he would have.

''You flatter me, sir! I don't have one as yet, but I do not doubt whatever reputation I gain will be inextricably linked to your good name.'' A devilish little smile played on her lips as she slowly lifted her gaze to his.

Michael lifted a brow. ''I believe you have just thrown down the gauntlet, Abigail.''

''Oh, no, sir—you did! I merely picked it up.''

The smell of defeat at his own game was beginning to irritate him. With a frown, he considered her for a long moment. Despite her ability to play the game, her violet eyes exposed an odd mixture of anger and hurt. He could hardly blame her; he himself would not have believed he could be such a cad, but circumstances had forced him. He decided to make one last attempt, and in three strides, he moved to stand directly in front of her, peering down at her with his fists planted on his hips and as grim a face as he could muster.

''I strongly recommend you not fight me on this; you cannot possibly win. I do not desire a wife, and if I am forced to *keep* a wife, I will exact my revenge on you every waking hour. Think long and hard about what I've said before you make up your mind, Abigail.''

''You should have thought about that before you signed that silly agreement, or whatever it was,'' she responded quietly. His eyes narrowed with undisguised rancor. She stood unsteadily. "If you will excuse me, I think I should like to freshen up. Anything would be infinitely more pleasurable than this interview." She looked him directly in the eye, brazenly daring him to say anything more.

The sparkle in those angry violet eyes captivated him. He surprised himself by suddenly catching her upper arms and jerking her to his chest. Abbey flung her arms wildly, but he easily caught them and pinned them behind her back. He held her close, her slender body pressed against the full length of his hard, muscular frame. His gaze swept from her flashing eyes to her mouth, pursed with fear.

"I am not given to assaulting women, if I correctly interpret that look. But you will be my *wife*, and I will touch you whenever I please." Fear clouded her eyes and he took pity. He continued, a little more softly. "Abigail, your father's will is clear in its stipulations. If we do not marry, your father's business associates will not receive their shares. My father's debts cannot be repaid. My family will lose our ancestral home and you will lose your dowry. But I can settle all of that if only you will agree to end this so that we can lead our lives as we wish. I will attempt to settle a sum upon you to compensate the loss of your dowry if you will but end this now."

Abbey could not think straight and stared helplessly at him. He seemed different now, almost sad. What game was he playing with her? Whatever his motives, she did not want to be chained to a man who did not want her and openly resented her. Her eyes stung with tears of bitter disappointment; she blinked and looked down. Michael gingerly slipped two fingers under her chin and tilted her face up to his.

"*I think I hate you*," she whispered before he could speak. A raw emotion flashed in his gray eyes just before his mouth swept down on hers. It happened so swiftly and so brutally that she could not react. He crushed her to him, pressing her into his hard chest and thighs. His tongue battered at her lips, insisting she open to him. Abbey struggled, but Michael pulled her even closer than she thought possible. His body, hard and lean, burned her like an open flame. Squirming against him, she gasped for air, and Michael plunged his tongue inside her soft, sweet mouth.

Abbey was immediately caught in a gulf between fear and a depth of emotion she could not possibly understand. His mouth was cruel until the roiling emotions crashing through her made her relent. Then he softened, his lips carefully molding hers, his tongue gently probing, willing her to him. Humiliated and deeply hurt, Abbey felt a single hot tear fall down her cheek, followed by the tender stroke of Michael's thumb as he swept it away. His kiss was drugging her, sweeping her from reality, sparking a flame in her she had never before felt. The assault on her senses seemed endless, and when he at last lifted his head, a shiver coursed her spine and made her shudder violently.

She had never been kissed, not like that. Stunned, Abbey could do nothing but stare at his lips, conscious of a lingering warmth that spread slowly down to her toes. He was smiling down at her, a cocky, self-assured smile, and as the magic of the kiss began to wear off, she slowly grew embarrassed and resentful. It was cruel thing to have done after everything he had said. Abbey pushed angrily against his chest, stumbling backward.

"*That* was badly done!" she spat. He laughed and folded his arms across his chest. Without so much as a glance at him, she brushed past him and walked with regal grace to the door. Michael reached it before her and yanked it open, standing in the doorway so that she would have to step around him to quit the room.

She could not resist looking at him. He stared deep into her eyes, and Abbey suddenly knew those piercing gray orbs could see right through her bravado. She raised her chin a notch.

"Think on what I have said, Abigail," he intoned with a bow.

She bestowed a sufficiently hateful glare on him and snapped, "My name is *Abbey*!" before sweeping out of the room.

# Chapter 4

Michael closed the door behind her and stood with his hand on the brass handle for a long moment, commanding himself to get hold of his conflicting emotions while he savored her taste on his lips. He had expected an ugly spinster! A dirty, ragged hellion! Not a woman like *that*.

Angry with himself, Michael marched straight for the sideboard, poured himself a large whiskey, and downed it in two gulps. She was absolutely radiant, and certainly more so than he would have ever dreamed possible. *Very good, Michael. Crush her then lust after her. Very charming.* He turned abruptly and walked to the mantel, deep in thought. He could not forget the look in her eyes when he told her he would not have her under any circumstances. The contagious smile and sparkle in her eye had dimmed rapidly, and he thought he had never seen a more dejected look in his life. But he was determined to feel no pity or esteem for her. He was determined to dissuade her from this ridiculous marriage.

But why, in God's name, did she have to turn out to be such a beauty?

He unconsciously gripped the back of a wing-backed leather chair and glared into his empty glass.

The circumstances were loathesome at best, and revolting in every way. From the day he had received the papers from Carrington's solicitor, Mr. Strait, he had been plagued with resentment and fury. Mr. Strait's letter made it very plain that if Michael refused, he would be breaking a very legal agreement and risk certain lawsuits from half of London. On top of that, Abigail Carrington would lose every penny her father had left her; all but a paltry annuity would go to pay his debts.

Michael could have lived with those two possibilities. He was sure he would be vindicated if he fought the absurd agreement in the courts. If the little beastie lost her money, well, he was sorry for that, and would have settled a sum on her that would at least allow her to live in relative comfort the rest of her days.

What drove him to despair was the reality that in trying to sort through all this mess, he might lose his family's ancestral home. He could not drag his family's name through the mud once more.

Moreover, Carrington had partnered with some of the most influential businessmen in England. If they were forced to suffer losses because Michael welched on the agreement, it was *he* who would suffer irreparable harm, even if he won in the courts. No one would do business with him; he would be shunned and his powerful shipping trade could be ruined. He would become a social outcast—again. In short, he would do just as well to leave England altogether and start life anew.

A frown wrinkled the bridge of his nose as he recalled how his own solicitors had confirmed Strait's interpretation of the legal documents. Resentment still boiled in his veins. Rationally, he understood that he had signed a legally binding document when he was nineteen and had been fully cognizant of what he was doing, even if he had not been fully cognizant of all the consequences. And he further understood that his own father had done his part to make sure Michael would pay all his days. He expected as much from the old man, but not from Carrington. Michael could only assume the captain had not told him about the debt so that he would be forced to marry the little hellion.

And Carrington had tried to sweeten the pot with the lure of a substantial dowry. But that was little comfort to Michael— he did not need or want the young woman's money. Just the thought of accepting it made his stomach knot.

But he would make do with the situation. He would live in his spacious Brighton town house, keeping to the seas, and leave her to rot at Blessing Park. Rebecca would not like it, but then again, there was little she liked these days. The woman was simply never satisfied, and Michael suspected until she had his name and a town house in Mayfair, she would never be. He had not as yet deemed it necessary to inform Rebecca that he had no intention of marrying her, a conclusion he had reached long before the documents came informing him he would wed the little hellion. No doubt Abbey would be relieved to marry a marquis. Her gratitude for being lifted from the bonds of obscurity and given the protection of his name likely would be so acute that she would undoubtedly pledge to make him a good wife and bear him many sons.

He would take the sons, but he wanted nothing else to do with her.

He poured another whiskey and began to pace. Despite what he told himself, he could not erase the memory of her remarkable eyes clouded with confusion. What in the devil was wrong with him? How had he expected her to look, happy? It was part of her punishment, was it not, her payment for her roll in this sham? Yet regardless of how much she deserved his disdain, he could not, at the moment, reconcile the image of her with it. He walked to the windows and angrily yanked the heavy velvet drapes apart and peered outside, unseeing. He did not turn when the door opened and closed softly.

"I would wager your reunion did not go well," Sam remarked casually. His steps fell silently on the thick Aubusson carpet as he strolled to the sideboard.

"What did you expect?" Michael asked coolly.

Sam wisely did not answer as he helped himself to a brandy. He took a drink and eyed Michael's back over the rim of his glass. "Now what?"

Michael shrugged. "I will go to Brighton and summon Rebecca," he said indifferently as he propped a booted foot on the window seat.

"I think there is something you should know, Darfield. That girl has no notion of the agreement. Thanks to Carrington, she believes you sought this marriage," Sam announced.

Michael grunted his skepticism. "That little hellion knows too well what her father did, Sam. Don't underestimate her ability to deceive."

"Don't underestimate Carrington's ability, either, for I am telling you, he greatly deceived her. That girl is in love with an image of a man her father created from thin air. Do you know that she believes you sent her gifts over the last years? That you wrote letters to her father reconfirming your devotion and desire to wed?"

"Really, Hunt, you do not honestly think she could believe such nonsense," Michael snapped.

"On my word, I think she does believe it. You should at least give her the benefit of the doubt," Sam responded quietly.

Michael glowered over his shoulder at his friend. "I wonder, if you found yourself in similar circumstance, what *your* reaction might be."

"I would hope that I would remember the young woman has traveled thousands of miles to marry a man she has not seen since she was a child. She believes—or *believed*—that man loves her and has romanticized that notion to her great satisfaction." He took a sip of brandy. Michael, saying nothing, turned his broad back again.

Sam sighed heavily. "Well, at the very least she seems to be a rather pleasant sort. There is no need to treat her ill."

Michael shook his head and pushed away from the window seat. He strolled toward the fireplace, absently swirling the whiskey in his glass. "There is no need to treat her in *any* fashion,'' he said after a moment. ''She shall be well attended here while I am in Brighton.''

''You might at least try to acquaint yourself with her. She's not the hellion you described. And after all, she may one day be the mother of your heir.''

Michael threw the whiskey down his throat, slammed his empty glass on the mantel, and turned to glare at Sam. ''You need not remind me of *that*,'' he said, yanking impatiently at his neckcloth. Suddenly the study was stifling.

''It is not wholly inconceivable that she is as much a victim in all this as you are,'' Sam continued, unperturbed, as he placed his snifter down.

Michael snorted scornfully. ''If she would but listen to reason, she would not be the helpless victim in your eyes now,'' he muttered angrily before stalking to the corner of the room and yanking hard on the bell pull.

''It's really none of my affair—''

''You are right.''

Jones appeared before Sam could respond.

''Jones, get the vicar here. Today. Straightaway,'' Michael barked. Jones bowed and left immediately.

''What are you about?'' Sam asked, startled.

''About? I am going to marry her. Or at least make her think I am,'' Michael growled and plopped unceremoniously into a leather chair. Sam gave him such a disapproving frown that he could not help wondering what feminine charms had swayed his friend so quickly. Good God, not two days ago the two had shared in his misery. Well, in a matter of a few hours Sam could join him at his wedding—or at least what he hoped would be enough of a wedding to frighten the little hellion away for good.

Alone in the room Jones had shown her to, Abbey grew increasingly inconsolate. She longed for the comfort of her aunt and her cousins and felt a pang of homesickness so deep that it doubled her over.

Her aunt had made her come here. She had reminded Abbey she had a fortune to collect and a man who loved her impatiently awaiting her arrival. Aunt Nan had put her on the first ship out of Newport after the papers and news of her father's death had arrived from the West Indies. But had Aunt Nan known what awaited Abbey, she would never have sent her. Aunt Nan believed Michael loved her.

With tears burning in her eyes, she cursed the memory of the man she held dear. The summer she had spent on her father's vessel had been one of the happiest of her life. Michael had been kind to her and, in her recollection, had indulged her childish fantasies. Of course, there was the one exception of the unfortunate doll incident, but the Michael she remembered with vivid clarity and admiration was *not* the Michael she had met today.

Abbey fought to keep the tears from falling, but failed. When had Michael's heart turned from her? Why hadn't he told her father? Alone in the large, unfamiliar room, she bitterly swallowed the fantasy. Not only had he made it clear he did not want her, he also made it clear that he resented her. She felt physically ill, and as she lay despondently on the bed, fighting down waves of nausea, she grudgingly recognized it was her own naïveté that was to blame.

At last she pulled herself off the bed and moved to the gilt-edged vanity.

She sank onto a silk-covered bench and began brushing her hair with a vengeance. "I shall return to America. There is no other answer," she stated firmly. It was the best thing to do. He could have her bloody fortune, or her father's creditors, or whoever wanted it, she thought bitterly as she regarded her pale reflection in the mirror. She should have agreed it was a ludicrous situation, thanked him for his candor, and gone on with her life. But no, she had to get angry and stubbornly refuse to give ground. At this more rational moment she realized she would not wed a man who so obviously resented her presence, not even for her own father, God rest his soul.

A rapid staccato of knocks on her door startled her. The brush stilled in her hand as she debated opening it, but before

she could react, the door flung open and the devil himself
strode through.

Abbey surged to her feet, dropping the brush. "I beg your
pardon!"

"Pardon granted," he drawled as he crossed the room and
picked up her brush.

Abbey's heart was pounding erratically, and for one insane
moment, she could not decide if it was from his ungentle-
manly behavior or his sheer magnetism. "What . . . just
who do you think you are, barging in here like that!" she
fairly shrieked.

"I think I am the master of this house. No door will be
barred to me."

"The door was not *barred*! It was *shut*. I should hope you
would have the common decency—"

"Decency"—he grinned devilishly—"is not something I
concern myself with. This is my house. My room. My door. If
I want, I shall enter." With that, he tossed the brush onto the
vanity and put his hands on his waist, regarding her closely.
Her dark hair, which seemed to be all curl, tumbled about her
shoulders, providing a stark contrast to her pale face and the
telltale sign of tears. It was exactly what he wanted. He was
moving in for the kill and ignored the thought that his kill was
a kitten.

"Well? Have you thought about what I said?"

Abbey folded her arms defensively across her middle. Of
course she had thought about it, the fool. "No," she said
hoarsely.

Michael arched a skeptical brow as he strolled casually to
one of her trunks and peered inside. "How much longer do
you need? An hour?"

All of Abbey's best intentions flew out of her mind at that
moment. He was bullying her, trying to force her hand, and he
had aroused a stubborn streak in her unlike anything she had
ever experienced. Her eyes narrowed.

"Five minutes is more likely." She strolled to the trunk he
was standing over and, with her foot, kicked the lid shut.

Michael lifted his gaze and frowned. So far, his reign of

terror was not having the desired impact on the kitten. "Then your time is up. Either you agree to end this abomination now, or you will marry me. Tonight."

Abbey merely shrugged.

"Well?" he demanded, his irritation mounting.

"I will not cry off."

Michael's heart skipped a beat. "Then come along. The vicar is waiting," he said with a snarl, and almost smiled in triumph when she paled.

The *vicar*? Abbey wanted to kick herself for being so incredibly stubborn. "No . . . not yet—"

"Yes, right now. Come along," he said, reaching for her hand.

Abbey took a quick step backward, shaking her head. "No, you see . . I must change. I must change! I cannot be married in this gown." Her eyes flicked nervously about the room.

Michael could not suppress his smile. Just as he had hoped, the threat of a real ceremony was scaring her.

"Fifteen minutes. I don't care if you are wearing the same thing in which you entered this world, you are coming to the chapel in fifteen minutes, understood?" Abbey's wide eyes fixed on him and she nodded slowly. Michael walked out of the room, shutting the door rather loudly behind him. Smiling to himself, he strolled down the hall to his rooms. It would be the crowning glory, he thought, to show up at her door in fifteen minutes in all of *his* finery. If he was not mistaken, he would be putting the little hellion on a coach first thing in the morning.

As Michael changed, Abbey stared at the ice-blue gown she had extracted from a trunk. It was wrinkled and several of the small pearl beads were missing. But it was the wedding dress Victoria had made for her, and by God, she was going to wear it. That man, that *devil* did not want to marry her, and at the moment, she would bet just about anything she had he would not go through with it. He was trying to scare her, and although he was succeeding—admirably—she was going to call his rotten bluff.

But God in heaven, what if she was wrong?

She was not wrong, she was certain. She quickly disrobed and slipped into the dress. It would have been a stunning wedding gown. A low-cut bodice decorated with tiny seed pearls was fitted tightly to her, the skirt pleated in the back. Abbey struggled with the buttons and realized, too late, that she could not fasten them all herself. She shrugged as she searched for the slippers dyed to match her gown. It did not matter. She was not getting married in this or any other dress. That horrid man would not marry her. He *despised* her.

She had not had time to do anything with her hair when the rapid staccato fell on her door again, and it swung open. Not only was he an ogre, but he was exceedingly rude, she thought, snapping to attention. She was hardly prepared for the sight of him. Dressed in formal attire of midnight black with a snowy white satin waistcoat, he looked even more impossibly handsome than before. A swath of regret cut across her as she stared at his magnificent features. The only thing she and her cousins had been right about was his looks. He was, quite certainly, the most handsome man she had ever clapped eyes on.

At the same moment, Michael thought she would have made a stunning bride even as he eyed her wrinkled gown. But not his, and not tonight. He leaned negligently against the door frame, his arms folded across his chest, and let his gaze wander her svelte figure. She was a gorgeous woman, that much he could not deny. It was a pity; in any other time or place, he would have greatly appreciated her beauty. But the only thing he would appreciate now was her refusal of the agreement. "Well? The vicar is waiting."

"All right," she said smoothly, and marched out of the room, passing him in a cloud of pale blue and lilac scent. A laugh caught in his throat as she passed him and he realized her gown was buttoned only halfway up her back.

He placed a hand on her shoulder. She whirled around, a look of wild panic in her eyes. Michael quickly held up his hands.

"Your gown," he said quickly.

Abbey's brows snapped to a frown. "I am sorry, but I did not come with a lady's maid. Surely if I had, you would have sent her back at once. Not responsible for a bevy of relatives or favorites, isn't that right?"

Michael chuckled and motioned for her to turn around. Abbey was having none of that and violently shook her head. He ignored her, put his hands on her shoulders, and forced her to turn. "Do not worry about your good name, Miss Carrington. I intend to button up this gown of yours as opposed to unbutton it. I rather doubt your bevy of relatives in America will hear of this little episode," he said as he quickly fastened her gown.

The light touch of his fingers on her back sent a queer, tingling shiver down her spine, but Abbey bit her lower lip and endured it. He was right; she could hardly appear in front of a vicar or anyone else with her gown undone, and as she had no cousins to help her, she was going to have to allow him this one indiscretion. She was amazed at how deftly he fastened the tiny row of buttons, and wondered madly how many times he had sent his fingers flying in the opposite direction on a woman's back. As soon as he finished, she jumped away from him, practically to the other side of the corridor. When Michael motioned toward the grand staircase, Abbey walked quickly to avoid any further contact, even though Michael was right on her heels.

"It's your own fault," he casually observed. "If you could but give up this absurdity, there would be no call for you to come running out of your room half dressed."

Abbey bristled. "I did *not* come running out of my room half dressed! If you will recall, *you* are the one who decreed fifteen minutes. I am not the one acting irrationally here, *you* are."

"Don't be ridiculous. I have explained to you my hands are tied. You are the only one who can stop this madness, yet you refuse to do it. You are, apparently, as stubborn a wench as you ever were," he shot back.

Abbey lifted her chin and deigned not to answer that as they raced to the bottom of the stairs. In the foyer, she turned to proceed down the corridor she had been in earlier, but his hand on her waist stopped her.

"Miss Carrington," he said. Startled by the intimate contact of his strong hand on her waist, Abbey stopped and reluctantly glanced up at him.

With his head, he motioned in the opposite direction. "The chapel is this way," he said dryly, a thin smile playing at the corner of his lips.

Abbey snorted with exasperation and, pivoting on her heel, began to march in direction he indicated.

"For your information, I am not nor have I ever been a stubborn wench," she muttered angrily as they strode, side by side, down the corridor. "You undoubtedly believe anyone who does not instantly agree with you is stubborn. You certainly showed signs of that aboard the *Dancing Maiden.*"

"If I were you, I would not begin to recount the slights you perceive as being at my hand, because your transgressions will outnumber mine significantly. You were an impossible, willful, and most extraordinarily undisciplined child."

She had been nothing of the sort, and she groaned disdainfully at his fiction. He was simply trying to goad her. Well, he was going to have to do a lot more than make up stories about her childhood before she would give in to his strong-arm tactics. No, if anyone was going to cry off, it would be he.

He grabbed her elbow as they neared the end of the corridor and turned into an alcove from which the chapel was entered. Abbey could see the small sanctuary, could see the heads of Lord Hunt, Sebastian, and Jones simultaneously turning toward them.

"Here we are, Miss Carrington. This is your last opportunity to release us both from this insanity," Michael said evenly.

Abbey was very sure he would not go through with it. So sure that she looked up at him and smiled brilliantly. "Not on your life, Darfield," she whispered sweetly.

Michael's gray eyes clouded over as if warning her of an impending storm. And a storm was definitely brewing inside him. He could not believe the nerve of this chit. He had been as disagreeable as possible, and yet she was standing there beside him, her hair tumbling about her shoulders in a gown pulled rumpled from her trunk, her face a study of very pretty mortification. He had no idea what compelled her to this other than a stubborn streak a mile long. One thing was certain. She was an obstinate woman, and *that* came as no surprise.

He tightened his grip on her elbow and propelled her toward the altar, halting abruptly just in front of it. He had given her a last opportunity before he pushed her to the brink of humiliation, but she would not relent. No doubt she would falter if the ceremony was begun, but by then her humiliation before his best friend and the vicar would be complete. She had it coming, in his humble estimation. He looked down at her flawless face. She was looking at the altar, her violet eyes wide with the chagrin she could not hide. He sighed wearily as he decided to reason with her one last time.

"Look at me," he commanded her softly.

Abbey did, her expression revealing her uncertainty. He considered her very carefully, his eyes sweeping her face. "Think on what you are about to do, because it will not easily be undone. Are you quite sure this is what you want?" he asked softly.

"I have thought about it for a very long time—for what seems almost a lifetime," she answered truthfully. She felt compelled to tell him everything she was feeling, but Michael's eyes hardened again before she could speak.

"I see. If you will turn this way, Miss Carrington." She did as he asked and was surprised to see the vicar standing there. Funny, she had not noticed him until this very moment.

To the vicar, Michael said, "Get on with it."

Stunned, Abbey stared at the vicar, who began, "Dearly beloved, we gather here today in the sight of God—"

"*Wait!*" Abbey cried and placed her hand on Michael's folded arm; the steel muscles flexed tightly beneath her touch. His gaze shifted to her face with a distinctive look of cool impatience. This was not right, not right at all. Abbey was now extremely uneasy, and searched his icy gray eyes for something, *anything* that might indicate he was bluffing. He was bluffing!

"Is this . . . I mean, are we . . ."

"It is a marriage ceremony, Miss Carrington," he said casually. Abbey could not believe her ears. This man did not look as if he was about to stop this charade, but she knew he would. He had to!

She looked frantically at the vicar, who conveniently turned his attention to his prayer book.

Michael's gray eyes flicked to her open mouth and back to her eyes. "It's what you wanted, is it not?" he asked quietly through clenched teeth.

"Yes! *No!* I mean, Michael, of *course* I want to marry you, I have always wanted to marry you, but not like *this,*" she whispered frantically.

Michael sneered. "What were you expecting? A grand affair in London? An event that the *Times* would report? The social event of the season? Did you think your terms granted you all that?" he hissed.

Abbey was suddenly frightened. This man was nothing like the man she remembered at all, but an impostor in Michael Ingram's skin, a hateful man who looked so resentful at this very moment that she thought he could easily strangle her.

"I am not sure what I was expecting, but it most certainly was not this," she whispered hoarsely.

"I warned you," he muttered angrily. "You know how to stop it."

Confused, Abbey could not respond. Her little game had spiraled out of control. For some inexplicable reason, she was paralyzed, knowing she should stop this *now* but completely incapable of doing so.

Michael turned his cold gaze to the vicar. "Get on with it. Miss Carrington can sort out her expectations later," he said abruptly. The vicar glanced sheepishly at Abbey, then began again. Stunned, Abbey stood unmoving, unthinking, while the vicar quickly ran through the ceremony and vows, waiting for the moment Michael would halt this ridiculous charade. Only vaguely aware that she was answering, she mumbled something incoherent when the vicar pressed her for a response, and next to her, Michael did much the same. When she heard the horrifying words "man and wife," Abbey thought she would faint.

Before she could, Michael's arm encircled her waist and jerked her hard to his chest. "Lady Darfield," he muttered, then lightly brushed his lips across hers. The intimate contact of his soft lips on hers jolted Abbey senseless. A strange, alluring fire raced up her spine. His lips lingered on hers for a long moment, and when he lifted his head, she was sure his stone-gray eyes had softened. She was equally sure, judging by the way he was looking at her, that he had felt the heat race up his spine, too.

Apparently, she would be the last to know if that was true. He immediately dropped his arm from her waist, pivoted on his heel, and marched out of the chapel. Abbey stared after him in horrified amazement. Sebastian and Jones shook their heads sadly at one another, and Sam glared angrily at the vicar for want of a better target.

# Chapter 5

Abbey, having cried herself to sleep, awoke the next morning with a dull headache. As her gaze adjusted to the room about her, melancholy descended on her. She was in *his* house. Unfortunately, nothing had changed overnight, and therefore, she would demand he return her to America. His incentive, as if he needed one, would be her bloody dowry and the satisfaction of her father's debts. He could keep it and she would never darken his door again—no, his name would never so much as pass her lips. The vicar could certainly be persuaded to forget what had passed for a ceremony last night had ever happened. Reluctantly she rose and fished through her things for a plain gown. She was startled a moment later when a young woman with blond hair peeking from beneath her maid's cap entered. The maid seemed just as surprised, and she hastily curtsied.

"Morning, mum. I didn't expect you about quite so early. My name is Sarah. Lord Darfield has instructed me to tend to you," she said nervously.

Abbey had never had anyone tend her and felt very self-conscious. "Good morning, Sarah. If you would be so good as to fasten these buttons, then perhaps you could show me to the breakfast room?" Abbey suggested just as nervously.

"Of course, mum." Sarah quickly moved to fasten her gown. "You're younger than I would have thought, if you don't mind me saying so, mum. When we heard Lord Darfield might take a wife, lord, we couldn't imagine. I never thought him the marrying type. He has been alone all these years, you know, and he rather prefers the sea," Sarah blurted. She patted Abbey's back to indicate she had finished.

"Withers, he had me half convinced you'd be rather homely," she continued as she moved to the bed to straighten the covers. "He said my lord wouldn't marry unless it were for money, and it's only the homely ladies that has the money. I don't know why I give Withers one bit of time, to tell you the truth."

"Withers?" At the same time Abbey wondered what fool would come to such a ridiculous conclusion, she thought the name sounded very familiar.

"He's the head gardener, mum."

Abbey perked up at that. There was nothing she had enjoyed more than tending her garden in Virginia. "Head gardener? That sounds as if there are more than one."

"Oh, indeed there are, mum. There are three, and of course the groundsmen."

"Three?"

"It's a rather big house, mum, with rather big gardens, but you can't see them for all the snow. In the springtime, you'll have a lovely view from your window. In the winter, Withers spends his time in the hothouse. I'll show you if you like."

"I thought I would breakfast with Lord Darfield," Abbey said shyly. It would be best to confront her terrible situation immediately, not spend time exploring an estate that she intended to leave immediately, no matter how grand.

"Oh, mum, the master is away already. He takes his breakfast very early when he is in residence; he's usually gone before the sun is up." Sarah giggled to herself. "Cook is not very fond of the morning. She is quite beside herself when he comes. She says eating that early ain't good for the body.

Been grousing all morning, she has. Wouldn't have been so bad if the master hadn't gotten her up in the middle of the night to show him where the cheese was kept."

Abbey missed the reference to Michael's sleepless night. "Lord Darfield has departed?"

"An hour ago, mum, with Lord Hunt."

Abbey was sorely disappointed. She very much needed to get this ugly affair over and done with. He might have at least mentioned when they would have opportunity to speak again. That is, if he ever intended to speak to her again. Sarah finished with the bed and straightened up, regarding Abbey closely. "Aye, you are quite lovely, mum. Won't Withers be surprised."

Embarrassed, Abbey shrugged and moved toward the door. Sarah happily bustled in front of her and opened it. "I'll unpack your trunks first thing," she said as she opened the door and gestured for Abbey to precede her.

The corridor could have doubled as a ballroom, it was so wide. Abbey had not noticed yesterday that it was much like the ground floor, with small tables and vases of fresh-cut flowers lining each side. Paintings were also in abundance, as were artifacts from a more ancient time. Just ahead of her, Sarah pointed to a large oak door across from the landing.

"That would be your sitting room, mum. And there, that's the library."

"The library? I thought it was downstairs."

"Yes, mum, the main library is downstairs. This is *your* library." Abbey gave Sarah a puzzled look. "The master says you are to have your own rooms. Your library doesn't have many books in it yet, but Sebastian says you may purchase your own." Sarah wrinkled her nose and whispered, "The master's reading tastes are a bit strong for a lady. Latin and such."

Abbey's stomach lurched involuntarily. She should not care; she should be ecstatic. She did not *want* to be with him, but it hurt terribly that he had so blatantly planned a separate life for her. He intended her to live on the first floor when he was in residence, and he in his rooms on the ground floor.

"How perfectly arrogant," she muttered.

Sarah's pale-blue eyes widened at her remark. "I beg your pardon, mum?"

"I suppose I am to dine and sleep up here alone? Like some prisoner?" she asked, making no effort to conceal her bitterness.

A bit of color seeped into Sarah's pale cheeks. "Well, no, mum. The dining room is on the ground floor. And, of course, the master's chambers are next to yours."

Abbey was not expecting that and suddenly remembered the door in her room adjoining another suite. Had he slept there last night while she cried herself to sleep? She quickly looked away and pretended to study a priceless Chinese vase as she tried to collect herself. She could be such a fool at times. Of course he would have chambers next to hers. Of course he would want her company for *that*. He wanted the obligatory coupling to produce an heir. Beyond that he wanted nothing to do with her. So exactly when was it she should expect *that* to happen? Before or after he spoke to her again? Would he come barging in, claiming to own her now, in addition to the house, the room, and the door?

As Abbey followed Sarah down the grand staircase, she had to pause and blink several times to clear hot tears of frustration so she could see where she was stepping. In front of her, Sarah chatted away, pointing here and there as she explained the surroundings. Abbey heard nothing. She was too overwhelmed by the reality of her bleak situation to concentrate.

On the ground floor, Sarah reached the corner room well ahead of her, and when Abbey crossed the threshold, she was busy at the sideboard with Jones. Sebastian, the Devil's secretary, sat at the table sipping a cup of tea. The nook was brightened by the sun streaming through a long bank of windows. A large, round table dominated the center of the room, surrounded by four chairs upholstered in yellow damask that matched the fresh-cut tulips in the center of the table. A fire warmed the room from a marble hearth, and a sideboard full of food was set across a long wall. On any other morning, in any other circumstance, Abbey would have delighted in the cozy room.

She was glad to see Sebastian; at least he seemed to care about her welfare. He had looked in on her twice the previous evening, each time looking terribly concerned when she had sent him away. She told herself to shore up and inhaled a deep breath.

"Good morning, Mr. Sebastian," she forced herself to call.

Sebastian greeted her with a cheerful smile. "My lady! You are looking quite refreshed after your long trip," he said, artfully skipping any reference to her so-called wedding and solitary evening. "Shall Jones pour you some tea?"

"Perchance, have you any coffee?"

"Ah, yes. I've heard Americans prefer coffee," he remarked with a smile.

Abbey settled into a seat next to Sebastian as Jones placed a cup of coffee in front of her, a caddie of toast, and a plate of fruit. "I am not really an American, sir. I lived there for some years with my aunt, but I was born in England, near York."

"Pardon me, madam," Sebastian apologized. "Your accent causes me to forget."

"Oh. That. Well, I gather it's because I have not been to England in a very long while."

Sebastian smiled politely as Abbey took a sip of the hot coffee. She managed to keep from gagging; she could have stood a spoon upright in it. Sebastian smiled and very breezily launched into a story about his digestive system and the coffee of the Orient. After a while, Abbey had lapsed into comfortable dialogue with the secretary and was trading stories with him.

"Sarah said that Lord Darfield has left for the day?" she asked nonchalantly.

Sebastian glanced surreptitiously at Jones's back before answering. "He has gone to Brighton," he replied disapprovingly. "He shouldn't be gone more than a day or two."

Brighton! Abbey was surprised by her sudden anger and by the fact that it made her angry upset her even more. "He said nothing of going!" she blurted. But he *had*. He had told her very clearly he intended to live there and leave her at Blessing Park. But would he go without so much as a cold good-bye or even a well-deserved I-told-you-so?

"The master has a ship in port there and some business to attend. It was unavoidable," Sebastian clarified.

Abbey pushed the plate of fruit away and sagged against the chair, unconsciously wadding the napkin in her lap. The fact that he had left her one day after their wedding infuriated her. He might despise her, but to leave her like some dockside wench without a word was reprehensible. He was not only an arrogant, snobbish boor, but a rake as well!

At just past ten o'clock, Abbey bundled up and wandered outside. Contemplating her circumstances, she decided that her best course of action was to ignore this damnable situation and carry on as she normally would. She could not very well flee this rural estate and board a ship to America; she would have to wait for his very exalted lordship's return for that. For the time being, she was stuck at Blessing Park, and therefore, she should try to make it as pleasurable a visit as was humanly possible. The Devil of Darfield was not going to keep her locked away in some room, pining for her aunt.

She would draw from the most pleasurable time of her life—America. Four women overseeing a small farm brought freedom that none of them would have enjoyed had they been married. They spent their days working and their nights gathered around a fire engaged in a variety of unsophisticated activities. They did not entertain, they did not go to town to meet eligible young men. They just existed. Peacefully, freely, and without restraint. If she was going to survive this awful predicament, then she would do the same here. Why not? *He* would not be in attendance, and apparently he did not care what she did with her time.

Abbey trudged out onto the snow blanketing the great circular drive, bashfully declining the offers of help from various servants who seemed almost alarmed that she was outside at all. She shrugged off their concern as she introduced herself and asked each their names. Looking warily at one another, they reluctantly responded. Abbey then asked each of them to show her what work they did at the estate. Completely astonished, the groomsmen pointed to the stables.

Inside, they exchanged anxious looks when Abbey climbed into the stalls and cooed to the horses, then marched over to a very pregnant milk cow and lovingly patted her sagging belly. The groundsmen, who had followed their new marchioness with great curiosity, convinced her they could not show her the estate's park land because of the snow. And they steadfastly refused to take her to the hothouse when she asked, swearing Withers would have their heads if they so much as stepped inside.

So Abbey insisted on being taken to the kennels next. Dismayed, the kennelmaster looked on as she befriended a hound that had been mangled by a trap. The master had told him to put the dog down, the kennelmaster told her, but Abbey would not listen to him and soon had the maimed dog following her about. She even went so far as to announce the name Harry would be bestowed on the hound in honor of a sailor she once knew with a similar gait. At that declaration, the kennelmaster exchanged a frantic look with a groom. Lord Darfield *never*, under *any* circumstance, named his hounds.

After spending the morning with the animals and a group of very confused, very enchanted servants, Abbey decided to visit the hothouse by herself. She laughed at their pleas of caution and, with a jaunty wave and a promise to return—alive, she assured them—she set out across the wide expanse of a winter wonderland that was obviously the garden. It appeared to cover several acres. A tall wall of hedges shaped into various characters bordered the garden all around. Wide paths allowed access between carefully manicured plots. In the very back were two large lawns with iron benches placed around the perimeter. Abbey was certain she had never seen anything so grand, and imagined it was quite spectacular in full bloom.

She gasped with delight when she stepped inside the hothouse. A riot of color greeted her: roses in full bloom, asters, geraniums, gardenias, and tulips were everywhere. Terribly pleased, Abbey stroked the petal of a pristine white rose.

"You there! Don't be handling me roses!" a deep voice barked. Abbey whirled around to face one of the biggest, ugliest men she had ever seen. He had a thick patch of gray hair atop his enormous head. Beady little eyes glared at her from folds of flesh. His nose was terribly misshapen, and his lips thick and wet. His hands, which rested on a shovel in front of him, looked like two hams. His shirt and waistcoat strained across his barrel chest and protruding belly.

Abbey recognized him immediately; she remembered her father's first mate very fondly. He always had a dour exterior, but he also had a heart as big as the ocean.

"Withers!" she cried with glee, and impetuously threw her arms around his neck.

Surprised, Withers dropped his shovel and stumbled backward. "Come now," he said gruffly, and pulled her arms from his neck.

"Withers, don't you recognize me? I'm Abigail!"

*"Who?"* He searched her face, then slowly, a rare smile began to crack his thick lips.

"I'll be. Little Abigail? The terror of the high seas?"

Laughing, Abbey nodded furiously. "The very same! Oh, Withers, how *truly* delightful to see you again!"

A slow blush crept into Withers ruddy cheeks. "It's ain't *you* Lord Darfield married?" he asked uncertainly.

Abbey flinched. "Uh . . . well. As a matter of fact, it is," she said as cheerfully as she could.

"Well, I'll be. Heard he was marrying but I had no inkling . . ." he remarked thoughtfully. "Never thought I'd see that. No, sir, never thought I'd see that," he marveled, chuckling. "When you were but a wee lass, the marquis didn't care for you a'tall! Always on him, you were. Why, I think if your papa hadn't put you off the ship, he'd've jumped overboard!" He laughed.

Abbey felt the slow creep of embarrassment stain her cheeks. To have it confirmed that he had despised her even then was humiliating.

"That was a long time ago!" she declared shakily.

"Aye, it was indeed. Well, look at you now, lass. As pretty a lass as I ever did see!" he said fondly. Then his expression turned stern. "Now see here, Miss Abigail, I don't work from sunup to sundown just so's you can come in here and handle the flowers to death."

"I am truly sorry, Withers, but they are so beautiful!" Abbey exclaimed. Withers's fleshy cheeks jiggled like jelly as he shook his head in furious disagreement.

"I don't care if you be the Queen of England, you ain't allowed to touch me flowers without asking!"

Abbey could not help smiling broadly. She had always admired the gruff old man, and his adamant protection of his garden was something she understood very well.

"I will not touch your flowers without permission, Withers," she said agreeably.

"See that you don't," he mumbled, and pushed past her to examine the rose she had touched. Satisfied that it was not damaged, he turned around and swiftly eyed her up and down. "So you be the marchioness now."

"I suppose."

"Didn't expect that."

"So you have said."

Withers raised a wiry gray brow. "Still know how to whittle?"

"I haven't in a long time, but I don't think I've forgotten. Do you?" she teased.

Withers scowled. "Course I do," he grumbled, then retrieving his shovel began to move down the graveled aisle. Abbey followed closely behind.

"You know, Withers, I could help you here," Abbey suggested hopefully as she stopped to examine the waxy leaves of an ivy hanging overhead.

"Don't let just anyone in here. Bailey and Hans been with me a long time," the man responded quickly.

"I shall be quite careful. I am not without experience, you know. I had quite a large garden—well, not as large as this, of course, but large by Virginia standards. It was quite successful too.''

Withers settled back onto one hip and perched his great hands on top of the shovel. ''Virginia don't have the same climate. We grow roses almost year round here. They are a hardy strain, and I won't have any practice that will weaken them.''

''Of course not,'' she agreed cheerfully.

''They ain't easy to grow. Takes work.''

''Absolutely. Hard work.''

''Can't do it part o' the time, either. Got to be committed.''

''Yes, of course. One must be *very* committed. Rain or shine, they need their care.''

Withers scratched the thick patch of gray hair as he considered her. ''Well,'' he said with a growl. ''I might let you visit me here. But you got to mind that you do as me or Hans says. And don't listen to Bailey; he's so simple no telling what he'd say.''

''I promise.'' Abbey nodded and smiled brightly.

Withers's gruff facade melted, and he straightened. ''Got work to do. See that you don't touch anything,'' he muttered as he walked away.

Abbey smiled at his great departing back and gleefully went about exploring the whole of the hothouse, being extremely careful not to touch anything. She was aware that Withers watched her closely, just as he had done aboard her father's ship so many years ago, but he never said a word. When Abbey finally began to make her way back to the house, he appeared from nowhere at the entrance of the hothouse and thrust a white rose in her face.

''Here,'' he said, then stalked away.

Abbey smiled fondly as she brought the rose to her nose. The heavenly scent had a soothing effect on her. In here, it was possible to forget her circumstances, forget that Michael apparently had despised her even as a child. She would not think of that now. She had arranged her day so that she would not have to think of him, and so far, it had gone very well. She certainly was not going to start now. Stuffing the rose behind her ear, she marched back to the house, determined to rearrange that godawful chamber they called a sitting room.


Michael did not return as expected, which was just fine with Abbey. The next few days flew by as she delighted in exploring her surroundings. She attended the stables every morning with her maimed dog Harry always on her heels, and finally extracted a promise from a stableboy to teach her to ride one of the fabulous horses. Although she had spent a little time on the back of a mule in Virginia, she had never learned to ride, but reasoned it could not be very different. She also took a great interest in the pregnant milk cow. She made the boy who tended the dairy to promise to send word when the cow showed signs of birthing. She had, after all, helped birth other calves, and she could be counted on to assist when the time came. The color had drained from the boy's face when she had volunteered, but he had solemnly given his word.

In the afternoons, Abbey visited the hothouse. Withers had given her a small section of roses to work with—under his strict supervision, of course. Every day she appeared in a black skirt and simple white blouse and an outrageously decorated straw hat that looked something like a misshapen fruit basket. She patiently explained to anyone who looked particularly pained by it that her cousin Virginia had made it specially for her, and therefore, she was obliged to wear it. Even though she knew it was perfectly hideous.

By the middle of the week, the weather turned warmer and drier, and she took to exploring Blessing Park. It was more beautiful than any land she had ever seen; lush carpets of grass and tall, stately trees abounded. Beyond the walls of the expansive garden were a small lake and a gazebo, and behind the lake, soft, rolling hills fell away to small dales. One day Abbey happened across the old ruins of a castle in her exploration and spent the next two days exploring every nook and cranny while Harry slept in the sun.

Sometimes she even allowed herself to imagine the Michael of her memory roaming the ruins. Try as she might, she could not get past the tendril of longing she had held for years, a tendril for the memory of him that was so inextricably wound up in the real man. The real man looked like the Michael of her memory, moved like him, and even sounded like him. But the words that came out of the real Michael's mouth were so wrong, so unlike the memory. Fortunately, at the ruins, she could substitute her own words in place of the heartless ones.

At night, after an early supper, Abbey retired to her new sitting room. She always had Sarah in tow, sometimes even Cook, and they would wile away the hours much as she had in Virginia. When two younger maids had come with fresh linens and the weekly papers from London one evening, Abbey eagerly invited them to stay. By the end of the week, Abbey played hostess to a sitting room full of female servants from Blessing Park.

They tried to teach her needlework, but to no avail. Undaunted, Abbey began to embroider a picture of Blessing Park for a draught screen. None of the servants had the heart to tell her how poor her skills were. When her patience with the needlework wore thin, she would read outrageous *on dits* from the London papers that had the women laughing hilariously. Or she would read from the history books that graced her room and private library. Apparently the Almighty Darfield enjoyed purchasing expensive volumes of history and in a matter of days, the women were quite well acquainted with Persian history.

She also played her violin for them. The first time Abbey had produced the instrument, she claimed she was rather a mediocre talent compared with the great virtuosos and could not sing or play the pianoforte as might be expected. But the beautiful strains of music that lifted from her strings kept the women in awe and brought a tear to Sarah's eye. Every night after that, the same luscious strains of music would drift through the house, and before long, Sebastian, Jones, and the master's valet, Damon, would hover about the hallway, along with an occasional footman, enraptured. Sebastian remarked one morning that there was nothing the marquis enjoyed more than music. Abbey had wrinkled her nose at that; she would have sworn they had absolutely nothing in common.

Several more days passed and the Devil of Darfield still did not return. Abbey was proud of herself for almost forgetting the King of Rude and settled comfortably into the world she had created for herself. It was a bucolic and simple existence, one she found more and more to her liking as the days passed. She began to relax for the first time since coming to England, and decided that she could very easily make a life at Blessing Park if she were forced to do so. She convinced herself that the absence of a loving husband—and naturally, children— would not be so hard to bear as she feared, as long as she had Blessing Park and the many diversions it offered her.

One morning she received two letters. The first, much to her delight and surprise, was from her second cousin, Galen Carrey. Even though she had not heard from him in some years, she recognized the handwriting immediately. Quite ex- cited about receiving a note from her *dearest*—and only— male cousin, Abbey danced a little jig about her sitting room before carelessly breaking the seal.

My dearest Abbey, greetings and salutations. I had in- tended to visit you in America but received word of your father's untimely demise just prior to departure. I am greatly saddened by the news, as I harbored the most tender of feelings for the captain, much like those for my own father, may they both rest in peace. I learned from Aunt Nan that you have gone to England. As business has kept me on the continent till now, I have not had the opportunity to see you as I have desperately hoped to do. However, I find my circumstance has changed, and I shall very soon be on England's green shores again. I should very much like to see you, as there is much I would tell you. Hoping this letter finds you well, I shall look ever forward to our reunion. Fondly, your cousin, Galen.

Abbey was thrilled with the prospect of a visit from Galen. She remembered him very warmly. The son of her father's cousin, as best she could recall, Galen, who was just a few years older than she, had spent a few summers aboard the *Dancing Maiden*. She had worshipped him; he had paid special attention to her, particularly on those long voyages to the East. It was Galen who had given her her first and practically only kiss beneath an Indian Ocean moon. She sighed at the memory, wondering absently why she had not heard of him in the last few years.

She shrugged happily as she reached for the second letter, which was from a neighbor inviting her and Lord Darfield to Sunday dinner after church services. Delighted, Abbey returned word that if they did not mind, she would attend alone, as Lord Darfield was away.

When Sunday came, and a rather plain carriage was brought to the front of the house, Michael still had not returned.

Wringing his hands, Sebastian followed Abbey to the door like a fretting governess. "Lady Darfield, I would be remiss in my duty if I did not tell you that the marquis will not care for you dining at the Havershams' without him. He was quite insistent you not leave Blessing Park."

Abbey smiled sweetly at Sebastian's reflection in the mirror as she adjusted her bonnet. "I am only attending church services and a friendly dinner, Sebastian. He should not care in the least."

"He *expressly* bade me to keep you at Blessing Park until such time as *he* has the honor of introducing you!"

"Ha!" Abbey snorted and turned to face Sebastian with her hands on her hips. "I am sure that if he truly wanted the honor, he would be here to do it. Really, he has no grounds to object!" she replied cheerfully.

"I beg your pardon, Lady Darfield, but I must *insist*—"

Abbey had already skipped down the steps to the waiting carriage. With a sigh of resignation, Sebastian stood beside Jones and watched as she chatted amicably with the Havershams' footman, who looked stricken by the unusual familiarity.

"She will cause trouble if Lord Darfield does not return

soon," Jones remarked dryly. He struggled to suppress a smile when Abbey patted the footman on the arm before climbing into the carriage. The poor man looked helplessly at Jones and Sebastian.

"He shall have no one to blame but himself," Sebastian replied with a sniff as the carriage pulled away from Blessing Park.


The Havershams, an elderly couple with no children, were more than delighted to host a marchioness, and a pretty, youthful one at that. Abbey was delighted with her hosts. They were open and warm, and Abbey found herself talking freely about her life, the Havershams hungrily hanging on to each and every word. They laughed loudly as Abbey regaled them with tales of her year in Egypt, where she had learned the very tasteless belly dance. Pressed to demonstrate, Abbey reluctantly agreed despite a gnawing sense of impropriety, and by the end of the afternoon, Lord and Lady Haversham were coaxed into trying.

When she returned to Blessing Park late that night—a bit in her cups, Sebastian ruefully noted—Abbey could hardly contain her glee as she recounted how Lord Haversham had slowly gyrated while peering through his monocle, and Lady Haversham, who could not gyrate, had instead bounced up and down. Sebastian had listened politely, bid his lady a good evening, then marched straight to the study and poured himself a big, stout whiskey.

The very next day the Havershams appeared at Blessing Park to fetch Abbey for an outing to Pemberheath. Once again Sebastian pleaded with her to remain, and once again Abbey blithely ignored him.

"There is an old priory there I should very much like to see. Do you know that Simon de Montfort spent a fortnight there?" she asked him, her enthusiasm infectious.

"Yes, madam, I am aware of that. I am quite certain the priory will still be standing when Lord Darfield returns. Please, could your visit not wait until then?"

"Really, Sebastian, is he such an ogre he would deny me a simple excursion to a *priory*?" she asked as she smoothed her hair.

"Certainly not!" Sebastian had answered too quickly.

"There you have it, then. I shall return before nightfall, and there will be no harm done, I promise you," she said cheerfully, and once again turned on her heel and marched out the door, pretending not to hear his blustering objection.

Several hours later and well after nightfall, an exhausted Abbey returned and patiently explained the axle grease on her gown to a stunned Sebastian. The Haversham carriage had encountered a wagon with a broken wheel carrying a rather large family. As there had been several small children in the party, they could not very well leave them to wait for assistance. The Havershams had asked their driver and coachmen to help lift the wagon onto a stump so that the wheel could be reattached. But they had not had enough strength, Abbey reported, and she had offered to lend a hand. After some wrangling, they had managed to reattach the wheel. Abbey's reward had been an ale that the stranded family gratefully shared with the Haversham party. She confessed that both she *and* the elderly Lady Haversham, who had held the team of mules during the repair, found the homemade brew much to their liking.

As Abbey wearily climbed the stairs to her room, Sebastian felt as if he might faint for the first time in his life. He hoped desperately that Lord Darfield would return before something awful happened to shame him any more than what had already transpired.


It was late in the evening, two weeks after his departure from Blessing Park, that Michael galloped into Pemberheath and stopped at the local inn to clear the dust from his throat. He entered the common rooms and spoke politely to his tenants as they greeted him with great enthusiasm. He was mildly puzzled; their excitement at seeing him was far greater than it had ever been, and certainly much more than was warranted.

The round innkeeper wiped his hands on his stained apron and quickly poured the ale Michael requested.

"Lord Darfield! It's been awhile since we had the pleasure of your company," the fat man rasped, his red face beaming with delight.

Michael nodded curtly as he tossed two coins onto the scarred bar.

"The whole village is talking about your lovely wife, milord. What a beauty!" the innkeeper continued.

Michael stopped his tankard midway to his lips and slid his gaze to the man. "My wife?" he asked quietly.

"Lady Darfield! Oh, what a *pleasure* she is, my lord. The lads are *still* talking about the game!" the innkeeper said with a happy shake of his head.

Michael slowly lowered the tankard. "*What* game?"

"Darts. A particular forte of hers, I am sure you'd agree. After the first night she was here, the lads, you know—they had to see if it was true talent or just luck. You never seen anything like it, the way she marched right up to the line and hit the king's eye without nary a blink! When she came back, the lads wouldn't leave 'er be till she agreed to a rematch. She'd've won it too, had Lindsay not hit the king's eye at the very end," he remarked jovially.

Michael could not believe what he had just heard; there had to be some mistake. A horrible mistake. "Are you saying my wife was in here playing darts?" he asked evenly.

The innkeeper's perpetual grin faded. "She *was* in the company of Lord Haversham, milord," he replied indignantly.

"*The Havershams? Here?*" Michael choked. The innkeeper frowned and lifted his double chin.

"*Aye*, the Havershams. They have been here before, my lord," he said haughtily.

Michael could not believe it. He had not spent years of his life restoring the family name only to have the little hellion destroy it by cavorting with seamen and playing barroom games. He did not know whom he would throttle first: Sebastian, to whom he had given strict instructions to mind Abbey at all times, or the Havershams, for bringing her to

Pemberheath. Or that little hellion Abbey, his *pleasure* of a wife whose *forte* was darts! He downed the ale and left the inn without another word, ignoring the disgruntled look of the innkeeper.

He ruthlessly pushed his mount Samson toward Blessing Park, hardly able to contain his anger. He had left the morning after his wedding night because he had tossed and turned, thinking of the incredibly beautiful woman just on the other side of the door—crying. The taste of her, the feel of her in his arms had not dissipated, and it had alarmed him. But he was a fool to have left, for the little hellion could not be trusted! In the two weeks he had been gone, he had gained control of himself—with some difficulty—and was prepared to face her again. He was so much in control of his unusually unsettled emotions that he was ready for a verbal pummeling for having left her. The tables had certainly turned. Now *he* was going to give *her* a verbal pummeling for having spent time in an inn like a common wench, *throwing darts*.

As he galloped up the long drive, he was relieved to see only a few lights. If most of the servants had retired for the evening, he could throttle her without interruption. He vaulted off his horse, ignoring the groom who scrambled to meet him. He marched inside and tossed his hat, gloves, and riding crop to a footman, barely nodding in response to his polite greeting. Without a word, he walked swiftly to the green drawing room and threw open the door.

Inside, Sebastian sat with his head in his hands.

"Where is she?" he asked bluntly. Sebastian looked up and grimaced.

"Good evening, my lord. So good to have you back—"

"Where is she, Sebastian?"

"In her sitting room, my lord."

Michael regarded his secretary with such a scathing look that Sebastian winced. "I know I was quite clear in my desire to keep her at Blessing Park until my return, so I am sure you have a perfectly reasonable explanation for why she has been cavorting about Pemberheath with the Havershams, haven't you, Sebastian?"

Sebastian's thin shoulders drooped. "On my mother's grave, it certainly was not from a lack of trying," he said wearily. Michael raised a brow at his normally stoic secretary.

Sebastian glanced warily at his lord. "You see, my lord, the calf was finally birthed today, and the Havershams, naturally having been infected by her excitement at the impending birth, had very closely followed the progress. Unbeknownst to me, she sent word to Lady Haversham this morning, telling if she truly desired to assist in such a birth—at which, by the by, Lady Darfield seems to be quite practiced—to come at once. Well, Lady Haversham *did* come, and the two of them assisted that old milk cow to bear a healthy calf, and now, naturally, they are celebrating," Sebastian said weakly.

"Naturally," Michael ground out. "If you are telling me what I *think* you are telling me, sir, I am seriously considering sending you out on the *La Belle* next week as a deckhand."

Sebastian groaned. "I did *everything* in my power, my lord, but she is, well, she is rather *willful* at times, and the truth of the matter is, she takes such joy in the simple pleasures of life that it is really rather hard for one to *resist* her—"

"Putting aside, for a moment, the fact that she is a *marchioness,* and therefore expected to adhere to certain standards of behavior, I trust it has not gone unnoticed by you that she is also a young woman. Are you telling me that it is not within your power to restrain a young woman from birthing calves and *playing darts*?" Michael asked acidly.

"Or changing wagon wheels," Sebastian muttered miserably. Michael clenched his jaw tightly shut to keep himself from exploding. Sebastian's misery was apparent. Sebastian, who had been with him forever, who was always so damned unflappable, was telling Michael that he had not been able to control a slender young woman! Michael sighed and tried to summon a little pity. She was, after all, a hellion. No one knew that better than he.

"I want to see her directly after breakfast, Sebastian. Do you think you can persuade her to do *that*?"

Sebastian sighed heavily. "I will certainly try, my lord," he muttered helplessly.

Michael nodded curtly. "Now, if you will excuse me, I intend to bathe and go to bed," he snapped, and marched out of the room. Behind him, Sebastian downed his port and slumped wearily against the chair cushions.

When Michael's boot hit the soft blue carpet at the top of the stairs, he thought he heard muffled laughter. He stopped abruptly and listened for a moment, but heard nothing. With a shake of his head, he started for his rooms, then heard it again. He cocked his head to one side. It was coming from the library directly in front of him. He listened carefully and could hear the feminine and cheerful giggles behind the solid oak door. The little hellion seemed to be having a soirée in there.

Impulsively he knocked on the door. His rap was followed by a moment of silence, then the muffled flurry of movement. His irritation mounting, he knocked a little more forcefully. The door opened just a fraction, and Abbey peeked out from behind it with laughing violet eyes and a smile on her lips that faded rapidly when she saw him.

"Enjoying yourself?" he asked coolly.

Abbey blinked. "Uh, well, yes, thank you. I, uh . . . we . . . weren't expecting you."

"That's obvious," he remarked sarcastically, and slipped his boot in between the door and its frame.

"Was there something you needed?" she asked cautiously.

"You and I are going to have a discussion in the morning, madam," he said icily.

"Oh! Certainly!" she replied politely, then smiled enchantingly. She might as well have punched him in the gut, so powerful was the effect of that smile on him.

Michael swallowed and glanced past her, trying to peer into the room. He put his hand against the door and pushed a little, but Abbey held fast.

"What are you about?" he demanded.

Abbey's eyes darted quickly over her shoulder then back to him. "Nothing of interest. We are sewing."

"Who is *we*?" Michael asked as he pushed again, this time managing to open the door a little wider. Abbey took one step back, but would not budge from the door.

"Well . . . Sarah. Sarah is here. And Lady Haversham, too. And then we invited Cook . . ." She laughed nervously.

*Cook?* Stunned, Michael inched inside, wedging his shoulder between the door and frame, and peered about the room. He was greatly astonished at the sight that greeted him. Sarah was sitting cross-legged in an overstuffed chair, her head bent over a cloth in which she pushed a needle up and down, as if it were the most natural thing in the world for a servant girl to loll about with her mistress. More surprisingly, Lady Haversham sat at a table, and the broad back across from her belonged to none other than Cook.

The room itself had been transformed from a library into a sitting room, and looked as if it had been hit by a cyclone. Papers, books, and magazines were strewn across every conceivable surface. A basket of sewing articles on the floor next to the green settee was open, and its contents spilling carelessly over the sides. Cushions were tossed about the floor and a dozen or more candles flickered light about the room. Two vases stuffed full of hothouse flowers graced a low table between the chairs. There was something so utterly feminine about the room that he did not want to enter; it seemed almost sacrosanct. Instead he nodded curtly to Lady Haversham.

"Lord Darfield! I daresay I was beginning to despair that you would *ever* return to your lovely wife!" she called, and waved a handkerchief at him in greeting.

"As you can see, madam, I have returned," he said abruptly, then looked down at Abbey. Her violet eyes were sparkling as if she harbored some happy secret.

"I shall expect a word with you directly after breakfast," he said stiffly.

"Yes, that's what I understood you to say," she said agreeably.

He glanced one more time about the room, then gave her a curt nod and stepped back. In a moment's hesitation, he quickly changed his mind and stepped forward again, intent on telling her at exactly what time he would see her. But she closed the door so quickly that it collided with his forehead.

"*Damnation!*" he muttered angrily, rubbing his forehead.

A burst of laughter on the other side of the door brought his head up, and irrationally he believed that those women were laughing at his expense.

"Damnation!" he muttered again as he marched down the hall to his rooms.

# Chapter 6

Abbey was not ready for another one of Lord Boorfield's interviews. She had really begun to enjoy herself at Blessing Park, but his return had cast a gray pall over everything. She believed she had come to terms with his callous indifference and did not want to see him. But when she had opened the sitting room door last night, she was dismayed to discover the small kernel of desire that had taken root so many years ago and sprouted within her had not diminished in the least.

Especially after His Insufferable Arrogance had kissed her two weeks ago.

As she dressed, she mulled over what she would say. She had heard enough gossip from Lady Haversham to know that he was very much sought after among the ladies, a tidbit she found terribly disquieting. Lady Haversham had even suggested that the widow, Lady Davenport, was his lover. That had not surprised her; he had said as much himself. In fact, Abbey had deduced that Lady Davenport must be the reason for his aversion to this marriage—perhaps he felt love for the widow. Lady Haversham said she was a celebrated beauty, a petite blonde and closer to Michael's own age. Abbey, on the other hand, was too tall, her eyes too wide for her face, and her unruly hair unfashionably dark. It was no wonder that Michael preferred the beautiful Lady Davenport to her.

She finished dressing and paced in front of the cavernous fireplace to avoid the inevitable. She had to be logical about this. If she returned to America now, it would be in disgrace. Michael loved another, but had honored his commitment to marry her. She apparently had landed at an inopportune time; Michael probably had thought to end his liaison before he married. Perhaps he had not considered he would be married so soon.

Perhaps he needed time to resolve the matter of Lady Davenport before he could give himself to her. It certainly explained his desire to lead separate lives. However, if there was any hope that he could love her again, she would gladly give him the time and space he needed.

She resolved to abide by his terms. He had said she must ask his permission for all purchases. She would certainly agree to that. She really did not care much for fashion, and she could not possibly imagine anything she might need. If he needed to control her allowance as was the practice, then so be it.

He had said he wanted an heir. Now, that was a little stickier. She could not bear the thought of carrying his child when he loved another. She would suggest at least a year should pass so that he would have ample time to finish with Lady Davenport. Besides, she hardly knew him. Shouldn't they find some middle ground on which they could coexist peacefully before parenting children? Not to mention that the thought of his powerful body coupled with hers almost sent her to her knees with fear.

And if he wanted, she would go and not look back, even it was the least desirable option for her and would mean her disgrace. Even so, she refused to listen to the part of her that argued she was not ready to give up on the man she had loved all her life, even if it meant a battered pride.

She was ready to give him everything he wanted—no, *demanded*. In the meantime, she would live as she had the last two weeks, enjoying the wealth of diversion Blessing Park offered, staying well out of his way, and striving to increase her indifference to him. He, on the other hand, could take the time he needed to end his relationship with Lady Davenport.

Pleased and admiring of her ability to muddle through to a workable plan, Abbey went to the breakfast room.

She appeared in the doorway wearing a beguiling smile and a cream day dress covered with a pattern of tiny violets. She felt remarkably fresh despite the early hour and even a little giddy when she saw Michael sitting at the table. He was clad in a dark-blue coat and dove-gray pants that matched the color of his eyes. He looked extremely beautiful this morning, but she was strong enough to ignore that.

"Good morning, Michael!" she said cheerfully.

*Good God,* Michael thought, she actually looked happy to see him as she rocked gently back and forth with her hands clasped demurely behind her back. Lord, but she had a strong effect on him. His gaze swept over her. He had been with many pretty women in his time, but something about her eyes, something about the way she looked at him made him weak. He was not weak, he reminded himself angrily.

"May I join you?" she asked politely. He barely nodded his consent and surreptitiously eyed her feminine figure as she settled into a chair. Her breasts strained against the muslin cloth as she reached across the table for sugar. A vision of those breasts—bared—danced uninvited in his mind's eye.

All right, perhaps he was a *little* weak.

Jones entered through a side door and looked genuinely pleased to see her, an occurrence, Michael thought as he buried his head behind his paper, that was highly unusual.

"Good morning, Lady Darfield! Shall I bring you the usual?" Jones asked in a too-cheerful, singsong voice.

"That would be wonderful. And please, Jones, tell Cook that yesterday's pastries were her best yet! Simply divine!"

"I will relay your compliment, madam. Cook will be pleased."

Behind his paper, Michael raised a brow. Since when did

anyone dare speak to Cook this early in the morning? And since when did Jones have more than two words to say?

Uncharacteristically, Jones tapped a finger on the other side of Michael's paper. "And for you, my lord?" he asked in a cool tone.

Surprised, Michael lowered the paper. "Porridge."

"Porridge," Jones repeated irritably, and disappeared through the side door.

Michael scowled and buried his head behind the weekly again. He tried to ignore Abbey. He tried to absolve Jones for being smitten with her. He tried to pretend he did not smell the enticing scent of lilac and tried not to count the number of sugar cubes she dropped into her tea. He had much more important things about which to speak with her.

After a rather sleepless night, he had decided that some of his displeasure was his own doing. She did not know all the social dictates of this country, and he certainly had not bothered to explain them to her. He suspected some of her outrageous behavior during his absence had been directed at him for leaving. The most logical course was to have a firm discussion with her, brooking no argument, and give her a fair chance to behave properly. He would magnanimously forestall throttling her for the time being. He thought, given the circumstances, that he was being a model of charitable behavior.

"No more than two, Abbey. Five cubes is quite excessive," he heard himself say—much to his own surprise. There was a moment of silence, and he waited for the barrage to begin behind the cover of his paper.

Instead, she began to hum softly.

Against his better judgment, he lowered his paper so he could see over the edge. She was still smiling. Damn that smile! He jerked the paper up again. Several moments passed. He sat rigidly, not comprehending what he was reading, and wondering what in the hell she was doing.

"Michael?"

Her pleasant voice startled him. Slowly he brought the paper down an inch. He would have sworn by the way her eyes sparkled that she was laughing at him. Bloody hell, she was beautiful when her eyes sparkled like that.

"I trust your business was taken care of?" When he did not answer, she spoke again. "There is quite a lot of correspondence that has arrived in the last several days. If you would like, I would be happy to respond to those you think appropriate." His eyes narrowed. At last, here it was. Whatever she had up her sleeve, it was about to unfold.

"Oh no, madam, oh no. *No!*" he said emphatically, shaking his head. He put the paper in his lap and stared at her in a silent challenge to continue.

"As you wish," she said with an agreeable smile.

Surprised again, something that so rarely happened to him, he had to concentrate on keeping his expression bland. He was about to ask her what she was up to when Jones bustled into the room.

"Cook is happy you are pleased with the pastries," he announced joyfully. "She has made you a special treat this morning. Raspberry tarts!" He proudly held up a plate piled precariously high with pastries for her to see. Delighted, Abbey gasped and gleefully clasped her hands together.

Michael's eyes darted first to Abbey, then to Jones. "Cook made raspberry tarts before dawn?" he demanded.

Jones answered with a scowl and plopped a bowl in front of him without ceremony. "Porridge," he drawled disapprovingly.

"Oh, these are delicious! Would you care for one?" Abbey purred.

Vaguely irritated and unsure as to why, he muttered, "No. Thank you." Abbey made a little sound as if she were perplexed by his response, then devoured her tart. Ignoring his porridge, Michael watched her blissfully reach for another tart and devour it, too, smiling at him all the while. After daintily dabbing at the corners of her mouth with a linen napkin, she carefully put aside her teacup, stood, and reached for the plate of tarts.

"Just where do you think you are going?" Michael demanded. Her eyes widened in innocence.

"If you will excuse me, I have rather a full day in front of me. Oh! You mean the tarts. Sarah is quite fond of them, so I thought to take some to her. Unless, of course, you would prefer them."

"I do not want any tarts," he said with a growl.

Abbey shrugged indifferently. "Very well then. Good day."

Michael could not think of what to say as she turned from the table and stopped to examine some fresh-cut flowers before starting for the door.

"Wait!" he barked. Abbey glanced over her shoulder at him. "Did you not understand that I wanted a discussion with you?" he snapped.

Abbey smiled cheerfully. "I quite understood. I suppose I thought we just had it."

"No, we did not. Sit down," he commanded, trying gamely to ignore the unnerving sparkle in her eye and forcibly reminding himself of the role she had played in the agreement.

Abbey placed the tarts on the table, then dutifully sat and folded her hands demurely in her lap. Her lovely face watched him expectantly.

Michael's pulse began to quicken. "Abigail—"

"Abbey."

"Abbey," he conceded. "Pay close attention to what I say. I have been remiss in not explaining certain things to you. There are . . . activities . . . a marchioness does not engage in, no matter what the circumstance."

"Indeed? I had no idea!" she said with genuine surprise, then frowned slightly at Jones, as if he had also been remiss in not explaining to her.

"To begin with, a marchioness does not"—he could hardly say the words—"*play darts* at the local inn, no matter how skilled she may be." Abbey blinked.

"Or change wagon wheels. Or birth calves," he continued evenly.

Abbey's brilliant violet eyes began to darken. There was no hiding a single emotion in those eyes; they were a window to her very soul. And at the moment, her soul was clearly irritated.

"Pray tell, what does a marchioness do?" she asked coolly.

"She amuses herself with gentle activities. Embroidery, the pianoforte, riding, etcetera. *Not* manual labor, and most certainly *not* barroom games."

She considered that for a moment, then asked with feigned innocence, "Do you mean to say there are *rules* a marchioness must follow?"

"Not *rules* exactly."

"Then how should one know what a marchioness must do?"

Michael rolled his eyes and glared at the ornately plastered ceiling. He had the distinct impression he was being trifled with, or the girl was too artless for her own good. "There are certain dictates, societal norms, if you will. Standards that members of polite society are expected to follow," he tried again.

"Are you expected to follow them, as well?"

"Of course."

"Hmm . . . you mean something like a card game. There are certain rules, and if one does not follow them, one loses." She nodded helpfully, then turned a beguiling grin to Jones. "Unless one *cheats*, of course!" she added. Jones chuckled but stopped abruptly when Michael glared at him.

"I wasn't exactly speaking of cards, Abbey. No one dictates what members of the *ton* will do, but there are expectations." She looked puzzled. He began to rub his temples.

"Then perhaps you mean rules that govern a solicitor? Like the law?" she asked.

"No, I do not mean that, either," he said behind clenched teeth.

Abbey frowned slightly and tapped a manicured nail against her bottom lip. "Then are you referring to procedures that govern the working of something, like a ship? There may not be exact *rules* to guide a ship, but one must certainly *guide* a ship in such a manner that one does not sink it," she said, as if playing a game.

At the sideboard, Jones nodded enthusiastically and looked hopefully at Michael, who drew a long, tortured breath.

"I hardly mean guiding a ship, Abbey," he said impatiently, despite his best effort to remain calm.

"Then how does a marchioness *know* what is expected if there are no rules or procedures?" she asked again.

"There are no *rules*, Abbey. No rules!" he snapped irritably, helpless to explain himself.

Abbey was silent for a brief moment. "I see," she said cheerfully.

He certainly hoped she did. He returned to rubbing his temples.

"Then the *ton* can really do whatever they please?" she asked sweetly.

"Yes!" he ground out.

"Thank you, this has been very useful," she said amicably, and stood to go.

Michael, quite unaccustomed to having to explain himself to anyone, was speechless at how she had twisted his words against him. The scent of lilac drifted over him as she swept by and suddenly, he could not let her get away so easily. "Just a moment, Abbey."

She paused at the door. "Yes?"

"I forbid you to play darts, birth cows, or change wagon wheels. Those are *my* rules. You will behave in a manner befitting your station, do I make myself clear?"

"You mean my station as a marchioness?" she asked carefully.

"Yes, that of a marchioness," he said, his patience wearing thin.

Abbey cocked her head prettily to one side. "You make yourself quite clear."

"Now, what have you planned for today?"

"Oh. Embroidery, the pianoforte. Nothing remarkable," she replied sweetly.

"You will remain at Blessing Park. Do not visit the Havershams and do not go to Pemberheath," he snapped. An unmistakable cloud of disappointment covered her violet eyes, and Michael instantly regretted being so churlish.

"As you wish. Good day, my lord." She closed the door softly behind her.

Jones immediately turned from the sideboard and uncharacteristically bestowed a hateful glare on Michael. "If I may be so bold, sir—"

Michael still had not recovered from his decided inability to explain himself and was very much taken aback by the remarkable utterance from Jones. "You may not!"

"A little kindness would not be too much to ask, I should think. She is deserving of it."

"My God, Jones, I think you should fetch a physician. For a moment I was certain I heard *you* instruct *me* on how to treat a woman!" Michael said incredulously.

"My humblest apologies, my lord, I would never instruct you on how to treat a woman," Jones said smoothly. Michael nodded smugly and turned back to his porridge. "I was referring to your wife."

The spoon froze midway between Michael's bowl and his mouth. "*Jones!*"

But Jones was already out the door, leaving Michael to stare into his coagulated porridge. In frustration, he dropped his spoon and stared at the door to the breakfast room, silently willing her to come back and chiding himself for being weak.

Michael eventually made his way to the library to look for the correspondence the silly chit had mentioned. It was not in there as he expected, so he went to the main sitting room. He opened the door and faltered. The room had been completely transformed. The furniture had been moved to the middle of the room, forming cozy circles around tables heaped with books. Gone were several of the old portraits that had hung on the wall, and those that remained had been rearranged. He was not sure, but he thought several smaller objêts d'art were missing, as well. The French doors that led onto the terrace were open, and a soft breeze, unusually warm for late winter, lifted a sheet of paper on one table. Those doors, to the best of his recollection, had *never* been open. The room, now airy and bright, was a stark contrast to the dark, solemn room to which he was accustomed. A maid paused in her dusting and dropped a polite curtsey as he slowly came across the threshold.

"What happened to this room, Ann?"

"Lady Darfield rearranged it, my lord. She thought it too formal."

"I see," he muttered. He walked slowly to the mantel, where a silver tray stacked high with letters sat next to a vase of fresh-cut flowers. He took the bundle and absently began to sift through them. Invitations, business letters, more invitations. He suspected the whole Southampton region was eager for a look at the new Lady Darfield, assuming, naturally, that Lady Haversham had been her usual loquacious self with a piece of news. Yes, his neighbors were probably in a frenzy by now, what with his quick and unplanned marriage. No doubt flagrant rumors of inappropriate behavior on his part were circulating freely.

The sound of laughter coming from the gardens snapped him back to the present. Unless Withers had completely lost his mind, someone was in the gardens who should not be, and he had a good idea who.

He dropped the papers on the tray and marched through the open doors onto the terrace.

Abbey was below him on a grassy lawn. She had changed into a plain black skirt and white blouse. Her mahogany hair was knotted simply at the nape of her neck, and soft curls drifted down her back. Atop her head she wore a strange, floppy straw hat that looked like a giant fruit basket. A dog, one that looked to be from his kennels, was chasing a ball Abbey tossed for him. Withers was there, too, working in the garden. He seemed oblivious to her presence until Abbey said something that made the big man throw back his head with laughter. Michael would not have believed it had he not heard it himself. What was it about her that had his normally humorless staff swooning?

He stood silently watching the scene below him for several minutes. Abbey tossed the ball and in a lilting voice urged the dog to bring it to her. Once the dog had returned the ball, she gathered her skirts in one hand, revealing a very shapely calf, and skipped about the lawn, keeping the ball from the dog before throwing it again. Michael inhaled a slow, deliberate breath before moving toward the stone steps leading to the garden.

Abbey and Withers did not notice him approaching down the main path. By the time he reached them, Abbey was breathless, her cheeks stained the color of Withers's roses. A familiar and unwelcome longing tugged at Michael as he sauntered toward them.

She still had not seen him when she sent the ball sailing. It ricocheted off a tree and knocked squarely into Michael's leg. In a whirl of skirt and satin hair, Abbey turned to retrieve it, laughing, but drew up short when she saw him.

He was aware his expression was one of stone. He clasped his hands behind his back and shifted his weight to one leg as he regarded her behind cool gray eyes. She glanced anxiously at Withers, who grunted as if he were afraid Michael might touch one of his precious roses. She approached him slowly to retrieve the ball.

"Would you like to join us in a game? You will find it's quite invigorating, particularly on such a glorious morning."

"I think not," he responded coolly. He picked up the leather ball and tossed it to her. She caught it deftly in one hand, tossed it carelessly in the air, and caught it again.

"Is there something you wanted?" she asked, and nervously flipped the long tail of silky hair over her shoulder.

"No," he managed. He might have thought of something more profound to say, but he was mesmerized. He realized he was staring and abruptly shifted his weight to the other leg and glanced upward. "Fetching hat," he remarked dryly.

Abbey wrinkled her nose. "Do you really think so? I think it rather hideous," she said as she pulled the hat off her head and examined the outrageous fruit decoration.

Michael raised one brow in silent question as to why she would wear a hat she thought was hideous but said nothing.

The dog, having wandered over in search of his ball, began sniffing Michael's boots with abandon.

"That dog should be in the kennels," he remarked, for wont of anything better.

"Harry? Unfortunately, he has been expelled from your kennels."

"I beg your pardon?" Michael asked, shifting his gaze to her.

"Do you see his paw? He was injured in a steel trap. The kennelmaster was set to put him down, but I couldn't bear it. He's rather a cheerful hound, and but for his mangled foot, he does quite nicely." She patted her thigh and the dog wobbled across the lawn in a half lope, half walk, blissfully unaware that one front paw was permanently disfigured and faced the other at a right angle. Abbey squatted down to pet the dog, and Michael could see the voluptuous line of her thigh against her skirt and her breasts straining against her blouse. He forced himself to look at the ground. He was mad, quite raving mad. He was standing there admiring the pirate girl, for chrissakes!

"He is useless," he muttered impassionately.

Abbey peered up at him with one hand across her eyes to shade the sun. "He may well be useless for the hunt, sir, but he is quite a good companion." She stood up and brushed her hands lightly against her skirt while his gaze swiftly swept her figure. His jaw clenched tightly, and for some inexplicable reason, he could not summon his tongue. She waited patiently, looking about, anywhere but at him. After several, long, painful moments, she nodded politely and started to turn from him.

"Shall I expect you at supper?" Those were definitely not the words he was trying to summon; it was as if his tongue had a mind of its own. He did not want to be with her, a small fact his tongue apparently had forgotten.

Abbey's cheerful smile faded. God, he could be a dolt at times. He added softly, "I do not intend to interview you if you choose to dine with me." She smiled shyly but did not answer him. Michael stood, regarding her without expression, waiting for her to agree. When it became apparent she had no intention of responding, he began to feel like an awkward schoolboy. He did *not* want to be with her. He did not want anything to do with her. Good God, he could call on Rebecca if he was suddenly so desperate for companionship! He turned abruptly on his heel and strode purposefully toward the house.

Withers slowly shook his head as he watched him march away from the corner of his eye.

"Oh, God, Withers, he *despises* me!" Abbey moaned.

Withers snorted irritably. "You are naive and apparently blind. That man doesn't despise you, gel, he wants you in his bed."

Abbey blushed furiously. "He wants nothing of the sort," she said, and stooped to pet Harry. Not that she wouldn't have given anything for Michael to want in her some small way, but not just to bed. She was now convinced he did not want her even *there*. She had every intention of telling him this morning she would abide by whatever rules he laid down, but he had been so devastatingly handsome and so predictably cold that she could not bring herself to do it.

"I am not so much as allowed to leave Blessing Park, you know, or to visit the Havershams. That is hardly because he holds me in great esteem."

Withers chuckled. "I reckon it has more to do with his esteem for the Havershams."

"But it's so unfair! Galen is coming all this way to visit me, and I suppose I will not be allowed to see him, either," she sniffed.

Withers stopped what he was doing and glanced over his shoulder. "Galen? Who in the devil is Galen?"

Surprised, Abbey smiled at Withers. "My cousin Galen. Do you not recall him? He was aboard the *Dancing Maiden* the year we sailed to Africa. He wrote me and said he is coming to visit, very soon. That is, if *he* will allow it."

Withers's fleshy face darkened noticeably, and he turned slowly back to his roses. "If he don't, it's for your own good, silly gel," he muttered.

Puzzled by his reaction, Abbey straightened and stared the

gardener's broad back. "Withers, he is my cousin. Surely even Lord Darfield wouldn't begrudge me a visit by my own cousin!"

"He won't put you in harm's way, you can count on that! Now, don't be looking at me like 'at!"

Abbey frowned and examined the leather ball in her hand. She did not believe Withers and chalked up his blustering to a seaman's superstition. In her experience, sailors had a superstition for just about everything under the sun. She shrugged and tossed the ball for Harry. She still owed the Black Marquis a graceful way out if he needed it. Perhaps she would join him at supper. Perhaps she would cry off then, and perhaps he would be so enormously thankful, he would allow her cousin to visit. How happy she would be to see Galen. God knew she could use a friend just now.

# Chapter 7

Except for two cool brief encounters during the day, Abbey managed to think little of Michael until it came time to dress for supper. Now, the prospect of seeing him again made her oddly nervous, and she insisted Sarah help her select an appropriate gown and arrange her hair.

While Abbey dressed, Sarah chatted endlessly about Lord Darfield. To hear the gushing young maid tell it, he was even more a saint than Captain Carrington could have imagined. But Abbey was wise to her new friend and her desire to see the Darfields firmly united, and politely ignored her chatter.

She could not really concentrate, anyway. Inside, she was a jumbled mess of confused emotions. She wanted to look appealing, but she did not want him to notice her. She wanted him to like her, but she wanted to remain aloof and separate.

When she was finally ready, she slowly descended the winding marble staircase and paused at the foot of the stairs. She was in no hurry to join him; more and more this was seeming a very bad idea. She should keep her distance from him, maintain a distinct separation, speak only when spoken to. She walked languidly toward the drawing room, her fingers trailing carelessly over furniture, admiring the portraits that lined the walls. One portrait in particular caught her attention. It was a woman who closely resembled Michael, except that she had light hair and a beautiful smile. The Marquis of Bitterfield had a beautiful smile, too, but he so rarely used it.

"It's my mother," Michael said from behind her.

Startled, Abbey jumped and whirled around. A faint smile touched his lips as she sucked in a deep, calming breath and turned back to the portrait.

"She was beautiful," she murmured, gazing up at the portrait.

"Yes, she was," Michael agreed.

Abbey sighed wistfully. "You must miss her very much."

Michael politely offered his arm, which she reluctantly took. "Indeed, I do," he said simply, then led her to the gold drawing room and seated her on a gold, chintz-covered chair before moving gracefully to the drink cart.

Through the veil of her lashes, Abbey watched him. He was wearing formal black evening attire. The whiteness of his pristine collar and neckcloth made his face look even more bronzed, and his thick black hair seemed to melt into his broad shoulders. Abbey bit her lower lip and looked away so that he would not catch her practically drooling over him.

"A sherry?" he asked politely.

"I much prefer a rum, if you have it," she responded.

With his back to her, Michael arched a brow, but said nothing. He brought her the drink, then settled in a chair next to her, casually crossing one leg over the other.

"I wonder where in America a girl would develop a taste for rum," he said lightly.

"I don't have a taste for it yet, but I thought I should try it." She missed his curious look and sipped cautiously. She immediately shut her eyes and wrinkled her nose.

"Not to your liking?" he asked with a smile of amusement.

She opened her bright eyes. "I like it better than the whiskey," she said hoarsely, "but not as much as ale."

Michael chuckled.

"I was only in America for three years."

"Indeed? I was under the impression you had not been to England in some time," Michael said.

"Not since I was a very young girl, that's true." Abbey caught a breath in her throat. He *knew* she had lived most of her life at sea! He knew every place she had lived, did he not?

"What of you?" she asked hesitantly. "Have you been to America?"

"Twice. My ships are built in Boston."

Abbey perked up at that. "I am quite fond of Boston. We always had such a grand time when we went there. Last year they had a rather large festival on the waterfront. There were big ships from all over the world, and one was actually permitted to tour them! They are much larger than those my father owned."

Michael nodded. "I attended that festival. I had quite a grand time of it myself."

Abbey's smile faded. He had been in Boston only last year and did not attempt to see her? He had been at the same festival. She glanced away as she tried to collect her thoughts. She was jumping to conclusions again, a practice she definitely had to stop. He obviously had not known how to contact her. Or perhaps he was involved with Lady Davenport at the time and did not *want* to contact her. She put her rum down, a little harder than she would have liked.

"Is something wrong?" he asked.

Abbey took a steadying breath and composed herself, determined not to let him see her disappointment. "I think the rum does not quite agree with me." She smiled nervously.

But Michael could plainly see it was not the rum. Her violet eyes had darkened with an emotion he would have termed misery.

Jones entered the room just then, smiled broadly at Abbey, and announced that supper was served.

"Are you ill?" Michael asked, a bit alarmed at the sudden change in her.

Abbey's thin smile did nothing to assuage his concern. "Not in the least. Truly, it was just the rum," she said, and stood. Michael came to his feet, offering his arm. Abbey stared at it, then reluctantly put her elegant hand on his forearm. Staring straight ahead, she fell in beside him and marched off to what a casual observer might have reasonably expected was the hangman's noose instead of the dining room.

Once seated Abbey decided she had to divert the subject from their past until she could talk about it without getting so abysmally emotional. She could not do it at supper; he seemed too relaxed, and that pleased her enormously. Except for her doubts about his presence in Boston, their conversation was amicable. She asked him about his ship, the *La Belle*, and he lit up with excitement. It was the latest design, he explained to her, built to speed over the water. It had made its maiden voyage six months ago and was now ready to be launched for a voyage to the Mediterranean. That led her to ask about his life at sea, and he talked with great animation, regaling her with tales of various ports he had visited, many of which Abbey had been in at one time or another. She tried to ignore the feeling that something was not quite right. Ships went in and out of port every day; it would have been impossible for him to have known where she was at any given point in time.

But he had known where her father was.

After supper, they retired to his private library. Abbey peered into the dimly lit room before taking a small step across the threshold. She eyed the fine furnishings and stood shyly next to the servant waiting attentively at the door. The walls were covered with dark paneling and bookshelves full of leather-bound volumes. A globe stood near the hearth, where a fire crackled brightly. Rich velvet draperies, the color of wine, adorned two large windows. Big, soft leather chairs faced each other in front of the hearth, next to a long leather couch. Two upholstered chairs were in the center of the room, with a low polished table separating them.

Michael removed his coat as he crossed the thick Persian rug and dropped it carelessly across the wing-backed leather chair stationed behind a massive mahogany desk. He then strolled casually to the hearth, nodding imperceptibly to a footman, who immediately brought two snifters of brandy.

When Abbey moved slowly to the fire, Michael surreptitiously perused her feminine figure. In the green dress, her soft, curving figure was well displayed. Her gown was a soft velvet gathered at her natural waist—not a currently fashionable design, but certainly very comely and elegant. She looked something like a goddess, and the idea of pulling the gorgeous creature onto his lap flitted swiftly across his mind's eye.

"That's a lovely dress," he remarked genuinely.

Abbey blushed prettily. "My cousin Victoria made it for me. She's rather handy with a needle, fortunately, as I don't have a single notion of what is fashionable."

"Indeed? I rather think your gowns are quite becoming."

"Really?" she asked, clearly pleased. "I owe it all to Tori. Fortunately, she is *much* better with her needle than Virginia is with her paste." She laughed lightly.

"Virginia?" Michael asked.

"My other cousin. She is responsible for the hat." She nodded.

Michael grinned. "Ah, yes, the hat. And what are *you* handy with, Abbey?" he asked as he brought the snifter to his lips.

Her blush deepened, contradicting her careless shrug. "Oh, nothing, really. I'm very poor at navigating cloth with a needle, and I certainly have no eye for hats. I helped Aunt Nan manage the farm." She moved to the chair across from him and settled in a cloud of green. With the firelight flickering against her skin, she easily could have been an artist's creation.

"And what did you do before that?" he asked, more interested in the creamy skin of her breasts rising softly above her bodice than her answer.

"You know," she replied nervously. His eyes flicked to hers.

"Do I?" he asked, the lazy grin snaking across his lips again.

"You *know* you do," she insisted. He had no idea of what

she was talking about and merely smiled. Abbey stiffened noticeably in her seat and set aside the brandy, untouched.

"I think we should talk," she announced suddenly.

"Of what?" He gestured subtly to the footman, who quietly quit the room.

"I think we should establish some rules now, don't you?" she asked carefully.

Michael's eyes suddenly hardened, and he slowly crossed one leg over the other.

"I believe the rules have been established," he said coolly as he swirled the brandy in his snifter. His intent gaze made her terribly self-conscious, and she stupidly wondered if he was comparing her to Lady Davenport.

Flustered, she bit her lower lip and looked intently at her lap. "After hearing your preferred arrangement—

"It is not my *preferred* arrangement, it is *the* arrangement—"

"After hearing the *arrangement*, I thought we should mutually agree upon a few simple ideals. For example, you shall live in Brighton, and I shall live here, is that not correct?"

"I shall live where I see fit, Abbey. *You* shall live here."

"You implied you would leave me to Blessing Park. I think that, given the unfortunate circumstances in which we find ourselves, I prefer you to remain in Brighton unless there is some compelling need for you to be here."

Michael actually looked surprised for a moment, but his expression quickly gave way to bland indifference. "I did suggest I would spend my time in Brighton. But I may change my mind at any given moment, and it is best you understand that I will do as I please."

Abbey released a small, weary sigh. He was suddenly so cold and distant, her courage was beginning to crumble. "I see," she muttered, and stood abruptly. She crossed to a library table and absently fingered the books that lay there as she tried to muster her resolve.

"Then let me broach the subject of my allowance," she finally continued. "I have no need of money. You may have it." She thought he would appreciate her straightforward manner with such a sensitive topic. If his sarcastic snort was any indication, that was hardly the case. His resentment of her had seemed to vanish at supper, but it had grown by leaps and bounds in the short time they had been in his private library. It was obvious Lord Rude would make an appearance tonight after all.

"I know by law it belongs to you—rest assured, that fact was made perfectly clear before I ever left America—and I am telling you I relinquish it freely," she clarified. She waited for him to respond, but the room was filled with only the sound of a ticking clock. At the very least he could thank her for being so reasonable about the whole thing! Why did he not say anything? His silence made her even more nervous, and she whirled around, leaned against the table, and studied him for a long moment, as he did her. He did not seem the least bit appreciative of what she was trying to do; instead he looked angry. She wondered what he could be thinking as his gaze swept her.

"If I may be perfectly frank, Michael—"

"Please," he said coolly.

She sighed with great exasperation. "If I may be perfectly frank, I think you should know that I understand your, uh, *circumstance*, and I do not mind in the least. In fact, I think it rather explains a lot, and I have no animosity toward the situation whatsoever."

Michael's brows lowered with his suspicions. "My circumstance?"

"I have no desire to interfere, but I would ask for some consideration in return for my . . . *discretion*."

"Of what circumstance do you speak?" he asked slowly.

Abbey sighed impatiently. "I supposed there is no delicate way to say it, is there? Very well. I am trying very hard to say that I understand about you and Lady Davenport, and I—"

"Lady Davenport," he said acidly.

Abbey flinched. "Yes. Lady Davenport. I'm trying to tell you that I don't—"

"Trying to tell me what? That as far as you are concerned,

it is perfectly all right for me to have a *circumstance* with Lady Davenport?'' he half stated, half asked.

Abbey was momentarily startled. ''No, I was . . . well, on second thought, I suppose I was,'' she said thoughtfully.

''That's what you suppose,'' he echoed, his frown deepening.

''Yes!'' she declared impatiently. She was being as charitable as she knew how, and he actually seemed annoyed with her! The Devil of Darfield certainly had audacity. He put his snifter down and stood slowly, drawing to his full height of more than six feet, and started toward her, slowly and deliberately. The muscles in his jaw were working, a sign she intuitively knew was not a good one.

''Really, I think I am being quite reasonable!'' she fairly shouted as panic filled her. ''Your resentment of me is quite evident, and you have made it perfectly clear your affections may lie elsewhere! I have been told Lady Davenport is very beautiful, and I can hardly blame you!''

Michael continued his slow approach, moving like a cat preparing to catch its prey. Abbey instinctively braced herself against the table, gripping it so hard that her fingers ached. His cold, stone-gray eyes were impenetrable, and she knew that she had hit a deep, dissonant chord.

She frantically attempted to explain again. ''Really, Darfield, I do not know why this angers you so! I am trying to convey that I quite understand your circumstance and will not stand in your way!''

Michael came to a halt just inches from her. She could feel his brute strength, thinly restrained, emanating from beneath his expensive clothing. His breath fanned lightly across her face, and Abbey could look no higher than his mouth, which was drawn in a tight, grim line. She was, for once in her life, truly frightened, and could feel the quaking in her limbs and the pit of her stomach. He suddenly grabbed her arms and gripped them tightly.

He jerked her to him and smiled sardonically when she gasped. ''The only *circumstance* I shall have is with my wife, Abbey. Whatever is in that devious little mind of yours, know this: If I ever suspect, even for a moment, that you are cuck-olding me, I will have your pretty little head on a platter. Do I make myself clear?"

Abbey recoiled from his deadly tone. "I would *never*," she whispered.

His grip tightened painfully; his eyes slipped to her mouth. "You are my wife, Abbey, for better or worse, and I expect you to act the part.

She inhaled sharply and leaned backward in a vain attempt to escape him, forcing herself to look into his inviolable eyes.

"You misunderstand me, sir," she rasped. "This is obvi-ously an unbearable situation for you, and I only wish to chart a course we can both abide in relative comfort," she mur-mured helplessly.

The corner of his mouth lifted in a twisted grin. "I shall dictate a course that makes it bearable, I assure you," he muttered coarsely, then covered her mouth with his.

Abbey struggled against him. Forcing her lips apart with his tongue, he plunged deep inside her mouth. The sensual attack ignited a smoldering fire within her, and against her will, for-saking every shred of dignity she had, she responded. He released his painful grip on her arms and slid his hands behind her back, caressing her spine and pulling her more closely to him. She instinctively arched against him and could not contain a small moan when he pressed his swollen manhood against her belly. Michael's kiss became more urgent then, and she clutched his shoulders as her body responded to a desire that seemed to batter uncontrollably for release.

He groaned and tightened his embrace, crushing her to him. His lips slid to her lobe and he flicked his tongue in her ear. Suddenly adrift on a sea of consuming desire, Abbey closed her eyes and dropped her head back. Michael pressed his lips against the warm hollow of her throat, while one hand began to travel slowly up her side. When he cupped her breast, she almost came out of her skin. Her eyes flew open and she pushed hard against his chest.

Michael growled. "You are my *wife*," he insisted against her lips.

Trembling uncontrollably with a peculiar mixture of fear and desire, she panicked. She wrenched her head away from him and desperately pushed against his chest. "*No!* I can't do this, I can't!" She gasped.

Michael groaned, but released her and took a step back. Gasping for air, Abbey's gaze unthinkingly traveled his masculine frame, her eyes widening at the sight of his manhood straining against the fabric of his trousers. She dragged her gaze to his face; he wore an expression of pure lust.

She thought she would be ill.

"What's wrong with you?" he demanded.

"I . . . this is rather inconvenient."

"*Inconvenient?*" he all but shouted.

With a trembling hand, Abbey brushed a strand of hair from her eye and searched frantically for an excuse.

"I have my monthly flux," she lied, blushing furiously. Michael blinked. He ran a hand through his thick hair, then turned his back to her.

She stumbled away from the sideboard as Michael fell into a leather chair and reached for his brandy. He shook his head violently, ran a hand through his hair again. Snarling to himself, he tossed his head back to drain the snifter of brandy. Still reeling wildly from the heated kiss and the terrifying emotions that roiled within her, Abbey stared at him in silence.

"Perhaps you should retire." The cool, steady aloofness had returned to his voice. Abbey unsteadily wiped her mouth with the back of her hand.

"What about our arrangement?" she asked nervously.

"Good God, woman, to *hell* with your bloody arrangement! Go to bed!"

Abbey wanted nothing more than to do just that, to be gone from him. She had tried to be magnanimous, had tried to indicate she knew he needed time, and now he was acting as if she were the most distasteful thing he had ever encountered. He was a scoundrel of the worst kind, and she suddenly wanted nothing more than to get away from him. She began to move toward the door.

"Abbey." His voice, cold as ice, sent a shiver through her. She stopped and turned slowly to face him.

He ruthlessly studied her face for a long moment before speaking. "If I ever discover you are cuckolding me, I may very well kill you. Believe me."

The mere suggestion was so vile, Abbey recoiled. "How *dare* you insinuate such a thing?" She gasped.

"How dare *I*?" he asked, laughing cruelly. "You come into my home and give me your *blessing* to have an adulterous affair and think I will not understand? What possible motive would you have for that, unless you think it gives *you* license to seek your own lover?" he asked nastily.

Abbey's gut lurched; she stumbled to one of the leather chairs and gripped the back of it for support as she realized she could no more love another man than she could take her own life.

"No, no . . ." She moaned at his misunderstanding. "I only wanted to give you time! I know you need time to remember that you once cared for me!" she blurted.

Startled, Michael's brows knit in confusion. "I beg your pardon?"

Abbey swallowed hard to keep tears from falling. "I thought you would want time to end your liaison," she rushed. "I know you had to wait a very long time, and I am sorry for that, because *I* didn't want to wait, either, but Papa said it wasn't the right time, and I *know* things may happen beyond our control! If you need time to end your liaison before you remember how you waited all those years, then I would gladly give it to you!"

As if watching some fantastic play unfold, Michael leaned forward in his chair. "I haven't the slightest notion what you are talking about," he said quietly.

Abbey took a deep breath. She must be babbling; she obviously was not making any sense. "Even though you waited all those years, I can understand that you were not ready for my arrival—"

"*Waited* all those years?" he asked incredulously, and looked at her as if she spoke a foreign language.

A feeling of sick dread began to descend on her. She nodded slowly, uncertainly. "The years we have been promised. You were waiting for me, Papa said you—" The dark look of pity that washed over Michael's face told her everything. In that one instance, with that one look, he told her that her papa had lied. He had never *waited* for her. He had never *loved* her. He probably did not even remember she existed! He had not come to see her in America because he had not known she was there! He saw her realization, and his pitiful expression only deepened. Abbey suddenly clutched her hands to her stomach and whirled away from him.

"*Oh—oh my God!*" she stammered. "*Oh my God!*" In a single, defining moment, her whole world, everything she had ever known or believed, came crashing in on her. A wave of nausea rumbled over her and the room began to surge to the right. Sickened, Abbey lurched for the door.

"Abbey!" Michael cried from behind her. She stumbled forward, away from him, desperate to find the door and flee before he could see her crushing humiliation. He caught her from behind and dragged her up against his chest, his arms tightly around her middle. Abbey sagged against him.

"I think I am going to be sick," she managed to get out. He muttered an oath under his breath and swept her into his arms.

"Please let me go!" she begged him, mortified he should see her engulfing shame at having been so *stupid*. What a fool she had been! What a naive, hapless little fool! He had told her the truth, but she had not heard it until this very minute. He had *never* loved her, he had not even liked her! Everything that had happened to her since she had set foot in England tumbled roughly in her mind. Michael had told her he married her because of her father's will. He had begged her to end it before they both suffered irreparable harm. Withers had told her he did not like her when she was a little girl. She had heard none of it. With a choking sob, she finally understood that all her life she had believed he loved her and was waiting for her, and he had been sailing around the world not even *remembering* her! The painful realization that her dreams had been nothing more than a fantasy concocted by her father was surpassed only by the revolting realization that her father had *lied* to her about everything.

Michael moved with incredible swiftness down the long corridor. Abbey buried her face in the soft wool of his coat, desperately swallowing her nausea.

"How could he? He could he have done this?" She moaned, not realizing she had voiced her thoughts aloud.

"I don't know, sweetheart," Michael responded tightly. She heard his boots strike the marble staircase and felt herself being propelled upward. She heard Sarah cry out when he kicked open the door to her chamber and heard him mumble something to Sarah when he gently lay her on the bed. Abbey instantly rolled away from his probing eyes and buried her face in a pillow. She could feel him standing there, staring down at her, and thought she would die of shame. After what seemed to her to be an eternity, he turned and left her bedside. She barely heard the soft exchange of voices as the tears she had tried to hide now seeped out of her uncontrollably.

Michael cursed long and colorfully as he slowly made his way back to his library. The physical longing he felt for her had not been diminished by the sudden and awful realization that she had been duped by her own father. No, it had actually intensified. For the first time, he saw in her eyes very painful evidence that she might not be a part of Carrington's plot but a victim. She had been a mere child when the agreement had been struck; at least he had known what he was doing when he signed the blasted thing. But now they were two adults, each caught in the grip of betrayal from beyond the grave. Each forced into an untenable situation by their fathers.

He poured a brandy as a servant picked up the glass he had dropped when it looked as if she would faint. He walked to one of the windows, pushed aside the thick drapes, forced the window open, and took several deep breaths of the gray night air. Against his will, he had enjoyed this most pleasurable evening. He had basked in the glow of Abbey's natural beauty, feeling a vague longing every time she smiled at him.

He had never known anyone like her, not really. She was so wildly unconventional, so worldly and innocent at the same time. And her natural and unfettered response to his kiss had startled him, unleashing a passion he had not known since he was a young man. He might very well have taken her there, on the library table, had she not come up with the obvious lie about her monthly flux.

He did not want to be attracted to her, much less desire her touch. He did not want to know the feel of her exquisite body in his arms. He did not want to know the taste or smell of her. He did not want to depend on her company. He did not want to pity her. In fact, he did not want to feel anything for her.

Thus his sudden feeling of tenderness was unwelcome as was his desire. He drained his brandy as he stared out the window. In that moment he decided that he would not become some foppish slave to her beauty and feisty charm. He had not wanted this marriage. She was another of his father's messes he was having to clean up, and he resented the hell out of the whole damn situation. Her physical allure aside, he did not want to be burdened with her.

Yet he could not forget the first day he had seen her, the look of adoration brimming in her eyes, or that beguiling smile. He could not forget that any more than he could forget the painful hurt that had darkened her beautiful eyes a half hour ago.

Bloody hell, he could *never* forget her.

# Chapter 8

Michael was not surprised when Abbey did not appear at breakfast the next morning, not after seeing her devastation at her father's treachery. Vaguely worried and more than a little disconcerted by his own traitorous feelings, he tried to listen to Sebastian but had no idea what he was saying. After a few attempts to eat his eggs, he finally pushed his plate aside.

"We will continue in the library, Sebastian," he said, and stood abruptly. "Jones, send a tray up to Lady Darfield."

"I have done so, my lord, but she refused it," he replied, casting an accusatory look at his employer. He said nothing and impatiently quit the room; behind him, Jones exchanged a frown with Sebastian.

After an hour in the library with Sebastian, Michael realized he was staring out the window as his thoughts repeatedly wandered to Abbey. He recalled her in the garden the day before, happily tossing a ball to a maimed dog. He remembered how enticing she had looked when he had happened upon her afternoon walk—her cheeks flushed from the exercise and her eyes sparkling gaily. And at supper, he had been pleasantly entertained with her playful banter as he recalled some of his more interesting ventures into the world as a young man.

"Are you quite certain?" Sebastian asked.

Michael forced himself from his preoccupation and slid his gaze to his secretary. "Certain of what?"

Sebastian cleared his throat and busied himself neatly stacking the papers on his lap. "You instructed me to accept the invitation to Lady Davenport's next weekend," he said sheepishly.

"Did I?" he asked, momentarily confused. Rebecca. He had to do something about Rebecca, but for the life of him, he did not know what. The back of his neck grew warm with a very rare feeling of embarrassment. He leaned forward on his desk and rubbed his temples. Bloody hell, he was useless in his current state. He could not concentrate on a single item Sebastian placed in front of him and could not remember being so damned distracted in all of his adult life. "I have not as yet decided. If you will excuse me, I think I shall go for a ride," he said, rising from his chair.

"It looks like rain, my lord," Sebastian called after him as he strode briskly across the room, and was answered with the sound of a door shutting firmly behind his employer. Left alone, Sebastian turned in his chair to face the window, a deep smile on his face. He had never seen the marquis so disagreeable, and he was quite aware of the cause. "It's about bloody time," he muttered cheerfully to himself, and gathered up his papers.

Michael took the marble stairs two at a time, landing silently at the top, and turned toward the master suite of rooms. A sound caught his attention, causing him to stop abruptly. The most mournful strains of music he had ever heard a violin make were wafting through the thick walnut door of Abbey's sitting room. Shocked, he walked slowly to the door and gripped the door frame.

It was Abbey, he knew it. He had no idea she played the violin, and dear God, how she played. The strings were achingly stroked; with every caress of the bow he could feel her heartbreak. He recognized the Handel piece, one that carried the weight of the world in its notes. He had never heard the violin played so elegantly in all his life, nor had he ever been so moved by a piece of music. She continually surprised him, but this . . . *this* struck a chord in him so deep it shook him.

The music abruptly ended. Michael jerked himself upright and stared at the door. Suddenly self-conscious, he backed away, looking sheepishly about the corridor, half expecting someone to jump out and laugh at him for being so emotionally touched. Greatly unsettled by her music and his own confused emotions, he strode swiftly to his chamber.

He changed into his riding clothes and went straight to the stables, almost running past the sitting room door so he would not have to hear her wrenching music again. He had to get away from the house so he could think. Her scent, the silken feel of her skin, and, good Lord, those eyes, were making it impossible. When he reached the stables, he waved the groom away and tossed a saddle onto Samson's back himself. He did not want anyone near him for fear they would discover the depth of his confusion. *Confusion!* He had been many things in his life, but *confused* was never one of them.

Perhaps a visit to Rebecca Davenport would set everything right again.

Abbey dried her last tear, and with chin up, she marched to the large window of her library and stared out at the gray day. She had, at last, come to terms with the horrible fact that her father had lied shamelessly and had caused her to humiliate herself beyond compare. But she had pitied herself enough.

She was ready to take the situation in hand.

At least now she understood Michael's attitude. She frowned as she thought of her own behavior over the last weeks. Despite her initial feelings to the contrary, he had been remarkably kind to her given the foul circumstances. No longer did she see him as the aloof, icily distant husband she would be forced to desire from a distance. She saw him as the real victim of her father's farce.

Naturally, she could not expect Michael to put up with this sham of a marriage one more moment. If it was within her power to end this, she would. She did not care about the money. She cared how awful it was for him to have been forced into this. The only decent thing she could do for him was request an end to their farcical marriage and return to America.

It was not such a bad solution. At least in America, she had an aunt and cousins who loved her; they would ignore the disgrace she brought back with her. At least there her spirit would thrive, not like here, where she would be reminded of the cruel hoax her father had played each and every time she looked at him.

She debated how she would tell him. Still feeling the sting of humiliation, her first thought was to send him a note apologizing for her deplorable naïveté and her decision to return to America. Naturally, it was only right he should keep her dowry. A twinge of consciousness pricked at her. It was also only right that she tell him in person. She could not be the coward now; it was only fair that he should have the opportunity to speak his peace.

As she stood contemplating her options, she saw Michael gallop into the drive atop a massive black horse, his shirt open at the neck and his coat slung haphazardly over his lap. His sleeves were rolled up over his thick forearms. She smiled as she watched him gracefully alight from his mount. Regardless of what happened, she would never forget how handsome he was. She would never forget how his lips felt on hers, or how he sparked a need in her that she could not even identify, much less quell. She watched him disappear into the stable and turned from the window.

She would tell him this evening.

He would be relieved.

Abbey picked up her violin and began to play a bright Bach composition.

\*   \*   \*

At a full fifteen minutes after eight o'clock, Michael still had not appeared in the drawing room where he usually took his brandy before supper. Abbey paced the broad expanse of room, smiling nervously at the footman who stood against one wall waiting to do her bidding. She was quite certain Jones had told her Michael was never late for his evening rituals.

"Do you think," she said to the footman, breaking the insufferable silence, "that perhaps Lord Darfield might be in another drawing room?"

"No, milady. His lordship prefers the gold drawing room as it gets the late-afternoon sun," the footman intoned. Abbey nodded politely and resumed her pacing. Perhaps he was not feeling well. Perhaps he was feeling perfectly fine but could not bear the thought of facing another episode like the one he had witnessed last evening. She should hardly be surprised; she could not recall ever falling completely apart like that, scattering her emotions all over the place like a handful of marbles.

"Perhaps," she suggested brightly, "you could ask Jones what is keeping his lordship?" The footman nodded and quietly left the room. The moment the door closed behind him, Abbey's pacing grew frantic. The last thing she wanted him to think was that she was some sort of hysterical chit. She was not hysterical, and given a proper amount of time, she had calmed considerably.

She jerked her head up the moment the door opened and smiled brightly, then gamely tried to keep the smile in place when Jones appeared. He looked grim, as grim as she suddenly felt.

"Milady. There seems to have been a misunderstanding," he said politely.

"A misunderstanding?"

Jones looked pained for a moment, then announced blandly, "Lord Darfield has left Blessing Park. He is not expected back for a day or two."

Abbey felt as if she had been kicked squarely in the stom-

ach. He had left her? *Again?* She half turned from Jones and
tried valiantly to calmly absorb that piece of news. He had left
her again. She did not know if she was more infuriated than
hurt. How dare he leave without so much as a word? She did
not care what the Devil of Darfield thought, he should at least
have had the common decency to say *something*! At least a
note! *Decency is not something I concern myself with.* She
could hear it as plainly now as if he was standing before her,
and a painful fury rifled through her. He did not concern himself with decency, particularly when he loathed her as he must
now!

"Madam?"

Abbey jerked her head to Jones, realizing for the first time
that he had been speaking. "I'm terribly sorry. You were
saying?" she said as sweetly as she could, knowing perfectly
well her expression betrayed her.

"Perhaps you would like to take your supper in your
room?" he asked.

Abbey smiled so brightly her cheeks hurt. "Thank you, but
no. I am really not the least bit hungry." She started to walk
toward the door, ignoring Jones's skeptical look.

"I should be happy to send a tray—"

"Really, I am not hungry. In fact, I just came down for a
sip of wine," she lied, inwardly cringing when Jones obviously did not believe her. She slipped past him and headed for
the door. "Thank you, Jones. That will be all," she called
over her shoulder, mimicking the phrase she had heard Michael use. She walked calmly down the long corridor, smiling
kindly at the footman in the foyer, then glided up the long
marble staircase. When she reached the landing, she glanced
furtively over her shoulder and, seeing no one, bolted to her
rooms.

Safely inside, she began to pace ferociously. Part of her
said she had no right to be angry. This was, after all, nothing
but a sham of a marriage, and she had acted so revoltingly last
evening he had probably fled to Brighton just from sheer disgust. Another part of her said she had every right, for even if
it was a sham, he should have the common courtesy to tell her

he was going. And for how long this time? Two weeks? Two years? She flopped down on a settee and buried her face in her hands.

Well, if he so despised her, she could not stay another moment at Blessing Park. She was a silly, naive young fool who had crossed the ocean after him like a lapdog, ignorantly believing he loved her, and acting absolutely giddy upon seeing him again. Good God, she could just die.

Well, there was nothing to stop her from leaving now. *She,* of course, would have the courtesy to leave a note. She would explain it all, how she had finally realized everything he had said was true, and therefore, her leaving was simply inevitable. She would even save him the trouble of arranging it for her. Tomorrow she would go to Pemberheath and arrange her own passage to America.

The next morning Abbey asked Jones to have a carriage brought around. Jones started to deny her, but Abbey had patiently explained that she was quite certain the rules that governed a marchioness must also extend to what a marchioness *could* do, and she was equally certain that a marchioness could go to Pemberheath in search of bath oils if she so chose. Jones had pressed his lips firmly together and turned away from her, marching resolutely toward a footman with her command. Abbey had stifled a laugh as she flew up the stairs in search of a reticule and proper bonnet. Today she would purchase passage to America. Tonight she would pen her note to the Devil of Darfield, releasing him. Tomorrow, or the next day, or the next, she would leave Blessing Park forever.

He would be exceedingly happy.

In Pemberheath, Abbey cheerfully instructed her driver and coachman to call for her in two hours. She might be going home in disgrace, but she would not go empty-handed. She spent a contented afternoon strolling among the little shops in search of trinkets. She selected a broach made of lapis for her aunt, and a china teapot for Virginia. For Victoria, her adventuresome cousin, she purchased a tweed hunting jacket from a haberdasher.

Pleased with her purchases, she began to make her way to a small office at the end of a narrow alley, where she had been directed to arrange for passage to America. Rounding the corner, she almost collided with a man coming out of the narrow door of a small house. Startled, she caught her packages before they fell, then smiled upward, prepared to offer her apologies.

The apologies died on her tongue. Dear God, it was her cousin Galen standing before her, looking more shocked than she. Abbey dropped the packages she had so carefully caught only moments before and threw her arms around his neck. "*Galen!* You didn't tell me you had come!" she cried.

Galen hugged her fiercely but briefly, and quickly set her away from him.

"I intended to surprise you, but it would seem you have surprised me." He smiled, glanced surreptitiously toward the main thoroughfare, then up the alley in the opposite direction. "Come, let me help you with those things," he said, and bent to gather her things as Abbey happily plied him with questions. When they had gathered the packages, Galen paused to look at a beaming Abbey. A smile slowly spread his lips.

"My God, little one, what a beauty you've become," he said appreciatively as he gazed at her for the first time in many years.

Abbey laughed and glanced demurely at her toes. "Galen, really. I'm the same as the last time we met."

"Indeed you are not! That was a full five years ago, I am quite certain, and though you were beginning to show signs of natural beauty . . ." He trailed off and lifted his hand, brushing his knuckles lightly across her cheek. "I could not have guessed how truly breathtaking you would be," he said softly.

Abbey, blushing furiously now, gazed shyly into his dark-brown eyes. He was one to talk with his dark-blond locks and dancing brown eyes. He had sent her into a bout of severe adolescent devotion many years ago, as he undoubtedly was still doing to unsuspecting maids. He was as tall as she remembered, his face tanned from years at sea, and his eyes still twinkled just as mischievously.

She grinned as a flood of warm memories invaded her. "I am so thankful you have come! I have so longed to see you, you could not imagine!"

Galen grinned charmingly. "I've missed you, too, little one. Have you time? There is a place I know where we might take tea. There is much we have to discuss."

"Of course! I have so much to tell you," Abbey agreed, and began to walk toward the main thoroughfare.

"Not that way!" Galen called sharply. Abbey glanced curiously over her shoulder; Galen smiled sheepishly and motioned toward the far end of the alley. "It's just here, a small, quaint little place I am sure you will like," he said, walking slowly away from the main street until Abbey caught up with him.

The place he took her could hardly be called a tearoom, but there was a scarred table, and a woman did bring them a pot of tea and some stale biscuits. Abbey sipped her tea, listening attentively as Galen told her of his many adventures since leaving the *Dancing Maiden*.

So many, in fact, she had to wonder if there was more than he might have possibly been able to squeeze into his twenty-five years. He talked of fighting in strange wars Abbey had never heard of, and having captained his own ship that unfortunately went down around Cape Horn. Then there was the time he spent apprenticing in the offices of the East India Trading Company in Amsterdam, which naturally led to his joining a small but independent shipping firm in Copenhagen sometime later.

As she listened to his thrilling stories, she felt as if she were listening to her aunt read from one of her adventure novels. In all honesty, she was not terribly sure she had not heard some of the stories Galen told in those books. But she did not care. Her adored cousin had come to visit her, and if he wanted to embellish a bit, that was perfectly all right with her.

"And what of you?" Galen finally asked after eating the last biscuit and helping himself to the last cup of tea. "When I last saw you, the captain was sending you to a Geneva finishing school."

Abbey laughed. "Geneva, dear God, how long ago that was! I should be ashamed to confess I lasted only a month in that school. I was much too old for it, I think, and I had a particular dislike for the headmistress, and she for me. She was quite appalled that I had been sailing about with a bunch of scalawags, as she called them. Anyway, it wasn't very long afterward that Papa's condition worsened, and he sent me to live with Aunt Nan."

Galen looked aggrieved at the mention of her father's consumption. "I can't tell you how terribly sorry I was to hear of your father's death. He was like a father to me, you know, but I never had the opportunity to tell him just how fond of him I was. I was just about to depart for the West Indies when I heard the news," he said sadly.

"I thought you were preparing to depart for America," Abbey remarked, recalling his letters.

Galen colored slightly. "Well, I was, in a manner of speaking. To the West Indies first, then to America. I had planned to do a grand tour of sorts and see the entire family in one long trip," he said with a dismissive smile. "But the news of his death came, and right on the heels of that, the company I was working for collapsed with debt. An amazing thing, really. I had thought it completely solvent, but apparently it was just making ends meet. One ship was lost, and the whole enterprise crumbled like a house of cards."

"Oh, no!" Abbey exclaimed, completely unaware that he had artfully turned the subject. "What did you do?"

"Fortunately, I had put a small amount aside in savings. It was enough to see me through for a time, and I had actually planned to join another vessel when I heard you were in England." He turned a charming grin on her. "I simply had to come and see my little cousin," he said, and covering her hand with his, squeezed gently.

"Oh, Galen, you shouldn't have used your savings to visit me!"

"And why the hell not? I've missed you terribly, little one, and I didn't know when I might have the opportunity again. Family is too important to ignore, don't you think? Don't look so surprised—the seas will wait!''

Abbey was not immune to the struggle of most seafaring men to make ends meet, and immediately worried. Galen was trying very hard, at the moment, to make light of it. He had always been so carefree; she could remember her papa complaining he was too carefree, too eager to shirk responsibility. But Papa would have been proud of the man he had become. "Have you sufficient funds? I mean, while you are here?" she asked boldly.

Galen shrugged and looked at the scarred tabletop, his face clouding a moment with what Abbey thought was regret.

"You haven't, I can see it plainly in your face!" she cried, alarmed.

Galen smiled sheepishly. "You shouldn't worry about me, little one. I've enough to get by. Granted, I won't be staying in the finest inns, and I won't be hiring a curricle for your fancy, either." He laughed.

Abbey shook her head and reached for her reticule.

"I have no desire to go about in a curricle, Galen. I cannot bear the thought of you sleeping in some barn! You'll come to Blessing Park with me—"

"No, no. I am quite fine in Pemberheath for the moment. I shall be all right," he assured her weakly. "And in fact, I am off on the morrow for a few days. I've some business in Portsmouth." Unthinking, Abbey reached inside her reticule and withdrew the cash she had put aside for her passage home. "Take this," she said, and as Galen started to shake his head, she grabbed his hand. "Please, Galen, I want you to have it! I would feel so much better if I knew you had a decent roof over your head!"

Galen laughed nervously as his fingers closed around the money she held in her hand. "It's not nearly as bad as all that, little one. We shall consider this a loan. And for a very short time, I assure you. I am expecting some important news very soon that I think will alter my situation completely."

"Really? What?"

Galen shook his head and grinned enigmatically. "In due course I shall tell you everything. I shouldn't be surprised if this very important news affects my little cousin, too. In the meantime, however, I should very much like to spend some time with you, as circumstances permit."

*Time.* Abbey was about to ask how his news could affect her, but her eyes flew to a clock across the room. She was a good quarter of an hour late for her coach. "Oh, dear God! I told the driver to call for me at precisely four o'clock!" she exclaimed, and started reaching for her packages. "I shouldn't want them to worry something has happened."

Galen looked oddly distracted by her remark for a moment. "No, we would not want them to worry," he muttered, and taking the things from her hand, escorted her outside and began to lead her toward the main thoroughfare.

"So, you've been in America all this time, have you?" he asked as they strolled down the alley.

Abbey nodded. "Until a little more than a month ago, when I came here."

They came to the point where the alley intersected the thoroughfare. Just down the street, the Darfield coach was waiting for her, and Abbey waved until she got the driver's attention.

Galen thoughtfully eyed the ornate coach over her head. "We hardly had time to talk about you! So, my little cousin is to marry the Marquis of Darfield. I suspect the happy event will occur sometime this spring?" he asked as the coach swung out onto the road and moved toward them.

Abbey hesitated. She was not prepared to tell Galen that her marriage had ended the moment it had begun, or that she was returning to America very soon. She was not quite ready to face her humiliation, not yet. She turned as the coach pulled to a halt and smiled at the driver, blithely ignoring the suspicious look he gave Galen. A coachman leapt down from his post on the back runners and with a definite, challenging glare for Galen, took Abbey's packages. Galen surrendered them easily, watching both men with a look of amusement.

"You should engage these two to drive you to the church,

little one," he teasingly muttered. "I am quite certain they won't allow anyone to stand in your way!"

"Actually, I have already married the marquis," Abbey said as matter-of-factly as she could.

Galen jerked a startled gaze to her. "You did *what*?"

Nonplussed by his reaction, she asked, "What is wrong?" Next to her, the coachman made a great show of opening the coach door.

Galen quickly recovered with a deeply charming smile. "You caught me by surprise. I had thought there would be a period of engagement, that's all."

"There *was* a period of engagement—of about thirteen years!" Abbey giggled nervously. "I assure you, it was all quite proper!"

Galen smiled down at her. "I should like to meet your marquis, little one. Perhaps I shall call in a few days. There is so much more we shall have to discuss." He took a step forward, his arms outstretched. "An embrace for a long-lost cousin?" Abbey happily obliged, hugging him tightly to her. Galen kissed her on the cheek, slowly released her, and, with a wink, took a step back as the coachman crowded between to separate them.

"Then you will come to Blessing Park? Very soon?" Abbey asked as she let the coachman help her inside.

"I shall, just as soon as I return form Portsmouth," he assured her as the coachman slammed the door shut.

Abbey smiled and waved at him through the window of the barouche as the coach lurched forward, watching him until she could not see him any longer. Only then did she wonder how she would return to America after giving all the money she had to Galen.

Facing the mirror, Michael finished tying his neckcloth, ignoring Rebecca's continuing tirade about broken promises. It had been a mistake to come here, a colossal mistake. A figurine went flying past him, crashing into the wall, and Michael impassively looked down at the broken pieces. With a final inspection of the knot he had just made, he turned and glanced at the pretty blonde, his eyes drifting over her filmy negligee and the curvaceous figure underneath.

"I never promised you a damn thing, Rebecca," he said impassively. "You and I had an arrangement that suited us for a time, but it no longer suits me."

"You heartless cretin! How *dare* you waltz in here and take me like some rutting stud, then announce this is the end!" she shrieked.

"No, it was not particularly satisfying, was it?" He sighed and shoved his hands in his pockets. Michael had not thought himself as heartless as she accused him of being, but at the moment, he felt . . . nothing. It was the end of another series of assignations, an event almost as routine as his business deals. Granted, his liaison with Rebecca had lasted a little longer than most, but in the end, they all ended. Always. He was mildly surprised she could evoke any emotion in him. From the moment he had arrived, he had realized he could not summon a true desire for her anymore. It was simply over. Irretrievably over. He suspected she had realized it, too, as they had gone through the motions rather mechanically.

"Rebecca, darling—"

"Don't call me that!" she spat, her eyes welling again.

"Stop acting like a child, love. You know there has been little to bind us to one another, except, perhaps, a shared physical attraction."

"That's not true!" She sobbed.

Michael frowned disapprovingly. "Isn't it? You do not like the country, or have you forgotten? I do not like town. You do not like that I engage in shipping—the Merchant of Darfield, I believe you called me. And I do not like lolling about tearooms, feeding on the latest *on dits* you so rabidly follow. Come now, love, you knew there would be an end."

Rebecca sank wearily to the bed, grabbed a satin pillow, and clutched it woefully to her breast in genuine sorrow. "I knew there would be an end for you," she murmured. "But not for me."

Michael felt a small twinge of pity. He walked slowly to the bed and placed his hand on her smooth shoulder. "Rebecca. We always knew it would end. It was only a matter of which of us would end it first," he said softly.

"No," she insisted, shaking her head. "I didn't. I never—"

"I am sorry, love," he interjected before she could finish. "Apparently it is better it ended sooner rather than later."

Pain glanced Rebecca's features at that remark, and she reached up and covered his hand with hers before he removed it from her skin forever. "Do you . . . *love* her?" she whispered. Michael did not immediately answer. He had told Rebecca he had married, but nothing more. He certainly had not suggested his marriage was the reason for ending their affair. Because it wasn't. He simply did not desire her anymore.

"Do you?" she whispered. Michael looked down at Rebecca and pondered her question. He did not love Abbey. But there was something there, something that had held his interest even when Rebecca had tried every feminine trick she knew to lay claim to his body. Something that made him feel a faint but definite twinge of guilt for being here. Something different, something he could not quite name, and something Rebecca did not have. She lifted her lashes and looked at him with wet green eyes.

"No," he said kindly.

"But you want her." She sniffed miserably.

Michael sighed impatiently and withdrew his hand. "There is no *her,* Rebecca. Try and understand. It's just . . . over." Without another word, he turned and walked out of her bedroom and her life.

# Chapter 9

Two grooms met Michael that afternoon when he arrived home and, as usual, Jones stood at the door. Michael strode up the stone steps, mildly perturbed that he had wanted to see Abbey standing where Jones was now.

"Welcome home, my lord," Jones said blandly, and extended his hands to receive Michael's hat and gloves.

"Thank you, Jones. Have a bath readied, will you? I seem to have found the muddiest road in all of Southampton," he said as he moved past the butler toward the grand staircase. He jogged up the marble stairs to the first floor and turned down the corridor, hoping Abbey would appear before him. For reasons he did not fully understand, or care to understand, he wanted to see her.

He did not see her, but he heard her. A bright, rapid piece of music drifted through the upper chambers; if he had to guess, he would say Bach. He smiled to himself as he walked casually to his rooms. The notes from her violin immediately answered two questions for him. She was nearby, and she was in good spirits.

Michael entered his chamber and nodded to Damon, his

valet, who was putting away some freshly laundered shirts. He went directly to a small writing desk, shaking his head at Damon as he immediately started for him, his eyes on Michael's boots. "As I am quite sure I can remove these boots myself, I will not be in need of your assistance." He smiled at the stoic valet, who bowed and made to quit the room as Michael pulled open a drawer and found some paper.

"One moment. I would have you deliver a note." Michael sat on an upholstered maple chair and dipped a quill in the inkwell. He quickly dashed off a note to Abbey, informing her of his return and requesting she dine with him that evening. By the time her reply was delivered, he was up to his neck in steaming hot water. Michael motioned for Damon to bring him the missive, and careful not to smear the ink, he quickly scanned her note.

*Thank you. That would be lovely.* That was it, the extent of her note, but Michael realized he was grinning.

Ten minutes after the supper hour he was pacing impatiently in front of the long windows of the gold drawing room, the wait for Abbey becoming interminable. He was famished; his stomach growled in protest as he paced, and he was infuriatingly anxious. When at last Jones entered the room carrying a tray of crystal glasses, Michael demanded, "Where is Lady Darfield?"

"Here," Abbey said quietly as she glided in behind Jones. She was wearing a gown of silver brocade trimmed in tiny seed pearls. Above the squre-cut bodice, a strand of pearls rested against the voluptuous flesh of her breasts. Her hair was pulled back from her forehead and fell down her back in a curtain of dark silk curls; one silken strand brushed against her cheek. Beneath long, black lashes, her violet eyes sparkled. "Welcome home." She smiled.

"Thank you." Michael slowly inhaled, marveling at how he could have managed to marry such a beautiful woman without even trying. "I was beginning to think you were not coming," he said, crossing the room to her.

Abbey smiled a little timidly. He looked glad to see her,

which seemed very strange, given that he had felt it necessary to escape to Brighton again just to get away from her.

"What will you be drinking this evening? Rum? Whiskey?" He smiled as his gray eyes probed her face. His nearness was making her skin tingle.

"I think I would try the port," she finally answered, trying her best to ignore the soft look in his eyes. Michael motioned to the footman, then took her hand and slipped it through the crook of his arm to lead her to a settee. Abbey forced herself to draw a slow, steadying breath; in his black dinner jacket and gray waistcoat, he looked every inch the swashbuckling hero about whom she had once dreamed. Just walking with him, she could feel the power of his muscular body, and blast it all, she was trembling by the time she sat. She flushed, hoping to high heaven he would not notice what his touch did to her. His masculine attempt to be as charming as he knew how—out of pity, or relief, no doubt—did not help her. It only made her task all the more difficult. And her task had not changed. She was determined to release him and go home.

"I was not aware you played the violin," he remarked with a lopsided smile as he settled into a chair across from her.

Abbey blanched. Until two days ago, she had believed he had sent her the violin in hopes she would learn to play for him. "I took it up when I was a girl, in Rome," she managed to say without choking on her words.

"You play beautifully. I heard you earlier—Bach, was it?" Pleasantly surprised, she nodded.

"I am a great lover of music, too," he added with a warm smile.

"I know—well, I have heard—" Abbey stammered.

Michael said nothing, politely ignoring her nervousness. He wanted to say her musical talent was brilliant. He wanted to tell her she was the most beautiful creature he had ever seen, stunning him in yet another celestial gown. Instead, he sipped his whiskey and watched Abbey's long fingers drum rapidly against her thigh.

"How else do you occupy your time, I wonder? I know you play darts, but what of other games? Chess, perhaps?"

"Chess? No, I never learned. I know a variety of card games, and billiards, of course . . ."

"Billiards?" he asked with some surprise.

"Brussels," she admitted by way of explanation.

Michael chuckled and shook his head. "Brussels, of course," he said agreeably. "And where did you learn to play cards?" he asked, standing to refresh his drink.

"Aboard Papa's ship, I suppose. But I learned to cheat in Cairo," she added absently.

Michael grinned as he returned and took a seat next to her on the settee. Abbey's eyes widened slightly with guileless consternation. "Cheating, indeed? That is quite scandalous, Lady Darfield."

"I do not cheat as a rule, only when circumstances dictate," she said softly. She was staring at his mouth, an innocent act that made Michael's blood boil.

He placed his untouched drink on a table and moved closer to Abbey. "Exactly when, may I ask, do circumstances dictate?"

Abbey's mouth parted slightly as if to respond. Michael leaned toward her and caught the lilac scent of her hair.

"When I am losing badly."

"Hmm?"

"Wh-when I am losing. Badly," she stammered. He was so close, she could smell his mild cologne. He was touching her hair, his fingers brushing lightly against her temple, sending a thousand tingling jolts down her spine. It was suddenly very hot in the room. *Very* hot. What on earth was he doing? Did he hope to frighten her off? If so, he was succeeding admirably.

Michael was reaching for the glass of port she held in a vice-like grip when Jones entered the room and announced supper. Michael glared at the butler, who pointedly ignored his lord as he opened the door wide, ready to attend them. With a heavy sigh of frustration, Michael rose slowly and helped Abbey to her feet. Grateful that her wobbling knees managed to hold her, she walked woodenly next to Michael to the dining room. It seemed so unfair that a simple touch from

him could turn her mind—and her resolve—to little more than
mush.


Seated at the end of the long, mahogany dining table, Michael
glanced surreptiously at Abbey, on his right. As the servants
bustled about them, he could tell she was extremely nervous,
and tried to think of inane topics that would put her at ease.
He did not have to think long. As soon as the first course was
served, Abbey suddenly began chattering like a magpie.

She started with a report of the two weeks she had been in
Blessing Park while he was away, as if it were perfectly natural that she should have been abandoned on her honeymoon.
She admitted to him that she had made some small changes in
the house, including rearranging the main study, and then, of
course, switching the sitting room and library upstairs. When
she had fully recounted each and every activity of those two
weeks, she artfully skipped any reference to his latest absence
and segued effortlessly into tales of America.

She talked of her cousins, Virginia and Victoria, and her
Aunt Nan at length. It sounded as if the two sisters argued
with one another all day while Abbey cheerfully played the
arbiter. After the soup bowls were cleared and the main
course of trout was served, Abbey chattered endlessly about
the places she and Harry had explored. That, naturally, led her
to thoughts on various chapters of history, and one by one,
every single thought that popped into her brain spilled out of
her mouth. She talked about Roman history, then Egyptian
history—with several references to Persian history—then Eu-
ropean history, then American history. She peppered her re-
cital with interesting, lesser-known facts she had gleaned
during her travels. She lamented she did not know as much as
she would like about the Orient, but vowed she would learn it,
as if it were all at once the most important thing in the world.
All the while, Michael quietly ate his food, listening politely
to her stream of unending commentary, making suitable,
monosyllabic comments as necessary, and resisting her en-
chantment.

He had no idea what made Abbey so extremely nervous, but she was. Her cheeks flushed prettily, and she looked everywhere about the room but never at him. She hardly ate a thing, and instead pushed the food around her plate as she talked. She was, he admitted to himself, a beguiling creature.

With a quiet smile on his lips, Michael finally leaned over and covered her hand with his. "Abbey. You can stop now," he said simply. He fully expected her to deny she was rattled, but the look of relief that washed over her was enough to make him chuckle.

"I suppose I should meet it straight on," she said wearily as she slumped back in her chair. She withdrew her hand from his and folded it demurely in her lap. Her long, sooty lashes just brushed her cheeks as she cast her gaze to her hands.

"What would you meet straight on?" Michael asked.

"Michael, I suppose you know . . . that is, I believed . . . well I *thought* that perhaps things were somehow different than they are, really, and I am quite mortified that I was so wrong about it, and, you see, I want to . . . I want . . ."

Michael did not like the reminder of her abject pain upon realizing her father had badly duped her, nor did he like the interruption in this extremely pleasant evening.

"Abbey, you don't have to do this," he said gently. She did not seem to hear him.

Her eyes remained fixed on her lap as she took a deep, steadying breath and continued. "I want to apologize. I never meant to cause you any discomfort, in fact, I would rather *die* than hurt you in any way, and really did not think I had, because, of course, I thought things were quite different than they truly are, apparently, despite the fact that you *clearly* stated the contrary, which of course I didn't believe, because I obviously—and *stubbornly*, I should add—believed something entirely different altogether, and it was a very foolish of me, but it's done now, and one cannot dwell on one's own stupidity without the risk of becoming *completely* stupid—"

"Abbey, don't," Michael said insistently before she tumbled into another long-winded monologue.

But Abbey plunged on. "I know how absurd this must all

seem to you, and believe me, I think it the *height* of absurdity, really, over the top so to speak, and I am sorry for that, but I really think there is no recourse other than my immediate return to America.'' She squeezed her eyes shut as if expecting some verbal assault from him, then slowly opened them, glancing up through her lashes when he did not.

Michael was stunned she was apologizing to *him* for having been duped by her father. He was about to tell her it was not her fault, but before he could speak, she rushed ahead in an effort to fill the momentary silence between them.

''I understand that my . . . your . . . fortune is all bound up in my father's will, and I really don't mind, I don't want it, truly. You see, my Aunt Nan, she has a small farm, and we all work on it, and we make a decent living from it, and with the annuity, it really would not be a hardship for me at all, and it seems to me the only logical thing to do, because I rather think you should not be made to suffer my father's reprehensible lies,'' she finished, an octave higher than she began.

Michael regarded her for a long moment. Her violet eyes pleaded for his understanding while she unselfishly attempted to shoulder the burden of blame for her father's misdeed, irrespective of her own future or happiness. He was touched by her offer but did not consider it for even a moment. He was not sending her back to America in disgrace and without a farthing to her name. The thought of her toiling for food made him angry; the idea of losing her was entirely unthinkable at the moment.

''That will not be necessary,'' he said brusquely, wondering why he could not tell her how brave and perfectly noble he thought she was to offer such a thing.

''Not necessary?'' she asked quietly.

''No,'' he answered curtly.

''Had I known, I *never* would have . . . that is to say, *you* are the victim in all this, and I will not be party to a marriage that you clearly made against your free will,'' she explained.

Michael fought for control, the muscles in his jaw working furiously as his mind raced. How could he say he had no intention of letting her go? He was hardly sure that was true.

How could he tell her his behavior had been abominable thus far and she deserved better? He was only just realizing it himself.

Abbey frantically wondered what was going through his mind and wished desperately she had her passage to America in hand. She assumed he was too honorable to think he could agree to her suggestion, but at the same time, she assumed he surely wanted to. She suddenly felt a need to make it easy for him. "I do not want to stay with you," she said bluntly.

He raised a brow as if surprised by that fact. "Don't you indeed?" he drawled.

"No, I do not! Now that I know the truth, I cannot abide this ridiculous pretense!"

His brows bunched across the bridge of his nose. "You seem to have done rather nicely at Blessing Park, madam. You have all that you need: a dog, a garden, and friends. What more could you possibly want? Certainly not to toil away on some farm in Virginia," he said evenly. Abbey wanted to scream that at least in Virginia, people *loved* her, but she bit her tongue on that point.

"I can't possibly imagine what would cause you to object!" she insisted.

"Abbey, you do not seem to understand the basic concept that *I* will decide what is best for you. Your notion of returning to America without a farthing to your name is unacceptable. Furthermore, we are quite married now, and there are many legal restrictions on what you can or cannot do. It is my obligation to see to your welfare," he said stubbornly, wondering once again why he could not seem to say that he did not want her to go. Not yet.

Abbey jerked her gaze to her half-eaten trout. The only thing this man could think of was obligation, and she was trying to *free* him of an unwanted obligation. She was obviously a burden to him, an idea she could barely stomach.

"I understand clearly," she said icily, and pushed away from the table. A footman rushed around the table to assist her, but Abbey was already on her feet, and collided with the poor servant in an effort to quit the dining room.

Michael was much quicker and surer than either one of them, catching her before she could get halfway to the door. "That will be all," he barked to the servants. With a firm grip on Abbey's elbow, he propelled her through the door, down the hallway, and into the main study.

Leaning against the door with his arms folded across his chest, Michael regarded her sternly. "Suppose you tell me what you are about," he said calmly.

Abbey planted her hands on her hips and glared at him. "What am I *about*? About *you*, and *me*, and a *horrid* deception! About your sense of *obligation*! About releasing you from that *obligation* and leaving your sight!" she shouted angrily.

"You are not returning to America," he said authoritatively.

Abbey gasped her outrage. "Do you not understand? I am *releasing* you! It's what you want! You are the most *frustrating* man!" she fairly shrieked. Michael pushed away from the door and began to stroll casually toward her. Abbey darted around a couch in front of the hearth, keeping the furniture between them. A slow, lazy grin spread across Michael's lips as he steadily changed course.

"Madam, you do not know the meaning of the word frustrating," he said smoothly.

"Ha! I know the meaning of rude and arrogant, and you are both! To think I actually felt *sorry* for what you have suffered! I am returning to America, for I will *not* stay here like some poor, burdensome relation!" she insisted as she slowly circled the settee, staying just out of his reach.

Michael's mocking grin deepened. "Burdensome relation? Is that what you think I believe?"

"I know it is!" Abbey cried, and felt the well of tears begin to build in the back of her throat. A burden, all right, a situation made all the more painful because she *loved* him—as much as she ever had, ever would, and more than she had ever dreamed possible. Aware that he moved, she darted quickly to one end of the couch. Michael stood at the other, his powerful legs braced apart, his hands on his hips.

"I merely said I had an obligation. Every man has obliga-
tions. Why should that upset you?" he asked calmly.

Abbey shuddered. It was not that so much as it was merely
an *obligation* to him and *love* to her. She had her pride, and
her pride told her to go, to leave him to Lady Davenport.
Instead of answering him, Abbey whirled and started for the
door. In three powerful strides, Michael caught her by the
shoulders and twisted her around to face him.

"You will not go to America," he said hoarsely.

Abbey recognized the look in his eye, and turning her head,
managed to get her arms between them. If he kissed her like
he did last night, she would lose all control.

Michael only pulled her closer. "Don't resist me!" he
breathed, his breath tickling her ear.

Abbey's resolve was crumbling rapidly, and she suddenly
felt hopeless. She was so weak where he was concerned that
she was, at that very moment, contemplating spending her life
with a man who did not love her. A man with a pretty mistress. When Michael cupped her face in his hands, Abbey
could control herself no longer. The rejection she had suffered
in the last weeks erupted deep within her, and she blinked
back hot, angry tears.

"I don't want to be an *obligation*! I don't want to be a
constant reminder of my father's trickery! I don't want to see
you look at another woman and wish you had been free to
marry her! I don't want to *love* you like I do and see that
distant look in your eye." She choked, appalled and horrified
at what she had just said, and began to weep uncontrollably.

Speechless, Michael stared down at her, then cradled her
head against his chest while grief flowed in torrents from her
slender body. He tenderly stroked her hair while she cried, a
protective arm around her shoulders. He never wanted to see
such pain in her eyes again, and at the moment, he believed he
would do anything to ensure he never did.

"You are not thinking clearly," he finally murmured
against the top of her head, acutely aware that he was not,
either.

"*Please* d-don't make me stay!" she stammered. His heart broke at the wretched sound of her voice.

"Abbey, you've been through too much recently, and you aren't being rational. I think it better if we postpone this conversation until another time, until we have thought clearly about our options."

"I *am* being rational, and there are no other options." She sniffed.

"We will not discuss it now," he insisted, and slipping a forefinger under her chin, tilted her head up so he could see her face. Abbey sniffed; the path of her tears stained her cheeks. He was overcome with a peculiar desire to soothe her, and he gingerly touched the wetness before bending to kiss the tears from her cheeks.

Abbey stood very still as his lips brushed her skin. He slid his lips to hers, painting them gently with his tongue, very tenderly asking her to open. It was a kiss so unlike the others, so sweetly seductive, and more than any woman could resist. When her lips parted of their own accord, he slipped inside slowly, gently urging her with his hands and lips to want him.

The warm, gentle desire behind his kiss rocked her toward oblivion. She felt as if she were spiraling downward and clung to him to keep from slipping into that oblivion. His hard frame was pressed against the full length of her; she could feel every sinewy muscle, could feel her body attempting to meld with his. When she at last realized what she was doing, what she was *feeling*, she began to panic and suddenly wrenched her mouth free. She could not do this. She could not feel the strength in his arms, the urgency behind his kiss, or the taste of his mouth without losing every last remnant of common sense she had.

"It's been a rather long day," she said apologetically.

Michael paused to brush the errant strand of hair from her face before respectfully stepping away. "A truce, then. Perhaps you would enjoy a game of billiards? It would be a pleasant diversion," he asked as he moved toward the hearth.

Abbey considered that. She could not speak of America at the moment without dissolving into schoolgirl tears again. A game of billiards would keep her mind occupied—and his as well—until she had regained her courage and could speak to him, make him understand.

"I think I should warn you that I am prone to wagering," she said softly. Surprised, he gave her a sidelong appraisal, at which she smiled tremulously.

"Should I be so bold to inquire if you intend to cheat, madam?"

Abbey's smile deepened. "I *never* cheat at billiards."

"Aha. Unless you are losing, I suppose."

"Very badly," she said nodding.

Michael's laugh was full and deep. "Terribly inappropriate for a marchioness, but in this instance, I will allow it," he said, and motioned toward the door. Abbey self-consciously smoothed her hair, then preceded him through the door, her brocade skirts swishing softly behind her with the gentle swaying of her lips. Michael rolled his eyes heavenward in a silent prayer for strength.

As he was beginning to grow accustomed to her unique talents, Michael was only mildly surprised that she played the game quite well. With one hip propped against the railing, he leaned against his cue, watching Abbey slowly circle the game table, her brow wrinkled in concentration and her elegant hand trailing along the polished railing. Settling on a shot, she leaned across the table, revealing the enticing crevice between her breasts. Michael missed the fact that she sank her intended ball until she straightened and beamed at him. Her next shot gave Michael the opportunity to admire her softly rounded hips.

"Bloody hell," she muttered unthinkingly under her breath when the ball scudded wide.

Michael chuckled. The little hellion had a foul mouth, a trait he was quite sure she learned at sea, and quite tame considering the total of what she likely had heard all those years.

"How much have you won?" he asked as he eyed the four remaining balls.

"You do not know?" she asked, surprised. "One thousand pounds."

Michael glanced up from chalking his cue. "Quite certain of that, are you? I had thought it one *hundred* pounds."

"You should really pay closer attention. It is one thousand pounds if it is one."

He smiled inwardly; he *would* pay more attention if she were not so damned captivating.

"It is hard to keep one's mind on the game when one is so distracted by such . . . skill," he said absently.

Abbey looked terribly pleased by that counterfeit compliment.

"One thousand pounds you say?" he continued as he circled the table and studied the lay of the four remaining balls. "Are you brave enough to raise the stakes?"

Abbey giggled irreverently. "I should think I have nothing to fear, since I have won one thousand pounds. Perhaps I should ask if *you* are brave enough to raise the stakes," she challenged.

A charming, lopsided grin broke his face. "I assure you, madam, I have courage enough."

His confidence was truly seductive. She studied him under the veil of her lashes as she pretended to consider his offer. He slowly circled the billiard table, intently studying the remaining balls. He had removed his coat long ago and had rolled up his sleeves, revealing his granite forearms. His waistcoat hugged his trim waist, and his black trousers looked as if they had been painted onto his powerful hips and thighs. Abbey exhaled a soft schoolgirl sigh as she admired his lean figure; he had never looked more relaxed to her, and certainly never more handsome.

"Well?" he prodded.

"What did you have in mind?" she asked demurely.

He grinned devilishly. "I'm afraid," he drawled, "what I

have in mind would offend your tender sensibilities. However, I have a second wager you might consider.''

Frankly, Abbey was more interested in the wager that would offend her sensibilities, but responded nonchalantly, ''I'm listening.''

''If I sink the remaining balls with one shot, you will wait a period of three months before you decide to return to America,'' he said, and lifted a pointed gaze to hers.

Abbey hesitated—that was hardly the wager she was expecting. Three months? Three months of wanting him, of loving him, with no return of her affections?

''Why?'' she blurted.

''Why?'' He hesitated, only for a moment, then shrugged and looked at the table again. ''Three months gives me ample opportunity to clean up the last details of your father's will and is sufficient time to ensure there is no danger of losing your dowry,'' he remarked casually.

His response, while not surprising, was hugely disappointing. Abbey wanted to kick herself for romanticizing every kind word he said to her. Each time she did that, the plunge back to reality took a harder toll on her. He plainly did not want her; but he needed time to fix the business aspect of their marriage. He loved Lady Davenport, not her, she reminded herself. She was his blasted obligation.

''And if you don't?'' She was irritated that her voice squeaked like that of a small child.

''You may decide tomorrow, and I will not stand in the way of your decision.'' His gaze did not leave her as she looked at the table. She frowned; she could not see how he could sink all four balls in one shot. What did that mean? It meant he wanted her to go, obviously. Or did he truly think he could do it, which meant he wanted her to wait three months? She glanced at Michael, who was expressionless, then back to the table. Good *God*, but she was going to have to get a serious grip on herself and stop these childish ruminations! She should return to America right away—it would destroy her to stay. *He does not love you! He hardly knows you!* she chided herself. *Three months is a long time to love a man who loves another. Three months is a long time to hang on every little word, hoping for something you will not find.*

"All right," she said stupidly.

"Quite sure?" he asked as he leaned across the table and lined his cue behind a ball. She did not answer; she was frozen, her eyes darting from ball to ball as she tried to understand how he would do it. "Abbey?" he asked again. She jerked her gaze to him and nodded slowly. Michael turned his attention to the table.

"Wait!" she cried. Michael glanced up expectantly. She frantically sought something to say, something to distract him so she could think. She had to think! "Wh-what of the thousand pounds?" she stammered.

"You won it. It's yours." He shrugged and turned back to the table.

"Bank draft or cash?" she asked hurriedly in a bid for time.

"Bank draft or cash?" He chuckled. "Why, whichever you prefer, Lady Darfield. And before you ask, I shall have Sebastian deliver it to you first thing in the morning," he added, anticipating her question. Abbey nodded numbly, still staring at the table.

"Would you like to reconsider?" he asked. Abbey flinched; this was just fabulous! Now he would think her an unwelcome obligation, a silly child, *and* a coward.

"Absolutely not," she said imperiously, then, for good measure, added, "What are you waiting for?"

Michael laughed and turned back to the table. As he concentrated on the shot, Abbey turned slowly away; she could not bear to watch. After what seemed to be an extremely long time, she heard him strike the ball, and closed her eyes tightly as she counted the balls dropping into the pocket. *One, two, three* . . . Her eyes flew open. Only three! Her heart sank on a wave of bitter disappointment.

*Four.* Elation surged through her, and clutching her cue tightly, she whirled toward the table.

"You missed an amazing shot of truly incredible skill, wouldn't you say, Anderson?" Michael drawled.

"Yes, my lord," the footman replied blandly.

Abbey grabbed the railing and gaped at the empty table. "How in God's name did you do that?" she demanded. "Did you *cheat*?"

Michael shouted his laughter, then swept a hand to his heart and bowed deeply. "Madam, you wound me."

Abbey laughed nervously, but inside, she was reeling. *Three months.* She had promised to wait three months before deciding if this was heaven or hell. Good Lord, what had she done? She felt the color drain from her face and impulsively thrust her cue at the footman.

"The excitement has exhausted me, I'm afraid. With your leave, I think I would retire and contemplate how I shall spend my thousand pounds," she said with forced lightness. It was the truth; she was emotionally drained. Her heart was thudding against her chest, threatening to break free and spill, raw and exposed, on the billiards table.

"Of course, madam," Michael said with mock formality. He was hardly ready for her to retire. "By the by, I have some business associates who will be here in the morning, but afterward, I would like to take you riding," he said as he took a brandy the footman handed him. Abbey stopped cold, and he could have sworn her spine snapped a little straighter.

"*Riding?*" she asked. A little hysterically, he thought. It occurred to him that she might not *want* to ride with him. Perhaps she did not want to wait three months, either. Perhaps he had foolishly pushed her to remain with him when she preferred to go. Perhaps he was the biggest fool of all. He had his chance to end this sham marriage, but he had let a pretty face cloud his judgment.

"That is, if you want to go," he said coolly.

Abbey half turned toward him. "I would enjoy it very much," she said politely, but Michael could see it was a lie, and it disturbed him greatly.

"Two o'clock, then," he said curtly, and turned away. When he heard the door close softly, he jerked his gaze to Anderson.

"Not a word about the fourth ball if you value your employment, Anderson," he warned.

Startled, the footman shook his head furiously. "*Never,* my lord." He gasped, truly affronted, then smiled approvingly.

# Chapter 10

"Talk with Mr. Hanley, the stable master. He will see that a tame mount is saddled for you," Sarah said in an attempt to soothe Abbey the next morning.

"It won't do any good!" Abbey despaired, squirming as Sarah tried to fasten her gown.

"Really, it's not so difficult, mum! After a few minutes, and you'll think you were born astride. You will make yourself sick if you keep fretting so!"

"Fretting?" Abbey laughed hysterically. "You call this fretting? This is panic. Sheer, unadulterated *panic*!"

"Mr. Hanley will see to it," Sarah said emphatically.

Abbey sighed. This was really a bad idea. She had stupidly agreed to risk her fool neck just to be with a man who didn't care for her. Spending time with him would only make it harder to leave when the time came. And she would have to leave, her foolish wager notwithstanding. Nothing else was fair, nothing else made sense. Least of all her absurd agreement to go riding when she had never before been on the back of a horse.

"Go and see Mr. Hanley," Sarah said again as she finished with Abbey's gown.

Abbey marched woodenly from the room, her imagination running wild. She could envision herself being trampled beneath the hooves of a high-spirited horse like the one she had seen Michael ride. Mounting anxiety caused her to fairly fly down the stairs and out the door in search of Mr. Hanley, the only one who could help her now. Outside, she picked up her skirts and raced for the stables, careering ungracefully about the curving path to the stables, and almost colliding with Sam and another gentleman who appeared around a corner. In the face of her impending doom, she had completely forgotten Michael's mention of appointments this morning.

"Oh, my!" she exclaimed genuinely, knowing full well she looked ridiculous running down the path. "I was . . . that is, I was . . ." she stammered, then smiled brightly. "I'm off to the stables!" she said cheerfully, bobbed a curtsey, and circled widely around the two men.

"Lady Darfield, it's a pleasure to see you again. You are looking quite well," Sam said with a playful smile on his handsome face.

"Thank you, Lord Hunt. You look to be in remarkably good health yourself," she said, frowning slightly at him.

Sam's grin deepened. He obviously was not content to let her sidle by. "It would appear we detain you from an important . . . ah, appointment?"

"Not at all," she said coolly. "It's just a bit chilly this time of morning. I was hurrying along to keep warm."

"Might I suggest a wrap?"

Abbey glanced at the stranger. "You might," she forced herself to reply.

Sam almost laughed, but caught himself after seeing her pointed look. He glanced at the gentleman with him; his smile faded as a distinct change came over his hazel eyes.

"Allow me to introduce Mr. Malcolm Routier," he said, his voice noticeably cooler. "Mr. Routier, Abigail Carrington Ingram, the Marchioness of Darfield." Abbey slid her gaze to the tall, amber, almost yellow-eyed man and immediately noticed his look of shock. She lifted her chin and sank into a polite curtsey.

"Surely, madam," Mr. Routier exclaimed, "you are not Captain Carrington's daughter?"

Surprised, Abbey blinked. "Malcolm Routier? My father had a business associate with that name. Why, of course!" she said, recalling the name.

"I am he." Routier's amber eyes took on an odd glint. "We have had the pleasure of meeting once before, my lady." At Abbey's puzzled look, he added, "Perhaps you do not recall? It was in Bombay, at the governor's soirée."

Abbey could hardly remember the governor's party, much less meeting the man. "I confess I do not recall," she admitted.

With a winsome grin, he said, "It was several years ago, madam. You were quite young." Abbey glanced at Sam, who now seemed oddly perturbed.

"Perhaps we did," she said uncertainly.

"Lady Darfield, if you will excuse us, we won't keep you any longer," Sam interjected. "Lord Darfield is undoubtedly waiting," he continued, and gave Routier an uncharacteristically dark look that puzzled Abbey.

"Of course. A pleasure, Mr. Routier. Good day," she said, and slipped through the paddock gate. She did not turn back and walked as slowly as she could make herself until she was quite certain they were far enough along the path they could not see her, then she dashed into the stable.

She paused inside so her eyes could adjust to the dim light. A horse in a nearby stall snorted right above her shoulder, surprising her, and she let out a little shriek as she whirled toward the beast. Michael's huge black stallion snorted again, impatiently, and studied her closely with one enormous black eye. Abbey gaped at the horse. She had never been so close to the huge animal; he had to be at least a foot taller than she and was as terrifying as he was large.

"A magnificent piece of horseflesh, wouldn't you agree?"

For the second time, Abbey started and turned abruptly to see a tall, dark-haired man.

"My apologies, I did not mean to frighten you," he said, flashing an apologetic smile that was all white teeth. He nodded toward Samson. "Darfield has fine taste in horses, I'll give him that."

"I suppose," Abbey muttered, and glanced warily across her shoulder at the huge beast.

The man cocked his head to one side as he considered her. "I suppose Samson seems a bit intimidating."

Abbey yanked her gaze to the stranger, assessing him. "A bit," she admitted suspiciously.

"I am Alex Christian," he said, extending his hand.

"Abbey Carrington. Ingram. Abbey Carrington Ingram," she clarified. If the man was shocked, he was careful not to show it, but smiled broadly.

"I have some business with your husband, but I had not anticipated I would have the extreme pleasure of making your acquaintance, Lady Darfield. Are you interested in horses?" Forgetting he was a stranger, Abbey sighed unconsciously and looked at the stallion again.

"I am really rather unfamiliar with horses. I had hoped there would be one a little . . . *smaller.*"

Alex Christian laughed and strolled to Samson and stroked his nose.

"Most are considerably smaller than this beast," he said fondly. "I noticed several mares; you would be much happier astride one of those."

"Really?" Abbey said quickly, and pivoted on her heel to examine the other stalls.

Alex strolled casually from Samson's rather spacious stall to a smaller, neighboring stall, where a roan stood patiently.

"This one is much smaller, and I rather think a gentle sort," he said, and patted the horse's neck. Abbey was quickly at his side.

"How can you tell?" she asked anxiously, hoping something as obvious as a marking would indicate gentleness in a horse.

Alex glanced at her from the corner of his eye, a faint smile of amusement on his lips. "See how she keeps her head down? And she doesn't snort and stomp about like Samson. This horse is used to having many riders on her back." As if hearing him, the roan dipped her head and nudged his pocket.

"Ah! I see!" Abbey exclaimed gleefully. "And if one was to ride her, do you suppose she would, say, go *left* if one wanted?"

"Yes," he laughed, stroking the roan's nose. "I suppose she would." Abbey glanced at Alex as he cooed softly to the horse. He had a warm, inviting smile, one that made the corners of his green eyes crinkle. With dark-brown hair just a shade lighter than hers and a face tanned by the sun, he was a very handsome man, almost as handsome as Michael. Almost.

"And then I suppose it follows she would also go right?" she asked shyly.

Alex laughed again and nodded. "I think if one were to tug on her rein just so, she would do just about anything. If I were to ride her, I would do thus." He smiled and, taking a bridle from a post nearby, looped it loosely over the roan's head and demonstrated. Abbey watched attentively, trying to memorize everything he showed her. He had just suggested they look at a sidesaddle when the stable master, Mr. Hanley, bustled inside. Alex and Abbey turned simultaneously turned toward him; the stable master stopped dead in his tracks and gaped at them.

"Your grace!" he exclaimed, and hurried quickly to the stall at which Abbey and Alex stood. Startled, Abbey looked at Alex. *Your grace?*

"It's quite all right," the duke said, waving Hanley off. "Lady Darfield was showing me some of the mounts."

Mr. Hanley looked nervously at Abbey who, having quickly recovered from her shock, smiled beguilingly at the flustered stable master.

"His grace is quite enamored of the stallion," she offered cheerfully.

Mr. Hanley turned red in the face. "Lord Southerland, my humblest apologies. Had I known you were within, I would have attended you *immediately*," Mr. Hanley said, emphatically emphasizing the last word.

"Not to worry, Hanley. Lady Darfield and I have quite enjoyed our chat." He turned to Abbey and smiled, bowing slightly. "I believe Lord Darfield is expecting me. If you will be so kind as to excuse me."

Abbey smiled and nodded, dipping lightly into a belated curtsey. With a warm smile, he strolled away, his gait at once graceful and powerful.

"Thank you!" she called after him. Looking over his shoulder with a warm grin, he nonchalantly waved a hand. Abbey turned her attention to Mr. Hanley, who was still a little pale after finding the duke unattended.

What in God's name had she been thinking? Abbey wondered helplessly when she emerged from the house at promptly two o'clock, dressed in a turquoise riding habit Tori had made for her in the event she should encounter a mule in England. She nervously fidgeted with her borrowed riding crop as she watched a young man lead an enormous gray mare from the stable outfitted with a sidesaddle. Michael followed behind on Samson, who pranced impatiently beneath him, forcing Michael to rein hard to control the beast as he neared her.

"Good afternoon, madam. I took the liberty of selecting Desdemona for you," he announced with a succinct nod. "She's perhaps a little green, but I think you should have no trouble."

Abbey's heart sank. Mr. Hanley had promised she would be given a very, *very* tame mount. Michael gave her a curious look, then motioned toward the mare with his head.

"If you please, Lady Darfield," he said expectantly.

Abbey peered up at him, then slowly slid her gaze to the horse, who was yanking her head against the stableboys tight hold. Abbey's stomach lurched.

"Is something amiss?" Michael asked suspiciously.

"Oh, no!" she exclaimed a little too loudly.

He lifted a dark brow. "Is there another mount you prefer? Mr. Hanley informs me you have not ridden as yet and did not know if you had a particular favorite—"

"Desdemona will do nicely," she said, nodding to emphasize she was quite fine. If only she could move her legs.

The stallion snorted with anticipation. "Abbey, if you are ready," Michael said again.

She nodded, mustered all her courage—which wasn't much—and walked purposefully toward the mare. She stopped and bravely stroked the mare's nose, just as Lord Southerland had suggested.

"Be gentle, Desdemona," she whispered, "and there will be a bucket of carrots at the end of the day." Feeling the stableboy's eyes on her, she walked to one side of the horse. Another young man appeared at her elbow and bent over, cupping his hands together. Abbey stared at him as if he were insane.

"Pardon, mum, but don't you want a lift up?"

Abbey regained her composure and laughed lightly. Naturally she would have to get on the horse to ride it.

"Yes, of course." She placed her foot in his cupped hand and gasped loudly when he vaulted her upward. It was a miracle that she landed in the saddle at all. She took a moment to adjust to the terribly awkward sidesaddle, feeling ridiculous perched precariously high on top of the horse as she was. She doubted she was sitting correctly, but fortunately, the thick folds of her habit concealed any glaring errors on her part.

One of the young men handed her the reins; she grabbed them hastily, gripping them with all her strength. The two young men exchanged a look before the older one spoke.

"My lady," he muttered quietly, "don't pull so hard. Give the horse a little slack and she'll do all right by you."

Abbey nodded, then gave him a slight frown that suggested he might have insulted her by explaining something so fundamental. With her riding crop stuffed tightly under one arm, and her hands gripping the reins for dear life, she turned a serene smile to Michael.

"We are wasting daylight," she chirped, but strangled on her words when the mare began to move. Smiling enigmatically, Michael reined in next to her.

"I think we've plenty of daylight. Why don't you lead?" he suggested.

Abbey swallowed a lump of fear and gripped the reins even tighter. "Surely you would rather. Lord only knows where I would lead you." She laughed nervously.

"Lord only knows," he agreed with a chuckle, and kneed his stallion forward. "Follow me," he called cheerfully, and cantered forward. Had the stableboy not slapped the mare's hindquarter, Abbey might have sat in the drive until Michael returned from his ride. With a small shriek, Abbey grabbed the saddle horn and prayed for mercy as the mare trotted after the stallion.

They had not gone far when Abbey decided she had mastered riding. In spite of the constant jarring, it really was not so difficult. In her mind, she went over and over what Lord Southerland had told her. *Tug right to go right, tug left to go left. Rein in to stop, slack the reins to run. Do not let the horse know you are frightened, for she will surely take advantage of you.* The only real discomfort she experienced was the fear she would topple from the saddle at any moment given the odd way in which she sat. With Michael in front of her, she managed to slide one leg awkwardly over the side of the saddle and let it dangle below her bunched habit. That position was much less comfortable, but it felt vastly more secure. She smiled happily to herself before tentatively testing her heels in the mare's side. The mare lurched forward and Abbey was soon bouncing along next to Michael.

"You ride well," he said when she caught up to him. Abbey smiled in response and cautiously reached up to adjust her slipping bonnet. "I'm surprised you found the opportunity to ride with so much time at sea. Where did you learn?"

Abbey laughed. "Oh, here and there . . . catch as catch can. One must seize opportunities when one is handed them," she said in a very confident voice. "You know, *carpe diem,* that sort of thing."

Michael rolled his eyes. Carpe diem, indeed! She was bobbing along atop a fat old nag like apples in a tub of water. Had his good friend, Alex Christian, the Duke of Southerland, not laughingly explained their encounter in the stables, he might well have had Black Widow saddled for her. He wanted to wring her slender neck for not telling him but had determined a little lesson was in order. Fortunately, the nag she was on could be trusted to do nothing faster than waddle. He glanced down at the shapely calf and booted foot that hung uncomfortably across the lip of the sidesaddle and swallowed a lump of desire.

There was at least one other lesson he wanted to teach her.

They rode along at what Michael thought was an excruciatingly slow pace for over an hour. Samson chomped at his bit to be given his head, but Michael held him tight. Abbey looked exhausted. Her bonnet had long since fallen behind her, and wisps of mahogany hair fell from her pretty coif. She still had not released her death grip—one hand on the saddle horn, one on the reins.

A cool breeze had picked up strength, and thick clouds were beginning to form above. A storm was coming and Michael decided it was time to turn back, but not before he had one last laugh at her expense.

"See that great oak just ahead?" he asked. Abbey peered ahead and nodded. "What say we race for it?" He had to turn his face so she would not see his smile at her look of horror.

She studied the tree for a long moment, then looked down at Desdemona. "I—I think Desdemona is tired?" she said hopefully.

"Hardly. Desdemona *loves* to run."

"She does?" she asked in a voice gone from hopeful to hopeless.

Michael could not suppress a grin. "Come now, on my mark," he called to her, and bent over Samson's neck.

"Ready . . . set . . . *go!*" he shouted, and spurred Samson forward, giving him free rein. He heard Abbey's shout behind him, and when he reached the tree, he yanked Samson around, instantly doubling over with laughter at the sight of Desdemona walking along with Abbey on her back, shouting furiously.

"Did you do something to my horse?" she demanded angrily when at last she reached him.

"Certainly not! That was Desdemona's top speed," Michael choked through fits of laughter.

Abbey's eyes narrowed. "You *knew*!" she shrieked.

He dismounted and caught Desdemona's reins when she flung them at him. Michael's sides began to hurt with laughter as she flung a string of very unladylike oaths at him and slid, or rather rolled, from the horse's back. He caught her when her legs buckled on impact.

"Abbey, you should have told me," he said when he at last caught his breath. "You could have been seriously hurt. Why didn't you tell me?"

"Because," she said stubbornly.

"Because?"

Abbey avoided his gaze and glanced to the meadow. "I thought you would not want to go if you knew," she said softly.

Michael felt an uncharacteristic rush of elation. So she *had* wanted to go with him! "No, Abbey, I would have driven you in a carriage," he replied sincerely.

Abbey's violet eyes grew wide with a spontaneous hopefulness he found enchanting. And bothersome. *Bloody hell.*

"Why did you never learn to ride?" he asked leading her to the oak.

"I never had the opportunity. In Egypt I rode a dromedary, and I thought *that* skill would lend itself at least in some small way to a horse's back. In Paris we took carriages. In Amsterdam boats were the preferred mode of travel. And in Virginia, well, we had a mule that would occasionally agree to having someone on his back, but only under extreme duress."

Michael laughed. "I will teach you to ride."

"If you are sincere, Darfield, I want to learn to ride like you. That contraption you call a saddle is positively from the Middle Ages!" she said, gesturing wildly toward Desdemona.

Michael removed his coat and laid it on grass beneath the tree. "I will teach you to ride sidesaddle, bareback—any way you want." He sat on the grass and leaned against the tree with his legs stretched and crossed at the ankles, peering up at her.

The look in his eye made Abbey nervous. *Three months*, she told herself. "The clouds are thickening. Do you think we should linger?" she asked, looking up at the sky. Michael unexpectedly grabbed her hand and yanked her down. In a *whoosh* of woolen turquoise skirt, she landed next to his muscular thighs.

"We have plenty of time." He slid a hand around her nape and pulled her toward him, brushing his lips across hers in slow, deliberate movement. Just as she feared, the familiar warmth began to spread through her. Self-control was leaking out of her. She would have been lost altogether had not the thought *three months* popped into her mind. She jerked away from him and sat back on her haunches.

"That's not at all how it's done!" she snapped irritably, for lack of anything better to say.

"I beg your pardon?" Michael's surprise twinkled enticingly in his eyes.

"It's simply not done that way!" she insisted. Certainly Galen had not kissed her like that, nor had she ever felt weak in his arms as she did in Michael's. Not that she had exactly ever been in Galen's arms, really, but had she *been* in his arms, she was quite convinced it would not have compared to this.

"Exactly how is it done?" he asked.

Abbey avoided looking into his gray eyes and being pulled into their depths. She plucked a blade of grass. "Not like that!" she mumbled.

"You speak with the authority of a woman who has been kissed many times, Abbey," he teased.

She blanched at the insinuation and pulled several more blades of grass. "All right, Galen did not kiss like that!"

Michael arched one brow over the other. "Galen? Who the bloody hell is Galen?"

"Indian Ocean," she said lamely.

Michael suddenly grabbed her hand and pulled her closer,

pressing his lips to her palm while his other hand anchored her to him.

"Did he kiss you like this?" he murmured, and lightly brushed his lips across hers. The tingling sensation swept down Abbey's spine again.

"No," she said stubbornly, and because it was true. Galen's kiss was planted on her lips. Short, sweet, and to the point.

Michael chuckled low in his throat. "Did he kiss you like this?" he asked, and brought her bottom lip in between his teeth.

"N-no," Abbey said shakily.

Michael dragged her across his lap, splaying his fingers against her neck and jaw while his other hand traced a soft line down her spine.

"Then perhaps it was like this," he said as he gently pressed his lips to hers.

"Y-yes. That's it. That's how it is done," she agreed in a daze.

Michael looked at her violet eyes, wide and a little glazed. Desire raged through him like wildfire. Everything he had told himself, every caution his mind could dredge up, was tossed aside like the blades of grass that fell from Abbey's fingers. "If this Galen had the opportunity, I can assure you he would have kissed you thus," he said, and swept down on her, his lips pressing gently at first, then insistently as his tongue probed her lips and the soft recess of her mouth. With his hand on the small of her back he pressed her into him. Her hands traveled slowly up his rock-hard chest, across every taut muscle. When she twisted on his lap, he groaned deep in his throat, and when she timidly touched her tongue to his lips, Michael went wild.

He plunged his tongue into her mouth again and again in seductive rhythm. She met him there; her tongue dueled with his and, finally, slipped into his mouth. Michael moved his hands slowly up her sides until he splayed his fingers against her breasts. Abbey did not object; when he cupped her breast and squeezed lightly, she sighed softly into his mouth and sent him reeling.

He tore his mouth from hers and pressed his lips against the swell of her breast beneath her clothes. Abbey instinctively threaded her fingers through his thick hair as Michael swiftly unbuttoned her blouse. He cupped the soft, pliable mound of flesh before gently pulling it free from her chemise and molding the hardening peak between his thumb and forefinger. Abbey gasped, and when he lowered his head to swab it with his tongue, she jumped.

"It's all right," he murmured as he took her full into his mouth. Abbey clutched at his shoulders, her fingers digging into his muscles, unconsciously lifting her breasts to him. Her breathing grew ragged; his own desire was mounting at an alarming pace. If he did not stop now, he never would. With sheer determination, he tore himself away from her.

"We have to stop," he muttered as he ran the palm of his hand over the peak of her breast.

Abbey pulled her lower lip between her teeth and looked at him with such seductive innocence that Michael came dangerously close to losing all self-control. He eased her off his lap and leapt to his feet, walking blindly into the meadow. He sucked in several deep breaths of the cool air before finally turning around. Abbey had buttoned her blouse and was sitting on her legs, watching him. Her coif, destroyed by the ride and the passionate kiss, was an alluring, tousled mess around her shoulders.

"You," he said as he strolled toward her, "are too enticing for your own good." He gracefully dropped down next to her.

"That doesn't sound very good."

He wrapped an arm around her shoulders and pulled her into his chest in a casual embrace. Over the top of her head, he looked out over the meadow. "It's not very good for me."

Abbey wondered what he meant by that but did not ask. She was too swept up by the feeling of safety and comfort she felt cradled in his arms. Michael pulled a long stem of grass from the ground and began to chew contentedly. They sat in silence for several long moments, each enjoying the cool breeze and the comfortable, quiet intimacy.

"Where did you go after you left the ship that summer?" he asked idly.

"To school. In Rome."

"Is that where you learned to play the violin?"

Abbey shifted uncomfortably in his arms as she recalled the day she had received the violin. Her father had told her it was Michael's Yuletide present to her. "Yes," she said softly, hoping he would change the subject.

He did not.

"It's unusual. Most young girls learn the pianoforte, don't they? How did you decide on the violin?"

"It was a gift," she said simply.

"From your father?"

Abbey hesitated. She was so awful at lying about anything. Her aunt had complained time and again that she was too straightforward for her own good. *You are as open as a book, girl. I can take one look at you and know what you are thinking, and if there is any doubt, you will tell me straightaway,* she had said. Abbey couldn't help it, and in that moment decided the best way to handle the horrible, cruel lie her father had perpetuated at every moment of her life was to make light of the whole thing.

"Actually, it was from you," she said nonchalantly, and felt him tense. "Papa said you wanted me to learn to play, and at the time, well, I simply *pined* for you, so I was happy to learn it. Do you remember when we were aboard the *Dancing Maiden*? I thought you were the most handsome man in the world. You know how little girls are," she said, then laughed lightly in an effort to demonstrate that it was a little girl's fancy, nothing more.

Michael was stunned. He recalled Sam saying that Carrington had given her gifts ostensibly from him, but he had not believed it. "You learned to play for me?" he asked hesitantly.

"I suppose you could say that, but I think it was the *only* way to get a headstrong, uncivilized little girl to play anything, if you ask me. I'm sure that's why Papa did what he did,'' she said dismissively. She suddenly sat up and stretched her arms above her head.

Michael stared at her svelte back. "What else?" he asked cautiously.

"Pardon?"

"Did you father give you anything else . . . from me?" Abbey's laugh sounded forced.

"Oh, I think a pair of earrings once," she said casually, and came gracefully to her feet without looking at him. "Nothing spectacular—just some amethysts," she said airily and strolled into the meadow. Michael clenched his jaw as he watched her glide across the tall yellow grass. She was speaking of the amethyst earrings that so complimented her eyes, he thought angrily. She had worn them every day, but he had not seen her wear them since . . . since she had learned of her father's deception. He could not help feeling angry. Whatever had possessed Carrington to trick him was one thing, but his deception of Abbey bordered on vile.

He stood up and grabbed his coat. He angrily brushed the grass from it, then shrugged into it as he watched Abbey stroll toward Desdemona from the corner of his eye. He turned to see where Samson had gotten off to when a shot rang out.

Michael whirled toward the sound, crouching low as he pulled a pistol from his boot. Desdemona, for all her laziness, bolted like a young colt at the sound and collided with Samson, who bolted after the nag. Abbey stood frozen in the meadow, peering curiously toward the woods from where the shot had been fired. Panic swelled in Michael when she started to move in the direction of the shot.

He sprang to his feet and ran, hurling himself at her. He managed to avoid crushing her, but felt a slash of pain across his chest when they struck the earth. Ignoring it, he scrambled on top of her, covering her body with his while he searched the tree line. They were out in the middle of the blasted meadow, with no cover or protection. Michael jerked around and spotted a large rock boulder protruding from the ground across the meadow. Beneath him, Abbey was struggling to rise, but he held her down.

"Abbey, when I tell you, you will run like the wind to that rock and get down behind it," he said. Abbey nodded. Michael slowly slid off her back and trained his pistol on the wooded area. *"Now,"* he said gruffly, and Abbey scrambled to her feet and ran.

She was crouching behind the rock and peering toward the tree line when Michael dove in next to her. "What happened?" she asked as she tried to catch her breath.

Michael did not answer as he carefully scanned their surroundings. "I don't know," he answered truthfully. He turned to look at her. Her expression scared him; gaping at his chest, her eyes were wide and the color had drained from her face. Bewildered, Michael looked down. A dark stain had appeared on his shirt and was spreading.

*"Oh, God! Oh, my God! Michael, you've been shot!"* She shrieked and threw herself on him. Startled, Michael fell backward as Abbey frantically sought the wound. He caught her face in his hands and forced her to look at him.

"Abbey, it's all right, it's all right, I have not been shot," he cooed in a vain attempt to soothe her. She jerked her face from his hands and frantically searched him, her hands fluttering across his body and probing for the wound. Michael grabbed her hands. Through clenched teeth, he reassured her. "I'm all right. I must have landed on a rock," he said, and struggled to sit up. He had to dump her off his chest to do it; she landed in a heap next to him. He gingerly inspected his chest. A long, deep gash just under his clavicle was the source of the blood. He pulled a handkerchief from his pocket and pressed it against the wound.

"A cut, all right, and a good one at that," he remarked as he looked around for the horses. Samson had come to halt at the far end of the meadow. Desdemona was nowhere to be seen, and Michael guessed the nag was waddling as fast as she could for the safety of her stable. He sighed and looked at Abbey, who was intently studying his gash.

"It's very deep," she said, a worried frown wrinkling her brow.

"Yes, I think it is. Apparently we find ourselves in a predicament, Lady Darfield. Desdemona is long gone, and Samson is across the meadow. You'll have to make a dash for him and ride to the house. You can do it," he added hurriedly as she began to shake her head.

"No!" Abbey cried immediately, shaking her head so violently that wisps of satin hair swirled about her. "No, no, no! You are seriously hurt, and I'm not leaving you!"

Michael glanced up at the darkening sky. A storm was fast approaching from the west. He grimaced; there was no time to argue with her, especially if their assailant was still training a gunsight on them. "We will both go, then," he said as he struggled to a squatting position. She started to leap to her feet, but Michael caught her wrist.

"Pay attention to me, Abbey. On my mark, run for Samson." Abbey nodded gravely, and Michael cocked the pistol he was holding.

"Go." Abbey picked up her skirts and ran. Michael was close behind her, his gun trained on the tree line. She ran like lightning until she collapsed against Samson's neck. Michael, fast losing blood, could hardly keep up with her. He had to admire her; for a woman who had just been shot at, Abbey was behaving remarkably well. He would have expected her to fall into a fit of hysteria. He glanced up at the sky. The storm was moving in quickly; the temperature had dropped dramatically since the shot was fired.

"Please hurry. The storm is almost upon us," Abbey said, having reached the same conclusion, and held out her hand to him. With chagrin, Michael realized he was light-headed. He glanced down at the small, turquoise jacket she had stuffed into his waistcoat and swallowed. It was soaked in blood.

"Give me your leg," he said to Abbey, and pushed her up onto Samson's back. With what strength he had left, he clumsily scrambled up behind her, and sent Samson galloping toward Blessing Park.

\*    \*    \*

In blinding sheets of rain, Samson made his way home without help from either rider. Abbey gripped the saddle horn as Michael's weight sagged against her. Half afraid he was dead, she was too frightened to look at him and kept her eyes glued to the path in front of them. When at last the horse entered the long, circular drive, Abbey shouted to a groom coming from the stable.

"He's been seriously hurt!" She shrieked as she slid awkwardly from Samson. The groom caught Michael and helped him to the ground. Abbey gasped with fear when she saw him; his dark curls were plastered to his ashen face. He attempted a weak smile for her benefit, but she whirled toward the house and ran, screaming for Sebastian as she crashed through the front door. Sebastian, and Sam, who had stayed on after Routier and Southerland departed, heard her screams and bolted from the front drawing room, meeting her halfway down the corridor.

"It's Michael!" she cried. "He's been hurt! Someone shot at us, and he fell . . ." Sam was already striding swiftly down the corridor, ordering Sebastian to send for a physician right away. Sebastian dragged a dazed Abbey into the drawing room, where he yanked frantically on the bell cord several times. Jones appeared almost instantaneously, and with one look at Abbey, soaked to the bone and a look of horror on her face, he barked at a footman to fetch Sarah. Abbey pushed past the stalwart butler and ran to the foyer in time to see Sam dragging Michael through the door and Sebastian rushing to help them up the stairs.

Shocked, Abbey watched them struggle up the marble stairs with Michael hanging limply between them. It was not until Sarah firmly grabbed her elbow that Abbey allowed herself to be led to her chamber.


Sam had assured her Michael was in no danger of dying. Sarah had persuaded her to bathe and change, and except for that one diversion, she had paced her sitting room, where Sam had banished her while the physician attended to Michael's wound. When she heard a door close down the hall, she rushed into the corridor and accosted the physician as he made his way to the stairs.

"How is he? Is he all right?" she asked desperately.

The elderly doctor peered at Abbey over his round spectacles. "Allow me to present the Marchioness of Darfield, Dr. Stephens," Sam mumbled.

"When did Darfield take a wife?" he demanded.

"A few weeks ago," Sam muttered uncomfortably.

The physician frowned as he perused Abbey from the crown of her hair to the hem of her skirt, then glanced disdainfully at her wringing hands. "Stop your pouting, young lady—I've sewn him up and he shall be good as new on the morrow," he commanded gruffly.

"You're quite sure?"

"Certainly I am!" he barked.

"Thank you, Doctor." Abbey sighed, relief evident on her face, and disappeared into her sitting room.

"What the hell is Darfield doing with a wife?" Dr. Stephens demanded again of Sam. "I've not heard a word of it."

"It's rather a long story, Doctor. I will save it for Lord Darfield to tell you," Sam said as he showed the doctor out.

Sam immediately returned to the master chamber and strolled in, ignoring Michael's annoyed glare from his bed, where he lay propped against a mountain of pillows.

"I was not jesting, Sam. I am not going to lie here like some infirm old man," he barked.

Sam settled into an armchair of soft suede and stretched his legs onto the matching ottoman, crossing them at the ankles. "You lost a good amount of blood. The least you can do is lie there until the morning and replenish the black stuff that runs in your veins. If you don't, you'll scare the staff half to death. Some of them already believe you are not quite human."

Michael grumbled irritably.

"Now that we are alone, what the hell happened?" Sam asked.

Michael exhaled loudly and shook his head. "I don't know, other than someone fired at us. She was standing in the open, in the meadow, and I was near a lone oak. We were in the bloody open, and I knocked her to the ground. Must have sliced my chest on a rock."

"Do you think it was poachers?"

Michael quickly shook his head. "No. We were in a meadow—not any large game there. It may have been a trespasser, but I think not. We were too deep within the estate."

Sam was clearly startled. "But who in the devil would want to harm you?"

"I don't know if the shot was fired at me or her. I am sure Carrington made some enemies along the way, but I can't think of what anyone would hope to gain from her death."

"He probably added some strange codicil to that blasted will of his," Sam muttered angrily.

"He may have, but that doesn't make any sense now that she's married. Her fortune belongs to me; in fact, I have put it in trust."

"But it cannot be widely known she is married, or that she is here," Sam speculated. "If someone were after her money and thought she was the orphaned daughter and sole survivor to the Carrington fortune, that might explain an attempt on her life. If money is owed and stipulated in the will, I suppose one would have an easier time collecting through the courts if there were no survivors."

Michael moved his arm and grimaced at the pain. "If that is true, then I should let it be known widely that I have married her. Can you get a notice to the *Times*?"

"Of course, but still, it makes no sense. Who besides your staff would have known you were riding today? It's not likely someone could stake out the whole of Blessing Park and happen to have been there this afternoon. Whoever it was had to know where you were going."

Michael's eyes narrowed as he considered Sam's remark. "Abbey doesn't know how to ride. I had her on that damned nag Desdemona. If someone had been following her, they could have easily skirted around and waited ahead—it took us more than an hour to go a distance of only a few miles. However, I can't believe it was anyone in my employ—they all adore her."

"Then who?" Sam asked, bewildered.

"In addition to the locals, my solicitors, you, and Southerland, there is only one other who knows she is here . . ."

Sam's eyes narrowed and he nodded. "Routier. I was rather surprised to see him with Southerland in Pemberheath."

"Quite by accident, Alex assured me. Routier was on his way here to collect on the settlement of Carrington's estate."

"Indeed?" Sam frowned and pressed his fingertips together. Malcolm Routier was a ruthless rake and unsavory businessman. Long ago he and Michael had usurped Routier's supposed trade routes. It had been too easy. Routier had not really fought it, which led them to suspect Routier made his money from pirating, and not the legitimate trade he would have everyone believe. When Michael had threatened to expose his scheme, Routier had done his best to shame Michael by spreading vile rumors about the Devil of Darfield. And then, purely by chance, Routier had had the singular misfortune of falling in love with Michael's sister, Mariah. Michael had, of course, refused his offer. Humiliated, Routier had vowed in private circles to see Michael brought down, a threat at which Michael had laughed openly.

"What are you thinking?" Michael asked.

Sam reluctantly continued. "Could she be lying? I mean, is there not a possibility she could be mixed up in something? After all, you don't *know* her, not really."

Michael's chest tightened at the suggestion. "No! Absolutely not. In the first place, I have had her thoroughly investigated. In the second place, I would know if she had lied."

Sam looked doubtful.

"Sam, that woman can't hide a thing. Every emotion she ever has is as clear as a picture if you only look in her eyes," he insisted. "She could not hide an illicit arrangement with Routier. I will send a note to my solicitor in the morning and have him get Bow Street on it," he said, settling gingerly against the pillows, grimacing with pain. "In the meantime, I do not want her out of my sight," he added with a yawn.

Sam grinned.

"What's so damned funny?" Michael snarled, his ill humor worsening by the minute as the light dose of laudanum Stephens had given him clouded his mind.

"It wasn't so very long ago that you never wanted to see her again. Now you do not want her out of your sight," Sam observed happily.

Michael glowered at him. "Thank you for that astute observation, Hunt. I have an obligation to protect her, or have you forgotten she now carries the Ingram name?"

"How could I possibly forget that monumental fact?" Sam laughed.

"I should hope you are quite finished amusing yourself."

"All right, all right!" Sam laughed. "I'll leave you be." He left, chuckling as he walked out of the room. Michael frowned deeply. He did not like that Sam could see right through him, not one bit.

He was awakened from a peaceful sleep a short time later by the creaking of the door being opened slowly. He jerked upright and gasped at the stab of pain. The glow of a candelabra filtered silently into his room, and he relaxed, assuming it was Jones or his valet, Damon.

But to his surprise, it was Abbey who slipped through the door behind the light. With a candelabra in one hand and a violin and bow in the other, she took several steps into the room and peered toward the bed.

"Are you awake?" she whispered cheerfully when she realized he was watching her.

"I am now," he said dryly.

She pushed the door shut with her foot and crossed the room until she was standing next to him, holding the candle high. She leaned over and inspected his face.

"Sam said you were not shot after all, that it was only 'a

deep gash.' I was fairly convinced it was a bullet. Those hunters must not have seen you behind the tree," she said.

Michael did not say anything to that; a dim shadow of doubt scudded through his mind. *You don't know her, not really*, Sam's voice echoed.

"The doctor said you will be fine, perhaps a bit sore," she announced.

Michael smiled lazily. "Have you come to nurse me back to health, then?"

Her laugh was melodic. "You would not want me nursing you. I can birth a calf, but when it comes to humans, I am quite hopeless. Ask Withers," she said, then flashed a cheerful smile.

Michael warmed at the sight of it; he was already feeling better. If she would just sit on the edge of the bed . . .

She moved away from the bed.

"I don't believe knowledge of a cow's anatomy will help me. Perhaps you would play for me instead?" he asked as he struggled to stack some pillows behind his back.

"What?" she asked, then glanced at the violin in her hand. "Oh! I was playing for Sarah and Cook—well, really, I was learning to play from them. They are teaching me a Scottish dance to play at the wedding of Sarah's brother. He's a groom in your stable, you know." Of course Michael knew that, but said nothing, admiring her as she wandered about his room and examined his belongings. "It's next month. They are having the wedding here, did you know? Withers said next month should be exceptionally fine for a garden wedding. It took me two full days to convince him that we could rope off the roses just so, and no one would touch them. That man lives in constant fear of someone touching his roses! Doesn't it seem lovely? A garden wedding?" She sighed wistfully as she leaned over a dresser to inspect a small portrait of his sister.

"I was on my way to bed," she continued, seemingly unaware that he was not participating in the conversation, "and although Jones said you were not to be disturbed, I thought a look wouldn't be so very harmful. I thought I would see for myself that you are quite all right. That shot came terribly close to you, I think." She stopped her perusal of items on his vanity and glanced at him from the corner of her eye. "I am sorry if I woke you," she added softly.

"I'm not."

She smiled happily. "Well. Jones was rather emphatic when he said you needed your rest. *Quite* emphatic, really, so I suppose I should go," she said as she started toward the door, pausing to inspect some of his things on the hearth mantel.

"Won't you play for me?" he asked.

Startled, she glanced over her shoulder. "Surely you don't want to hear music now." She laughed.

"On the contrary, I would very much like it," he insisted.

"Jones said—"

"The devil take Jones."

Delighted, Abbey smiled. "All right," she said, placing the candelabra on a writing table, "but you must promise to bear Jones's wrath when he learns of this. What shall I play . . . Vivaldi?"

Michael nodded, pleased that she had selected one of his favorite composers. She placed the violin beneath her chin and plucked at one of the strings.

"I'm afraid it may sound a little peculiar. It's difficult to appreciate it without the whole orchestra, or at least a pianoforte to accompany," she said as she tightened one of the strings, and drew the bow quickly across, tuning the instrument. "You must imagine the rest. It's really not so very hard; I do it all the time. Just pretend there is an orchestra behind me, picture it in your mind, and you will begin to hear the music," she said sincerely. She turned around, her back to him, and with her bow, she gestured to the left. "Here are the strings," she said, and gave him a winsome grin over her shoulder. "I am the guest soloist this evening, so there are very *few* violins." She laughed gaily.

She pointed to her right. "Here are the cellos, the bass, and, or course, a viola to play tenor to my soprano." She winked conspiratorially at Michael, then waved her bow to the wall. "There are the horns, and there the percussion. You won't

hear them, because we are performing a concerto for violin.''
She turned to face him, curtsied deeply, then rose slowly and
carefully placed the bow across the strings of her instrument.
The candelabra cast dancing shadows on the wall behind her,
as if an orchestra did accompany her.

"Maestro, if you please,'' she said, and drew her bow.

Michael was startled by the first notes she played. A slow,
flowing rhapsody filled the room and sent a shiver down his
spine. He grew flush from the rich sound; the strains that rose
from her strings were possibly the sweetest notes of music he
had ever heard. In awe, he felt himself drifting away, and
turned his gaze to the wall as he listened to the soulful sounds,
imagining Abbey in a concert hall with an orchestra behind
her. Her skill was incredible; he was astonished and moved by
what he was hearing.

He slowly dragged his gaze from the wall to Abbey. She
was smiling at him, and he blushed—*blushed!* Without missing a beat, she asked sweetly, ''Do you hear the music?''

He did not know if he even nodded. Entranced, he watched
with admiration as the tempo of the music began to increase,
and the low, sorrowful notes transformed into higher, more
robust tones. She turned away from him, strolled to the floor-
to-ceiling windows, and stood bathed in faint moonlight as her
bow moved with fierce speed and grace across the strings. Her
expression was remotely serene; she seemed lost in the sea of
music she was creating.

When she drew the final passionate note, she threw her
head back and her arms wide, the bow in one hand and the
violin in the other, as if she were listening to the last stanza of
her imaginary orchestra.

It absolutely took his breath away.

She slowly lowered her head and smiled brilliantly.

"Did you hear it?''

Michael swallowed hard the emotion that had built within
him. ''Come here,'' he commanded roughly. She floated
toward him and knelt at his bedside.

He reached for her, cupping her face with his hand. She

lifted sparkling violet eyes to his and leaned into the palm of his hand.

"Did you hear it?" she whispered.

"I heard it," he choked as his chest filled with a peculiar ache. He stared into her lovely face, marveling that she had learned to play like that for him.

It the most priceless gift he had ever received.

# Chapter 11

In a few days, when Michael had regained his strength, he, Sam, and a contingent of men scoured thousands of Blessing Park acres for clues. Their very thorough search, however, turned up nothing. Sam theorized that it had been nothing more than an errant shot fired by hunters too far into Ingram property. Given that there was no evidence to support his own, darker theory, Michael did not argue, but he remained unconvinced.

He ensured Abbey was never without a guardian, whether she was aware of it or not, and for her own safety, Michael explained his suspicions and misgivings to her. She thought his theory patently amusing but, at his stern look, had promised solemnly to abide by his wishes and remain at Blessing Park. She returned to her sitting room and dashed off a note to Galen in Portsmouth, explaining that Michael had asked her to remain at the manor, but that she was very much looking forward to his visit.

On a cold, rainy day, Michael and Sam spent a good part of the afternoon sequestered in his library with work. But as usual of late, Michael found it difficult to concentrate. His fondness for Abbey was growing. She was so utterly beguiling and unusual, it was impossible not to be drawn to her. And since that day in the meadow, he had been overwhelmed by an instinctive need to protect her from harm.

The fiercely protective feeling only intensified as letters and invitations began to pour in after the *Times* announced their marriage. The sight of missives from the very people who had once deliberately shunned his family disgusted him. In spite of the very proper salutations, he knew what they wanted. They wanted to see the mysterious Devil of Darfield's bride, so that in the privacy of their parlors they could postulate about her background, connections, and suitability as a member of their very elite circle. They wanted to discuss her at dinner parties and weekend soirées across England, and God help her if she did not measure up to their lofty expectations.

So it was with trepidation that he had agreed to her request to have the Havershams to supper that evening. It was clear she considered the eccentric couple friends, but he was torn between his desire to please her and his need to protect her. The hopeful look in her violet eyes convinced him too easily, a phenomenon that he realized was happening more frequently. Abbey affected him as no other person had in his life, and as extremely disturbing as that was, he seemed powerless to change it.

Sam noticed it, too. "Bloody hell, Darfield, you've added that column three times. Since when have you had trouble with math? I always thought of you as something akin to a walking abacus," he remarked with a friendly grin.

"Since about a month or so ago," Michael replied dryly as he examined the ledger in front of him.

"Just a month or so ago you were a very confirmed bachelor with a distinct gift for math. Today you are married and couldn't add two and two if your life depended upon it."

"Circumstances beyond my control ended my bachelorhood; I rather doubt it has affected my ability to add."

Sam chuckled into his cup of tea. "It seems to me you are besotted."

"Besotted!" Michael protested. "God, Hunt, I am not

some lovesick schoolboy. However, I will admit that I am pleasantly surprised to learn that Abbey is not the little hellion I remember.''

Sam snorted. ''That's rather an understatement. If you ask *me*, I think you find yourself with a wife that far exceeds any expectation you could have even dreamed.''

''I do not believe I asked you,'' Michael remarked, but could not help grinning in unspoken acquiescence to Sam's assertion.


Abbey dressed carefully for the supper party that evening. Although he had relented, Michael had not wanted the Havershams to come. She could only conclude that he doubted her ability to host. After all, she did not have what he would consider proper training, not like the other women he had known. It was ridiculous, of course, since she had hosted at her father's side and had attended more posh affairs than she cared to remember. But she would rather be drawn and quartered than disappoint Michael in any way.

This would be a perfect supper party.

She had spent the afternoon going over the details with Cook, Sarah, and Jones. They had all sought to reassure her that is was a simple matter to have the Havershams to supper, but Abbey was adamant that the affair be flawless. Given the Havershams' delight in anything Eastern, she had decided upon an Egyptian theme. She even helped Cook prepare the Egyptian meal and an assortment of eastern pastries, all the while ignoring Jones's very vocal belief that a marchioness did not work in the kitchens.

In the red drawing room, she and Sarah hung diaphanous strips of red and gold silk across the drapes, and brought cushions down from her sitting room to scatter about the floor. When they were done, the room had a decidedly Egyptian look about it.

She dressed in a gown of lilac-colored velvet and chiffon, trimmed in gold, that accented her eyes. Another creation of her cousin Victoria, a piece of the velvet cloth swathed diagonally across her breasts, wrapped around her middle, then around her hips. From there, the chiffon skirt drifted to the floor, ending with a small train. It was an exotic, form-hugging style that accentuated her rounded bosom, narrow waist, and slender hips. When she finished dressing, Sarah squealed with delight.

"You look positively *regal*," she exclaimed.

Pleased, Abbey held up two small diamond earrings. "What do you think? I have a necklace to match."

With her head cocked to one side in serious consideration, Sarah slowly shook her head. "I think the amethyst earrings would be better."

Abbey flushed. She had not worn the earrings since she had uncovered her father's treachery; the sight of the glistening gems only reminded her of it. "I don't care for them, really. I think the diamonds," she said with a nod, and attached them to her lobes.

"Don't care for them? Why, they are *lovely*! You seemed to like them before; I never saw you without—"

"Really, Sarah, I don't. Would you like them?" she offered impetuously. Sarah's eyes grew wide as Abbey dug into a small box on her vanity and thrust the earrings at Sarah. The maid shook her head slowly as her eyes riveted on the earrings.

"I couldn't, milady, I just couldn't. They are beautiful!" she breathed.

Abbey pressed the earrings into Sarah's hand. "I want you to have them," she insisted.

Sarah gaped at the earrings. "I just *couldn't*," she mumbled weakly as she donned them. Her astonishment turned to a wide grin as she viewed herself in the looking glass. Impulsively Sarah whirled and hugged Abbey. "Oh, milady, this is the finest gift I've ever received!"


The Havershams had already arrived, unfashionably early, and were sitting with Sam in the gold drawing room just off the main foyer. When Michael entered, Lady Haversham jumped to her feet and promptly fell into a deep curtsey—so deep that Lord Haversham had to help her up.

"Good evening, Lord Darfield! What a tremendous pleasure it is to be invited to your beautiful home!" Cora Haversham gushed. When Michael bowed over her hand, he thought the woman might positively swoon on him. Beside her, the rotund William Haversham adjusted his monocle and bowed.

"It's been quite some time since we have had the pleasure of visiting with you, Lord Darfield. Been socked away here, have you?" he asked.

Michael clasped his hand in greeting. "I'd hardly call it socked away, Lord Haversham. I have been at sea," he answered blandly, and accepted his usual sherry from Jones.

"Lord Haversham was just telling me about a rather remarkable game of darts he witnessed in Pemberheath," Sam remarked from near the window as Michael strolled to the mantel.

"Indeed? I don't suppose the game involved Lady Darfield?" he asked dryly.

"Indeed it did, sir! She's rather skilled in the sport, surprisingly so! She could have easily won the match, but I think she threw it in favor of the seaman Lindsay, who was quite flustered with his inability to best her," Haversham said, then slurped at his whiskey.

Lady Haversham added, "Those men were rather *insistent* she play a rematch with them, so much so that I was rather uneasy, wasn't I, William? But Lady Darfield was *very* composed. She remarked that she had learned long ago that when one is in Rome, one must do as the Romans, and agreed to their challenge. I truly thought I would be ill with fear, for they were very rough-looking men, if you take my meaning. Fortunately, they seemed so awed with her ability that they could only stand and gape, isn't that so, William?"

Lord Haversham's ears had turned bright red. He looked sheepishly at Michael. "*I* was never afraid for her safety, my lord. It was all rather innocent," he insisted, then cleared his throat and glared at his wife.

"I know why they challenged her," Sam said nonchalantly.

"The night she arrived in England, the same lads threatened her if she did not play. She was quite feisty, really, and bargained with them. Said if she hit the king's eye, they would leave her alone. I thought I was going to have to do battle with the lot of them, but she stepped up and threw a perfect dart. You have never heard such silence fill a room so quickly." He chuckled.

"You were *there*?" Abbey gasped from the doorway. Michael momentarily forgot his desire to wring Sam's neck for allowing her to be threatened. Framed in the doorway, Abbey was a vision of grace and beauty. She looked like an angel, a very *provocative* angel in that gown, and unconsciously, his hand fisted in his pocket as he held his desire in check. God, but she never failed to strike a chord in him.

Sam was chuckling as he came to his feet. "I was behind you all the while, Lady Darfield, ready to come to your aid if needed. You seemed to be handling the situation so easily that I confess I wanted to see if you could do it."

"You might have at least introduced yourself," she said, grumbling.

Michael, having sauntered forward to greet her, slipped an arm around her waist, pressed a soft kiss to her temple, and surreptitiously breathed from the subtle cloud of lilac scent surrounding her.

"Darts not once but twice, madam?" he murmured.

She smiled sheepishly. "It really was not of my choosing *either* time."

"Oh, my dear, how *lovely* you look this evening!" Lady Haversham gushed from across the room.

"You are very kind, Lady Haversham," Abbey said with a demure nod.

"An exquisite creature, wouldn't you agree, my lord? When do you intend to launch her? The entire *ton* will be all agog, I can promise you that," she said authoritatively. Michael did not doubt that for a moment, but not for the reasons Lady Haversham thought. He ignored her question and instead asked Abbey what she would like to drink.

She frowned and tapped a finger against her full lips. "Have you Madeira wine?"

Michael could not suppress his smile. "I believe there is some in the wine cellar," he said, and nodded to a footman.

"Lord Darfield, you cannot intend to leave this darling creature locked away at Blessing Park, surely!" Lady Haversham persisted.

Michael reluctantly forced his gaze to his guests. "In due time, milady. I confess we have not planned too far ahead."

"Leave him be, Cora. They are newly married," Lord Haversham said gruffly.

"Well, I do not mean to *pry*, William, but even you have remarked that Lady Darfield is just too lovely to be kept hidden away at Blessing Park." Lady Haversham sniffed.

Abbey's cheeks pinkened with self-conscious embarrassment.

"I daresay Lord Darfield prefers to have her all to himself," Sam interjected, and Lord Haversham nodded in such violent agreement that his monocle popped from his eye. He leveled a second glare at his wife.

"Lady Haversham, in honor of your great interest in the East, we are serving an Egyptian supper this evening," Abbey said, artfully turning the subject.

Lady Haversham gleefully clasped her hands. "Oh, how perfectly *marvelous*!"

"Pray tell, what exactly might one expect of an Egyptian supper?" Lord Haversham asked eagerly. He was, Abbey had discovered, a man who favored his stomach over all other fundamental pleasures in life.

Abbey smiled up at her husband, causing his chest to tighten. "You must wait and see," she told her rotund guest. "I don't want to spoil the surprise!"

But Lady Haversham unwittingly spoiled the evening for Abbey. It began right after the first course of lentil soup, which the entire dining party proclaimed a huge success. When the chick-pea pâté and eggplant dishes were served and Madeira wine was poured for all, Lady Haversham remarked,

"It's a pity you could not have joined Lady Darfield in Cairo, my lord."

"I beg you pardon?" Michael asked politely.

"Oh, you know, when Lady Darfield was in Cairo, you wanted to join her there, but you were, of course, engaged on the peninsula," she remarked as she took more of the pâté. From across the table, Abbey saw Michael's face darken, and her heart sank. She was such a stupid little chit for having told the Havershams every little thing in those first two weeks!

"Do you know, Lady Haversham," she said nervously, shaking her head to the chick-pea pâté, "that I rode a dromedary in Egypt? There is a certain amount of skill to riding one, too. You must be slightly behind the hump, you know, or the beast is quite contrary."

"A dromedary, truly?" Lady Haversham squealed with delight.

"A dromedary?" Michael echoed in disbelief at exactly the same time. Abbey smiled tremulously.

"I suppose I thought one would situate *between* the humps," Lady Haversham added.

"A dromedary has only one hump," Lord Haversham offered.

"How could you possibly know that, William? I daresay you've never seen a dromedary in your life!" the older woman blustered, then pivoted in her seat to face Abbey. "How does one mount a dromedary, Lady Darfield?"

With a furtive glance at Michael, Abbey proceeded to explain the art of riding a camel, leaving out the more indelicate details, such as how to avoid being spit upon by the beasts. Lady Haversham was enthralled, Sam listened attentively, and Lord Haversham was blissfully unaware of anything other than the food on his plate. Abbey thought Michael was staring a little too intently at his food.

"You learned so many things in Egypt, dear girl," Lady Haversham said after a sip of wine. "I suppose you know your wife is fluent in foreign languages, Lord Darfield? I'm not speaking of French, either," she said to Michael, waving her hand dismissively at the notion. Abbey leaned over her plate and pressed her finger and thumb on the bridge of her nose.

"Tell him what you did just the other day," she prodded. Abbey winced. Things had been going well the last few days, and the last thing she wanted was for Michael to think she was some sort of bluestocking.

"It was nothing, really," she said, hoping Lady Haversham would take her hint and cease her prattle.

"Nothing indeed! I have a lovely book given to me by my good friend Clara Whitesworth. She obtained it in Egypt, and the front of it is inscribed with what I called chicken scratch. Didn't it look like chicken scratch, William?"

"Like chicken scratch," Lord Haversham agreed without lifting his head from his eggplant sautéed in ginger sauce.

"I handed it to your wife for her opinion, and she laughed and said, 'Oh, no, Lady Haversham, this says "God willing, may you be blessed with long life," ' "then she returned it to me as if that were the simplest thing in the world to decipher!"

Abbey felt Michael's gaze on her and blushed. "I had a lot of free time in Egypt," she muttered apologetically.

"Well, of course she did. She was waiting to marry you!" Lady Haversham declared happily.

Abbey wanted to die, right there in her chair at the end of the table. In all her angst for the supper party, she had never once given any consideration to what Lady Haversham might say. Aunt Nan was right—she was an open book. A silly, childish, prattling, open book.

"Then the dancing! Oh, how perfectly *unique* their dancing is! Lady Darfield was gracious enough to demonstrate and even game enough to instruct us on the art!"

"Rather invigorating," Lord Haversham added.

Abbey slumped against her chair in absolute mortification. Sam grinned broadly, clearly enjoying the conversation and Abbey's discomfiture.

"I am learning there is no end to my wife's special talents," Michael said graciously, then lifted his unreadable gaze to hers. She briefly considered walking out onto the balcony and hurling herself to the gardens below. Judging by Sam's grin, her discomfort was evident to everyone in the room.

"Food, dancing, foreign languages," Sam remarked gleefully. "Is there anything *else* you learned in Egypt?" he asked.

"How to cheat at cards," Michael said blandly. Abbey closed her eyes and moaned.

"How *delightful*! You really must show me!" Lady Haversham exclaimed as a servant placed a plate of steaming rice and specially seasoned, minced meat in front of her.

"Yes, Lady Darfield has learned a variety of skills most men only dream of knowing. Violin in Rome, cheating in Egypt, billiards in Brussels, birthing calves in Virginia. I don't suppose you had opportunity to fight the Indians, as well?" Michael asked before he tasted the dish.

"Really, Lord Darfield, I think you are making fun. Of course she didn't fight Indians!" Lady Haversham scolded him.

"It was cattle rustlers, was it not, Lady Darfield?" Lord Haversham asked. Sam howled with laughter at that, and from across the table, one of Michael's brows lifted high above the other. Abbey picked up her crystal wineglass and downed her Madeira, wishing she had planned a two-course meal instead of eight.

She was grateful at the conclusion of the dinner when Michael suggested that she and Lady Haversham withdraw while the men enjoyed a cigar and some port. In the drawing room, Abbey screwed up enough courage to suggest quietly to Lady Haversham that her life had not been so remarkable and that Michael was probably growing weary of hearing about it.

"You may be right, dear. After all, he has lived a rather extraordinary life himself," she agreed. Abbey knew a moment of panic upon hearing that, but told herself her elderly neighbor was referring to the numerous rumors that circulated about Michael. The tragic death of his mother, his sister's dishonor, his father's loathsome gambling and drinking. But Michael had risen above it all to amass a fortune and a good reputation. Lady Haversham had told her that repeatedly.

When the men arrived in the drawing room, Lady Haversham was seated on a mound of floor pillows with a pastry in one hand.

"Lord Darfield, we were just discussing your own unusual life," she said.

"My life?" he asked, a bored expression on his face.

Abbey nervously cleared her throat. "I am sure, Lady Haversham, that everyone here is familiar with Michael's life," she suggested in a voice that was a little too pleading.

"Oh, Lady Darfield, you misunderstand me! Of *course* I know those ugly rumors are false! It's amazing the lengths some will go to defame another, isn't it? No, I was referring to his renowned generosity."

"Ah yes, terribly generous," Lord Haversham echoed as he plopped into an overstuffed chair and folded his pudgy hands across his belly. Michael looked inquiringly at Abbey. She shrugged helplessly, turned her back to them, and moved toward the expanse of silk-draped windows.

"My life has been rather unremarkable, I'm afraid."

"Oh, please, Lord Darfield, you are overly modest! What of your giving that entire treasure to the Spanish orphanage? I can think of no man who would have been so generous, can you, William?" she insisted.

"Not another soul," he agreed as he strained to reach a pastry.

"I don't believe I have heard this story," Sam said through an amused grin at his post near the hearth.

"It would be just like him not to tell you, Lord Hunt. Allow me. Several years ago a pirate ship was wrecked off the coast of Spain. A veritable king's ransom was aboard that ship, and Lord Darfield retrieved it—after rounding up the scoundrels, of course. He returned what he could, but as not all of the treasure was identifiable, he gave what was left, in its entirety, to a small orphanage in Spain. He didn't keep one single trinket for himself!"

Sam glanced at Michael with a gleeful glint in his green eyes.

Michael prayed for patience and scowled thinly at Sam.

"Lady Haversham, nothing of the sort ever happened," he avowed.

Lady Haversham looked puzzled and turned to glance at Abbey. "Why, I am *sure* you are being too modest, my good lord! Captain Carrington told the whole story to Lady Darfield!" she insisted. Michael glanced at Abbey's back and saw her shoulders stiffen. He wanted to muzzle Lady Haversham. In one particularly long wind over the course of the evening, she had single-handedly revived the tragic deception. He casually crossed the room and slipped his arm around Abbey's waist. She sagged against his chest.

"I must warn you, Lady Haversham, that my wife has a tendency to embellish any action on my part to make it seem as if it were some heroic deed. But I assure you, I am not nearly as good or as righteous as she believes," he said, and caught a breath in his throat when she lifted a poignantly grateful gaze to him. He suddenly wished their guests were gone so he could gaze into those eyes at his leisure.

But his guests were not even remotely ready to depart. The rest of the evening was spent at the card table after Michael suggested Abbey show them what tricks she had learned. Abbey happily taught Lady Haversham how to cheat, despite Lord Haversham's strong objections, who was quite convinced his wife would never lay an honest card again. Michael and Sam exchanged several looks of amusement and surprise at what Abbey demonstrated. As with everything else, Abbey was remarkably good at cheating. Lady Haversham would never be able to cheat, Sam remarked, because she could not keep her expression blank. Lady Haversham objected to that, and insisted she was as blank as the next person, to which Abbey could not contain a fit of giggles.

When they finally attempted a game of loo, Lady Haversham's attempts at cheating ended up costing poor Lord Haversham more than she could have lost honestly. Abbey steadily gathered a small mound of coins and, in the last hand, threw the game to Michael. It was so flagrant that he gave her a disapproving look while Lord and Lady Haversham argued. Abbey met his look with a smile and a mischievous wink.

It was well after midnight when the Havershams departed with pleas for the Darfields and Sam to join them at their home soon. Once their carriage left the drive, Abbey mumbled her excuses to Sam and Michael and made a quick escape to her chamber to sulk over the humiliating evening.

Sometime later, Abbey stood quietly in front of the window, bathed in the moonlight that spilled into her room, contemplating how horribly turned around her life had become.

When she heard the door open quietly, she sighed and lifted her gaze to the full moon. "Thank you, but I don't require anything, Sarah." She heard the maid move across the room. *Not now,* she thought miserably.

"Really, I prefer to be alone," she insisted weakly.

"I prefer to be with you," Michael responded softly. Abbey caught her breath; she did not move, did not say a word. She felt him move behind her, felt his fingers touch her arms and gently caress them. Her skin tingled at the contact; she instinctively leaned against him when he slipped his arms around her waist and pulled her to him.

*"Abbey,"* he whispered softly in her ear, giving her a sharp bolt of pleasure. She imagined his gray eyes as they had looked in the meadow. God, how she had longed for him that day. Now, with his arms securely around her and his warm breath on her neck, she was filled with a stronger desire than she thought possible. It seemed to course through her of its own accord, begging for his touch.

His hand lifted from her waist and gently caressed the nape of her neck. Abbey remained silent as he grabbed a fistful of her hair and brought it to his face before letting it fall softly. His arms found her waist again, and holding her firmly to him, he began to hum an old English tune in her ear, swaying gently.

Several moments passed without a word; there was nothing but the moon spilling over them, the twining heat of their bodies, and his soft, low hum. Her desire was great; when he pressed his warm lips against her neck, Abbey closed her eyes and sighed softly, gratefully.

He grasped her shoulders and turned her around to face him. His gray eyes, dark, silvery pools, languidly swept her face as he carefully brushed a strand of hair from her forehead.

"You are an amazing woman, Abbey," he muttered as his gaze settled on her mouth. With his thumb, he traced the set line of her chin, then her lips. He slid his hand behind her head and took hold of a handful of her lush mane. It felt like silk as it slid through his fingers. He imagined her hair draping her body in his bed, resting against her bare breasts. He slowly pulled the thick, satiny tresses over her shoulder. Her violet eyes, wide and wary, remained steadfast on his face.

"You are not angry?" she asked softly, and shifted her gaze to the top of his chest, where tiny curls of dark, crisp hair peeked from beneath his pristine silk shirt.

"Angry? Why on earth should I be angry?"

"Because of the things Lady Haversham said."

Michael laughed softly. "I found it highly entertaining. But later I shall insist you explain your confrontation with cattle rustlers."

Abbey closed her eyes and softly groaned with remorse. His fingers brushed lithely across her cheek.

"Do you know how beautiful you are?" he murmured.

"I am not beautiful."

Michael responded by kissing her eyelids. "I would beg to differ, madam," he said thickly, then lightly brushed his lips across hers. She shifted closer to him. Pleased, he tenderly stroked the contour of her cheek while his lips descended again, gently molding hers.

Abbey quickly yielded; lightning coursed up her spine as Michael's tongue began to explore her heatedly. Any apprehension swiftly dissipated and was replaced by a desire that made her feel as if she were floating on air. His hands softly swept her body, leaving a trace of fire in their wake. She returned his kiss by carefully exploring his lips and mouth, and he responded by tightening his embrace about her. She was surprised at how her body responded with a will of its own, pressing against him as if it sought to melt into his sleek frame.

He finally drew back and gazed down at her. "You are magnificent, sweetheart," he whispered.

The small endearment made her heart pound, and she sighed.

That small, contented sigh ignited a flame within him.

He caught her chin between his thumb and forefinger and tilted her face upward. His kiss, both urgent and tender, made her dizzy with desire. He slipped an arm around her waist to steady her. Abbey's head fell back as he pressed his warm lips against her neck. His hand fluttered across her breast, sending a wave of sheer pleasure down to the tips of her toes, and she grabbed his shoulders, afraid for a moment she might fall.

"I want you, Abbey," he whispered against her skin. Abbey did not answer. He lifted his head and looked down at her, stroking her cheek with his knuckles. Desire mounted in him so quickly, its intensity stunned him. "I want to make love to you."

"I . . . don't know," she whispered.

He smiled seductively and brushed his lips across her forehead. "Are you afraid?" he asked, idly kissing the hollow of her throat.

Abbey went almost limp in his arms. "I don't think so. Are you?" she forced herself to respond.

He chuckled deep in his throat, then unexpectedly swept her into his arms. "No," he said emphatically, and turning on his heel, he carried her into his chamber, to the massive, four-poster bed. He set her on her feet, kissed her again with some urgency, then reached behind her and began to undo the buttons of her gown.

"Wh-what are you doing?"

"Unbuttoning your gown."

"B-but your *valet*!" she whispered frantically.

Michael grinned. "Would you prefer Damon do it?" he teased as he deftly moved down the long row of buttons.

Abbey blushed furiously. "You said—"

"Forget what I said, forget everything except the simple fact that I want you desperately." His hands came to her shoulders and gradually pushed the gown down her arms. It fell to the floor in a cloud of lilac and gold, leaving her in only a thin chemise.

"Good God," he breathed in genuine appreciation, to which Abbey's eyes widened. She was so unlike any other woman he had ever known; this was no feigned pretense of innocence. In spite of her incredible beauty, it was apparent no one had ever told her before. When he reached to untie the tiny ribbon that held her chemise, she nervously grabbed his hand.

"Michael, I don't know anything!" she suddenly pleaded.

He stopped, realizing how truly innocent she was, and wrapped her in a warm embrace. "What do you know?" he asked calmly.

"Nothing, nothing at all! Just that I am to lie there while you do . . . *that*." Michael kissed the top of her head, gently pried her fingers from his hand, and again pulled on the ribbon of her chemise.

"*That*," he said patiently, "is the most pleasurable experience a man and woman can share, despite what you may have been told." He saw her look of doubt and continued. "When a man makes love to his wife, he covers her with gentle kisses to show her how beautiful he finds her," he said as he pulled the second ribbon free, revealing her voluptuous breasts. The two succulent globes were as perfect as he had imagined. He palmed a dark nipple that rose quickly to his touch.

"That's all?" she whispered skeptically.

He laughed softly as his fingers splayed across her breast and nipple and squeezed gently. "Something else may arise, but I think it better if I show you." Before she could disagree, he covered her mouth in a stupefying kiss and slipped the thin chemise from her shoulders and down her sides. Her skin was like satin beneath his fingers. Abbey shivered; from desire or fear he did not know, and he gently eased her down onto his bed.

He quickly shrugged out of his shirt. She was lying there as he had imagined she would, dark luxuriant hair framing her voluptuous body. God, but she had a beautiful body, from her breasts, to her slender waist, to the flare of her narrow hips, and her long, shapely legs. In the faint moonlight, her skin glowed radiantly. Her dark eyes flicked over his upper body, but when he freed his rigid member she flinched.

*"Dear God,"* she whispered softly. Michael had been with only one other virgin in his life, and he had been a young, bumbling lad then. It had been painful for them both, but he had learned. He hastily lowered himself to her and crushed his mouth to hers until, at last, her hands curled around his neck. Michael lifted his head and looked down at her.

"You lie there as you are now, while I," he said as he slipped a hand to her breast, smiling when she arched at his touch, "cover every inch of you with kisses."

"But what . . ."

"Don't be afraid." He smiled, then kissed the tip of her nose. Her gaze slipped to his mouth. His pulse coursed madly in his neck as he lowered himself to claim her again. Her breasts, rubbing seductively against the fine mat of hair on his chest, were contributing to the urgent need building in him. He began a slow, seductive exploration of her body as his mouth slanted over hers, demanding more and more from her. He returned a hand to her breast, then let it slide down her side, pausing on her flat stomach while he rubbed subtly against her, his member thickening with the contact of her rose-petal skin. When his fingers brushed deliberately against the inside of her thigh, she inhaled softly, so softly that Michael had to grit his teeth in an effort to maintain control.

Abbey was not conscious of anything but his touch, both alarmed and titillated by the response it evoked deep within her. She gasped when he brought his mouth to her breast, but when his hand slipped between her legs and stroked the silken folds there she thought she would come out of her skin. She was fast losing control; her thighs parted for him as if they had a will of their own. He muttered something incomprehensible against her breast before he slipped his fingers deep inside her. Abbey lifted uncontrollably against his palm.

It was not supposed to be like this. She was not supposed to like it. But like it she did; in fact, she *reveled* in it. A curious mix of pleasure and budding anticipation swept through her. She needed him to do . . . *something*.

"You're ready for me, sweetheart," he whispered as his fingers gently probed her, then slowly withdrew, stroking her as he did, then repeated the excruciatingly pleasurable motion. Abbey felt herself falling away, and she pushed her hands against the headboard, moaning softly.

"Not yet," he murmured against her stomach. She did not know what he meant, nor did she care. Her body screamed for release from the sensual weight that pressed against her; she writhed as he moved his thigh in between her legs and lifted himself over her. Her breathing was ragged; he kissed her breast as he laced her fingers with his above her head. With his other hand he guided her to feel his passion. Abbey jerked away when she felt the velvet head, alarmed by the size of it. Michael, not deterred, guided her hand between her legs while he brushed the tip against her. Shuddering uncontrollably, Abbey was astonished at the waves of desire crashing through her.

"Something's *happening*!" She gasped.

It was all the encouragement he needed.

"It's all right, darling, it's all right," he cooed as he gently guided himself inside her, sliding deeper and deeper with small, rhythmic movements. Abbey's hands tightened about his, silently begging him to give her the fulfillment she did not even know she wanted.

Michael's control was at an end; he did not think he could contain himself one second longer. Her tight, hot sheath contracted around him; she arched her pelvis against him and instinctively demanded more. He felt the thin membrane of her virginity and stopped. Her eyes were closed, her swollen lips slightly parted as she softly sought her breath. He thought it terribly fantastic that he, a man of the world and no stranger to women, would want this sweet virgin more than he had ever wanted a woman in his life. He moaned, covered her mouth with his, and thrust powerfully within her. Abbey cried out against his mouth as her body convulsed around him. She went rigid, her eyes closed tightly shut against the pain.

"I'm sorry, sweetheart, it won't hurt again," he whispered hoarsely. Abbey lay very still beneath him and said nothing. He kissed her cheek, her throat, and her ear. When her grip on him began to relax, he began an unhurried, sultry movement, biting his lip to keep from spilling himself inside her. Abbey whimpered at first but slowly began to respond. As his strokes lengthened within her, her response grew passionate and incredibly instinctive. Her knees came up on either side of him, and she lifted her pelvis to reach him, matching his rhythm. Her hair, spilling wildly about her, covered part of her face, and Michael thought that the very fragile hold he had on his own raging desire was to be commended. He held steady, praying she would find her fulfillment soon.

Abbey felt as if she were on a cloud, slowly drifting away from the world, from everything but Michael. The oddly pleasurable pressure began to mount in her again, and as his strokes deepened within her, the pressure became unbearable.

"Come now, darling, *now*," he urged her, watching her eyes as she did.

"Michael!" she whispered, wildly anxious. She gripped his shoulders with fierce strength, her nails digging into his back, and lifted herself, meeting his hard strokes. *"Michael!"* she all but shrieked, demanding . . . *what?*

Until it happened. Suddenly wave after wave of pleasure erupted within her, carrying her swiftly away from all reality but the magic of Michael inside her. She threw her head back and arched her neck as the release flooded from every pore, then collapsed backward.

*"Oh, Michael."* She gasped. Not able to control himself another moment, he cupped her bottom and lifted her from the bed. She heard Michael's breathing quicken, heard him whisper "Sweet darling," as his strokes plunged and intensified. Abbey was only dimly aware of his own powerful need as pure rapture continued to sweep over her. She tightened around him, never wanting the incredible experience to end. He moaned and, with a final, powerful thrust, filled her com-

pletely. His seed poured deep inside her as he softly called her name, arousing an emotion so deep it could only be love. She slowly opened her eyes. Michael was staring down at her, an unfathomable look in his gray eyes. He lowered himself onto his elbows and cupped her face in his hands.

"God, Abbey."

She brushed the lock of damp hair from his forehead, traced his jaw with the back of her hand, and caressed the steely muscles bunched across his shoulders.

"That was more than just kisses," she remarked solemnly.

He smiled faintly. "I confess, I didn't tell you everything."

"I didn't know this could be so . . . so . . . *exquisite*!" she blurted.

"Neither did I," he responded in all seriousness, thinking how she had pleased him beyond his wildest expectations. Her inexperience was completely overshadowed by her natural and incredible response. He realized, a little uncomfortably, that he had never experienced such profound lovemaking in his life. He stood in awe of his complete sense of fulfillment, something he had never experienced with a woman. Not like this.

Abbey propped herself on her elbows to kiss his neck, then brought her swollen lips to his, kissing him passionately. He quickly began to grow hard again, and reluctantly lifted his head. Somewhat daunted by the depth of raw emotion he felt, he was also sensitive to the painful invasion of her body. He kissed her once more and withdrew, then rolled onto his back, propping one arm under his head while encircling her shoulders with the other. She sighed contentedly and rested her head upon his chest, one hand tucked securely under her cheek.

He looked down at the figure that rested against his chest, the dark crescents of her lashes contrasting sharply with her creamy skin and her luscious lips, still swollen from the passion they had shared. This beautiful, amazing creature lying silently in his arms was his wife, whose natural, incredible passion had been reserved for him and him alone. What they had just shared thrilled him, but it also disturbed him. He was in no way prepared for such strong emotions. He was, for the first time in his life, at a loss. He carefully lifted a strand of hair that draped her eye and tightened his grip on her.

His wife. His beautiful, passionate, extraordinary wife.

*Dear God.*

When Michael emerged from his chamber the next morning, he almost collided with Sarah, who hurried down the hall with her arms loaded with fresh linens.

"Goodness, my lord, I didn't see you!" she exclaimed, and attempted to curtsey under her burden. Michael nodded and turned away, but suddenly glanced back at Sarah. Her eyes widened at his dark scowl. He took a step closer to her and peered intently at her ears.

"What's that dangling from your ears?"

Sarah beamed. "They are a gift from the mistress, my lord. Aren't they lovely?"

Michael blinked. "Yes, they are," he said quietly, and turning on his heel, moved swiftly down the corridor.

Sebastian was the first to notice Michael's jaunty walk when he entered the breakfast room. He was also whistling a gay little tune—something Sebastian had never heard him do, not once, in all the twenty years of their association.

"Sleep well, my lord?" he asked dryly.

Michael grinned mischievously. "I slept very well indeed, Benjamin."

Startled, Sebastian could not recall a single time the marquis had ever used his given name. Or anyone at Blessing Park, for that matter, and Lord knew how many lonely months he and the staff had spent together there when the marquis was at sea.

Jones obviously shared his great surprise, judging by his look from the sideboard. "The usual porridge today, my lord?"

Michael smiled, as if remembering some forgotten joke. "Don't think Cook has any raspberry tarts today, do you?" he asked cheerfully.

Much to Jones's credit, his expression did not change. "I shall certainly inquire, my lord," he said, and disappeared through the side door.

"Better yet, Sebastian, have Jones bring coffee and tarts to my library. I need to get some work done this morning as I intend to teach my wife how to ride this afternoon." Blatantly ignoring Sebastian's curious look, he thrust his hands in his pockets and left the breakfast room, whistling again. Jones appeared through the side door with a plate of warm tarts in time to hear Michael's whistle echoing down the corridor. He frowned at Sebastian.

Sebastian sighed. "Bring them round to the library, Jones. The master is eager to get his work done so he can teach Lady Darfield how to ride," he said as he tossed his napkin on the table, preparing to follow Michael.

As he approached the door, Jones drawled, "Oh, *Benjamin,* there is the small matter of five crowns I believe you owe me."

Sebastian stopped. "I do not believe we can be *exactly* sure," he protested.

Jones raised an impertinent brow. "Indeed? If I am not mistaken, only one thing can put a hitch in a man's step like that."

With a sigh of great exasperation, Sebastian pulled a small leather pouch from his coat pocket and counted out five crowns. "If only he had waited one more week," he grumbled irritably as he slapped the coins into Jones's outstretched palm.

# Chapter 12

Over the days that followed, Michael spent less time tending to his work and more time with Abbey. It was highly unusual for him not to oversee every detail of his expanding business. Typically he would work long hours, poring over his accounts. Michael had suffered so long for sins that were not his that his whole staff was thrilled that he finally had found some happiness. Not that Michael would admit it, of course, but his actions spoke for him.

One day Michael stood at the French doors of the working study, staring out into the garden. He dutifully but absently answered every question Sam or Sebastian put to him. But when Sam asked for his thoughts on replacing two cannons on one of their ships, he did not immediately respond.

"Who is that? Milton, I think," he answered himself. "He shouldn't stand so . . . bloody hell! She just winged him in the knee. Excuse me, gentlemen, while I instruct my wife on the proper use of a croquet mallet," he drawled, and, without so much as a glance backward, disappeared through the open door.

"Extraordinary," Sebastian mused.

"It is." Sam chuckled. "I never thought I would see the day when the Devil of Darfield was smitten."

"Oh, that," Sebastian said. "I was remarking upon the fact that she can't master croquet."

In truth, to the residents of Blessing Park it seemed there was little the marchioness was incapable of doing well. But Michael had discovered at least three things for which she had no talent.

The first was needlework. She was working diligently on a rather large piece of linen, and one night he had asked to see over what she toiled so intently. Her face beaming with pride, she had proudly held up the creation for him to see. He studied it for a long moment, then turned it around.

"Oh, no! That's upside down!" she had exclaimed.

"Is it? I can't seem to make it out."

Her pretty face had fallen. "Why, it's Blessing Park."

"Blessing Park?" he had echoed incredulously, and peered closely. Out of the corner of his eye, he could see her hopeful look, and finally nodded. "Blessing Park, of course," he had said, then abruptly handed it to her before she could see the lie on his face. For the life of him, every time he looked at that fabric, he could not any more make out Blessing Park than he could the moon.

The second thing Abbey could not master was croquet. As the months turned warm, several of the staff would gather in Withers's gardens—much to Michael's considerable amazement—and play croquet. Invariably, someone was injured by a flying ball or Abbey's mallet. Michael had tried repeatedly to show her how to play, but she was much better suited to the game of golf they played in Scotland. She swung the mallet with such ferocity that the servants would scatter each time it was her turn. As the weeks passed, Abbey would be seen more and more often sitting on one of the wrought-iron benches during the matches, whittling. Withers was determined she would finish the wooden flute she had started, and had insisted she do it during the matches so he could oversee her progress. To the collective relief of the players, the former sailor would sit next to her with his great arms folded tightly across his chest as small wood chips flew in every direction. From his study, Michael would watch Abbey, frequently leaping from her bench to cheer a particularly good shot or to argue the finer points of the game.

The third thing his wife could not master was horseback riding. Initially, Michael insisted on taking her riding on the tamest mounts he could find. When Abbey refused Desdemona—citing irreconcilable differences—he even had gone so far as to purchase an old workhorse from a tenant farmer. They discarded the sidesaddle early on, but even astride she could not find her rhythm with the horse. The few times he actually could coax her onto a horse's back, she inevitably returned from their ventures battered from the constant jarring and the tension. As the number of lessons increased, Michael realized he more often than not pulled her across to his saddle and led her horse back to the stables. She never resisted, sagging against him as the tension poured from her body and apologizing profusely for her ineptitude. He tried every trick he knew, but Abbey was exceedingly wary of any horse, despite her adamant claims to the contrary.

Beyond that, there was little she could or would not do. His surprise had been great the day he found her, quite by accident, shearing sheep. He glared angrily at his men, who astutely avoided any eye contact with him, for each of them knew without a doubt it was something she should *not* have been doing. Abbey patiently tried to explain to a flustered Michael that it could very well be a handy skill to have one day. Michael had nonetheless hauled her away, insisting that a marchioness did not engage in such activities. She responded that she preferred not to be a marchioness if it was going to limit her activities. Despite his best efforts not to, Michael could not help smiling at that. She had to be the only woman in all of England who would see the title as *limiting* her activities.

When Sarah's brother married in the garden, Abbey entertained the guests playing old Gaelic music she had learned from listening to Sarah and Cook hum the tunes. Michael thought she bordered on genius where music was concerned.

One only had to hum a tune and she could translate it into a flowing melody on the strings of her violin.

With curious pride, Michael watched her interact with the estate tenants and employees. She was so vibrant, it was difficult for anyone at the small wedding to resist her. She danced with them all, her interpretation of the Scottish dances both elegant and lively.

What Michael most enjoyed was the lazy afternoons they would spend exploring Blessing Park. With Harry along, they often found themselves at the ruins, where Abbey would regale him with some fantastic tale straight from British history. One afternoon she was reliving the fall of Simon de Montfort, and he had watched, fascinated, as she had slowly twirled around, her arms extended, weaving the tale of Simon's quest against despotism and his tragic end. When she had finished, she turned to him with genuine sorrow in her eyes and had walked straight into his arms. He had stroked her hair while she stood silently, her face buried in his chest.

"Poor Simon de Montfort," she had murmured at last. "His vision was extraordinary, but he was on this earth too soon."

"When did you take such an interest in history?" he had asked.

She had smiled sheepishly and answered, "When you asked it of me."

As they had strolled back to the house, he had glanced surreptitiously at her several times, marveling at how she had lived all those years, pursuing interests because she had believed he desired it of her. He could not fathom such unquestioning devotion.

In the evenings, they often sat together in the newly decorated green drawing room, she working diligently on her monstrosity of a needlework, he reading in quiet, comfortable companionship. She used their evenings to experiment with liquors, announcing one day that she had determined ale was her preference. He, of course, made sure that ale was always available, just as he made sure sheet music came from London on a regular basis. Anything Abbey wanted, he provided, telling himself it was his obligation. His reward was her company, her smile. And her music.

Sometimes, late at night, she would play for him as she did that night so many weeks ago, and each time Michael was swept away with the passion and richness of the sound that filled his chamber. And as he did almost every night, he made passionate love to her. Sometimes he would delay her climax until she begged him; other times he took her with abandon, bringing them both to fulfillment quickly. She was an avid student, guilelessly warm and open in his bed. She exuded quiet sensuality and pure adoration for him, and he unwillingly discovered she held a certain power over him. He felt uncharacteristically helpless when she looked at him, ready to do anything for her or to her, intent on pleasuring her beyond her wildest expectations. Yet somehow it was his satisfaction and pleasure that was exceeded each time.

But there were times when Michael was plagued with lingering doubts about the agreement and a gnawing bitterness with his own father for having pushed her on him. That alone was enough to give him pause. In many ways, she epitomized the burden his father had been to him, a burden he had carried all his life and a burden from which he had thought he was finally free. He feared that when Abbey's star faded for him, and it would eventually—they all did, he was sure, just as Rebecca's had—she would remain his unwanted obligation.

Abbey was blissfully unaware of his doubts. For her, the weeks she spent with Michael were pure heaven, every bit the fantasy she had dreamed of all those years, and more, much more. He was incredibly tender and attentive, and could hardly be in the same room with her without touching her in some small, intimate way. She secretly delighted in the way he impassively indulged her every whim. She often wondered who could possibly have thought that magnanimous, handsome man the Devil of Darfield, conveniently forgetting she herself had called him that at one time.

He was terribly kind, too, although he denied it. He was

unusually considerate of his many servants and made sure
they wanted for nothing. The young children of the estate
adored him. More than once Abbey found him on the lawn
with them, his coat slung haphazardly across the shrubbery
and his neckcloth untied as he taught them how to fence, or
played ball with them. She loved the time they spent together,
strolling through the softly rolling hills, wandering through
Withers's magnificent gardens, or taking the coach to
Pemberheath.

Despite his gruff exterior, Michael even grew accustomed
to Harry. One day he had come into her room and found her
sitting on the green silk settee with the hound curled next to
her. She had jumped up and attempted to hide the dog behind
her skirts, but Harry's loudly thumping tail had given him
away. Michael had frowned and crooked his finger, beckoning
Abbey to him. She had come reluctantly, fully expecting the
tongue-lashing she deserved. But Michael had surprised her
by saying "Madam, how do you expect me to compete?" She
had laughed gaily and had kissed him ardently, and after a few
minutes of that, Michael had dragged her into his room, calling his apology to the dog when he shut the door behind them.

And, of course, their nights were pure bliss, a world of
sensual delight she never knew existed. He made her feel
beautiful, praising her body and her response to him. He
brought her to shattering fulfillment each and every time, and
she never tired of trying new things with him. It had not taken
her long to begin to experiment; she tried touching him in
different places, or moving in different ways, and his reaction
was always one of pure pleasure and gratitude. She told him
she loved him when they made love, and he would whisper,
"I know, sweet," or just smile.

But he never said the same to her.

Abbey knew he did not love her; he had never loved her.
But as time passed and the magic between them seemed to
intensify, she wondered how he could not have some small
regard for her. She sensed that he held back from her, did not
show her everything. But how could he not feel the power of
emotion when their bodies joined, or the depth of tenderness a

simple caress could bring? How could he not share her feeling of being one with him?

Regardless of her curiosity, she would not ask it of him. She had decided, as the three months drew to a close, that she did not care if he ever loved her, because she loved him too much to live without him.

Unaware one morning that it was three months to the day she had promised to wait, Abbey woke up to find Michael gone and a single red rose on the pillow next to her. She sat up, laughing as she brought the fragrant petals to her face. Withers likely would throw his spade and toss his beefy hands into the air in defeat if he knew Michael was now pilfering from his gardens.

She got up and wandered to her room, washed and combed her hair, then slipped into a simple black skirt and pale-blue blouse. She braided her hair, let it hang down her back, and donned her ridiculous gardening hat. Then she made her way down to the gardens and hothouse by way of the kennels. She could see Withers already at work with Hans and Bailey, trimming the hedges.

"Abbey!"

Abbey turned and gasped lightly with surprise. Galen was standing in the shadows of an arbor, which struck her as odd. But she was too exuberant at seeing him to wonder about it.

"Galen!" She smiled, hurrying toward him. "I wasn't expecting you! Oh, but I am so glad you have come! I don't know where Michael is, but he'll want to meet you, I am certain. Wait here and I'll fetch a footman—"

"No," Galen quickly interjected, then smiled as he encircled her in his arms and kissed her fondly on the cheek. "I can't stay long, little one, but I wanted to see you. How are you? Are you well?"

"I'm perfectly fine! Won't you come in for just a little while? I would so like you to meet Michael."

Galen dropped his arms and peered over her shoulder toward the front drive, his brown eyes dark. "I can't, really. I'm expected in Dellwood this afternoon. Abbey, there is something I must ask you." He shifted his weight to one leg, moving deeper into the cover of the arbor.

"Yes?"

"As I explained to you, I am expecting some important news, news that will enable me to return to the seas in my rightful position as captain of a merchant vessel."

Abbey grinned and unthinkingly touched his arm. "That's wonderful! Is it a commission of some sort?"

"No, it's . . . well, really, I am not at liberty to say. The final arrangements have not been made as of yet, you see," he offered, and looked at her hopefully. He seemed oddly nervous; she wondered what sort of deal he was making that required such secrecy. A fleeting memory of Galen and her father arguing loudly in the captain's cabin about his irresponsibility raced across her mind's eye.

"It must sound odd, I know, but I am too hopeful. I prefer not to say anything until I am quite certain of the facts. I would not want to invite bad luck." He laughed tautly.

Abbey opened her mouth to tell him she would give him what she had, but he quickly rushed to speak.

"You can't imagine how it burns me to have to come to my little cousin and ask for money. I have no one to blame but myself, but I could not have anticipated these delays, I swear to you, and once everything is arranged, I shall repay your generosity with interest," he pleaded earnestly.

Abbey did not care a whit about interest or if he ever repaid her. "Galen! You are welcome to what I have. I shall have to ask Michael—"

"*No!*" He glanced behind her again then grabbed her hand, holding it between his two gloved ones and pulling her under the cover of the arbor. "Abbey, listen to me. Let's agree to keep this our secret, just for a time. I would die of shame if you had to ask your husband on my behalf. He would think me a debtor, and as I am your cousin, it would not look well for you. I will not have him thinking ill of you because of some poor relation. I need only a little, just enough to see me through the next few weeks. Surely he gives you an allowance?"

Abbey's brow wrinkled. Galen was right; Michael had very clearly told her he would not entertain requests from her family. Granted, the relationship between them had blossomed since then, but she did not feel so secure with him that she was willing to risk his displeasure. She had no idea how he would react to Galen, particularly without a proper situation. Yes, Galen was right. It would go much better with Michael when he had a post.

But she had no money, other than the thousand pounds she had won from Michael at billiards. Beyond that, she had given Galen all that she had that afternoon in Pemberheath. "I don't think I receive an allowance," she said slowly, "but I've a thousand pounds."

"Ah, little one, your trust and generosity mean so much to me. I am quite ashamed that I must come to you, but—"

"Oh, Galen." Abbey moaned sympathetically. "You can *always* come to me. You are my cousin!"

He started to speak but something behind her caught his attention, and he immediately dropped her hand and moved forward. Abbey turned; Bailey, the simpleton, was making his way toward them, a curious look on his face. Galen quickly extended his hand, stepping forward to greet the old deckhand.

"Bailey, you old scoundrel. How are you?" He laughed.

Bailey looked confused as he peered closely at Galen.

"Bailey, you remember my cousin Galen Carrey, don't you?" Abbey smiled. "He was aboard the *Dancing Maiden* the summer we sailed to Africa, do you recall?

Recognition slowly dawned on his weathered face. "Mr. Carrey?" he said slowly.

Galen smiled, flashing a row of white teeth. "I've come to say hello to my little cousin. Abbey, darling, do you think you could fetch what we talked about?" he asked sweetly. "I'm in something of a rush for Dellwood."

"Of course! I shall be back in a moment," she said, and turned for the house.

*    *    *

Michael strolled to a bank of windows and looked out over the gardens, his thoughts on news he had received from Calais concerning a cargo from the Orient. He saw Abbey heading for the gardens and smiled warmly. He started to turn but his eye caught a movement near the arbor. Slowly he turned toward the window as a man embraced Abbey, kissing her. Surprise rocked him as the man dropped his arms and began to speak earnestly. As Abbey reached out to touch him, the man pulled her deeper into the shadows.

Michael's mind went numb; another movement registered, and his eyes flicked to Bailey, who was marching with a look of determination Michael thought curious. The simpleton rounded the path and made straight for the arbor. The stranger reappeared, smiling broadly, and extended his hand. Something about the exchange did not seem right to Michael, and as he puzzled over it, Abbey disappeared from view, heading toward the house.

Michael turned from the window and walked slowly to his desk. It was probably someone from Pemberheath. Bailey seemed to know him. It could not be more than a friendly greeting, not for all of Blessing Park to see. He would ask Abbey later, but it was hardly anything over which he should be concerned. He sat down and stared at a bill of sale, trying very hard to push the doubt from his mind.


An hour later, Michael rose to fetch an account book, and through the window, saw Abbey flying across the lawn with the giant azalea in her hands, her straw hat flopping furiously around her face. He couldn't help smiling; if he had to guess, he would say that azalea was coming to his study.

He strolled to the desk and perched his hip on the edge, his arms folded casually across his chest. Dressed in buff riding breeches, a white lawn shirt, and polished Hessians gleaming below his knee, Michael had every intention of taking his wife on a picnic that day. Today was the three-month mark they had agreed upon, and he would have her answer.

The corners of his mouth turned up as he thought how he would wrest the answer from her.

The barking in the hallway announced Abbey's arrival, and she fairly burst through the door holding the big potted plant with Harry nipping at her skirt.

"Michael! I thought you had gone out!" she said with surprise.

"I am waiting for you." She looked very pleased and stood smiling at him.

"Don't you want to put that down?"

"What? Oh!" she exclaimed, remembering the plant. She glanced about the room and finally decided it would do quite nicely in front of the door opened onto the terrace. She struggled to put it down, but Michael did not raise a finger to help, not when he could enjoy watching her derriere wriggle beneath the plant's weight. She stood up and brushed her hands together.

"Is that one of yours?" he asked as she admired the shrub.

"Indeed it is. Withers is rather stingy with his roses this morning. Do you like it? Withers said it would never grow, because I started it when it was too cold. I told him it would, it just needed some love and attention."

"Is that all it takes?" he asked softly.

Abbey nodded eagerly. "*I* think so. That old sailor is much more practical. He says water and sunshine are all these plants need."

Michael smiled enigmatically. "I have a surprise for you, sweetheart. Cook is preparing a basket for us—I'd like to take you for a ride in the coach."

"Really? Where are we going?" She grinned, clearly pleased.

"To the sea. There is a cove I would show you."

"Oh, how perfectly wonderful! I truly miss the sea, don't you?" she asked, already turning to leave. Oddly, he really did not miss the sea anymore. Not since she had come into his life.

"I must change—"

"No, go as you are," he said huskily.

Abbey glanced curiously over her shoulder, her violet eyes sparkling. "At least my hat, then. Will you wait for me, Michael? I shall be but a moment," she called over her shoulder, and disappeared through the door. Michael pushed off the desk and walked over to examine the azalea. *Yes, Abbey, I will wait for you. I think I shall always wait for you,* he responded silently.

The sun was bright, but there was a lingering frost in the air. As Michael tossed a few shillings to the coachmen and pointed them in the direction of the nearest public house, Abbey ran ahead, easily climbing down the thickly wooded hill to the cove. When Michael finally emerged through the brush, she was standing on the small beach with her feet braced apart and her hands fisted on her hips.

"Michael Evan Ingram, why have you kept this place hidden from me?" she demanded.

He laughed, dropping the basket he was carrying. "In truth, darling, I haven't been here since I was a lad." He glanced around the little cove in which he had spent many summer afternoons as a child. Afternoons when he and Mariah would escape the drunken tirades of his father. He strolled toward a tree that protruded from the natural tree line and checked the trunk. Running his fingers over the smooth bark, he found what he was looking for: the carved initials M.E.I. and, next to them, M.A.I.

"Whose are those?" Abbey asked.

"Mariah," he said as he ran his fingers over her initials.

"Do you miss her?"

Michael shrugged. "I miss her from time to time, but she's been gone a long while. She just had a son, her second child. I received a letter from her just a few days ago, admonishing me for not having told her about you before now," he said as he stepped away from the tree.

"She knows about me?" Abbey asked, surprised.

"Of course she does. Do you think I would not tell my sister about my own marriage?" Michael put an arm around her shoulder and pulled her into his side to lead her to the small beach.

"Did you tell her why?" Abbey asked.

"Why?"

There were times, Abbey thought, that Michael could be a little dense. "Did you tell her you were forced?"

Michael squeezed her shoulders. "I told her I had married, but I did not think to bore her with the details," he said reassuringly.

"Or astound her with them," Abbey muttered under her breath.

Michael playfully pinched her cheek and wisely ignored the remark. He retrieved the basket and rummaged inside, producing a blanket, which he spread on the sand.

"I'm going to gather some firewood. Don't wander off," he said, and headed back into the woods. By the time he returned with an armload, Abbey had spread out the small feast Cook had prepared. He requested laughingly that she save some for him before returning to the thicket for more wood. The second time he emerged, he was surprised to find a small fire. Abbey was sitting next to it, her arms wrapped around her knees.

"Who lit that fire?" he asked in genuine surprise and dropped the armload of wood. Abbey laughed. "I don't see any evidence of an intruder. There are no footprints in the sand save the small ones there," he said, pointing to her prints. "Madam, am I to understand that you lit this fire?"

"Of course I did!" Abbey giggled.

"How on earth—"

"With a flint and some kindling, of course." She frowned laughingly.

Michael slowly shook his head. "Good God, woman, is there no end to what you know?"

*I don't know if you love me,* she thought, but smiled up at him and said nothing.

"Are you hungry?" she asked.

Michael smiled sardonically. "Aye, I am hungry," he muttered, and dropped next to her. In one fluid movement, he pulled her onto his lap and sought her mouth. Abbey's hands instantly swept up his chest and around his neck. Michael groaned against her mouth as her tongue darted between his lips. She was aware of being lowered onto the blanket, of his hand moving deftly over the buttons of her blouse.

"Michael, you aren't thinking—"

"Oh, yes I am," he said, and covered her mouth before she could protest again.

In the cool afternoon sun, with a small fire to warm them, Michael made gentle love to her. It was exquisite, Abbey thought, as he thrust deeply within her, the muscles of his arms quivering next to her as he held himself above her. The sun was behind his head and blinded her to his face. But she could hear him, smell him, and when she ran her tongue across his nipple, she could taste him. As his strokes grew more insistent, he reached between them and stroked her, and after a few richly agonizing moments she imploded into a thousand dots of light. With one last powerful surge, Michael groaned and shuddered, spilling his seed deep within her, then he slowly lowered himself to her, resting his forehead on her shoulder.

"I love you, Michael," she whispered in his ear. He snaked his arms around her and squeezed her tightly to him in response. Neither of them said a word for a long while, and finally Michael sighed and withdrew. He made a show of rearranging her blouse before jumping to his feet and fastening his breeches. She lowered her skirt and sat up, then tried to rearrange her hair. Michael kissed the mess.

"I think you will find some ale in that flagon," he said, and moved to tend the fire. Abbey found two wooden cups and poured them ale, then filled a plate of food for him. Satisfied with the small, roaring fire, Michael settled next to her and regaled her with his youthful adventures in the cove with Mariah. After they finished their languid meal, Michael propped himself up against a tree. Abbey's lids were growing heavy, and she laid her head on his lap.

"Who were you speaking with in the garden this morning?" he murmured.

Abbey's lashes fluttered and a moment passed before she answered. Several things went through her mind, not the least of which was surprise that he had seen them. But that was followed quickly by the memory of Galen's warning to keep his secret. In the space of a moment, she decided her cousin was right. When he had a legitimate post, she would tell Michael everything. Michael had said very clearly he did not want to be burdened with her relatives, and she was not about to let him think he was burdened with Galen. Nor was she willing to do anything that might sour the intimate bond they seemed to have established and strengthened this afternoon.

"He was a hand aboard the *Dancing Maiden* a few years ago, from Pemberheath. Withers and the lads know him," she said softly. Michael watched her, looking for a sign of deceit, and slowly, reluctantly, accepted her explanation. He really could not believe she would lie to him; not when he could easily confirm anything she said with Withers. Given that she would embrace an old dairy cow if so moved, it seemed almost plausible she would greet an old friend thus. *Almost* plausible. He could not quite shake a feeling of doubt.

She made a small sound and snuggled closer to him. With the ever-present strand of silken hair drifted across one eye, she looked so young and innocent in her slumber. He tenderly brushed the tress from her face, and with a protective arm around her, he sat, staring out at the sea. He savored the contentment he had not known was achievable, and he marveled at the budding realization of how important it was to him.

Abbey slowly became aware that something was tickling her, and she grumpily batted the thing away. What felt like a feather next drifted across her face. She swatted at it again, then slowly opened her eyes. She was still lying with her head on Michael's lap, and when she looked up, he was smiling down at her, holding a feather in his hand.

"Wake up, sweetheart. You have slept the afternoon away," he murmured, and brought her hand to his lips.

"No, I only closed my eyes for a moment," she insisted, and pushed herself to a sitting position.

"I assure you it was more than a moment," he chuckled. He watched as she sleepily brushed the hair from her face, then glanced, bewildered, around the cove.

"There is something I want to ask you," he said. Abbey nodded and crossed her legs beneath her voluminous skirt.

"A few months ago, we played billiards, do you recall?" he asked, a smile playing on his lips.

"I remember very well."

"And do you recall the wager?"

"Better still," Abbey said slowly. Like a flash of light, it suddenly occurred to her that the three months was over. She blanched visibly; Michael's smile faded.

"Is something wrong?" he asked softly. Abbey swallowed and shook her head.

"Today is the three-month mark of our wager," he said, and impulsively covered her hands with one of his.

Abbey's throat parched; what did he want her to say? She felt uncomfortably exposed; the facts today were no different from what they had been that night three months ago. Michael had been forced into a marriage against his will and deserved to be released. But God, did he *want* to be released? Her breathing grew constricted. She could not bear to hear him say he wanted out of this marriage, but she owed him the opportunity. She closed her eyes; Michael's hand gripped hers tightly.

"Abbey, I would have your answer," he insisted. Abbey flinched. "But before you do, I think you should know that I will be sorely displeased if I must rescind my favorable reply to the Delacorte Ball next month." Abbey's eyes flew open and she started to shake her head. He came quickly to his knees and grabbed her shoulders; his gray gaze pierced hers with brutal intensity. She did not want to go, but she could not deny the very real truth of their marriage.

"It's . . . it's not *fair*! You deserve—"

"I deserve to have my wife on my arm in London. I deserve to have you in my bed at night. I deserve to see that devastating smile of yours every day, and I would have sworn on my mother's grave that you did not *want* to go!" he said gruffly.

"I *don't* want to go!" she cried.

"Then why in the devil do you look as if you could be ill at any moment?" he roared.

"I'd rather die than be without you, don't you know that? But I can't ask it of you, Michael! Papa *lied* to you!" she cried.

Something flicked across his gray eyes and he smiled ruefully. "Abbey, listen to me. That is past history and has nothing to do with us now. I would prefer you not go."

Shocked by the words she had so longed to hear, she suddenly threw herself at Michael, knocking him to his back. "Oh, Michael!" she cried, and covered his face with fierce kisses until her elation managed to manifest itself in a burst of tears.

"Good God," he murmured, and with his thumbs, wiped her tears away.

"Darfield, you d-don't know how happy you've m-made me!" she cried.

Made *her* happy? He had only managed to convey very awkwardly that he wanted her to stay. He crushed her to him in a bruising kiss, to which Abbey responded with abandon. He quickly rolled her onto her back and grabbed the hem of her skirt, pushing it up to her waist. He growled, fumbling with the buttons of his breeches, then thrust into her with such strength that Abbey cried out in ecstasy, lifting her hips to meet the next powerful surge. And as Abbey found fulfillment, she whispered her love, over and over again in glorious elation.

When at last they lay spent in each other's arms, Michael chuckled against her neck.

"What's so funny?" she asked lazily as she stared up at the pinkening sky.

"Have I your word that you will not cause me bodily harm?"

"Of course!" she said very seriously.

"Then I have a confession to make," he said cheerfully. "The wager was four balls, remember?"

"Yes."

"You turned your back, do you recall?" he asked, and swept a finger across her swollen lips.

"I could not bear to watch. I was afraid you would miss," she added sheepishly.

"I did miss. I made only three. I helped the fourth ball into the pocket," he said casually.

"You *what*?" She gasped.

"I cheated. Blatantly. I even threatened Anderson with his employment if he dared breathe a word," he grinned.

Abbey's eyes narrowed. "Michael Ingram, how despicable," she began. He nodded in cheerful agreement. "But I suppose I am hardly in a position to censure you."

Michael's brows rose slightly. "And why is that?"

"I only won one hundred pounds, not a thousand," she said sweetly.

Michael threw back his head and roared with laughter.

# Chapter 13

Abbey tapped the dry quill against the desktop and stared through the window at a branch dancing in the spring breeze. It was hard for her to believe she was actually in London; harder still to believe the town no longer held the same attraction for her as it had once. When Michael had first announced they were to go, she had told him she never wanted to leave Blessing Park. The time they had spent there had been idyllic; the most fulfilling, blissful days she had ever known. He had argued it was impractical to remain forever there, and the sooner she was introduced to the *ton,* the sooner the interest in her would ebb. She did not care a whit about being presented to the *ton,* but it was obvious he did, and Sam had not helped matters by agreeing with Michael. She smiled inwardly as she recalled how he had once threatened to leave her at Blessing Park. Sitting in the huge study at his London town house and going through the hundreds of invitations they had received, she wished that she had demanded those words in writing.

She had not yet really ventured out, other than to go to the exclusive modiste where Michael had insisted—no, demanded—on paying a small fortune to have her outfitted in the finest haute couture. Her cousin Victoria would have been awed by the fabrics and styles, just as she was. Her only other outing had been to accompany Michael's elderly great aunt to a tearoom one afternoon.

That outing had caused quite a stir. Her tea with the slightly senile Aunt Neva had begun uneventfully, but when other patrons realized she was the wife of the mysterious Marquis of Darfield, there had begun a steady stream of visitors to their table, all wishing for introductions. They were stifled in the corner of the tearoom, and Aunt Neva looked positively peaked. Abbey had been forced to speak with practically the entire room before she could get the older woman safely through the crush and to the awaiting carriage.

She thought the interest in her was peculiar, though, granted, Michael was something of a celebrity. She had heard enough gossip to know that the *ton* believed he had almost risen from the dead, but there was nothing particularly remarkable about her. Nonetheless, if the afternoon in the tearoom or the mound of invitations was any indication, the *ton* was very interested. And tonight, she thought with sickening dread, was the Delacorte Ball. Sebastian had told her it was *the* event of the season; everyone who was anyone would be in attendance.

"Lady Darfield, have you decided if you will accept the invitation from the Duchess of Kent?" Sebastian reminded her. Abbey dragged her gaze from the window to the secretary.

"Oh! I don't know, Sebastian, what do you think?" she asked apathetically.

"I think one does not refuse the Duchess of Kent unless one is on one's deathbed," he sniffed.

Abbey moaned and tossed the quill down and stood abruptly. "I can't seem to think today! Sebastian, please excuse me. I think I should like a short walk."

"But, my lady!" Sebastian protested as Abbey paused to smooth her skirts. "There is quite a lot of correspondence that should be answered!"

Abbey smiled and patted Sebastian on the arm. "I am quite

certain you will manage it nicely," she said brightly, and disappeared through the door, in spite of the man's protestations. She stopped only long enough to retrieve a bonnet and a pair of gloves, then walked briskly into the bustling street, headed for Hyde Park.

It was a glorious day, and in the park, she began to gain some serenity. She convinced herself she was being ridiculous. She had nothing to fear tonight; she was not going to do anything calamitous, like career off the dance floor and into a tray of drinks. Giggling to herself at that visual image, she noticed a group of elderly women calling to her and furiously waving white handkerchiefs from across the green. Abbey groaned, smiled and waved, and began walking as quickly as she could without appearing to run. They started toward her.

For elderly women, the trio gave her quite a race, finally catching her as the path turned toward the middle of the green. Abbey sighed and slowed when it became apparent they would chase her all the way to her front door if necessary, then turned reluctantly, pasting a thin smile on her face.

"I beg your pardon, my lady, but I should very much like to introduce myself! I am Lady Thistlecourt, your neighbor!" the slightly plump woman said in a raspy voice as she caught her breath. She beat a gloved hand at her red face in such furious fashion that Abbey was reminded of a hummingbird.

"A pleasure, Lady Thistlecourt, I am sure," Abbey murmured. "You are a neighbor of Blessing Park?"

"Oh, no! I meant your Audley Street residence! We are just across the park, near Belgrave Square." She panted, pointing in the very opposite direction of Audley Street.

"We have been so eager to meet you and welcome you to our country." She smiled and glanced at her two companions, who, peering closely at her, nodded in enthusiastic agreement. "May I introduce Lady Billingsly," she said, pointing to the thin woman on her right, "and Lady Fitzgerald." The short woman on her left curtsied in perfect unison with Lady Billingsly.

"Good day, ladies. It's a pleasure"—Abbey smiled, taking

a tentative step backward—"but I should not want to interrupt your turn about the park—"

"Nonsense! You shall walk with us!" Lady Thistlecourt declared, and reached up to adjust her slipping bonnet, knocked loose, no doubt, from her sprint down the path.

"Oh, thank you, but really, I have a rather pressing engagement this afternoon and just stepped out to take some air. Very briefly. For only a minute or two." Abbey took another small step backward.

But Lady Thistlecourt, who had not run since she was a girl, did not intend to lose the Season's elusive prize. "Lady Darfield, if you are not familiar with our park, it is quite possible to become lost. You would do well to stay with us," she insisted.

"Yes, have you been here very long? That is, long enough to learn your way about the park? Or did you only come recently to London?" Lady Fitzgerald asked, squinting intently at Abbey's gown. Abbey self-consciously looked down at the gold day dress she wore, realizing, in a moment of polite horror, that she was not wearing the obligatory walking dress.

"I just came out for a moment. Why, I am not even dressed for strolling," she said nervously, plucking a piece of imaginary lint from her lap. "I will not go very far," she promised hopelessly.

"That's a highly unusual color, isn't it dear?" Lady Billingsley observed.

Abbey bit her lower lip and told herself to ignore their frank perusal. Their reaction was *not* a portent of things to come tonight at the Delacorte Ball. They were simply three elderly women who wanted to meet her. And peer curiously at her gown. She unconsciously took another step backward, prepared to flee if she had to, and racking her brain for a polite excuse.

"She probably has a modiste from the continent," Lady Billingsly declared to her companions, then frowned at Abbey and demanded, "Do you? Have a modiste from the continent, that is?"

"Oh, dear, the time!" Abbey gasped. "Ladies, if you will excuse me, I really *must* be going."

"So should we. We shall escort you back Audley Street, madam. We would not rest if we thought you undertook that walk alone! Lord only knows what danger may lurk in these trees!" Lady Thistlecourt declared, and, with a conspiratorial look at her companions, shifted her weight to one leg and waited for Abbey to come forward.

Abbey sighed and cast her gaze to the ground. It was useless to point out they could almost see her home on Audley Street from here, so she resigned herself to the fact these women were going to escort her. No doubt they would expect to be invited in for tea.

Lady Billingsly made a strange sound. Abbey looked up; the trio were looking past her shoulder, staring very intently. She glanced over her shoulder and smiled with relief. The Duke of Southerland was walking toward them, on his arm an elderly woman with curls as fat as sausages dangling about her plump face. He was truly her neighbor, owning the grand town house just next door, and he and Abbey had exchanged polite greetings on a couple of occasions.

"Dear God, I can't believe it! It's the *duke*!" one of the women whispered in awe. "He *never* comes to London in the Season! Dear God, it can only mean he intends to offer for Miss Reese!"

"Miss *Reese?* Have you lost your mind, Rose?" another whispered just as frantically.

Abbey smiled gratefully as the duke approached; she could not have been happier if it had been Michael himself. He responded with an exceedingly charming smile that made the corners of his green eyes crinkle.

"Lady Darfield," he said, bowing low when he reached her. "May I introduce my aunt, Lady Paddington?"

Abbey curtsied and nodded politely at the woman, whose eyes grew wide. "Oh, what a *pleasure*!" Lady Paddington gushed. "I have so wanted to meet you! I could scarcely believe it when Alex told me Darfield had married! I thought he was trifling with me until I saw the announcement in the

*Times* with my own two eyes. The *Times* would not fabricate such a story!'' she blustered, smiling broadly.

"Apparently I would." Alex chuckled and smiled fondly at his aunt.

She responded by slapping his arm with a pair of gloves, her little eyes never leaving Abbey's face as the duke greeted her new-sprung companions. "Oh, my! It's true what they say, isn't it Alex? She is really quite lovely," Lady Paddington remarked. She then slid her gaze to the three women standing behind Abbey, and frowned. "Good day, Hortense," she sniffed, her tone cool.

"Oh, Clara, for heaven's sake! You're not still angry about that silly game, are you?" Lady Thistlecourt exclaimed.

"No, Hortense. I do not get *angry* over something as silly as a card game, thank you!" Lady Paddington shot back, and, releasing Alex's arm, waddled toward the three women, immediately engaging Lady Thistlecourt in an argument about said card game.

Alex smiled down at Abbey, his green eyes dancing merrily. "Someone should have warned you about the prowlers in this park," he said, and shifted his gaze meaningfully to the women, whose conversation was growing more animated as their collective voices became louder.

Abbey chuckled as they watched the women argue. "I did not think I would be accosted," she muttered.

He laughed and whispered, "Shall I see if I can rescue you from these prowlers?" When Abbey nodded, he winked slyly and straightened. "Aunt Paddy?" All four women stopped immediately and turned puzzled looks, as one, to the duke. "I would escort Lady Darfield home. Shall I retrieve you in a quarter of an hour?"

The ladies nodded in agreement. Alex offered Abbey his arm and after exchanging farewells, they began to stroll away.

Alex laughed. "Would you believe that there is a pack of those prowlers, numbering around a dozen or so, that roam the best homes of London? I have encountered them on more than one occasion in my aunt's salon. They quite enjoy their card games; in fact, one might say they are obsessed."

"No!" Abbey pretended shock. "I shall have to talk with Jones. He is usually quite good about warning me of danger!" Alex grinned, but Abbey quickly sobered. "I must confess, I cannot for the life of me understand why they seem so terribly interested in me."

"That's simple. You are a beautiful woman, new to London and the peerage." He flashed a row of even white teeth at her self-conscious flush. "But most important, you have married the scandalous Devil of Darfield," he said dramatically. "Naturally, the prowlers, having too much time on their hands, are overly curious."

Abbey rolled her eyes heavenward. "Naturally." She sighed. "It's so unfair they should call him that! There is not a devilish bone in his body."

"They remember the rumors."

Abbey dragged her gaze from the path to him. "You mean about the scandals surrounding his father? Surely that is all behind him now."

Alex considered her closely for a moment. "Lady Darfield, if I may be so bold as to offer some insight?" he asked after a moment.

*"Please."*

"It's quite difficult to explain, really. The *ton* is like a parasite, one that feeds off ill fortune. Darfield—Michael—in my humble estimation, has never done anything to deserve the vile gossip that has been spread about him," Alex started.

Abbey was momentarily reminded of Mrs. Petty and the despicable things she had uttered. "What *were* the scandals? I have heard he is quite popular with the ladies; is that what you mean?"

With an amused smile, Alex shook his head. "Who told you that? I am quite certain Michael would not approve of your being bothered by such ugly tales—"

"Then how am I to understand if no one tells me?" she asked, her exasperation showing.

Alex considered it, looking at her curiously. "If I have your word you will not repeat anything I am about to tell you . . . I tell you only so you may understand why the keen interest in your every move," he said reluctantly. Abbey quickly nodded her agreement. Alex was silent for several moments, staring at the path ahead of them as he gathered his thoughts.

"Michael and I were boys, attending Eton, when the first scandals occurred. His father apparently gambled away the family fortune, and he was removed from school. Lord Darfield was a man possessed, frankly. He would win a few pounds, then lose twice as much. He was not partial to any particular type of gaming—he would bet on anything. He borrowed from everyone—family, friends, business associates— ostensibly to repay his debts, but then he invariably gambled *that* away. The Ingram family owed virtually everyone, and for a period of a few years, they were shunned, treated as if they were lepers."

Abbey winced.

"Michael bore the brunt of his father's disgrace and, reportedly, his abuse. Before he was of age, he escaped to the French wars. He hid his identity, fighting in the trenches with common men. He told me years later a captain recognized him, and he was promptly sent home, as it was unheard of for an heir to a title to fight like a commoner. When he returned, I think he found things much worse than before he left. A little older and wiser, he did the only thing he could to save his family from complete ruin. He turned to trade, a profession wholly unacceptable to most of the *ton*. Nonetheless, Michael took to the seas, and over the years made a fortune to repay his father's debts. Unfortunately, even though he amassed a fortune far greater than what was needed to restore the family honor, his father continued to gamble it away.

"Eventually, the marquis became so ill with his liver ailment—brought on by his strong predilection for whiskey—he could no longer gamble. Michael was able to rebuild the family fortune and good name and the talk seemed to decrease. The Ingrams were not deemed the pariahs they once had been."

Abbey sighed as they strolled along, trying to imagine Michael, working hard to restore the family. And all that time, she had thought he was happily sailing the open seas, working to build a future. For her. She suddenly flushed, embarrassed by her foolishness.

"In amassing his fortune, your husband made some enemies along the way," Alex continued, his face darkening. "In particular, there was an Englishman who held himself up as a paragon of virtue but who was actually pirating. Rumors began to circulate that the pirate was none other than the Devil of Darfield. This news, of course, was easy for the *ton* to believe because he had amassed not one but *two* fortunes in shipping. The culprit behind the vicious rumor was a ruthless businessman whom Michael had occasion to meet in foreign ports. The man *was* pirating, and when Michael threatened to expose him and captured his routes, the man turned the tables and accused *him* of pirating.

"But as the charge was completely without foundation, Michael survived, and all was going well until his younger sister, Mariah, made her debut. I was on the continent at the time, but I was given to understand that the fragile goodwill that had been extended to Michael was not extended to her. There were no suitors for her hand. Her brother was in trade, after all, and the family stigma weighed more heavily on her than Michael. A lovely young woman, mind you, and not one single offer for her hand in her debut Season, which in some circles spelled the end for the poor girl."

Spellbound by his tale, Abbey leaned toward him, her eyes wide. "How horrible for her," she murmured.

Alex nodded his agreement. "When the *ton* turns its collective back, it takes a small miracle to turn it around again. Sometime later, I think Mariah believed the miracle had come in the form of a suitor. An Englishman, just returned from a voyage, saw her in Brighton and fell quite hard for her. He courted her in earnest, and when Michael returned home from the Mediterranean, he was presented with an offer for her hand, as his father was too incapacitated to act. Michael flatly turned it down. The suitor, you see, was the same pirate who had spread the rumors about him. Mariah was understandably devastated.

"A couple of years later, Ian McShane, a minor partner in

Michael's trade, had occasion to meet Mariah at Blessing Park, and the two fell in love. A handsome young fellow, but a Scot with no title. Nonetheless, Michael happily gave his blessing to the union. After the wedding, McShane took Mariah to Scotland, where I believe they reside to this day. It was a proper courtship, to be sure, but when the *ton* learned of her marriage, rumors started to build that it hadn't been proper at all, that McShane had defiled her—some went so far as to say she was with child.''

Abbey's hand flew to her throat. Alex frowned as they neared Park Lane. ''All lies, of course, but because McShane was a Scot and untitled, the vicious rumors persisted. Thankfully, Mariah has never been aware of the scandal that followed in the wake of her wedding. It all fell on Michael,'' Alex said solemnly. He stopped at the park entrance and looked down at Abbey.

''And, as you know, Mariah's wedding was followed by the tragic death of Lady Darfield. Her untimely death came but a fortnight after the wedding, and rumors abounded that she had hanged herself to escape the shame of her daughter's ruin. Lord Darfield died soon after that.''

''Dear God.'' Abbey gasped softly, cognizant of the rage building in her. There was never a kinder, gentler, or more generous man than Michael, she thought angrily, and she felt nothing but scorn and intense rage for those who would tear him down. She stared at her feet in speechless frustration until Alex patted her hand.

''In the last few years Michael has chosen to remain at Blessing Park when he is not at sea. He has quietly and consistently rebuilt the family honor by earning a reputation as a shrewd and fair business partner and by erasing all the Ingram debts. Time and absence has helped heal the old wounds, to be sure. Just last year he happened to be in London during the Season and uncharacteristically attended a ball. Since he had kept to himself all those years, he was suddenly deigned the elusive Marquis of Darfield, and just as suddenly, everyone wanted to know him. He became the most coveted guest at all events. He didn't attend more than a handful, and returned to

Blessing Park as quickly as he could. The mystique has only intensified since then. When his marriage was announced, you can well imagine the frenzy. Now *you* are the most sought after person of the Season.''

Abbey paled. "Oh, dear God, how will I cope?" She moaned.

Alex chuckled. "I have every faith you will cope, Lady Darfield. Quite frankly, I believe you could charm an old billy goat into your bidding with a single smile. You will be fine, and I daresay the fairer half of the *ton* will be wild with envy.''

Abbey blushed and shyly looked at him. "Lord Southerland, you have been too kind. Thank you for rescuing me,'' she said, and started to step away. She hesitated, then turned back and took one of his large hands in hers. "I needed to hear that. Thank you,'' she said softly, and with a gentle squeeze, stepped away, darting gracefully across the street.

Alex Christian stood at the park entrance and watched her walking briskly toward Audley Street, an appreciative smile on his lips. When she had disappeared from view, he sighed with a bit of longing and turned back to the park, in search of his aunt and her fellow prowlers.

In the early evening, Michael returned from White's where, for the first time in many years, he had actually enjoyed a card game. It was odd how easy it was to get along in Polite Society when one was not the object of scornful gossip. That realization did not endear the *ton* to him in the least, but he had enjoyed a relaxing afternoon nonetheless.

He smiled to himself as he climbed the stairs to his rooms. The anticipation among the same Polite Society of seeing Lady Darfield was particularly evident. Every single acquaintance he had greeted at White's had asked if he were attending the Delacorte Ball and if his lovely wife would accompany him. One man had even asked him what she would be wearing, a question that had startled him. When Michael responded he had not the vaguest notion, the man had sheepishly confessed that his wife was curious.

Sam, too, had grumbled that he could not get any work done because of the number of callers pestering him with questions about the Marquis and Marchioness of Darfield. His friend was obviously weary of the attention, but had grinned with great amusement when he related how some of the more illustrious patrons of the *ton* were scheming to meet Abbey. Michael chuckled under his breath as he untied his neckcloth and tossed it aside. He was half tempted to skip the ball. It would serve his former—and numerous—detractors right to be led down a path of great anticipation, only to wait all night for the woman who would never appear. He had no doubt Abbey would agree; she had been a bundle of nerves about the ball when he had left her that morning.

Michael ordered a hot bath and stripped out of his clothes. As he shrugged into the dressing gown Damon held out for him, he caught Abbey's scent on the black velvet. He brought the fabric to his face and inhaled deeply. The truth was that he *wanted* to show the *ton* the prize that was his. After years of abuse, he *wanted* men to look at him with envy and know he was the victor. He *wanted* women who had so shamelessly thrown themselves at him last Season to understand the kind of woman he would make his. In truth, he anticipated this evening more than anyone else in London.

Strains of music drifted into his room from the adjoining chamber as he bathed. Abbey was playing a lively tune, a very good sign.

"It would appear her ladyship is in a festive mood, sir," Damon muttered as he handed Michael a towel.

Michael smiled. "It would appear." He secured the towel around his waist and walked to the basin, lathered his face, and began to shave.

"What do you think, Damon? Black attire this evening?" he asked as he scraped at his whiskers.

"Yes, my lord, and, if I may suggest, the silver silk waistcoat."

"Fine. You will find a box on the dresser with some amethyst studs. Lay those out as well," Michael said, and toweled his face dry. As he dressed, the music continued to drift in his room, and he found he could hardly contain himself.

"Get on with it, Damon. There is a beautiful woman calling to me," he said lightly, and the normally stoic Damon chuckled. When he was fully dressed, the valet uncharacteristically whistled in appreciation.

"If I may say so, my lord, you look remarkably . . . fine . . . this evening."

Michael smiled as he adjusted his neckcloth one last time. "With talk like that Damon, you may just turn my head," he replied, and laughed when Damon turned crimson red. He picked up a box from his dresser and strolled through the door adjoining Abbey's chamber.

Abbey did not hear him enter her room. She was standing in front of the hearth, her violin on the settee next to her. Staring into the fire, she was lost in thought, her head bowed and her hands clasped behind her. The flickering light of the fire shadowed the fine angles of her face.

Dear God, how easily she took his breath away.

She was wearing an exquisite pale-pink satin gown. The neckline was squared and revealed the very enticing swell of her bosom. The gown was fitted to her midsection, then flared out into a full skirt. The bodice was embroidered with tiny seed pearls, as was the hem and sleeves, and the skirt bore an elaborate design of the tiny pearls. Her hair was swept up in the unusual and very becoming simple style she preferred. A strand of pearls was threaded through her thick, dark locks. She looked every inch a princess, and Michael swelled with unconquerable pride.

"I must be dreaming. You look like an angel," he said appreciatively from the door.

Abbey started at the sound of his voice and gave him a bright smile beneath the rose blush of her cheeks. As he strolled into the room, Abbey curtsied deeply. "Good evening, my lord husband," she said demurely.

Michael frowned suspiciously as he pulled her up. "My lord? You've not deigned to address me—"

Giggling, she put a finger to his lips. He caught her hand and kissed her palm before brushing his lips across hers. The scent of lilac drifted between them, and Michael reluctantly drew back.

"Pray tell, how is it possible that you can look even more stunning than I have ever seen you?" he murmured.

She laughed nervously. "You flatter me unduly, especially when *you* look so beautiful. I thought *I* was supposed to draw attention."

"Do not doubt for one moment that all eyes will be on you, sweetheart," he said truthfully, snaking an arm around her waist and drawing her close when her smile faltered. "Nor should you doubt that I will be ever at your side," he added, kissing her forehead. He grasped her slender hands in his and stepped back to admire her again.

"Why do you never wear your amethyst earrings, Abbey? They compliment your eyes so very well," he remarked.

She colored slightly. "I suppose I grew tired of them."

"I rather like them. Why don't you put them on?"

Abbey guiltily averted her gaze from him. "I gave them to Sarah."

Michael gasped with feigned shock. "To Sarah? Whatever possessed you?"

"I just grew tired of them," she insisted. "Don't you like my pearls?"

"I like the amethysts. So much so that, had I known you on your sixteenth birthday, I *would* have given you a pair," he said casually.

Clearly surprised, Abbey's violet eyes grew wide. "How did you know that?" she demanded.

"It doesn't matter." He laughed and then presented the velvet box.

"I want you to have your amethysts, sweetheart." Abbey drew a long breath as she slowly opened the lid. Inside was a pair of large, pearl drop amethyst earrings dangling from two small diamonds, and a matching necklace and bracelet of amethysts interspersed with diamonds. In addition, there was a ring that boasted a large, square-cut amethyst stone.

*"Oh, Michael,"* she whispered. Her hand fluttered at her throat as she gazed in astonishment at the gems. Michael reached behind her and unclasped the pearl necklace she wore and put it aside. Still staring at the gems, she had not even noticed as he removed the pearls and draped the necklace around her slender neck. He put his hands on her shoulders and turned her around so she could admire the jewels in the mirror. Abbey slowly inhaled at the glittering necklace, then quickly donned the earrings and bracelet, her violet eyes sparkling like the stones.

"They are beautiful," she whispered.

Michael, who thought the gems did not compare to her, kissed the back of her neck before taking the ring from the box. "I am, at last, providing you with a proper betrothal ring," he said softly.

Abbey's eyes grew misty as he slipped the ring on her finger. She held out her hand to admire it.

"Have I ever told you how much I love you?" she asked after a moment.

"Not since this morning." He laughed. He was cut short when she threw her arms around his neck and jerked his mouth to hers, kissing him with a passion that set fire to his blood. If she kept that up, damn the Delacortes. He had to force himself to disengage from her before he ruined her hair and gown. Abbey laughed lightly at his discomfiture, then turned once more to admire the amethysts, and proclaiming them a perfect match with her gown. Michael did not know if that was true or not; but between her sparkling earrings, her sparkling eyes, and her brilliant smile, he was almost blinded, and blissfully so.

"Now, my darling marchioness, if you are ready, I believe we are expected at a ball," he said, and with a bow and a sweep of the arm befitting a queen, he very gallantly offered her his arm.

# Chapter 14

Abbey's heart began to pound with anxiety when she saw the crush at the gate in front of the Delacorte mansion. Ornate carriages, brightly clad footmen, and dozens of guests crowded around the front steps and into the street. The Delacorte residence was at least as big as Michael's, if not larger, and bright lights glittered from every window. Michael helped Abbey from the coach, then tucked her hand in the crook of his arm and covered it with his own. He smiled reassuringly and began to lead her to the entrance. She moved woodenly, acutely conscious that several people turned to gape at them. Fans snapped up and open and women's heads bent together, peering at Abbey over the tops. Michael noticed it, too, and put a comforting hand on her waist. When she glanced up at him, he winked and gave her a smile that suggested he found it all highly amusing.

"It's Darfield!"

Abbey heard the frantic whisper, then watched as more heads turned toward them and more fans snapped open. "Dear *lord*," she murmured.

"Mmmm, overly curious, are they not? Reminds me of

chickens gathered about their feed,'' he whispered into her
ear. Abbey smiled at that, and the whispers seemed to grow
more frenzied. Michael led her through the crowd, bowing in
polite greeting to those he knew. His hand rode her waist,
never leaving her, and Abbey found it to be a huge comfort.
Inside, Michael gave his coat and hat to a footman, then
helped Abbey with her cloak. She heard a muffled gasp behind her as her gown was revealed.

"Michael!'' She frantically clutched his sleeve. "Am I
properly fastened?''

Michael very smoothly ran his hand down her spine until he
reached the small of her back, where his hand lightly rested.
He leaned down to her. "You are completely fastened, sweetheart. They are just admiring your gown.''

"Or their feed,'' she murmured. Chuckling, Michael
guided her forward through the crush to the top of the stairs
where the Delacortes were receiving guests.

Abbey momentarily forgot her anxiety when they reached
the landing where their hosts stood. The house was magnificent; candles blazed in crystal candelabras hanging from huge
plaster medallions across the ballroom. The walls were covered with silk paper, except one, which was covered from
floor to ceiling with mirrored panels that had the effect of
making the room look even larger than it was. Thick carpets
covered the floors, but the dance floor was of marble tile.
Below them, women in fantastically bright pastel gowns and
men in formal black attire paraded about. At one end of the
ballroom was a small orchestra situated on a platform just
above the dancers, partially covered with a row of potted
plants. The music could just barely be heard above the din of
the crowd. On the other end, four sets of open French doors
led out onto a balcony. Of all the places Abbey had been in
her lifetime, she had never seen so many people squeezed into
one place.

Michael nudged her, and she became aware that he was
speaking. She quickly turned her attention to the couple in
front of them. Lady Delacorte was a short, squat woman with
spectacles and a large ostrich feather protruding at an odd

angle from her silver hair. Her husband was just the opposite; tall and lean, his eyes sparkling beneath his bald crown.

"A pleasure," Abbey heard herself say, then dipped into a perfect curtsey.

"Lord Darfield, I did not for one minute believe the announcement in the *Times*, but as I live and breathe, it appears you have gone and got yourself married!" Lady Delacorte chirped cheerfully. "Lady Darfield, welcome."

"Thank you, my lady," Abbey said with a polite nod.

Lord Delacorte grabbed her hand and brought it to his thin lips. "Well done, Darfield," the older man said as he smiled down at Abbey.

"I would humbly agree." Michael laughed.

"You are from America, no?" Lord Delacorte asked, turning his twinkling eyes to Abbey.

"I am English, my lord, but I last resided in America."

The man lifted his wiry brows. "English?"

"My wife has had the good fortune to live a variety of places around the world, and therefore her British accent has been somewhat subdued," Michael explained.

"I daresay that's the *only* thing that has been subdued." Lord Delacorte laughed and glanced knowingly at Michael. Abbey blushed; Michael said something more to the Delacortes and moved her toward the butler who was announcing the guests. There were three couples in front of them, and Abbey had the misfortune of being in a position to stare down at the ballroom while they waited to be announced.

She was unaware that she had a vice grip on Michael's arm, and when he glanced at his wife, he saw the terror that widened her eyes.

"I was at a ball very much like this once," he said impassively. Abbey's eyes flicked to him for a brief moment, then back to the crowd below them.

"*The right honorable Earl and Countess of Wellingham*," the butler called.

"It was several years ago, when men still wore knee britches. I recall a particularly stout chap who wore a pair of purple satin knee britches, a bright green waistcoat, and a yellow coat. He looked like a fat parrot,'' Michael continued.

*''Mr. and Mrs. William Saunders, and Miss Lillian Saunders.''*

Abbey's grip tightened on his arm.

''The man had the grave misfortune to step on a woman's foot at the top of the stairs,'' Michael said as he stepped forward and handed the butler the engraved invitation. ''She screeched and frightened the poor man to death, and when he jumped away from her, he tripped.'' Abbey thought he was mad to be telling her this story now, of all times, and she frowned up at Michael.

*''The right honorable Marquis and Marchioness of Darfield!''* The din below them lessened noticeably as all eyes turned toward the top of the stairs.

''He bounced like an Indian rubber ball all the way down the stairs and ended in a colorful heap right at the feet of the Prince Regent!'' Abbey couldn't help picturing the ridiculous scene and laughter bubbled from her.

She thought she sounded hysterical.

Michael thought she sounded lyrical.

The crowd saw an elegantly beautiful woman laughing serenely with her husband as they descended the stairs.

The minute they reached the ballroom floor, the crowd seemed to move as one toward them, all eager for an introduction.

''Brace yourself, darling,'' Michael muttered, and immediately began to greet the faces swarming around them. Abbey swallowed hard. Miraculously, she managed to respond appropriately to everyone Michael introduced. There were so many that the names and faces were soon nothing more than a blur. It seemed that the men generally greeted her bosom and the women greeted her behind forced smiles. Throughout the ordeal, Michael stood close by, keeping her calm with subtle touches to her elbow, her hand, or her back. At one point, she turned and bestowed a grateful smile on him; his gray eyes sparkled in response.

Someone put a glass of champagne in her hand, and Abbey

drank it quickly. Another glass appeared, and Abbey drank that, too. The bubbly wine helped; she began to feel the tension in her body ease a bit. Even her toes began to tingle. When a waiter came by, she helped herself to another glass and was halfway through it when she noticed Michael had raised a questioning brow. She smiled sweetly and downed the rest of it.

"One would think it was the Queen of England herself judging by the fawning crowd."

Abbey turned and grinned at Sam. "Thank God you are here!" she whispered frantically.

"The crowd's a little overbearing, is it?" He chuckled and moved to stand between her and an overtly curious group of young debutantes.

"A bit." She sighed.

"It's quite understandable. Michael has always been very intriguing to this set, even more so now, but fear not. I have come to save you," he whispered with a wink. He looked over her head to Michael, who was engaged in a boring conversation with the elderly Viscount Varbussen.

"Say there, my good Lord Darfield, if you aren't going to dance with your wife, may I?" he asked loudly enough for several to hear.

Michael grinned. "I think not, sir. I am quite confident Lady Darfield has saved her first dance for me," he responded to the delight of the circle around them.

Michael nodded politely to Varbussen, and, with apologies to the small crowd around them, he took Abbey's champagne flute and handed it to Sam, then led her to the dance floor.

And it was no easy feat. They were stopped no less than three times by guests who acted as if they were Michael's long-lost cousins. When they at last reached the center of the dance floor, Michael bowed to her as was customary, and with a wink, Abbey curtsied. She opened her mouth to speak, but the music began and Michael quickly swept her into a waltz. He looked down at those remarkable, slightly unfocused violet eyes and felt a strong stirring in his loin.

"They cannot keep their eyes off you, sweetheart," he remarked sincerely.

"Ha! You mean they can't keep their eyes off my bosom, or this unfashionable dress." She blew away a tendril of hair that had worked its way free of her coif only to stubbornly drape her eye again.

"What are you talking about? Your gown is beautiful."

"Miss Stanley remarked she was surprised I found the fabric, since it was not at all a fashionable color this Season. Lady William agreed, and said that she hadn't seen such an unusual design, and was surprised I could find a modiste to sew it," she said, grumbling.

"I see." Michael smiled down at her. "No wonder you are frowning. It's not easy being the object of envy, is it?"

"Envy?" She looked so innocent, he could not suppress his chuckle.

"Those women are insanely jealous, and will grow even more so when the objects of their affections leave them standing alone to clamor around you, begging for the opportunity to stand up with you," he said as he pulled her closer and moved toward the orchestra.

"Oh, no. I'm not dancing with anyone but you!" she said with great authority.

"Oh, yes you are," he said cheerfully. "As much as I would like to, I can't allow you to snub every man in here. You must dance."

"Oh, no! No, no, I do not want to do that," Abbey insisted with a shake of her head that knocked the strand of hair across her eye again.

"What's wrong? You dance beautifully!"

"I don't know them, Michael! What if I say something wrong?" she whispered frantically.

"My dear, you are far too charming to offend anyone. Do not fret so, everything will be all right," he assured her, then pressed his lips against her cheek, well aware that the affectionate gesture sent up another round of frantic tittering among the onlookers.

"I mean," she whispered, pausing when Michael pulled

her into his chest to avoid a collision with another couple, "what if I say something that they will talk about? I don't want them to *talk* about us."

"If they are talking about us, darling, it's because they can't believe my good fortune."

She sighed and smiled up at him. It was a beautifully charming, trusting smile. God, but she was enticing. And everyone in that ballroom watching them dance thought so, too.

When the dance ended, Abbey did as she was told, but not before she helped herself to another glass of champagne. Michael nudged Sam and inclined his head toward Abbey.

"If you would be so good as to help me keep an eye on my wife, Hunt. She is attracting men like moths to a flame and has discovered a liking for champagne that may match her thirst for ale," he said dryly, and Sam chuckled with a nod of agreement.

"I shall do my best, but the line is already forming for a chance at her dance card," Sam said before dutifully pushing his way through a growing crowd and asking Abbey to stand up with him.

Abbey enjoyed dancing with Sam. Like Michael, he was a very polished dancer and regaled her with quips about the *ton*, keeping her laughing as they whirled around the floor.

When Sam escorted her from the floor at the conclusion of the dance, she was intercepted by the Earl of Westchester. He was shorter than she, and while they danced, the earl, who was inebriated, stared blatantly at her bosom.

"They say you come from American money," he inquired of her bosom.

"No, my lord, I believe you misunderstood." Abbey sighed wearily. "They say I come from American monkeys." Just as she had suspected, the earl was so enthralled with the swell of her breasts that he did not hear her outrageous response. She tried to ignore the lecherous old goat, praying for the dance to end, and caught a glimpse of Michael dancing with another woman. She did not like the feeling it gave her. Of course Michael would be expected to dance with other women, she knew that. But the sight of him smiling down at another woman made her chest tighten.

She lost sight of Michael during the next two dances. After the earl, a very kind, elderly gentleman was her next partner. Abbey liked him instantly.

"I knew your father, child, and was a great admirer. I happened upon him in India several years ago," the old Baron de Sevionton said.

"Truly?" Abbey asked, warmed by the memory of her father.

"Indeed. He was quite handy in assisting me with a small problem there. Suffice it to say I needed to get out of port quickly, and had it not been for your father," he said, his rheumy eyes glistening, "they might have found me dangling from the masts. If you ever are in need of anything, my dear, you must call upon me. I owe your father for his help in that *very* indelicate matter." Abbey thanked him for his kind offer, wondering what in the world a kind old gentleman like himself could have done to warrant such assistance.

When the baron finally escorted her from the floor, she caught sight of Michael, his shoulder propped against a pillar, watching her above the heads of the admirers circled about him with a peculiar smile on his face. She beamed and began to make her way toward him when someone stepped in her path.

Mildly irritated, she slowly looked up to see Malcolm Routier smiling down at her, his yellow eyes glinting as they swept her face.

"It's a pleasure to see you again, Lady Darfield. Might I have the favor of a dance?" he asked in a low, rich voice.

Abbey glanced past his shoulder to Michael, whose smile had faded. She was uncertain what to do; she had no desire to dance with Routier but thought it improper to refuse, as she had a space on her dance card. She drew her bottom lip between her teeth as she peered at Michael, then glanced again at Routier. Her sense of propriety had been dulled by the champagne, but she knew it simply would not do to refuse him.

"Perhaps another time," he said, his disappointment evident.

"Oh, no, Mr. Routier, I did not mean to imply—I would enjoy it very much." She forced herself to smile at him. He smiled, too, but it did not quite reach his eyes. With a quick, helpless glance to Michael, Abbey reluctantly returned to the dance floor.

It was a waltz, and Abbey felt a slight revulsion when Routier took her in his arms. She was puzzled at her reaction, for she had not felt this way when she had danced with other men. Yet there was something about Malcolm Routier that she could not quite identify, something that made his attractive features almost loathsome to her.

"Are you enjoying yourself this evening?" Routier asked politely.

"Oh, yes, very much so," she replied with feigned enthusiasm.

His gaze flicked to her lips. "You have caused quite a stir. Everyone is talking about Lady Darfield," he said. "You are what one would call an instant success."

Abbey gamely attempted to smile. "Forgive me, Mr. Routier, but I cannot agree. I'm not sure what the fascination is all about, but one never knows what to expect when one is new to a particular setting, do you think?"

"Especially given your husband's circumstances."

Abbey bristled beneath her smile. "I beg your pardon?"

Routier showed his affected smile again. "I beg your forgiveness. I spoke without thinking." He nodded curtly and moved her toward the center of the dance floor.

Abbey looked up at the glowing chandeliers to avoid looking at Routier. The champagne she had drunk still had her feeling mellow, and when she looked at the twinkling light twirling above her, she could not suppress a smile.

Or the dizziness. She dragged her gaze from the lights to Routier's stiff collar and frowned.

"Are you unwell Lady Darfield?"

"No, I just made myself a bit dizzy." When he grinned,

Abbey noticed for the first time that his genuine smile was rather nice.

"If I may be so bold, madam, I think you the loveliest woman in the room," he said softly. A warm, uncomfortable flush crept up Abbey's neck and to her cheeks, and she slid her gaze away, landing unintentionally on Michael, who was leading a very pretty blond woman around the dance floor. The two were engaged in a deep conversation, and Abbey could not tear her eyes away. When Routier moved himself between her and Michael, she tried to see over his shoulder.

"Lady Davenport," Routier said dryly.

"Pardon?" Abbey croaked, jerking her gaze to him.

"Your husband is dancing with Lady Rebecca Davenport." Abbey could not believe her ears. *That* was Lady Davenport? He was dancing with his lover? Dear God, she was as pretty as Abbey had feared.

"*Who?*" she blurted before she could think.

Routier smiled wickedly. "Have you met her?"

Abbey was acutely embarrassed, aware that Routier was watching her reaction very closely. "Actually, I have not had the pleasure," she murmured miserably.

Routier's wicked smile deepened. "No, I would think not."

Abbey resisted the urge to look at Michael again and, instead, stared at Routier's ruffled chest. "So you attended the governor's soirée in Bombay, Mr. Routier?" she asked in a feeble attempt to change the subject.

A slight smirk cracked the corner of Routier's lips. "I did. Do you not recall the governor's affair?"

Abbey shook her head. "Only vaguely. I was very young."

"As I recall, you were ten or eleven years of age. But what I recall in particular was that you had fixated on an older gentleman, one who wore a turban," he said.

Abbey could not help laughing. "You can't be serious!"

"Oh, but I am." He smiled. "Your father told me later that you were quite determined to see what was under that turban but found the soirée a rather daunting place to unmask him, so to speak. So you marched up to him, declared your intent, and offered to meet him on the docks the next morning before you sailed.''

"I arranged to meet a perfect stranger on the docks?" She giggled.

"So I have been told. But it was all for the sake of science," he said with mock solemnity.

"My father"—she smiled as he whirled her about—"was not always, how shall I say, as *insistent* with me as he should have been." She chuckled, shaking her head.

Routier smiled thinly, his eyes taking on an odd glint. "But he was insistent you marry Darfield, wasn't he?"

His remark surprised her. She assumed that Michael had told him the circumstances of the marriage the day he had come to Blessing Park. "I suppose," she muttered. Michael and Lady Davenport had come back into view and were nearing them. Michael had not noticed her; he was too engrossed in his conversation with Lady Davenport. Abbey began to feel queasy.

They neared the edge of the tiled floor as the dance wound to a close. Mr. Routier smiled and bowed deeply.

"Thank you, Lady Darfield." He paused and peered curiously at her. "You look a bit flushed. Shall I fetch you some water?" he asked, and tucked her hand in his arm, leading her toward the refreshment table before she could answer.

Abbey felt a hand grip her elbow. "If you are through dancing with my wife, Routier, please excuse us," Michael said behind her. Routier's yellow eyes turned hard as he glanced at Michael over Abbey's head. Michael was looking at him with no expression at all.

Routier smiled at Abbey. "Thank you again, Lady Darfield." With a curt nod of his head, he stepped away. Michael gripped Abbey's elbow and immediately began to propel her toward the French doors leading onto the balcony.

"Enjoy your dance?" Michael asked coolly. He seemed perturbed, which Abbey found highly amusing, given that he was just dancing with his lover.

"I tolerated it. And did you enjoy yours?"

Michael frowned slightly as he pulled her onto the balcony

and pushed her toward a dark corner. "I would not even call it tolerable," he muttered.

"Is something wrong?" Abbey asked, growing a little irritated with his sudden cool demeanor.

"Yes, something is wrong, Abbey. I have not kissed you all damned evening," he said, and jerked her to him, claiming her mouth in a bruising kiss. Having heard the tinge of jealousy in his voice, she melted in his embrace, whimpering with pleasure in the back of her throat. His mouth slanted over hers with an urgency she understood very well, and as his hands began to travel up her side, Abbey pulled back.

*"Michael,"* she scolded him, then smiled seductively.

He groaned and brought her hand to his lips. "Will there ever come a time I don't want you?" he whispered hoarsely, then slowly lowered his head to hers, lingering there for a moment, in a very light, very provocative kiss.

"Bloody hell, I hope not," she whispered when he finally lifted his head.

Michael laughed and led her further into the shadows. "You seem to enjoy dancing."

"I like dancing with you. I don't like dancing with other men." She wanted to tell him it was hardly gratifying to see him with other women and positively infuriating to see him with Lady Davenport.

He laughed low and slipped his arms around her waist. "I don't either," he agreed, and claimed her mouth again before reluctantly leading her back to the ballroom and a waiting throng of men eager to dance with his wife.


At a little after four in the morning, Sam elbowed Michael and inclined his head toward an exhausted Abbey. Standing apart from any of the remaining guests, she was leaning against the wall with her arms folded across her middle, that ever-present strand of hair over one eye. She could barely keep her eyes open and wearily covered a deep yawn with her gloved hand. Michael winked at Sam, then casually strolled toward her. She attempted a weary smile.

"Tired, sweetheart?" he asked. She nodded.

"I will take you home," he said softly, gently brushing the hair from her eyes. "I think we've made enough of a splash for one evening."

As the coach rolled through the fog-shrouded streets, Michael gazed at Abbey, fast asleep against his chest. He had never thought himself a jealous man, but when he had seen her in the arms of so many other men, the seeds had taken firm root. In his mind's eye, he could still see her clearly in Routier's arms, looking up at the chandeliers and smiling that dreamy smile of hers. That was *his* smile, reserved for him alone, and he resented Routier having the opportunity to be graced with it. Had he been within a foot of them, he might have snatched Abbey from the blackguard's arms and handed over a very irate Rebecca. He had not visited her, nor had he answered her pathetic letters since he had ended their liaison. Rebecca had gone from hurt to angry over the last few weeks, and when she had actually seen Abbey, she had bared her fangs. The realization that Michael was never coming back to her had made for a rough exchange.

Abbey sighed in her sleep and shifted against his chest. He glanced heavenward.

When the coach rolled to a halt in front of his home, Michael helped her from the coach. She staggered against him when her feet hit the pavement, and he immediately swept her into his arms and carried her inside and up the stairs to his chamber, calmly ignoring her sleepy protests. He dismissed Damon, lay her in the middle of his bed, and quickly shed everything but his trousers. Then he moved back to the bed, admiring the sweep of her lashes against her skin, the relaxed line of her lips, her arm dropped carelessly across her waist. He gently rolled her onto her side and swiftly unfastened the row of tiny buttons down her back. She did not open her eyes, but she smiled sleepily as he removed her jewelry.

"Lady Delacorte said, 'You simply must come to supper Wednesday next,' " Abbey said, quietly mimicking the rotund woman's chirp. " 'The Earl and Countess of Middlefield will be in attendance, and they've just returned from

America, my dear. I am quite sure you would enjoy hearing their news.' "

Michael smiled to himself as he removed her shoes and stockings. "And what did you say?" he asked as he leaned over her to slide the gown from her smooth shoulders.

"I told her I was flattered, but that I had to consult with my husband's secretary. Lady Delacorte said, 'Why, of course, Lord Darfield is in great demand.' "

"Mmmm," Michael said idly as he leaned down to kiss the satin skin of her shoulder.

"But then she clarified she was asking *me* and not you." Abbey giggled. Her light, tinkling laugh was too provocative, and Michael moved over her, covering her body with his own.

"So that's the way of it, is it? You make a successful appearance among England's elite, and suddenly I am relegated to lonely suppers while you gad about?" he asked, kissing the hollow of her throat. Abbey sighed softly at the touch of his warm lips and tenderly stroked his hair.

"The way of it, my handsome lord, is that Lady Delacorte and her countess can rot," Abbey said, giggling as Michael tried to kiss the smile from her face.

Later Abbey lay with her back to Michael's chest, her arm draped across his thickly corded one that possessively held her to him. The evening had gone well, despite some of the rude ogling and untoward questions. Michael had enjoyed himself and she had enjoyed most of it too. But the best part was that it was finally over.

"Abbey?" Michael asked against her hair, his voice heavy with sleep.

"I love you, Michael. You have made my life perfect," she whispered.

He grunted, unable to choke out a proper reply. But in his heart he acknowledged that those words made a grand evening perfect. He was truly glad to be home.

# Chapter 15

Abbey's life was perfect until the next afternoon. After a late and leisurely breakfast with Michael, Abbey retired to her chambers to put a dent in the correspondence over which Sebastian was nearing apoplexy. She had made good progress when Jones interrupted to tell her that a gentleman, Mr. Galen Carrey, had come to call.

Galen was standing at the window of the blue drawing room, nervously fingering his dark-brown neckcloth when Abbey bounced in.

"Galen! You surprise me again!" She laughed, opening her arms to embrace him.

"I missed you at Blessing Park, little one." He smiled, returning her warm embrace. He released her and stood back, smiling appreciatively as he eyed her sea-green and cream gown. "I must say, London seems to agree with you."

Abbey smiled self-consciously and led him to the settee, where she settled daintily, her hands folded in her lap. Galen sat beside her.

"Have you been in London long?" she asked.

"Just a few days." He shrugged. "I concluded my business

in Portsmouth and went straight to Blessing Park, then I followed you here." Galen looked at her hands and drew one into his and clasped it, studying it intently. He was expressionless, and Abbey wondered if his deal had fallen through.

"Well?" she prodded. "Was it concluded successfully?"

"One could say it was." He kept his eyes on her hand as he spoke.

"Oh, Galen, that's wonderful! So you have a post now, do you? As captain?" she asked excitedly.

Galen slowly released her hand and leaned forward, propping his forearms on his thighs, and stared at the floor. "Abbey, I have some important news. Perhaps you could dismiss your footman?" Abbey lifted her brows, silently questioning what he could possibly have to say that could not be said in front of Hanson. "I rather think it best if you heard it alone," he muttered, his eyes still on the floor.

An odd sense of foreboding swept through her. "But what—"

"I can assure you it's a matter of some . . . delicacy. I'm only thinking of you." He lifted his gaze and looked at her with such concern that Abbey's heart skipped a beat. Her first thought was that something had happened to Aunt Nan or one of the girls. She tried to read his expression, but he quickly averted his eyes again and clasped his hands tightly together.

Abbey glanced over her shoulder. "Please excuse us, Hanson." She waited until the footman had quietly closed the door. "Oh, God, what has happened? Has something happened to Aunt Nan?"

"Oh, no!" He laughed nervously. "It's just that the news I have is rather important . . . for you as well as for me."

A vague sense of panic pricked her. "What is it?" she asked slowly, quite certain she did not want to hear his answer. Galen had been waiting for his news with enthusiasm, but at the moment, he looked sickened, as if he could not bear to say it aloud.

"Well, it's very hard to say, really, something of a long story. I wonder if you were aware that your father and I were estranged for some years." Abbey blinked. "He considered me to be a bit irresponsible,'' Galen quickly explained, ''and I was, in my youth. But that changed, and happily, in the last three or four years, the captain and I reconciled.''

"I had no idea,'' Abbey admitted truthfully. She could recall her papa complaining about Galen's irresponsible ways, a terrible row or two between them, but no estrangement had been mentioned. And if there was some sort of rift between them, she could not, for the life of her, imagine what it had to do with anything now.

Galen took a deep breath. "He took me in after my father died and was like a father to me himself, you know. I very much respected him, Abbey, I truly did,'' he said softly, his gaze riveted on the Oriental carpet between his feet.

"And I am sure he felt the same for you, Galen,'' Abbey replied earnestly. "But I don't understand. What has this to do with your new post?''

Galen blinked, shifted his gaze to the ceiling, and took another deep breath. "When we reconciled, the captain promised me a living of sorts. He informed me that he intended to leave one of his larger merchant vessels to me, so that I might carry on with the family trade. That is why I accepted the apprenticeship in Amsterdam, so I could learn every aspect of the business. But when he died, I discovered a rather unfortunate mistake.''

Abbey was sure she had not heard him correctly. Her father had never mentioned any such thing to her, and there was certainly no mention of Galen in the papers she had received. Perhaps there had been a codicil? She was not sure what happened to the vessels; all she knew is that they were somehow entailed in the final settlement of his estate. "What mistake?'' she asked softly.

Galen turned to look at her, his brown eyes almost pleading. "Abbey, what I have to tell you is quite extraordinary. Apparently, your father's solicitor, Mr. Strait, dispatched a will to you before the captain actually died. It was quite natural for Mr. Strait to do so; the captain was very near death, and he wanted to be sure the last will was executed. But . . . you see, the captain had a change of heart.''

"A change of heart?" she echoed incredulously.

"Yes. Unfortunately, Mr. Strait had already sent the papers he had in his possession. What I am saying is that he did not send the final papers."

Panic began to swell in Abbey's throat. "*What* final papers? I received my father's last will and testament."

He smiled sadly and shook his head. "No, little one, you did not. I have the last will here, one that supersedes yours."

Abbey blinked, unable to absorb what he was telling her. She came quickly to her feet and unconsciously began to pace. "Forgive me, but I don't understand. I don't recall that he left a ship to you, but perhaps there was a codicil, something detailing his wishes for the fleet. Surely that is what you have?" she asked, nodding hopefully.

"No, Abbey. I have, in my possession, his final will and testament. It does not bequeath a ship. It bequeaths a considerable sum."

"A sum?"

"Of almost five hundred thousand pounds," he said weakly.

Abbey laughed, a little hysterically. "That is the sum of my dowry!"

Galen sighed heavily and withdrew a thick document from his coat. "Try and understand, little one. He had a change of heart on his deathbed and let the half million pounds to me. Your dowry is the cancellation of Darfield's debts. Unfortunately, the revised will did not reach you in time." With that announcement, he opened the document and showed her the captain's distinctive signature.

Abbey was stunned, absolutely and thoroughly stunned. It was too outrageous to believe, but then again, she hardly knew what to believe about her father anymore. He had, after all, lied to her about Michael all those years. But this was different; it was inconceivable. She stared blankly at the document in Galen's hand as she tried to comprehend it. "It's *impossible*," she muttered to herself.

Galen smiled thinly and stooped to pick up a satchel she had not previously noticed. "I assumed, naturally, that you would find it hard to believe. The courier I hired to retrieve the papers also returned a few personal items. Apparently Mr. Strait did not think to return them to you, as he had already deemed it unnecessary to travel personally to America." As Abbey gaped at him, he reached into the satchel and retrieved a pair of ivory cuff links cut in the shape of small elephant heads that she immediately recognized as being her father's.

"Where did you get those?" she whispered. "They belonged to Papa." Galen did not answer as he placed them on a table. She swallowed hard; there had to be some explanation.

"The captain wanted you to have this," Galen said, nodding to something in the satchel. "He saved it, believing you would one day want to give it to one of your children." As he pulled a doll from the satchel, Abbey gasped. It was an exact replica of the doll she had dragged over the decks of the *Dancing Maiden*. She sank heavily into a damask chair as her head began to swim. It was impossible, completely improbable.

*But was it really?*

She had discovered things about her father since his death that made her question everything about him. She felt an odd stab of guilt; what if her father had changed his mind and left her money to Galen? But had her father really done something so rash? Had he really, in the throes of death, attempted to provide for Galen?

"I do not know what to say," she murmured.

"Little one, I know this is all very difficult. Your husband will understand, I am quite certain of it."

Abbey moaned; she was not nearly so certain. Suddenly she rose to her feet and reached for the will that Galen had put on the table with the other things, and frantically scanned the pages. It looked just like the one she had, except that it bequeathed the Carrington fortune to Galen, not her. Just as Galen had said, the will specified the cancellation of Michael's debts as her dowry. And if she had any doubt, her father's characteristically bold handwriting stood starkly on the page, confirming everything, and dated a month or more past the one she had. Abbey took a deep gulp of air to fight down her spiraling hysteria.

She knew, instinctively, how very bad this would look to Michael. Her father had duped him once before, and now he was adding the crowning glory of his deception from his grave. He had left her dowry to Galen. Not a ship—her dowry. Dear God, what would Michael think? That he had been duped into an unwanted marriage with her? Only to learn that she had come empty-handed to this union, and therefore it was all for naught? He would not have married her under those circumstances, he had made that painfully clear. But would he now assume he had been *tricked* into marrying her?

*"No!"* she whispered hoarsely, and whirled toward the mantel, clutching the will to her chest. She told herself frantically that Michael would never believe she had tricked him, but she hardly believed it.

"Dear God," she heard Galen mutter, and felt a strong hand on her elbow, as she was pulled to the settee and forced to sit. Galen knelt next to her, her hands in his. His brown eyes, full of worry, searched her face. "Abbey, don't be upset! It shall be all right, I promise you!"

But Abbey could think only of Michael, who would soon hear of yet another deception.

*"Please* don't fret!" Galen was saying. "I will support you when you tell him; I will explain you could not have possibly known. The matter can be kept very quiet; no one need ever know! Don't fret! Darfield will understand! Men on their deathbeds change their last testaments all the time, they do!" Galen's voice was low, rushed. Abbey doubled over with sickening dread.

"Look, I've brought all the proof you need. His ivory cuff links, that doll from your youth, for God's sake, and the will! What more proof could your husband need?" The nausea that swept over Abbey prevented her from speaking. Too shocked and confused to do anything, she stared helplessly at the cuff links on the table, the doll tossed onto an armchair, and the will Galen had taken from her and placed on the table.

She dragged her gaze to Galen, whose genuine concern was

etched around his eyes. She shifted her gaze to the doll across the room, sprawled in the chair, its black eyes staring blankly at her. It was a replica of the doll she had carried all those years ago, but the last time she had seen it, it had no head. Did her father repair it? Had he truly saved it for her?

And in that moment, the enormity of her anger with the captain hit her. A flood of tears erupted, and in painful fury, she buried her face in her hands. Galen quickly rose to put a comforting arm around her shoulder.


Michael looked curiously at the footman stationed outside the drawing room door. "What are you about?" he asked kindly.

The footman cleared his throat. "The marchioness is receiving a visitor, my lord."

Michael assumed it was Sam, a frequent visitor to his home. He opened the closed door.

He was not prepared for the sight that greeted him. Abbey, with her back to him, was bent over. A man was seated next to her, his arm draped around her shoulder. When he looked over his shoulder, Michael immediately recognized him as the stranger from Blessing Park. The stranger she had so warmly embraced.

"What in the hell is going on here?" Michael's voice boomed in the drawing room as he strode across the carpet. The man sprang to his feet, but Abbey did not move. Michael went quickly to her, leaning down to look into her tearstained face. "Good God, Abbey, what has happened?" he asked, suddenly and oddly frightened.

*"Oh, Michael!"* she muttered hopelessly.

Michael jerked upright and glared at the man. "By God, you had better speak!"

"Please, my lord, I am Galen Carrey—your wife's cousin." The name, vaguely familiar, registered somewhere in Michael's brain. "I am afraid I have brought her some disturbing news," he said softly. At Michael's increasingly dark look, Galen spoke quickly. "It's about her father. It is troubling news. Perhaps you would like to sit—"

"You had best tell me before I force it out of you." Michael's voice had gone from angry to deadly calm.

Galen blanched visibly. "Lord Darfield, it is with extreme displeasure that I must inform you Captain Carrington composed another will. A later will, I should say. Not the one you have in your possession."

Dumbfounded, Michael glared at Carrey. Of all the idiotic things. Of all the completely insane, reprehensible things. "*What?!*"

"It would appear that Mr. Strait was too efficient. He began disposing of the estate before the captain died. Unfortunately, the captain had a change of heart and signed another will shortly before his death that effectively invalidates the first."

It was preposterous and a little too convenient for Michael. "Impossible," he muttered angrily.

"I beg your pardon, my lord. It is quite possible," Galen said quietly.

"And I suppose this new will has something to do with you, does it?"

Galen colored slightly as he reached down to retrieve it from the table. Holding it out to Michael, he said calmly, "It leaves his estate to me, my lord. The dowry you received belongs to me."

That was absurd. Michael did not give a damn about her dowry, but he was not about to believe for one moment that the captain had penned another will. He took the document from Galen's hand and quickly scanned it. It was all there, the blasted agreement, the payment of debts—everything, but instead of a sum for her dowry, he was supposed to have accepted the cancellation of his debts. Carrington's estate was left, in total, to Galen Carrey.

"This is a forgery!"

"It's his signature," Abbey said softly.

Her words slammed into Michael's head; he dragged his gaze from the document to her. She looked up at him, her eyes red-rimmed and dull, then flicked her gaze to Galen Carrey. *All right, Galen did not kiss like that.* Michael felt as if he had been punched in the gut. Galen. The embrace. Dear God, it

was inconceivable, but he had to consider that she was somehow a part of this fraud. His expression remained inscrutable
despite the thoughts racing through his mind. He carefully
folded the vellum and placed it on the table.

"My lord, your wife could not know of the second will, as
she was already in England. And I did not mention it in my
correspondence to Blessing Park, only that I was expecting
some important news," Galen interjected.

*Correspondence?* Astounded, Michael stared blankly at the
man across from him. She had corresponded with him? He
clenched his jaw as he recalled the day he had seen this man
at Blessing Park. She had said he was a deck hand aboard the
*Dancing Maiden,* a friend of Withers's. She had not mentioned any correspondence. Or their kinship. Indeed, there had
been a decided omission of any kinship.

"You, sir, are a fraud," he announced flatly, his disgust
apparent.

Galen blinked nervously. "I am truly sorry, my lord. I
know this comes as quite a surprise, but I am not lying to you.
Abbey told you herself it is the captain's signature. And I
have brought some other articles, articles only her father could
have had, along with the will." Galen motioned to the cuff
links and the doll. Chafing from the familiar use of her name,
Michael stared at the articles Galen indicated. The doll trig-
gered a distant memory, one he could not quite grasp.

"These are articles that could be acquired anywhere. I do
not believe they signify." Galen swallowed a visible lump in
his throat. "Mr. Carrey, my solicitors thoroughly documented
and authenticated the papers I received from Captain Carrington. If Mr. Strait wishes to inform me of a mistake, I shall
be obliged to listen." He did not miss the flicker of Carrey's
eyes at the mention of Mr. Strait. "Until such time, however,
I will consider anything you bring me, including your trinkets,
as nothing more than a pathetic attempt to defraud me. I will
thank you to leave my home," he said calmly.

"Michael," Abbey said weakly, "I think my father did
this, not Galen."

Michael could not believe what he was hearing. She was

*defending* the bastard. Ice began to run through Michael's veins; he could hardly contain his desire to throttle Carrey. And Abbey, good *God*! The last few months had not been a lie, he was certain of that—wasn't he? Was it possible she could have deceived him so completely? Michael's chest tightened painfully and he turned an icy gaze to her. "I will speak with you in a moment," he said coolly, then flicked his gaze to Galen. "Leave now."

Galen moved from the settee. "Clearly you need time to absorb the unfortunate news I bring you. Naturally you will want to review the papers," he said as he walked to the door. He paused and smiled reassuringly at Abbey. "I shall give your butler my direction. But I will call on you in a few days, little one."

Galen's endearment for his wife rifled through Michael like a shot; his hands clenched at his side. He stepped in front of Abbey, blocking Galen's view of her.

"You will not, under any circumstance, call on my *wife*, Mr. Carrey. Now leave!"

With a final look at Abbey, Galen walked out the door.

The silence in the wake of Galen's departure was almost deafening. Abbey touched Michael's sleeve, but he reacted by moving away from her. Her soft gasp did not daunt him as he turned, his roiling emotions masked beneath an expression of stone.

"You lied to me. I asked you who he was. You said he was a deckhand aboard the *Dancing Maiden*, not your kissing cousin."

A shot of fear and remorse rumbled through Abbey. Michael's granite eyes blatantly searched her face. "I did not lie to you, I just did not—"

"Tell me the truth?"

Abbey winced, realizing how horrible it all seemed. "I could not tell you then," she blurted. "He was embarrassed because . . ." The words were no sooner out of her mouth than she recognized the deep hole she was digging for herself. She needed to *think*, to gather her wits so she could explain everything coherently.

"You were saying, *little one*?" he spat. "He was embarrassed to present himself to me? Why? Because it was exceedingly bad form to do so before he defrauded me?"

"No, no," Abbey replied hoarsely. "He . . . did not have a post," she said lamely as her mind raced. Terribly shaken by her father's latest betrayal and Michael's anger, she felt completely inept to explain. Obviously, her responses were not easing him in the slightest. If it was possible for a man's face to harden any more, Michael's did.

"I suppose his *correspondence* was quite illuminating on that front," he said in a low voice. Before she could respond, he pivoted away from her. "I think you should retire to your rooms."

Panicked, Abbey debated how to explain to him. God, she was *so* confused! She could mess it all up, much worse than she already had. But she could not leave it like this. Against her better judgment, she took a step forward. "Michael, please listen to me! Galen didn't tell me about the other will. He said only that he was expecting some important news, a *post* on a merchant vessel! He was reluctant to present himself because he felt . . . *inadequate,*" she blurted. "I honored his request—for God's sake, he is my *cousin*!"

"That," Michael drawled icily, "is a fact you should have mentioned when I asked you."

He stalked to the sideboard and poured a whiskey as Abbey stared at his back. He did not believe her. Dear God, he did not believe her. She closed her eyes and quickly, painfully, decided that until she had collected her wits and could think, she was doing more harm than good.

"You are upset, and so am I. It's extraordinary news, for both of us," she heard herself saying.

Michael glanced over his shoulder at her with a look of disdain that made her flush.

"I would rather wait until we can both discuss it rationally," she said with a croak, and pivoting on her heel, walked unsteadily to the door. She paused at the threshold to glance at Michael's rigid back before fleeing upstairs to the sanctity of her room.

Michael stared at the window, gripping the whiskey glass with all his strength as his emotions warred. It did not occur to him even once that Galen Carrey could be telling the truth; it was simply too preposterous. All he could think was that Abbey's eyes did not lie. *She* did not lie, goddammit!

But she had lied to him in the cove.

And she purposely had not told him of Galen's correspondence. Bloody hell, could she have done this to him? Could she have participated in a scheme with her cousin to embezzle him? Could she have perpetuated such a lie over the last months? Standing in the middle of the room, he weighed the fantastic thought. He recalled every conversation, every night spent in his massive bed, every stroll about Blessing Park, every single meal. And not once, not once had she shown him anything but genuine esteem and affection. Not once had her story changed.

No, it simply could not be true.

He moved stiffly to a chair and sat heavily, staring into the amber liquid he swirled in the glass.

It *could* be true.

Could he have been so wrong about her? Could she have played him so completely false? Could he have mistaken her response in his bed or the look in her violet eyes every time their gazes met? Bloody hell, she had professed to love him! Oh, and he had fallen for that like a stone sinks to the bottom of the river. For Chrissakes, he had never, in all his thirty-one years, been a victim of a woman's charms. Not once! Was it possible he could have been so completely unguarded this time?

It was definitely possible.

He recalled with some bitterness the night she had realized Carrington had lied to her. She could not have manufactured her devastation. Or was she as fine an actress as one would hope to find on Drury Lane?

Michael shifted his gaze from the glass he held to the table where the will lay next to some cuff links. He sat forward, reached across the table to pick up one of the links, and examined it closely. As he replaced it, his eye caught the doll sprawled haphazardly across a chair near the window. The toy struck a faint chord in him. He stared at it, blinking, until it registered. In two strides, he was at the chair.

The moment he picked it up, he knew unequivocally that Galen Carrey was a fraud. The doll was a copy of one Abbey had carried more than ten years ago. How could he forget the little gingham dress he had torn? He lifted the skirt of the curly-headed doll. It had bloomers, just like the ones he had ripped apart to make knee britches.

An ill feeling swept over Michael as he looked down at the doll he clutched in his hand. *What I recall is being terrorized by an older boy, who incidentally decapitated the one doll I had as a child.* Abbey had said that the first day she was at Blessing Park. He dropped the doll and strode quickly to the bell pull.

Jones appeared almost instantaneously. "There is a leather trunk in the attic," Michael said gruffly. "Have it brought to my rooms immediately. Fetch Sebastian and have him dispatch a messenger to Blessing Park. I want Withers here first thing in the morning." He pushed past the startled butler and headed for his room.

When the trunk was brought to him, Michael threw the lid open and peered inside. It was stuffed with articles from his youth. He ignored the keepsakes and dug through, intent on finding the long-forgotten item. After tossing aside a rusted knife, a pair of heavy boots whose leather had long ago cracked, and a weathered hat, he found what he was looking for. There, buried beneath some old clothes at the bottom of the trunk, was a small doll made up to look like a little pirate. It was the same doll he had doctored after severing the head in a moment of anger. It was the very same doll he had intended to return to the distraught little girl after seeing her search the decks for her damaged toy. But Carrington had put her on the boat for Rome before he had the opportunity to return it. Why he had kept it all these years, he did not know.

He sank down on the edge of the bed and stared at the doll in his hand. It was all beginning to make some sense, or at least he tried to convince himself it was.

Galen Carrey, or someone behind him, was trying to destroy him. Suddenly he needed to talk to Sam. He stood abruptly, dropped the pirate doll carelessly on the bed, and paused only long enough to shrug into a forest-green coat before vaulting down the stairs, calling for his mount.

Michael found Sam at White's and dragged him from a game of whist. Sam protested loudly—he was winning, for once—but Michael ignored his objections and pushed him toward a private room in the back. Sam sat in a huff, but as Michael began to relate the whole fantastic tale, he watched his friend's eyes widen with astonishment, then narrow with suspicion. Sam slowly shook his head as the weight of Michael's words registered.

"What do you think, Darfield?" he asked softly.

Michael sighed and thrust a hand through his dark locks as he thoughtfully eyed Sam. "I don't know. The will is a forgery, I would stake my life on it. This purported cousin of hers was a bit nervous, and I find myself wondering if someone has put him up to it, someone like Routier." Sam sighed wearily. Michael watched his friend silently consider the facts. Sam's loyalty was one of the most admirable qualities about him, something Michael had relied upon time and again. But until this very moment, he had never known how important it was to him.

"What about Abbey?" Sam asked slowly.

Michael shrugged and looked at his drink. "It is rather hard to believe she could carry on such a fantastic lie. That woman cannot hide a single emotion, much less a deception so huge that it implies she *acted*—" He stopped short of saying that she must have acted in his bed, in his arms, at his table—it didn't matter; Sam instantly understood what Michael was thinking, and nodded slowly.

"Yes, but I can't help thinking . . ."

"What?" Michael prodded.

Sam sighed again and lifted his gaze to Michael. "Think about it, Michael. She obviously has known him for many

years, and despite having corresponded with him, she lied to
you about his identity. For the sake of argument, suppose she
and this Carrey fellow were attached and wanted to be together. It would explain her lie and the embrace you witnessed.'' A rush of heat invaded Michael's neck.

''Michael,'' Sam continued, his expression tense, ''you are
my oldest friend. Believe me, I do not want to think it any
more than you, but I cannot help thinking you have known her
for less than three months. It would not be the first time you
were the target of some nefarious scheme.''

Michael understood the direction Sam's thoughts were taking, and his heart slammed against his ribs in denial. ''But
what about the shot?'' Michael protested.

Sam shrugged. ''Perhaps it has nothing to do with this and
was truly a mishap. But then again, perhaps someone wanted
you dead, someone like Carrey. It would be much more convenient for them, if she was married, to collect a fortune without you in the way,'' Sam said slowly.

Michael glanced away, remembering that day. He had been
proud of Abbey for not panicking and falling into a fit of
hysterics. But was that because she was expecting it? Had she
been waiting for the shot to fell him? The thought was devastating; God, she could not have deceived him so completely!

''I believe that Routier is somehow behind this. I needn't
remind you he has publicly vowed to ruin me on more than
one occasion,'' Michael insisted.

''Perhaps,'' Sam agreed weakly.

''Come now.'' Michael huffed. ''Short of killing me, what
could she have hoped to gain?''

''I don't know,'' Sam answered slowly. ''I only know that
she stood to lose her inheritance if she did not marry you. *If*
she married you, her chances of getting at least something had
to be improved. And despite your most callous efforts to convince her otherwise, she did not cry off when given the opportunity. Michael, if she and Carrey wanted to be together, the
only thing they had was an ill-conceived, dated contract. Perhaps they planned this together. Perhaps he thought to put you
out of the way. Perhaps they hoped to embezzle the funds

from you. But you cannot deny that the evidence points to at least the *possibility* she is involved."

Sam's argument put a voice to Michael's worst fears, yet he could not wholly believe it. There had to be another explanation, he thought, shaking his head in furious disagreement. "It is Routier, I am certain. Abbey may have lied to me about her cousin, but she most certainly did not connive to have me killed, Sam. She may be that idiot's lover, but she is not a killer. No, Routier is behind it."

Sam nodded thoughtfully. "I cannot deny that he would do just about anything to see you ruined. But consider this. Routier would not possibly know what the doll looked like. Abbey would."

Michael inhaled sharply; the thought had not occurred to him. But Carrey could have known what the damn doll looked like, and a half-dozen other sailors. It looked bad, very bad, but he simply could not believe she had betrayed him so thoroughly, not yet, not without more proof.

"What do you intend to do?" Sam asked softly.

"Find Strait," Michael responded bitterly. Until he talked to the solicitor, he did not know what to believe. He gulped his brandy to dull the twist he felt in his gut.

# Chapter 16

Abbey stared blindly at Jones. "He wants to see me?" she asked for the second time.

"Yes, madam." Jones looked pained. Abbey stood unsteadily from the chair she had been sitting in since she had fled the drawing room. She must have sat for hours, staring blindly at a portrait on the wall. Her thoughts were a tangled mess. In one moment, she fretted over Galen's struggle, seeing him as victim of another lie perpetuated by Captain Carrington. In the next, she wondered if her father really could have changed his plans so abruptly, plans he had obviously been building for over a decade. And she bled for Michael, the real victim in her father's twisted dealings. Then she would panic that he somehow thought *she* had done this to him, not the captain. That was followed by anger that he was so quick to judge her. If the last few months had meant *anything* to him, he would know she had not. But then again, why should he? The Carringtons had not exactly been paragons of truthfulness thus far.

And if he did not believe her? Abbey could not face that possibility.

"Did he say anything?" she asked, her voice trembling under the strain. Jones shook his head.

Abbey nodded dumbly. "Thank you, Jones," she muttered, and started slowly for the door. Her legs were leaden; she could scarcely make them move. But she could not and would not avoid him, no matter how much she feared him at the moment. When she reached the ground floor, she stopped in front of the closed oak door that led to his study, staring at it, trying to muster her courage. Several minutes and several deep breaths passed before she grasped the brass knob and pushed the door open.

She wanted to crumble when she saw Michael standing rigidly at the window, his back to her. She knew instinctively by his stance that he did not believe her. His hands were clasped firmly behind his narrow waist and his sinewy legs braced apart. She had a fleeting memory of the pictures she and her cousins would draw of the fearless captain standing at the helm of his ship. He did not turn.

"Why you did not tell me about your cousin?" Michael said, going directly to the point in a voice smooth as ice.

Abbey's hand fluttered instantly to her forehead, but she quickly dropped it and steeled herself. "He did not want to present himself until his circumstance had improved. He thought you would think ill of us."

"Of *us*?"

"He thought you would think ill of him for not having a proper situation, and me . . . he thought you would think ill of me because of him."

"So he asked you not to tell me of his existence?"

"For just a time," she murmured.

His shoulders tensed. "And you were merely honoring his request?" Although the tone of his voice was impersonal, almost casual, he still had not turned to face her.

"I—I did not see the harm."

"You did not see the harm in lying to me?"

Abbey's stomach flipped. "I did not lie to you. I just didn't tell you everything."

Michael said nothing. The silence seemed to create a huge

gulf between them, and Abbey was suddenly frantic to fill that void.

"I thought . . . I thought he would come to Blessing Park soon, with a post, a respectable post. He was quite embarrassed, not only for himself, but for me. He was afraid you would think he was trying to take advantage."

"Did it occur to you I might think he was taking advantage by virtue of sneaking around behind my back?"

Abbey faltered. Michael's voice was cool and even, and so detached she could not tell if he was angry or merely inconvenienced. "I thought . . . I guess I thought . . ." Her voice trailed off. Good God, what *had* she been thinking?

Michael slowly turned around. His face was devoid of any expression, except for his eyes, and they were burning. Abbey swallowed a surge of fear. "What did you think, Abbey? That I would receive the news about your cousin much better if he had a post? That I would forget you had lied to me? That I would readily accept his explanation for the sudden and improbable appearance of a second will?"

Abbey unintentionally shut her eyes. Her worst fear—that he would think she was part of her father's deception—filled every fiber. "On my honor, I did not know of the will. He said he was waiting for important news, but I did not know what it was. Like you, I thought my father's last testament was delivered to me in America."

"Are you being truthful with me now? Or shall I discover more facts you and this cousin of yours were ashamed to give me?"

"You cannot believe I had any knowledge of that second will, Michael," she heard herself say. She slowly opened her eyes to see a wickedly wry smirk twist his lips.

"Why not? Strange wills seem to follow you. If you are as blameless as you would have me believe, why did you not tell me about his letters or his visit?"

His accusatory tone sparked something inside her. Could he stand there before her and honestly believe she would betray him so completely? Did he think their lovemaking a lie? Was the day at the cove a lie? Was every day of the last three months a lie?

"I didn't tell you about his first letter because *you* had fled to Brighton," she snapped, "and as you made it quite clear you intended to live separately from me, I saw no point in boring you with the arrival of the second. As for his visit, I had no idea he was in Pemberheath and encountered him quite by chance. I might have told you then, but you had absented yourself for a *second* time without word to me!"

Michael's eyes narrowed dangerously. "Pemberheath? You had occasion to see him in Pemberheath?" he asked, clearly startled, but did not allow her to respond. "Putting aside, for the moment, that you were forbidden to go to Pemberheath without my express permission, you should have told me *immediately* of your encounter. I can't believe you could be so naive, Abbey. A distant cousin does not appear, unannounced, on the door of a wealthy young heiress without cause. Or perhaps you are not so naive. You did not seem surprised when he fired upon us."

"*Fired* upon us?" Abbey gasped with outrage. "How *dare* you impugn him?" she breathed angrily. "Galen would *never* harm anyone! As you don't know him, I do not see how you could possibly make such sweeping judgments!"

The sound of Michael's sardonic laughter ricocheted off the walls and hit her squarely in the face. "How terribly inappropriate of me. *My* one encounter with your beloved cousin was so that he could use a fraudulent document and demand five hundred thousand pounds from me! How silly of me to think anything amiss!"

Abbey turned abruptly so he would not see her painful confusion. He was right; it all seemed so wrong. But Galen had not defrauded him! He might be irresponsible, but he was *not* a thief! "I don't know *what* to think!" She moaned. "I am so . . . so . . ."

"So afraid? So exposed?"

"No!" she cried, turning to face him. "Astonished! Confused!"

"Astonished and confused. That hardly begins to describe

how I found this news, my sweet,'' Michael sneered, his voice dripping with sarcasm.

A dull sickness swept her. "Michael, he had things that belonged to my father! And as Papa had lied once before, I thought Galen was a victim, too!'' she pleaded with him. Didn't he understand how much she loved him? That she would rather die than hurt him?

"Michael, *please* . . .'' she said weakly, mortified that she sounded so guilty. "I can't explain it. All I know is that Mr. Strait sent the papers I expected. But when Galen showed me his, I did not think it wholly unbelievable that my father would change his mind at the last moment. I did not think it wholly unbelievable that he would have betrayed me a second time! Galen would not lie about this. He expected to be left a *ship*, not my dowry! He was as shocked as I!''

Michael clenched his jaw and cast a scathing glare at her. "I wonder how you thought you would secure the dowry after you were married,'' he said in a low, accusatory tone.

Desperate, she tried to think of something that would prove her innocence. "I told you once I would return to America if that was what you wanted, and you could have the money. I had every intention of leaving so that you could be free of me! Surely that proves that I had no part in it! Had it not been for that silly bet, I *would* have left! If this was some scheme, I would not have left!''

"You did not leave,'' he quietly reminded her.

Abbey inhaled sharply. God, how guilty he thought her. Devastated by what was happening, she took a step toward him. He stiffened. Her eyes darted helplessly about the room; she felt like a raving madwoman as she searched for something, anything that would show him she had not lied. How could she make him understand that she loved him with all her heart and would never do anything to hurt him? She walked forward to him and reached out to touch him, but he pulled away from her.

That single response killed her.

"I love you, Michael. I love you more than my own life,'' she heard herself whisper softly. The muscle in his jaw flexed.

"I would *never* do anything to hurt you, don't you know that? Do you honestly think everything we have been was a *lie*? That I have deceived you in your own house . . . in your *bed*?" she whispered.

Michael's jaw tightened. She thought for a moment that the hard glint in his eye softened, but through clenched teeth he muttered, "I do not know what to believe."

An involuntary cry of anguish escaped her, and she stumbled for a chair, praying she would not fall to her knees. Tears were beginning to seep from her eyes and an irrational shame engulfed her. "Michael!" she insisted hysterically. "Please, you must believe me!" He did not believe anything but her guilt, and she was breaking apart in front of him like the weakling she was. She forced herself to lift her head and look at him through wet lashes. The icy distance stretched between them; his face had a ghostly pall she took to be anger.

It was hopeless.

With what little pride she could muster, she straightened. "I won't beg you, Michael. I have never played you false, not once, and I swear to you on my father's grave I have not started now. If you believe everything we have is a lie, then so be it," she said evenly. "But I love you. I always have, and God save me, I always shall."

Michael said nothing. His cold, steady gaze did not waver from hers, and after several tense moments, Abbey bowed her head. It was over. This man felt nothing, and she could not bear it another moment. Dejected, she turned away from him and started unsteadily to the door.

"Abbey." The hoarseness in his voice betrayed his emotion. A surge of hope erupted within her, and she turned expectantly to face him. "Do not, under any circumstance, see him again."

With that, he very succinctly broke her heart. She whirled and ran to her room. She flung herself facedown upon the bed, and the tears she had held back now came forth in gut-wrenching torrents.

\*     \*     \*

Galen Carrey glanced at his pocket watch for the third time, then glanced up, peering through the thick fog that had begun to settle about the docks. He did not see the figure approaching from the right and stumbled backward when the red tip of a cheroot suddenly appeared in his peripheral vision.

"God, Routier, you startled me," he muttered irritably, and self-consciously straightened his neckcloth.

Routier ignored the remark. "What in the bloody hell are you waiting for?"

"I said I would give him a few days," Galen shot back.

Routier, disgusted, tossed his cheroot to the cobblestones, and ground it out with the heel of his boot.

He fisted his hands on his hips and glared at the younger man. "Look here, Carrey. From the moment I found you crying in your cups, I've taken the necessary steps to ensure your rightful inheritance is returned to you. I concocted the plan. I dealt with Strait. I retrieved those blasted articles for you to use. I am doing it for *you*. What the devil is wrong with you? You've hardly lifted a finger, and now you are balking!"

"I am *not* balking!" Galen loudly protested. "We cannot rush headlong into this, Routier. You know he is suspicious of me. We have to give him time to come to the realization that Carrington duped him."

"Right. And while you are giving him time, he is scouring all of London for Strait! Do you have any idea what that could mean? You must demand it of him!"

"Demand it? Do you think if I demand it, he will turn it over? God, Routier, you should know as well as anyone he will refuse such threats!"

"He won't. You have the documents as proof, and a court suit would threaten scandal. He can ill afford another one, and my guess is he will do what he must to avoid having his precious little marchioness subjected to the speculation of the entire *ton*," Routier said matter-of-factly.

At the mention of Abbey, Galen drew to his full height of six feet and glared at Routier. "I will not drag her into this any more than I already have, Routier!" he responded angrily.

Routier flashed an evil smile and leaned forward so that his face was only an inch or two from Galen's. "Then do as I tell you, Carrey. Look, the captain wronged you. He should have left you *something*. As his only male relative, you deserved the entire estate! Did you slave all those years on his ship to be tossed aside like a piece of garbage in the end? No! But I had to convince you to fight for what is rightfully yours! Now Darfield holds it, and he knows it. Are you a coward now? Are you going to let him get away with it?"

Galen shook his head weakly.

Routier relaxed a little. "Quit dawdling about then and go and demand what belongs to you. You can soothe your pretty cousin later."

Galen did not respond and regarded Routier with apprehensive dislike. Routier was right; he deserved his fair share of Carrington's estate. He had been the man's only living male relative, the son of his second cousin, and had served the captain faithfully for several years. Despite the rows he might have had with Carrington, he deserved something. Routier had helped him to see that when they had met, by chance, in Calais last summer.

But he had never meant to hurt Abbey. He had always been very fond of the lass, even more so upon seeing what a beauty she had become. Routier thought nothing of ruining her, as his motive went far deeper than the cut of the fortune he was promised. He practically spit venom at the mere mention of Darfield's name, and Galen feared he would ruthlessly use Abbey to get to Darfield and ruin him.

"If you are finding you are too weak for the task, Carrey, you can repay me the five thousand pounds you owe me, and we will go our separate ways," Routier said, interrupting his thoughts.

Galen's eyes narrowed. "I don't have five thousand pounds, sir, a fact you know very well."

Routier's smirk deepened. "Then you had best go and see Darfield, hadn't you?"

\*     \*     \*

The first thing Michael did was to move his things to a chamber as far away as he could get from those violet eyes that haunted him. The second thing he did was avoid her at all costs, refusing her one request to see him, and keeping odd hours so he would not risk running into her. The third thing he did was drink. A lot. But he could not drink enough to clarify in his mind her guilt or innocence.

For three days Michael waited, restlessly alternating between drinking and fitful sleep. On the morning Galen Carrey finally made an appearance, Michael was sprawled in an overstuffed chair in his study, staring at the mound of gowns for which he had paid a small fortune and a velvet box containing the amethyst jewelry he had given Abbey. She had returned the articles just that morning with a terse note saying they belonged to him.

The gowns and jewelry did not distress Michael. It was the violin case that lay next to the gowns. She had returned the instrument as one of the articles she claimed belonged to him. But it was a part of her, and it was impossible to imagine her without it. Just as it was impossible not to feel deep pangs of guilt and anger when he looked at the case.

When Galen Carrey was announced, Michael's anger gave way to white fury. He did not rise when the man was shown in.

"I had thought you would slither out from under your rock before now," Michael said dryly.

"I know this news is upsetting to you, my lord, and I had thought to give you some time to collect your thoughts," Carrey responded politely.

"Spare me your bloody platitudes. What do you want?"

Galen's faint smirk almost went unnoticed. "For both our sakes, I shall be blunt. As unpleasant as this is, surely you can understand my desire to collect from you what is rightfully mine."

"That's bloody well blunt, I'll give you that. But make no mistake, Carrey. I have *nothing* that belongs to you."

Galen's eyes narrowed slightly, and he shifted his weight onto one leg. "I beg to differ, my lord. The will I have shared with you is quite plain. You have my inheritance, and I respectfully request you return it at once.''

*God,* what a lying bastard he was, Michael thought angrily. ''You wouldn't be trying to extort a sizable sum from me, would you?''

''It is rather unfortunate that Captain Carrington chose to proceed as he did, but that hardly is of my doing. And you must not blame Abbey, either. She was quite unaware of the change.''

Michael smirked. Carrey was certainly quick to absolve Abbey. ''Was she?'' he asked sarcastically. ''It would seem to me that if anyone was unaware of the change, it was Carrington. It must greatly surprise you to know that he made sure a small fortune would be paid to her aunt the moment she was put aboard a ship bound for England. It must also surprise you to know that his associates and creditors would not have been paid had she not come here and married me. And no doubt it must astonish you to know that there was never a mention of any distant cousin who would be heir to her fortune,'' he said with a sneer.

One corner of Galen's mouth turned up in a mocking smile. ''I believe the papers I gave you clearly state those same things were to happen. The only change is the direction of his liquidated assets. In the will I brought you, there is mention of a cousin, sir.''

''How convenient. You miraculously appear *after* the captain's estate has been settled by marriage,'' Michael said.

Galen frowned at that. He paused to remove a small, white kerchief from his sleeve, and dabbed at the corners of his mouth before responding. ''My timing has nothing to do with the rightful settlement of the captain's estate. It has everything to do with a man's change of heart on his deathbed, my lord, I can assure you.''

''Um-hmm.'' Michael nodded. ''I wonder what prompted Carrington's change of heart? It wouldn't have been a pistol to his head, would it?''

Galen folded his arms across his chest and glared at Michael. "I take offense to that, sir! Men on their deathbeds change their minds all the time."

Michael almost laughed. "I've never heard of one changing his mind so drastically on his deathbed, Carrey. And how odd; I was given to understand by Mr. Strait's correspondence that as the end drew near, Carrington was rather adamant the estate be settled. Mr. Strait was quite clear that the goal was to have it done before he expired."

Galen's eyes flickered at the mention of Mr. Strait, and he shifted his weight unconsciously.

"How did you come across Carrington's personal articles?"

Galen's eyes slid to the mound of gowns. "They were delivered to me, with the second will."

"Who delivered them?" Michael asked quickly.

"A courier," Galen lied.

"And the doll?"

"The doll belonged to Abbey when she was a child. It was the captain's hope she would give it to her children," Galen patiently explained.

Michael slowly pushed himself to his feet. He walked to his desk and perched a hip on one corner, folded his arms across his chest, and brazenly considered Carrey. "Do you really expect me to believe that Carrington would have pressed this marriage if he intended to leave his estate to you? What possible motive would I have to marry his daughter without a dowry?"

Galen tossed his head indifferently. "Her dowry, my lord, was the elimination of your rather sizable debts. Did you think he would also *compensate* you?" He snorted sarcastically.

Michael bristled; a vein in his neck began to beat with the steady rise of his rage. "I'll tell you what I think, Carrey," he said in a dangerously low voice, "I think you and your *little one* concocted this scheme. I think the two of you determined you would have Carrington's wealth for your own. I think the two of you—with the help of a fraud of a solicitor—forged a will designed to force my hand and banked on the assumption that once we were wed, I would not divorce her in the face of scandal, and she would continue to live in the lap of luxury when you made your claim. Assuming, of course, you could not successfully kill me."

A cloud of bewilderment glanced Galen's features before he pressed his lips tightly together. "You may interpret it how you will, Darfield. But know that I will drag this through the courts if I must. Before you dismiss me out of hand, my suggestion is that you return what is mine. It is simpler for everyone and will invite far less talk for you and the marchioness than a lengthy court case!"

Michael laughed impertinently. "You sorely underestimate me, Carrey. I am not the least bit afraid of scandal, nor am I the least bit reluctant to divorce Carrington's daughter. And I will bloody well keep the Carrington fortune for my time and trouble."

Galen's face turned crimson. "This can *ruin* you," he hissed, slapping his gloves against his thigh for emphasis.

"I seriously doubt that," Michael said in return. "And I would think twice before threatening me, sir. You are a charlatan who deserves to be hanged, and believe me, I will see it done."

Galen paled. "Consider carefully what I am telling you, Darfield. The will has not been fully executed, and if I were to tie it up in the courts, Carrington's creditors will not be paid, and *that*, my friend, will fall on *your* head," he shot back.

"Get out of my house." Michael growled.

"You are a fool, Darfield!" Galen turned abruptly on his heel, almost colliding with a chair. He stormed to the door and jerked it open, then paused to look over his shoulder. "Your name will be dragged through the mud. *Again.*"

"Oh, I don't think so," Michael said calmly. "I'm quite certain I'll see you dead first.

Galen's lips pursed; he looked as if he would say more, but on second thought, he stalked from the room. Michael walked calmly to the door, shut it, and turned back to the pile of gowns. He lifted a blue one to his face and inhaled her scent, then dropped it and walked to the sideboard and the dozen decanters there.

\*    \*    \*

Galen cursed lightly under his breath as he strode down the hall. Routier was an absolute fool to think Darfield would roll over. That devil would not give into anyone's demands, Galen was quite sure of it. As he walked swiftly toward the foyer, he was startled by the opening of the library door. Abbey stood at the threshold, staring blankly at him.

She looked like death. Dark circles shadowed her dull, lifeless eyes. Her intrinsic sparkle was gone, doused. Her hair hung limply down her back, fastened at the nape of her neck with a leather tie. She wore a shapeless, plain brown gown and hugged a leather-bound book to her chest.

"My God," he breathed helplessly.

Abbey's stoic expression did not change. "I am forbidden to see you," she said flatly.

Glancing over his shoulder, Galen quickly stepped inside the library. Abbey made no effort to move, and he had to step around her to enter. The library was oppresively dark, and he went immediately to the windows and drew the drapes and blinds, then opened both windows. Abbey squinted painfully and turned away from the bright sunlight that poured into the room.

"Michael will be very angry if he finds you here," she said quietly.

"Dear God, Abbey, look at you!" he exclaimed.

Abbey shrugged and moved slowly toward an overstuffed armchair as if she carried some enormous weight. She dropped her book carelessly onto a table, then fell listlessly into the chair like a rag doll.

Alarm rifling through him, Galen demanded, "What has he done to you?" Abbey did not look at him, nor did she move a fraction of an inch. Suddenly frantic, Galen crossed the room in two angry strides and grabbed her by the elbow, jerking her upright with a force that surprised him. Abbey made no sound; her eyes were blank as they turned to him.

"What has he done? Does he starve you?" he barked, appalled by her complete apathy.

Abbey's gaze dropped to her lap. "What does it matter?"

Galen leaned over her. He gripped her chin and forced her drawn face upward so he could peer closely into her eyes. "*It matters.*"

Abbey's lifeless violet eyes flickered briefly, then slid away. Touched and disturbed by the devastation he saw there, Galen straightened slowly and pushed a hand through his hair. Darfield was a monster to have broken her spirit this way. But worse, far worse, was the realization that her devastation was of his own doing. Guilt soared in him, guilt he would do anything to quash.

"Bloody hell, I don't know what he's done, but you cannot go on like this!" She did not respond, did not acknowledge him. Galen inhaled sharply. "I never thought you a coward, Abbey."

Abbey's dull gaze flicked to her lap. "I am not a coward."

"You are acting like one," he interrupted. With his hands on his hips, he looked disdainfully down the length of his nose. "He accuses you of unspeakable crimes you did not commit. And you respond like this?"

She grimaced and pushed herself off the chair, moving sluggishly toward the bank of windows. "Pray tell, how should I deport myself? Should I pretend that everything is the same as it was four days ago?" she asked with her back to him.

"You should act like the innocent you are, an innocent wronged," he snapped.

Abbey's spine stiffened. "What would you suggest? That I put on my finest and gad about town as if everything is quite ordinary?" she asked angrily.

"I suggest *precisely* that," Galen said emphatically, his anger with Darfield spiraling out of control.

At the window, Abbey glanced skeptically over her shoulder. "You must be out of your mind."

Her profile against the bright sunlight was a poignant as any work of art he had ever seen. Her pale skin, shadowed by the light, made her torment clearly visible, a torment borne of a broken heart. He winced at the deep, painful stab of guilt.

"Has he touched you?" he asked quietly, angrily.

Abbey choked on a bitter laugh. *"No."*

"I will not allow this. I will not allow him to intimidate you like this!" Galen said hoarsely, moving to close the gap between them. She was fighting valiantly to keep the tears at bay, and her whole body quivered from the effort. He reached out and touched her shoulder.

Choking on a sob, Abbey lost her control. A torrent of tears burst from her, and she doubled over. Galen caught her and wrapped his arms around her. Cupping the back of her head, he eased her face into his chest as sobs racked her thin frame. Abbey clutched forlornly at the lapels of his coat and cried as if her heart would break. He held her protectively in his arms, swallowing bitter lumps of emotion until her tears at last began to subside and her grip on him began to ease.

"Abbey, little one," he whispered, "I am so very sorry. I never meant to cause you any harm, you must believe me."

A single tear rolled down her cheek, and she swallowed hard. "You did not cause me harm, Galen, Papa did. But do not be sorry—I am glad I know what Michael is," she muttered unconvincingly. "No more. I will not cry one more tear for him." She hiccuped.

"Good," Galen said soothingly.

"No, I mean it, Galen! He did not even *attempt* to believe me! He doesn't even know you, yet he instantly assumed you are evil! And dear God, you would not believe the incredible speed with which he concluded that I had lied! I deserve *some* consideration, don't I?" she demanded against his neckcloth.

"Indeed you do," he readily agreed.

"I should be *insulted*! I have never given him *any* reason to doubt me!"

"I know you have not, little one," Galen said, heartened by the spirit beginning to emerge.

Abbey suddenly pushed back from him and wiped her nose with the back of her hand. "Why should *I* stay holed up in this godforsaken house? I've done nothing wrong!"

"If you stay holed up like this, pining away, he will think you *do* have something to hide," Galen encouraged her.

Abbey's brows snapped together. "I have *nothing* to hide," she said vehemently, but her angry frown quickly turned to helpless wonder. "But what am I to do?" she asked forlornly.

Galen guided her to a chair. "You did nothing wrong, regardless of what *he* believes. It would seem to me that you should carry on. Let *him* bear the burden of his faithlessness," he suggested confidently.

"What do you mean?"

"You should go out into society as you have every right to do."

Abbey's brows knitted together as she considered that. "Go out?" she asked hesitantly. "But I cannot go out alone, can I?"

"I will escort you," Galen said, lifting his chin.

Abbey looked frightened by the mere suggestion and hesitantly shook her head. "I do not think that's a good idea . . . I mean, I am not allowed to see you."

"Lord, Abbey, will you allow him to control you so completely? Will you allow him to forbid contact with your own kin? Does he tell you when you may eat and sleep? Are you a *prisoner* here?" Galen demanded.

Abbey's eyes narrowed, flashing a brilliant shade of violet. "No, I am *not* his prisoner!" She leaned back against the cushions, considering the pattern on the arm very thoughtfully.

Galen looked nervously at the door. Darfield would kill him if he found him in there. He turned back to his cousin, going down on his haunches next to her chair. "Abbey, I must go before he discovers us. Harrison Green is having one of his infamous routs this evening," he suggested impetuously. "Meet me at the park, eight o'clock. Will you meet me there?"

Abbey did not lift her gaze from the arm of the chair for a long moment, but slowly, uncertainly, nodded her head. "I will," she murmured. "I will meet you. He cannot keep me prisoner—the king's *army* cannot stop me!" With that less than hearty avowal, she glanced up, smiling tremulously at her cousin.

# Chapter 17

Harrison Green was the untitled nephew of an influential duke who had gained a reputation among the *ton* for throwing the bawdiest of routs. The number of people in attendance that night attested to the immense popularity of his affairs. Abbey was acutely aware of the stares in her direction as she and Galen pushed through the throng. Tension began to knot in her stomach as her eyes swept the crush. She shuddered to think what Michael would do if her found her here with Galen. Even though they lived in the same house—at least she thought they did—she had not seen him since their altercation in the drawing room, but she knew the Black Plague went out every night.

*"Lady Darfield!"* The cheerful voice belonged to Lady Delacorte, who was pushing unceremoniously through the crowd, dragging her husband behind.

"Madam, what a pleasure to see you! Oh, I had so hoped you'd be able to attend our little gathering last evening," she said as she reached Abbey.

Abbey's eyes flew wide upon realizing she had forgotten the invitation. "Lady Delacorte, I am so sorry! You must

forgive me for being so rude!'' Abbey cried in genuine horror
at her faux pas. Lady Delacorte arched a penciled brow.

"Please, my dear, there is no need for an apology! Lord
Darfield explained the entire situation quite clearly," the
woman smiled. Abbey froze. Surely Michael had not publicly
derided her, surely not.

"The entire situation?" she asked weakly.

"What my wife means is that Lord Darfield explained you
had unfortunately discovered a previously unknown allergy to
shellfish, madam," Lord Delacorte said, politely lifting her
hand to his mouth. Her relief was great; Michael had not yet
denigrated her, at least not to the Delacortes.

"Shellfish. Quite so, I'm afraid," she murmured.

"Oh, he is *such* a charming man! We met him at the buffet
just moments ago—odd, but he did not mention you had
come."

So he was here. There was no escaping it; the slim hope she
had harbored that she would not see him this evening had
been dashed before she had barely stepped foot into the house.
Abbey forced a faint smile. "Ah, well, he does not
know . . ."

"What my dear cousin means to say is that she thought she
would be waiting at home for my late arrival, madam. As I am
a bit early, we had hoped to surprise the marquis," Galen
said, bowing low.

"Yes, that's it!" Abbey said nervously. "May I present my
cousin, Mr. Galen Carrey?"

"What fun, a cousin!" a voice boomed behind them. A
very rotund fellow dressed in a peacock-blue satin coat moved
unsteadily toward the small group.

"Lady Darfield, Mr. Harrison Green," Lord Delacorte intoned. Green's beady blue eyes lit up, and he clumsily
switched his glass of champagne to his left hand so he could
greet her properly. Abbey gently pulled her hand away from
his thick, wet lips.

"Mr. Green," she said demurely.

"Lady Darfield, what a tremendous pleasure. Your reputation precedes you, indeed it does, but it does not do you

justice," he said. Once again Abbey started. What did he mean by that? Had he heard something about her?

"I beg your pardon?" she asked, fully expecting the slightly drunken man to say Michael had accused her of lying.

"Forgive me, madam. They say you are a true beauty, but I think that does not begin to describe—"

"Before you begin to describe, sir, please remember she is the wife of the Marquis of Darfield," Galen bluntly interjected.

Green's bushy brows rose in feigned affront. "Of course she is, my good fellow, but can't a man admire?" he asked, pausing to stifle a drunken belch. "You need not be so protective, for I can assure you, Darfield will not let me forget to whom she belongs!"

"Oh no, he is quite proud of his treasure," Lady Delacorte agreed as Green slurped his champagne loudly. A slow blush crept into Abbey's cheeks. How would she ever live through this charade? She glanced helplessly at Galen, who smiled reassuringly.

"If you will excuse us, I promised to see Lady Darfield directly to her husband."

"Of course. We'll chat later, my dear," Lady Delacorte said.

"Oh, yes, let's do just that," said Green, who then tottered off to replace his empty glass. Abbey nodded graciously to the Delacortes and gratefully obeyed Galen's grip on her elbow.

"Don't fret," Galen muttered, pausing to acquire two glasses of champagne. "There must be five hundred people here. We can easily avoid him." Abbey strongly doubted that. She followed Galen into the ballroom, wondering what had possessed her to so brazenly risk Michael's considerable wrath.

Her anxiety was only heightened in the ballroom. She could feel everyone's eyes upon her. Nervously she smoothed a strand of hair from her face and tried vainly to keep her attention on her glass to avoid making eye contact with anyone. She was incredibly self-conscious of her gown and hair; she felt as if she were in a cage, on display for the entire *ton* to see. What were they thinking? Did they know about the rift between her and Michael? Did they eye her with disdain or mere curiosity?

She was studying the tips of her toes when her brain registered a conversation occurring nearby. The silky voice of a woman was saying, "Michael never did care much for the Season, you know. I had to practically drag him to Harrison's rout last fall." Every muscle in Abbey's body knotted. There were dozens, probably hundreds of Michaels in England alone. It was a coincidence. "He certainly prefers the quiet of the countryside. He emphasized as much to me a few weeks ago at my country house near Blessing Park."

Abbey jerked her head up and died a silent death. Lady Rebecca Davenport was standing a few feet away with two other women, dressed in a shimmering pale-yellow gown. Silvery white curls graced her crown, and she was openly looking at Abbey with a smile of superiority on her very pretty face. Stunned, Abbey realized she had been meant to overhear the exchange. But that was not nearly as stunning as the realization Michael had gone to *her* when he had disappeared from Blessing Park. Her stomach sank—how dare he accuse her of betrayal! A pain ripped through her that left her shaking. The Malevolent Marquis talked from both sides of his mouth! He had *lain* with that beautiful blond goddess while she was dreaming of him!

That *bastard!*

Dismayed, Abbey turned her back to the blonde. God forgive her, but she would have liked to strike the smug smile from that woman's face.

"This was a *horrible* idea," she muttered to Galen.

"Would you prefer another solitary supper in your rooms?" Galen responded. "Smile. Try not to look so distressed." He took the champagne from her hand. "I will get you a fresh drink." He slipped away. Abbey tried to do what he said. Her smile was frozen; she was miserably self-conscious and was so engrossed in her efforts to look perfectly normal that she did not hear *him* approach and had to catch a colonnade for support when he spoke.

"Your judgment is grossly impaired, madam," Michael said coolly. Determination suddenly failed her, and Abbey squeezed her eyes shut, summoning her strength. She would very much liked to have run and avoid looking at those gray eyes, but caught between him and the dance floor, she had no escape. With every ounce of courage she had, she turned toward him. He was standing so close that she almost collided with his brick wall of a chest.

The faint smell of his cologne drifted over her. She unthinkingly inhaled; dressed in black, he was undoubtedly the most handsome man in the entire room. Her knees started to quiver, and she slowly lifted her gaze past the white satin neckcloth, firm chin, the dark rose lips set in an implacable line, and his eyes. Beneath the dark curl that draped his forehead, he stared down at her with eyes of cold, hard granite. Abbey's stomach fluttered. It seemed as if she could do nothing but stare dumbly.

His eyes narrowed; he took a step closer, almost touching her. "How dare you defy me. I should drag you from here and lock you away at Blessing Park for disobeying me." His voice was silky, contradicting the deadliness of his expression.

His arm came up, trapping her against the colonnade. Nothing had prepared her for this. She had convinced herself she was angry with him and despised him for his inconstancy. Lady Davenport's contrived confession certainly had not endeared him to her. But the sight of him quite literally took her breath away. There was no denying how much she loved him, nor how it destroyed her to see the cold distance in his eyes. She stubbornly lifted her chin.

"You cannot keep me a prisoner, Michael. I have done nothing wrong." She sounded terribly weak and unsure.

"I beg to differ. You lied to me. You disobeyed me. And now you push my patience to its limits." His gray eyes flashed with pure loathing. It was more than she could bear, and she abruptly turned away.

Michael leaned forward and whispered in her ear, "What's the matter, darling? Can't look me in the eye?"

Abbey folded her arms protectively across her middle and turned her head slightly, away from him. "I prefer not to. What I see there sickens me," she answered softly.

"It sickens *you*?" he asked testily.

"If you had granted an audience when I requested, I would have been more than happy to answer your unfounded accusations. And then, perhaps, you could have answered a few of mine. But I hardly think this is the place, Michael. I would ask that you just leave me be," she whispered hoarsely.

"Leave her, Darfield!" Galen's voice shattered the tension between them. Gripping two flutes of champagne, he glared at Michael. A muscle in Michael's jaw flinched and he slid his granite gaze back to Abbey, locking with hers, piercing through to her very soul, silenty accusing her.

"I fully intend to," he retorted caustically, and, with a scathing glance for Galen, walked away. Abbey exhaled slowly. Why hadn't she gone straight back to America when she had first learned of her father's lie? Why had she allowed herself to fall so hopelessly in love with him?

She slowly became aware of Galen's soft voice. "Little one," he was saying, "drink your champagne. He won't bother you again, he will not risk a scene here. Listen, I am going to the gaming room. It will be easier if I am not with you. Come now, drink your champagne. Don't let him ruin this evening for you. Relax and enjoy yourself."

She nodded dumbly, unable to speak, her eyes riveted to the floor. Galen grabbed her hand and squeezed it before disappearing into the crowd. Standing alone at the edge of the dance floor with dozens of eyes on her, Abbey waged a battle against a tide of emotion that threatened to sweep her under.

Across the room, Michael sipped his champagne, languidly gazing at his wife. He should have left her alone, but he could not deny himself the chance to be near her, to inhale her sweet scent. As much as he distrusted her at the moment, he also missed her terribly. To him, it was nothing short of miraculous that a woman could affect him so, but he had no idea how much until he had seen her on Galen's arm. Bloody hell, she looked forlorn. And thin. But he had seen her look that way before, and for all he knew, it was part of her act. She had disobeyed him, had flouted his doubts in his face by coming here with Galen. God, but he ached with uncertainty.

Daniel Strickland, a rake renowned for his attraction to married women and, moreover, his success with them, strutted over to her and bowed very gallantly over her hand. Michael tensed. Bloody hell, he had never known how excruciating it could be to watch other men fawn over his wife. His chest tightened with jealousy as he watched Strickland lead her to the dance floor. Abbey glided on Strickland's arm, her dancing effortless. Good God, how long before his men found Strait? Carrington's solicitor was the one person who held the key to her innocence.

Or her guilt.

Michael remained rooted to his post at the column as he watched man after man escort Abbey onto the dance floor. He made polite but contrived conversation with those who braved his dark look. No one who approached stayed at his side long; it was clear that he was in no mood for light banter. After a while, the whispers about him grew to an almost fevered pitch as Harrison Green's guests watched the Devil of Darfield watch his wife. If the *ton* had not noticed the rift between them before, they certainly did now.

As he could not bear to see another man touch her, Michael had all but decided to leave, when Routier's tall, lanky figure stepped through the arched entry of the ballroom. Spotting Abbey, the villain glanced furtively about the crowded room. Michael suspected it was in search of him, and moved into the shadows. After scanning the room for several moments, Routier, with a decided smirk on his face, strolled casually to the far side of the room where Abbey was standing. Michael quietly finished off the glass of champagne he had been nursing for the last half hour.

\*     \*     \*

Abbey was escorted from the dance floor by a man who smelled to high heaven under his heavy coat. She made a polite excuse of needing the retiring room and, moving quickly away from the dance floor, did not notice Malcolm Routier until he spoke.

"Good evening, Lady Darfield."

Startled, Abbey lurched, glancing up at Routier. "Mr. Routier," she said coolly.

"I was hoping to find you . . ."

"I prefer not to dance, sir," she said weakly.

Routier's thin brow elevated slightly. "Forgive me, madam, but I think it is customary for a lady to bruise a man's tender ego *after* she has been invited to stand up."

Abbey winced at her unforgivable gaffe. "Oh, dear God, how perfectly horrid of me! Please accept my apology—I was not thinking," she said lamely.

"I took no offense." He smiled charmingly. The champagne she had been quaffing all evening had dulled her senses. It was mildly alarming to forget words, but the numbing effect it had on her was worth the discomfort. And in the fog that surrounded her, she thought that Routier actually seemed a very nice man.

"I received the cut direct once before. A Belgian lass did the honors," he was saying.

Her tension soared, making her light-headed. She put a hand to her temple. "Does that signify, sir?"

Routier smiled and bowed slightly. "I was making a jest. Apparently, not a very good one," he said gallantly.

Abbey silently scolded herself. He was being rather pleasant and did not deserve her biting remarks. She forced herself to smile; Routier's yellow eyes slipped to her mouth.

"Madam," he said roughly, "you are in the possession of a most extraordinary smile." His charm befuddled her, made her dizziness increase. The floral print on the wall behind Routier seemed to shift.

"Is something wrong?" he asked with genuine concern. The print began to swim, and Abbey tried to focus on the shoulder of his black coat.

"I am not feeling well," she murmured, concentrating on keeping her roiling stomach from worsening.

"Shall I get Lord Darfield for you?"

*"No!"* she all but shouted, then immediately brought a hand to her mouth. It was suddenly sweltering in the ballroom. "I mean, he is indisposed at the moment. I think I shall step outside. I could use some air—"

"Let me help you," Routier said, and moved hastily to lead her to the doors opening onto the balcony.

The cool night air rushed up from the garden and hit her face, and she immediately felt better. Gripping the railing, Abbey bent over the balcony and took deep gulps of air.

"Are you quite all right, Lady Darfield? Perhaps I should send for Lord Darfield?" Routier asked anxiously.

Abbey shook her head and took a deliberately deep breath. Leaning backward, she slowly exhaled. "I am really feeling much better, Mr. Routier." The cool air was helping considerably, and the queasiness was beginning to abate. She glanced at her companion, who looked genuinely concerned.

"Thank you for helping me," she said sheepishly. His yellow eyes flickered as he nodded politely. "So you have been to Brussels?"

Surprised, he nodded. "Yes, have you?"

"Some years ago," she said, taking a steadying breath. "I didn't see much of it, really. My father was quite protective." A memory came to her, the first one she had had in some time that did not pain her, and she smiled shyly.

"Was he indeed?" Routier asked softly.

"He certainly was. We spent an entire winter in Brussels with him constantly threatening to lock me in the hull of his ship. I never understood why he was so flustered; he would hardly let me leave the house," she said, recalling a terrible row she had had with the captain one day when he would not let her accompany two friends to a fashionable milliner's shop. *Absolutely not. There are pirates out there who would take one look at you and snatch you from the street!* he had said. *Papa, you read too many novels! What a perfectly absurd notion! Why on earth would they snatch me?* she had shouted in frustration. He had not responded, but had given her an obscure look and had pointed upstairs, indicating she was to return to her room. *I hate you!* she had screamed as she had run up the stairs, and had proceeded to lock herself in her room for the rest of the day.

"Were you my daughter, I believe I should have been tempted to do the same." Routier chuckled.

Abbey smiled. "How long did you know my father?"

"Many years."

"Were you friends?"

"We were business associates. I suppose we were friendly, but I never considered us friends per se," Routier said thoughtfully.

Abbey turned and settled her hips against the railing, watching the dancers through a pane-glass window. "I still miss him dreadfully," she said wistfully.

It was true—despite his betrayal, she missed him. Had missed him excessively in the last four days, which she thought rather odd, given that he was the cause of her misery.

"He was a big man, with a great crop of thick white hair and beard. I used to tease him that his beard was scraggly. It always infuriated him. He was quite proud of it," Routier remarked.

"*Very* proud. He always said you could judge a man by the strength of his whiskers," Abbey agreed.

"Then I would say he was a *very* strong man." Routier laughed. He watched admiringly as Abbey pushed away from the railing and walked slowly to a large potted evergreen. "I suspect you are, too."

Abbey flashed a smile over her shoulder. "I don't know. I don't feel very strong sometimes."

"I think you are quite strong," he said, straightening, and came to stand behind her at the window.

Abbey absently surveyed the room through the mullioned window, unwillingly compelled to find Michael. It was a stupid thing to have done, because she spotted him, all right, with Rebecca Davenport. The blond goddess was smiling up at him as if they shared a delicious secret. Michael's face was obscured, but he was standing close to her, and Abbey's pulse quickened with anger. He had betrayed her. Blatantly, easily, and very thoroughly. Seeing him so obviously engaged with his lover was humiliating.

"Lady Davenport is persistent, is she not?" Routier sighed.

No, Abbey thought bitterly, *Michael* was persistent. In that moment, she hated him.

"But then again, some liaisons are hard to sever." Routier added, and turned away, moving to the balcony railing.

*Apparently*. Anger coursed through Abbey's veins; how dare he question her about Galen when he was involved in his own, adulterous assignation? She raised her chin.

"Were you ever in Rome, Mr. Routier? I think Mr. Green has fashioned his ballroom after the Coliseum there, don't you think?" she asked.

Routier smiled at her transparent attempt to change the subject, but graciously went along with it. He chatted about the great Roman ruins and then began to enlighten her as to the Greek influence in the room. Abbey listened politely but found herself trying to snatch glimpses of Michael. He had disappeared from view, but Lady Davenport remained. The smug smile had faded from her lips, but seeing her standing there, so very beautiful, caused Abbey's head and stomach to protest violently. She closed her eyes and concentrated on keeping the nausea at bay. Tiny beads of perspiration erupted on her forehead and the color drained rapidly from her face.

"Good Lord, Lady Darfield, you have grown quite pale. Are you ill?" Routier demanded in the middle of his oration on Greek architecture.

"It's nothing, I am certain. Perhaps too much champagne," she whispered thickly, and swallowed hard past her nausea. Routier was quickly at her side, drawing her away from the window. Abbey stumbled toward the railing, horrified at the nausea that threatened to erupt. How embarrassing and absurd, she thought dumbly, that vomiting on Mr. Routier's shoes would be such a perfect end to a perfect evening. She inhaled sharply.

Routier placed his hand on the small of her back and leaned

over to peer into her face. "I am quite concerned, Lady Darfield—"

"No, please don't be. I will be all right," she whispered. Thankfully, her sudden rush of nausea was subsiding almost as quickly as it had come on her. She drew another deep breath.

Routier's hand moved up her back, resting between her shoulder blades. "Shall I fetch you some water?"

"No—I think if I stand still for a moment, I shall be quite all right," she said shakily. She blinked several times against the sway of the garden until the shrubbery finally stilled.

Routier bowed over her, anxiously watching her face.

She turned slightly and gave him a weak, reassuring smile. "I am quite all right, truly."

"Can't say I've ever made a lady ill with my company," he joked, "at least not that I am aware." Abbey laughed despite her nausea.

From the shadows of the balcony, Michael watched Routier and Abbey. The sight of Routier's hand on her back made his pulse pound furiously in his neck. With his hands opening and closing at his sides, he ground his teeth when Abbey's soft laugh wafted over his head. She was actually enjoying the bloody scoundrel's company!

At that precise moment, he believed he would rather give in to Carrey's fraudulent demands than allow Routier to touch his wife. He somehow forced himself further into the shadows and chided himself for losing control. He fought the desire to strangle Routier when Abbey's tingling laugh once again drifted upward. Of all the men she could have befriended, she had to choose Routier. It was a goddammed slap in his face. They looked like two lovers standing out there in the moonlight, and by God, it should be him standing with her. With anger spiraling out of control, Michael impulsively stepped from the shadows.

"*Abbey!*" he barked, surprised at the strangled tenor of his voice.

Abbey whirled around, her face falling instantly.

"What in the hell do you think you are doing?" he bit out.

"Your wife was ill, Darfield. Since you were otherwise engaged, I escorted her outside to take some air," Routier offered blandly.

"She does not seem ill to me." he said nastily. Abbey's dark brows snapped together in a scathing glare, and she actually turned her back on him. Michael clenched his fists.

"If you do not mind, Routier, I would like a word with my wife," he ground out. Routier did not step away from her, which Michael angrily considered was cause enough to call the bastard out.

"I will not go unless Lady Darfield requests it of me." Routier said behind a challenging smirk

Abbey turned: her gaze locked with Michael's. Her violet eyes were no longer dull—they were filled with fury. "I am sorry my husband is behaving so rudely. Mr. Routier, but he has been *quite* ill-humored as of late. If you would be so kind to excuse us," she said angrily.

Routier flicked a satisfied gaze to Michael. "As the lady wishes," he said almost cheerfully. "I have enjoyed our conversation, Lady Darfield. When you are feeling better, I shall look forward to the opportunity to stand up with you," he said with a bow.

"That would be lovely, Mr. Routier." Abbey smiled. In a supreme act of self-control, Michael managed to keep his expression neutral. Routier sneered triumphantly and casually strolled past him, across the balcony, and disappeared inside.

Michael's fists found his waist, and with arms akimbo and feet braced apart, he turned to glare at his beautiful wife. Astonishingly enough, his emotions warred between wanting to give her a sound thrashing and to take her in his arms and kiss any thought of Routier from her head. But all emotion quickly flew from his mind when she raised her chin a notch and began impatiently tapping her foot against the stone floor.

"Am I keeping you from your dance card?" he asked coldly.

"As a matter of fact, you are."

"Is that so? I recall a few short days ago when you did not care to dance with anyone else," he said snidely.

Abbey's eyes widened, then narrowed with anger. "That was *before* my faithless husband assumed my duplicity in some horrible, but purely imagined, dastardly deed," she snapped.

Michael took several steps forward, glaring at her. "And now?"

"*Now?* I would rather dance with *everyone else* but you!"

"I think you are well on your away to achieving just that," Michael retorted.

Abbey glowered at him; her fingers drummed furiously against her upper arm. "You have certainly shown yourself for what you truly are!" she grumbled.

"*I* have shown myself? Oh, madam, that is rich. The proverbial pot calls the kettle black!"

"I have done nothing wrong, Michael Ingram! If you are so pig-headed to believe that I have, that is your worry, not mine! I will not be locked away like some convicted criminal because *you* are faithless!" she fairly shouted. Despite her sure voice, her eyes gave her away, as they always did.

Michael swept in for the kill. "I don't give a damn what you think, Abbey. But heed me—if you cuckold me, I will rip your black heart from your breast and feed it to my dogs."

Abbey gasped with shock; then something sparked deep in those violet eyes. "*You son of a bitch,*" she breathed as he walked toward her.

He ignored her very unladylike curse. "I mean it, Abbey. Don't you dare cuckold me," he said low.

"My God, how easily you speak from both sides of your mouth! While you share your bed with Lady Davenport, you *dare* lecture me about fidelity?" she fairly shrieked.

That took him slightly aback, but he was too angry to retreat. "I think you forget yourself, *wife*. It is hardly your concern *what* I do with Lady Davenport, or any other woman, for that matter! I am the one who has been betrayed time and time again, not *you*."

That did it. Whatever Abbey may have felt when he first

appeared at her side this evening was plainly gone. He had never seen such outrage in anyone, and had she been a man, he might have feared for his life. Abbey's luscious lips clamped firmly together, her brows formed a dark vee above her eyes, and her eyes, God help him, her eyes said everything. She stepped forward and shoved forcefully against his chest before marching toward the door, muttering another oath that would have had the *ton* on its ear.

"Do not let me find you with Routier again, do you understand me?" Michael called after her. She stopped abruptly and, with her hands fisted at her sides, turned slowly to face him. Michael casually clasped his hands behind his back and stood nonchalantly, watching the fire sparkle in her eyes. She began to march back to him. He waited patiently until she was only inches from him.

The flash of her arm caught him by surprise as did the very strong punch in the mouth. The force of her blow propelled her off her feet, and she leapt to the side, shrieking softly and waving her hand in the air. The impact staggered Michael into the railing. Stunned, he brought his fingers to the corner of his mouth and probed gingerly. A small rivulet of blood had erupted where her ring had made contact with his lip and was tracing a slow path down his chin. The little hellion had actually socked him in the mouth! He could not help himself; he grinned broadly.

Abbey's surprise and anger at his reaction flashed across her face. This time he instantly recognized the sign of danger, but could not act quickly enough. She grabbed her skirt, and, with her very shapely and slender leg, she kicked him—hard—in the shin before whirling and fleeing the balcony. Michael grabbed his leg and rubbed swiftly to erase the pain, then withdrew a handkerchief from his pocket and dabbed at the blood on his mouth. When he looked down at the specks of blood on the white linen, he could no longer contain the absurd glee that was bubbling in his chest. He roared with mad laughter.

Bloody hell, he could not help loving that chit, and Jesus, she had a nasty right upper cut.

# Chapter 18

Rumors spread like fire through the *ton* about the rift between the Marquis and Marchioness of Darfield. In tearooms and drawing rooms across Mayfair, speculation was rife. No one could leave the tempting story of the Darfields alone—a dark man with an even darker past, suddenly married to a beauty who had seemingly appeared from nowhere. A glorious introduction to society, followed swiftly by an arcane falling out. Many who had witnessed the exchange between Lady Davenport and Lady Darfield at Harrison Green's believed Michael's lover was to blame. Still others hypothesized that the American woman had displayed a wanton side the marquis could not abide. By all standards, the Darfield story was better than the most popular novels currently circulating, and in the quest to feed the *ton*'s insatiable appetite for gossip, both Michael and Abbey were inundated with invitations to soirées, routs, balls, and supper parties.

After the Harrison Green affair, Galen told Abbey he did not think it wise to escort her again, given Darfield's appalling anger. Abbey had reluctantly agreed, but determined not to be put away while Michael dallied with his lover, she found Lord

Southerland to be a willing escort. Her anger had catapulted to the level of all-consuming fury, and the marchioness attended as many events as she could. The only course she had to escape the pain of it all was to submerge herself in the whirl of society. At least at those insufferable events, she was distracted from thoughts of him for the space of a few hours.

Well, almost. He was never far from her mind and, much to her chagrin, never far from her side. It seemed he attended every event she did, practically flaunting his disdain in her face by amusing himself with different women.

It angered and hurt her; she retaliated by dancing often and with as many partners as she could. If Michael noticed, he gave no sign. He blatantly ignored her for the most part, and if their paths did accidentally cross, he was extremely terse and distant. He made a practice of addressing his curt remarks to her escort, acting as if she did not exist. If he did speak to her, it was to make some coarse remark. Abbey replied hotly with such sharp retorts as "Let me be," or the equally stinging "Go away." She simply could not seem to find her tongue when he was near.

As furiously angry as she was, she could not help thinking Michael reminded her of a caged bird that had been freed. He flew about the room, from attraction to attraction.

Obviously she had been his cage.

She began to second guess herself. Had she imagined everything that had happened between them? Had she been so in love with him that she had attributed feelings to him that he did not have? When he finally realized the truth, would he want her back? She could not believe he would, given how he avoided her at all costs. But dear God, after all that had happened, she still wanted him. She could not stop loving him, no matter how desperately hard she tried. Even the rather daunting prospect of Lady Davenport did not quell her love.

Her dismay turned to abject misery when she began to suspect she was pregnant. She had never been terribly regular, but after forty-five days or more without her courses and bouts of extreme fatigue she could no longer deny it. Her pregnancy set her adrift on a sea of uncontrollable emotions. One minute she was elated about the prospect of bearing a child, *his* child. The very next minute her spirits plummeted. He did not want her; would he want this child? At night, she tossed and turned, unable to sleep from desperation about her predicament or because she so missed his arms around her. God, how she longed to talk to her aunt! There was no one she could trust as she did her aunt and cousins, no one she could talk to about her situation.

So she struggled with her warring emotions alone.


Michael attended the same affairs as Abbey, unsure as to why and unwilling to debate the issue with himself. He abhorred them; whatever his peers thought was happening between him and his wife did not deter other women from seeking his attention. In another time he might have found it amusing, but he utterly despised their inane chatter and obvious motives.

Abbey certainly seemed to enjoy the intolerable events. After watching her over the course of several nights, he thought it seemed too easy for her. She seemed to fall to a man's charms effortlessly, laughing gaily at their remarks and gracing every blasted one of them with that devastating smile. She was the one who had professed great love for him. If that were so, why wasn't she suffering as he was? When he listened to her melodious and carefree laughter, he could honestly believe that she *did* have some part in Carrey's fraud.

And it was surprisingly painful to think she had dismissed him so easily. Despite the fact that her eyes still seemed oddly vacant to him, he found himself wondering from time to time if she was the consummate actress a scheme such as this required. He envied Sam, who had come to the miraculous conclusion that she was innocent. He based his conclusion on nothing and everything. Michael wished he could be so sure.

It was Withers who gave him the most pause. The old sailor had confessed to Michael that he had seen his mistress give Carrey money, yet he firmly believed she had acted from the goodness of her heart. The stoic bear of a man had been adamant that it was impossible for Lady Darfield to be anything but guileless. Why couldn't *he* believe that? Because when he had given her the chance, she had chosen to take Galen's side and had lied to him. It was all so simple: He loved her. She had lied to him. He could not trust her.

Doubts consumed him. He roamed the spacious town house at odd hours, hardly eating or sleeping. He kept her violin on his desk in the study, and on occasion, he would lift the instrument from its case and examine the bow while he imagined her delicate fingers holding it, moving it across the strings. In those moments, he could almost *hear* her. More than one night he was haunted by the image of her strolling about his room, playing with her imaginary orchestra, and evoking a depth of emotion in him that made him shiver.

God, he missed her.

When Sam came by the morning of the Wilmington Ball, he found Michael studying the violin again.

"Bow Street has uncovered some interesting news," he announced dryly as he entered the library, dispensing with the usual pleasantries and dropping into a leather chair. Michael slowly put the violin away.

"Strait seems to have disappeared without a trace," Sam continued.

Michael's interest was immediately piqued. "How could that be? Perhaps he is on the continent?"

"Could be, but personally, I doubt it. According to the man's spinster niece who keeps his house, a Mr. Malcolm Routier was one of the last men she saw him with shortly before he disappeared," Sam said as he casually crossed one leg over the other.

Michael was still. That tiny piece of news confirmed his suspicions—Routier was behind this.

"I know what you are thinking," Sam remarked, reading Michael's expression. "It was not, apparently, out of the ordinary for Routier to call. He had engaged Strait's services from time to time."

Michael leaned forward on his desk and rubbed his temples. "He could be his bloody brother for all I care. Routier is behind it," he said patiently. "I had a message from Carrey this morning requesting an audience this afternoon. I shall inquire of the *cousin* just how unusual it might have been for Routier to call on Strait. And if he might have a notion where Strait is.''

A chambermaid, responding to Abbey's inquiry as to whether the study was in use, informed her that a man befitting Galen's description had arrived and waited there. Abbey's heart skipped a beat; after their ill-advised outing, she had heard nothing from her cousin. She had to see him; she had to know he was all right. And she had an idea.

She hurried downstairs and positioned herself in the library. After what seemed like hours to her, at last she heard the sound of boots echoing in the corridor and risked opening the door a crack. Galen was walking swiftly down the hall, his head down and his expression inscrutable.

''*Galen,*'' she whispered frantically from behind the door. His head snapped up and toward her. His eyes met hers, and he glanced furtively over his shoulder before slipping inside. Abbey quietly shut the door behind them and with a muffled squeal of happiness, embraced her cousin.

Galen grabbed her arms and pulled them from his neck. ''Abbey, are you all right?'' he asked, his expression strained. ''I have worried what that devil was doing to you; I left word where I could be reached, did the butler tell you?''

''I am very well, Galen! I told you, Michael would never harm me!'' Abbey assured him.

Galen shook his head. ''I cannot be so sure!'' His dark reaction surprised her. Not once had she ever feared Michael. She might be estranged from him, but she knew him well enough to know that he would never harm her. ''I know he seems . . . severe. But please forgive him, Galen. He has lived a terribly hard life and has been treated ill many times before. I know he is being highly unreasonable, and *extremely* obstinate, but it's because he assumes—''

''He assumes a lot. Maybe we should let sleeping dogs lie, little one. The man is unyielding,'' Galen muttered miserably.

"Don't despair. He will come around, I know he will. I've been thinking, Galen. There is one person who could give him the proof he needs," Abbey said reassuringly, and touched his arm.

"Who?" he asked skeptically.

"Mr. Strait! I do not know why I did not think of this before. It's perfectly logical, don't you think? At the very least he would confirm that he sent the first set of papers prematurely, probably because Papa insisted. Papa could be very insistent when he wanted to be, and I know from experience it was quite difficult to disagree with him at times, his deathbed notwithstanding—"

"Strait?" Galen choked, blanching visibly.

Puzzled, Abbey asked, "What is wrong?"

"Abbey," Galen said, catching her hands, "I do not think that's a good idea."

"But why not? He can help you, Galen. I remember him, he was a kind man. He can dispel Michael's doubt."

"There is nothing Strait could say that would dispel his doubts, little one. Your husband would not believe the king himself," he said, and turned abruptly, shoving a hand through his light-brown hair. He looked completely hopeless as his eyes roamed the small room.

"We must at least try, Galen! If we don't, Michael will never return your inheritance!"

"It won't work. Now is hardly the time to go chasing after some ancient solicitor!" he snapped.

Stunned, Abbey could not believe what she was hearing. She had racked her brain for a solution that would bring Galen his due and erase Michael's doubt. Mr. Strait was their only hope, and Galen was reacting as if it were the most foolish idea she could have conceived.

Before she could convince him, Galen closed his eyes in a painful grimace. "I must go; he will think we are colluding if he finds us here," he said bitterly.

"But, Galen!" Abbey exclaimed, distressed.

Galen's eyes softened. He quickly grasped her hand and brought it to his lips. "It will all be over soon. One way or another, it will be over very soon," he said enigmatically, and walked swiftly to the door. She watched in stunned disbelief as he cracked it open and, seeing the corridor clear, looked sadly at her and slipped outside. Abbey stood there for several long moments, grappling with his strange behavior. Why wouldn't Galen listen to her? Why was he so reluctant to find Mr. Strait? It was puzzling. And extremely bothersome.

Sullen and feeling nauseous, she returned to her rooms and winced when she noticed the time. She had accepted the invitation to accompany Lady Paddington to the Wilmington Ball, where the elderly woman had declared she would strip her good friend Mrs. Clark of every pence she had in revenge for their card game two nights past. Lord Southerland had been right; the group of elderly women he fondly referred to as the prowlers seemed to engage in a never-ending round of loo.

"You don't look so well, mum, if you don't mind me saying," Sarah observed later that afternoon as she brushed Abbey's hair. "Are you sleeping?"

She was sleeping, but her pregnancy was taking a toll on her. Illness was not confined to mornings; she seemed to feel as queasy at night as any time. "I am all right," she muttered, but was hit with a bout of nausea at that very moment that forced her into the water closet.

When she emerged, pale and unsteady, Sarah was frowning mightily, her hands on her hips. "You're carrying, aren't you?" she demanded. Abbey could not hide it from her maid, and nodded slowly. Sarah's countenance changed immediately, and beaming, she rushed to Abbey and hugged her tightly, squeezing the breath from her. "That's wonderful, mum! Oh, how wonderful! I'm so very happy for you, truly! It's just what my lord needs, if you want my opinion!"

Abbey accepted her congratulations with a thin smile. It *was* wonderful, but it would be so much more so if Michael could share the joy. She forced a bright smile. "Come. Lady Paddington said she would call at precisely eight-thirty, and God help me if I am not ready." She laughed shakily.

Sarah, always cheerful, brightened, too, and as she dressed Abbey's hair, she began to repeat the household gossip. Abbey nodded at the appropriate moments and smiled, but she could not really listen. She could not get Galen off her mind and, particularly, his refusal to seek Mr. Strait.

"Lord Darfield sulks about the house and never says a word to anyone, except *yes,* and *no,* and *thank you, that will be all,*" Sarah mimicked. Abbey smiled faintly as she imagined the servants gathered in the kitchens, mimicking the Devil of Darfield's determined stride and deep voice. She herself would never forget the sound of his voice the first time she had met him, deep and sure . . . and cold. "Then Wilson overheard us in the kitchen yesterday, and he said to quit prattling, that the truth of the matter was that some men were always trying to extort money from the marquis—"

Before Abbey could say anything about that stunning comment Sarah smiled and patted her shoulder. "It's just idle gossip, mum. If you ask me, they ought to be more worried that the marquis is so obsessed with those dolls—"

"The dolls?"

"He keeps them stashed away in the study. This afternoon he bade me bring them into the main drawing room. He gave me the key to his desk and told me to look in the bottom drawer. There was nothing there save some cuff links and a doll, so I brought them. It was all very odd, I thought, and he already had a doll with him."

Abbey shook her head in confusion. "What do you mean, he already had a doll with him?"

"Just that. He was holding another doll when he sent me to get the other things. It looked like the one I brought him, but it was different," Sarah explained casually as she finished Abbey's hair and moved to a wardrobe.

*"Different?"* Abbey asked breathlessly.

Sarah shrugged as she dug through a polished walnut box for earrings. "Lord Darfield's doll had the same face as the other, but his was dressed as a pirate. I couldn't imagine what two grown men were doing with those dolls—"

*"My God!"* Abbey fairly shrieked, and jumped to her feet.

Startled, Sarah dropped the earrings she had selected. "What?! What is it?"

Abbey did not answer but began to pace the small sitting room. A pirate doll! *The* pirate doll! A myriad of images suddenly invaded her consciousness. Her, standing in a small skiff headed for shore, shouting at her father for having put her off the boat. Papa, standing at the railing, waving cheerfully at her. And *Michael*, appearing on deck with the doll hanging from one hand. The doll he had decapitated. And it was *dressed like a pirate!* Galen's doll, she realized was a replica, a fake . . .

Abbey fell heavily into a chair, disbelieving her own thoughts. "He knows, Sarah! He *knows*! Oh dear God, he *knows*!" Abbey cried.

"Knows *what?*" Sarah gasped with alarm.

"He knows Galen is lying! Oh, God, Galen is lying, and Michael knows it because he had the doll! Don't you see? *He* had it all this time! He knows the other one is a fake! He knows Galen gave me an *imitation* . . ."

Her voice trailed off as she realized what she was saying. Everything was suddenly beginning to make sense, sickening sense. Suspicions about Galen now flitted rapidly through her mind. From the moment she had stumbled on him in Pemberheath, he had avoided meeting Michael. He had been mysterious about his business deal. He had surprised her with trinkets from her past and a second will. He did not want to find Mr. Strait, the one man who could clarify everything. She buried her face in her hands. Actions that had seemed rather innocent at the time now seemed to point to evasion, treachery, and deceit.

"My Lady, what is wrong?" Sarah cried with alarm.

"Sarah, I had *one* doll as a girl. Only *one*! And the summer we were on Papa's ship, Michael took it from me and tore its head from its body!"

"My goodness, he did *what?*"

"But he repaired it," Abbey rushed on, "and he dressed it up as a pirate, because *I* used to dress as a pirate! He was going to give it to me, but he never got the chance because Papa put me off the ship and sent me to school in the company of Mr. Strait!" Abbey paused. Mr. Strait was also one of a very few who could know what her doll looked like. Could the solicitor also be involved? Dear God, was everyone she had ever known determined to defraud Michael? But why? How? Abbey tapped a finger against her lips, staring blindly at the carpet.

"Mr. Strait could be involved. Galen, oh, how could he do this? It doesn't matter, he must confess. He must tell Michael everything," she whispered. Why had she not remembered this before? Why hadn't Michael told her he still had the doll? Did he want to be rid of her so badly that he had withheld information that would have exonerated her?

Abbey jumped to her feet and rushed to a writing table, where she quickly withdrew a sheet of parchment. "Sarah, you must get this note to my cousin, Galen Carrey," she said quietly as she wrote. "Jones should know where he can be found."

Sarah took an unconscious step backward as Abbey dripped candle wax on the missive asking Galen to meet her at the Wilmington Ball on a matter of grave urgency.

"I don't know, mum. The marquis said to tell him if you required messages to be delivered," she said unevenly.

Abbey jerked a heated gaze to her as she waved the missive in the air to dry the seal. "Did he?" she snapped angrily. "I don't care! I am begging you, Sarah, please take this to my cousin. It is extremely important, and you must not tell Lord Darfield." Satisfied the seal was dry, Abbey stood and marched to where the maid stood, grabbed her hand, and slapped the note into her palm.

"Shouldn't you tell Lord Darfield?" Sarah cried. "He was quite clear—"

"Sarah, it is imperative that I speak with my cousin privately! Give me your word you will not tell Lord Darfield!"

"But, my lady, if your cousin did something wrong, shouldn't the marquis know?" Sarah said, pleading.

Abbey hands flew instinctively to her abdomen. "I am begging you, as my friend, to do this," she said weakly, annoyed that tears were beginning to fill her eyes. "You don't understand, he won't accept . . ."

Sarah's gaze flicked to her hands on her abdomen, then back to Abbey's misty eyes.

Abbey took a deep breath. "I have to convince Galen to confess what he has done to Michael. It is my only hope," she murmured through her tears. She realized she must seem wildly out of control to Sarah; the poor girl had no idea what she was talking about. But Galen *had* to confess. He had to tell Michael everything so he would know she was not involved, had never been involved.

"Just do it, Sarah!" she suddenly shouted, hearing the edge of hysteria that had crept into her voice.

Sarah's face crumbled with fear, and she walked quickly to the door. "Yes, my lady," she murmured, suddenly eager to escape her raving mistress.


Sarah prided herself on being always cheerful and always obedient. Today was no different, with one exception. She sent a boy to her mistress's cousin with the note before she went in search of the marquis. She might lose her post, but she had seen the wild look in Lady Darfield's eyes, and it scared her. She had to do the right thing.


Michael helped himself to another whiskey and continued pacing. Galen Carrey had not been the least bit perturbed when he had denied his claim. Obviously Carrey had expected that, and oddly, he did not argue his case, as Michael had anticipated. When Michael demanded to know what had become of Mr. Strait, and why it was Routier had been one of the last to see him, Galen had not answered. He had remained silent throughout their encounter, and at the end, had asked quietly after Abbey. Michael had refrained from breaking his neck and had instead, told the scoundrel he would rot in hell before he would know. Galen had shrugged and left.

Michael lifted his head from his brooding when he heard the rap on the door. "Come," he said with a growl.

Sarah stepped through the door, scowling mightily.

With an impatient sigh. Michael asked, "What is it, Sarah?"

Uncharacteristically, Sarah raised her chin. "I have something to say, my lord." she said, and nervously cleared her throat.

Michael sighed and thrust a hand through his hair. "What is it?"

"I have been in your household since I was but a girl. my lord. and I never believed any of the things I heard about you, not a one," she began. Michael rolled his eyes; he should hardly be surprised that the staff would discuss the rift between him and Abbey.

"I shall forgive your breach of conduct—"

"I still do not believe them," she said. Michael stopped and quirked a brow in question. "No, my lord, I don't. Not even after the dolls and my lady's claims that you think her cousin is a fraud."

"The dolls?" Michael asked, his brows sinking into a scowl.

The maid lifted her chin a little higher. "*I* told her about the dolls, and good heavens, she jumped up and started shouting that you knew it was lie and for the life of her couldn't understand why you didn't tell her, and that Mr. Carry had lied, and Mr. Strait was involved—"

"Sarah, slow down!" Michael said, much more calmly than he felt, and motioned for her to sit in one of the chairs facing the desk. Sarah hesitated for a moment, then very stiffly took a seat. Michael waited for her to arrange her skirts and place her hands primly in her lap.

"Now, start from the beginning," he said, and listened in quiet amazement as Sarah related her earlier encounter with Abbey. That damned doll! She had remembered it after all.

"She'll never speak to me again, my lord, but I thought about it, and I don't think it's right, because I've seen you with Lady Darfield, and it's rather obvious you love her, and you've moped about the last several days, and when my lady said you *knew*, well, I couldn't think of any other explanation. She would realize it, too, if she wasn't so emotional. She can't think straight, she is so wrought up. I guess I should be grateful that she at least sent a note and didn't run off to confront Mr. Carrey because she was afraid for her . . . self,'' Sarah muttered angrily.

"Confront Mr. Carrey?" Michael echoed, confused. "Sarah, has she something to fear from him? Why is she afraid for herself?" he prodded, ignoring for the moment the fact that Abbey obviously knew Galen was a fraud.

"I cannot tell you," Sarah said softly.

Michael scowled and shifted his weight against the desk. He had little patience for a reticent maid. "Why not? You have told me every other thing," he asked calmly.

Sarah averted her eyes and pretended to be studying the embroidery in the arm of the chair.

"Sarah?" Michael coaxed, working to keep a hold on his patience.

"It's not my place to tell you," she muttered.

"*Sarah.*" It was not a request, it was a command.

Sarah's cheeks flushed. "She'll never speak to me again!"

"If there is something concerning Lady Darfield's welfare, you must tell me," he said, his patience quickly wearing thin.

"It's just that she's not herself! She is so emotional these days on account she's carrying," Sarah blurted without realizing what she had said. It hit her immediately, and her eyes flew wide with horror.

Dumbstruck, Michael gaped at her. "What did you say?"

Sarah wailed with despair. Michael lurched across the gap between them and grabbed her by the elbows, dragging her roughly to her feet.

"Is she with child?" he demanded in a threatening voice. Terrified, Sarah could only nod. Michael slowly released her. He felt something drain rapidly from him, only to be filled with another, stronger emotion that surged up in its place. He turned abruptly to the desk and braced himself against it, his mind quickly calculating the weeks. *She was carrying his child.* It was his, it had to be, there could not have been sufficient opportunity for it to be otherwise. It was more than he could fathom. Strong, tumultuous emotions raged within him. God in heaven, she was carrying *his* child.

"You have done the right thing, Sarah," he ground out, ignoring her wailing. "That will be all." He placed his arms on the desk and leaned into them.

"My lord—"

"*Go!*" he shouted. He heard Sarah scurry across the carpet and shut the door behind her.

He could not fully absorb it. A child. His child. The very suggestion had a powerful effect on him that he could not begin to understand or digest. A peculiar surge of pride washed over him.

And love.

Lord, but he had never wanted her more than he did at this very moment. He would deal with their situation later, but for now all he wanted was Abbey, and the consequences be damned. He pushed himself from the desk and marched across the study, flinging the door open with such force that it hit the wall. "*Jones!*" he roared as he made his way to his chamber. He could not wait to hold her in his arms, to lay his hand across her belly and feel the life within her, *his* life. He wanted her in his arms so he could show her what he would never find words to describe.

But Abbey had already left for the evening in the company of the rotund Lady Paddington.

# Chapter 19

Abbey's gaze swept the crowd in search of Galen. She had been at the Wilmington Ball for nearly two hours, and still he had not come. She leaned against a pillar with her arms folded across her middle, one slippered foot tapping steadily against the marble tile. She personally would throttle Sarah if she had not delivered the note.

A young fop she recognized as the younger son of the Earl of Whitstone approached her, smiling charmingly. Abbey frowned; the tempo of her tapping foot increased. She was in no mood for idle chatter tonight and had already thanked her lucky stars that the ebullient Lady Paddington was engaged in a fierce war of loo with the other prowlers.

"Good evening, Lady Darfield." The young man bowed.

"Good evening, sir."

"I was watching you from across the room. I noticed you had not stood up in some time and thought perchance that might mean there is space on your dance card?" he asked hopefully.

Abbey forced a smile. "Oh! Well, you see, I twisted my

ankle in a turn about the park this morning, and I'm afraid it's far too tender to contemplate dancing,'' she lied sweetly.

"Indeed? I had not noticed a limp,'' the young Whitstone remarked as he eyed her tapping foot skeptically. Abbey glanced down at her feet and frowned. Aunt Nan was right. She could not tell a falsehood convincingly if her very life depended on it. Even this little fop knew it. But not Michael, damn him!

"Lady Darfield.''

Abbey whirled toward Galen's voice, forgetting the young man. She gasped softly; her cousin looked horrible. His brown eyes were dull, set deep in his haggard face. She glanced uneasily toward the young fop. "If you will excuse me, sir,'' she muttered, and walked quickly to Galen, leaving Whitstone gaping at her perfectly fine stride.

"I was afraid you had not received my message,'' she whispered. Glancing furtively about, she grabbed Galen's arm and led him toward a corner of the room where a stand of large potted plants had been moved to make room for the dancers.

"I needed some time to think.''

Abbey fairly shoved Galen behind one of the giant plants and faced him, her hands on her hips. His gaze slid over her and landed on the floor, where it remained. Abbey's brows snapped together in a frown. He looked positively despondent, and she could only guess it was because he somehow suspected he had been discovered.

"Galen, I know about the dolls,'' she began.

Galen held up a hand and shook his head. "Say no more, little one—''

"No, *you* say no more! You have not been very truthful with me, Galen. It's all a lie, isn't it?'' she demanded.

Galen surprised her by nodding, immediately and effectively taking the wind out of her angry sails. She sagged against the wall, her arms dropping to her sides. A part of her had hoped he would deny it. God, why couldn't he deny it?

"But why?'' she murmured.

Galen shrugged and lifted his brown eyes to her. "He left

me without a farthing, Abbey. I was his only surviving male relative, and it just seemed so grossly unfair. Darfield is a very wealthy man—he doesn't need your dowry, and at the time, my plan didn't seem quite so horrible.''

Abbey's jaw dropped at his confession. She could not fathom her beloved cousin would do this to her. She simply could not accept it. Galen looked nervously at the crowd and took a step farther into the shadows behind the plants.

''I should have told him this afternoon. If only I . . . His pain is quite evident, cousin. I think he loves you very much.''

That was a laugh. A very painful laugh. Abbey found her voice. ''He doesn't love me, and I fear the opportunity has been lost, thanks to your little charade. He suspected you from the beginning, and like a fool, I defended you!'' she choked. Galen sadly nodded his head.

''How did you do it? The will, I mean. And the cuff links? The doll? How did you do it?'' she demanded.

Galen sighed wearily and shoved his hands in his pocket. ''Strait,'' he muttered. ''Apparently, out of necessity, the man learned your father's signature years ago. There were times when the captain was not present to sign, and he vested Strait with the authority. Over time, the solicitor became quite adept at it, and when pressed, he signed the forged document, for a percentage. As for the cuff links, they were in Strait's possession. He had intended to send them to you, as he knew they meant something to the captain. The doll? That was my idea. I recalled one you had dragged about as a little girl and recently, by chance, happened upon one very similar to it.''

''Mr. Strait was involved?'' she whispered.

Galen paused. ''Not willingly,'' he sighed.

His confession shattered her into what felt like a thousand pieces. For a brief moment, she recalled the Galen of her youth, laughing on the decks of the *Dancing Maiden,* his dancing brown eyes shining down on her. Her heart wrenched at the memory; she could not fathom her beloved cousin participating in such a scheme. A scheme that had destroyed her marriage.

''I cannot believe this, Galen,'' she whispered hoarsely.

"Why didn't you come to me? I would have given you everything I had." A tear slipped from her eye and traveled quickly
down her pale cheek.

Galen sullenly watched its path. "I know. That's why I
didn't press my claim. I could see it was destroying your
happiness—"

"Could you?" she shot back. "You've destroyed my marriage before it had a chance to begin. I can never win back
what I've lost, not now. You know that, don't you? I only
hope he believes you and does not continue to think that
I . . ." She caught a sob in her throat. "That *I* did this to
him!"

"We can go to him now, if you'd like. I will tell him
everything," he said solemnly.

Abbey stared at him, her mind warring with her heart. Why
did all the men in her life betray her?

"*You* go. Tell him everything," she ground out angrily. "If
I go with you, he'll suspect we are scheming. If he believes
you, I'll know it. One way or another, I'll know it." She
pushed away from the wall and backed away from him, shaking her head in disbelief.

Galen, with his hands shoved in his pockets, watched her,
misery etched on his face. "Abbey. Little one. I am so very
sorry. You cannot *know* how sorry," he said softly.

She bit her lower lip to keep a torrent of tears from gushing
forth. God, she was sorry, too. Sorry her father had not provided for him. Sorry he had felt compelled to go to such
incredible lengths. Sorry that he had ruined the near-perfect
life she had with Michael. "It's too late," she whispered, and
turning on her heel, walked away, her heart breaking for the
hundredth time.

Galen's own heart was breaking, too. She was right, his
apology was too little, too late. He had destroyed her happiness, and he had never, ever wanted that. If he could roll back
the clock, he would. If he could erase that fateful, chance
encounter with Malcolm Routier in Calais, he would. If he
could have undone the steps they had taken to defraud
Darfield, he would gladly do it. He had not understood how

deeply Darfield felt about her until he had seen him this afternoon. The man had a wild look in his eye, but when he spoke Abbey's name, something flickered in his gray eyes, something hauntingly touching. He should hardly be surprised. He could have loved her, too.

Over the last several days, Galen's distaste for this unspeakable scheme had grown so great, he should have walked away from it. But Routier had pushed him, threatening him. At first, he had used the fact that Galen owed him five thousand pounds. But Routier's motivation was not money. Galen had come to that realization rather slowly, but he had recently seen the incredible hatred the man bore for Darfield. What motivated Routier was a desire to see Darfield ruined, whatever the cost. He would never be able to undo what he had done, but at least he could stop Routier from ruining Darfield. Galen pushed away from the plants and began to make his way to the exit, determined to find the marquis.

He was nearing the door when a hand on his shoulder stopped him.

"Off so soon, Carrey?" Malcolm Routier asked blandly.

"You could say that."

"I was expecting to see you this afternoon, my friend. Were you favorably detained?" Routier asked slyly.

"I am not going through with it, Routier," Galen bluntly admitted.

Routier's yellow eyes went hard as stone. "Pardon?" he asked, forcing a smile onto his thin lips.

"You heard me. I'm not going through with it."

Routier laughed politely and, glancing around them, grabbed Galen's arm in a painful grip. "Surely I misunderstood you. You have no choice but to go through with it."

Galen jerked his arm from Routier's grip and walked outside, away from the heavily trafficked foyer. Routier followed him.

"Have you forgotten that you owe me?" he hissed at Galen's back.

Galen shrugged and shoved his hands into his pockets.

"No, I have not forgotten. Turn me into the authorities if you will, but you will not force my hand in this."

"What's the matter, Carrey? Your pretty little cousin not willing to warm your bed just now?" he snarled.

Galen whirled and shoved Routier up against the brick wall, ignoring the startled looks of guests arriving at the Wilmington home. "Don't, Routier," he muttered through clenched teeth, "or I will break your bloody neck."

Routier shoved back, then casually straightened his waistcoat. "You are a goddam fool, Carrey," he muttered as he straightened the cuffs of his sleeves. "Do you have any concept of what I've done for you? I planned it, I made sure we got what we needed from Strait so you could make your little claim to a half million pounds. I made sure he wouldn't get in the way—"

"*What?*" Galen gasped.

Routier rolled his eyes. "Did it ever occur to you that when asked, the honest Mr. Strait might talk about what I made him do? How would that have looked for your claim? Did you ever think of that?"

"I thought he agreed to do it for a percentage!"

"You thought wrong. He was an honest man if nothing else." Routier sighed coldly. At that moment, Galen thought he was the biggest fool in all the world. Not only had he destroyed his cousin, he had effectively had a man murdered. He might as well have pulled the trigger himself, and all because the captain had never forgiven his immaturity, his lack of responsibility. Good God, how ironic that was now! Carrington had been so bloody *right*! Look what he had done to Abbey. To Darfield. To Strait.

"You *disgust* me," he muttered angrily, speaking to Routier but also to himself. Then he turned on his heel, walking away from Routier for good, to find Darfield.

Routier's eyes narrowed. That bastard Carrey was about to cost him his one chance to ruin Darfield. He turned and walked back into the foyer, his mind racing. He was not through yet. Not yet. Darfield may keep his windfall, but he would know suffering at Routier's hand.

*    *    *

Abbey stood near the doors opening to the terrace, glaring down every would-be dance partner. As usual, she was a whirl of conflicting emotions. She wanted to go home, crawl into bed, and try to forget the whole, horrible affair. But she was afraid to go home. What if Galen was there? She was not certain what Michael would do when he learned the truth, but she could not think it would be good. And on top of that, she had the very real problem of no transportation. Until Lady Paddington was ready, she was stuck. So she stood, awkwardly and alone, deflecting gentleman after gentleman, completely preoccupied with thoughts of Galen. Oh, God, how his betrayal stung. It stung as deeply as the captain's, almost as deeply as Michael's.

"Good evening, Lady Darfield."

Abbey glanced to her right and smiled thinly. "Mr. Routier, what a pleasure," she said politely.

"No, lady, the pleasure is always mine. Forgive me, but you look rather tired this evening, if you don't mind me saying so. I hope your bout of nausea earlier this week was nothing serious."

"Oh, no, I am perfectly fine, thank you. I suppose I am a bit tired." She smiled.

"You don't say." Routier's yellow eyes held hers for a long moment, pricking something in the back of her consciousness, but she pushed it away.

"Actually, I have not been sleeping too terribly well. I think I've a touch of insomnia."

Malcolm raised a thin brow. "Indeed? I am sorry for that. Perhaps a turn about the gardens might help?" That actually sounded like a very good idea. Yes, a walk about the gardens would get her out of this stuffy room, away from the attentions of a dozen London dandies, and perhaps clear her head.

"I would like that very much," she agreed, and with a smile took his proffered arm.

*    *    *

After greeting the Wilmingtons, Michael walked swiftly to the ballroom. He made a quick scan of the room but did not see Abbey. He turned and headed for the grand salon, thinking Lady Paddington might have enticed her into a game of loo, but she was not there, either. He began to return to the ballroom, but spied his two friends, Sam and Alex, sitting together at a table in the library, chatting amicably over a snifter of brandy. In spite of his mission, he smiled to himself and changed course. No doubt every debutante within a fifty-mile radius was plotting how to get two of the most eligible bachelors in all of Britain onto an overcrowded dance floor. No doubt the bachelors were plotting just as fiercely to stay off it.

"Darfield, we did not expect to see you this evening," Alex said, stretching his long legs in front of him.

Michael took a seat at their table and accepted the brandy a footman offered him. "Wasn't expecting to be here," he admitted. "But I have something I would very much like to discuss with my wife." He could not help himself; a faint smile turned the corners of his lips. Sam looked at him as if he had lost his mind; Alex chuckled.

"I, for one, will be greatly disappointed if the Darfields determine to spend their evenings together," Alex whispered conspiratorially to Sam. "I have been extremely grateful for Lady Darfield's willingness to attend Aunt Paddy."

Sam was less hopeful. "I just hope there are no altercations."

Michael smiled enigmatically and sipped his brandy. "None that I anticipate, but then again, with Lady Darfield, one can never be too sure."

"Speak of the devil, isn't that the cause of your rift?" Alex asked quietly, nodding toward the door.

Michael glanced over his shoulder, his face immediately darkening at the sight of Galen Carrey. "How in God's name did he get in here?" he muttered. He placed the brandy snifter on the table and rose as Galen spotted him and walked quickly to him.

"What in the bloody hell are you doing here, Carrey?" Michael muttered through clenched teeth.

Galen flicked a nervous gaze to Sam and Alex, who both regarded him with disdain. He lifted his hands, palms facing outward. "Hear me out, Darfield, that's all I ask."

"I am through hearing you, Carrey. I would have thought I made that perfectly clear this afternoon."

"I would not have come here except that I am concerned for Abbey—"

"She is *none* of your concern—"

"Perhaps not," he interjected, "but I thought you would want to know that she is quite vulnerable at the moment."

That drew Michael up short. "What do you mean?"

"You were right about me, Darfield. It *is* a forgery," Galen muttered, looking over his shoulder. Michael's gaze did not waver from his face, but Alex and Sam exchanged startled glances. Simultaneously, the two men sat up and leaned forward.

"The devil you say. What a surprise," Michael mocked.

"Do you want to hear this or not?" Galen demanded.

Michael paused, considering whether he did or not, and finally, motioned the man to a seat. Galen sat gingerly, shook his head at the brandy a footman offered him, and clapped his hands on his knees, bracing himself. With a deep breath, he began speaking. In a calm monotone, he related a story of fantastic proportions, one that involved Michael's worst enemy, forgery, murder, and a scoundrel's change of heart.

His audience of three was completely absorbed by his tale. Occasionally one would ask a question, which Galen calmly answered. He made it very clear that Abbey had known nothing about his ruse but had simply tried to help him, a cousin for whom she held a special fondness. Galen's earnest entreaty did not fully exonerate her for Michael, because she had lied to him, but it went a long way toward healing an open wound. When Galen finished, he slid his gaze to Michael.

"Why are you telling me this now?" Michael demanded.

"Abbey discovered my scheme. She sent me a note, insisting I meet her here, and then demanded I confess. And as I was leaving to find you, I encountered Routier. I told him I would not go through with it. He was exceedingly angry, I am sure you can imagine, and I thought you should know—"

Michael was on his feet immediately. "Routier is here?" he asked with deadly calm.

"Yes, somewhere."

Michael did not say another word but turned abruptly and marched from the library. With a quick exchange of glances, Galen, Sam, and Alex followed him.


Abbey followed Routier's lead along the terrace, enjoying the cool breeze. Her companion was oddly quiet. "The air is refreshing, don't you think?"

"I suppose," he remarked, his voice strangely cool.

Abbey glanced at him from the corner of her eye. "You seem tense, Mr. Routier."

"Perhaps I am," he said curtly. A warning bell, so faint as to be ignored, went off in Abbey's head, but he looked at her and smiled. "Then again, perhaps not. Have you seen Lady Wilmington's maze? It is supposedly the grandest in London."

"No, I haven't."

"Now that's a sight you will not want to miss," he said, and began to lead her down the flagstone steps.

"But Mr. Routier, it's dark!" She laughed.

"There is plenty of light, I assure you. They post torches inside in case one is lost." Abbey felt an odd sense of foreboding as they strolled toward the maze entrance. "I don't think we should go inside. It hardly seems proper." She laughed nervously.

"Proper? Since when have you been bothered by propriety, Lady Darfield?" He smiled so strangely that her skin crawled.

She frowned at him, uncertain as to what he meant by that remark. "I believe the maze is reserved for lovers, Mr. Routier. Not casual strollers such as ourselves."

"I think it perfectly suitable for us," he muttered.

"I beg you pardon?"

"I am quite certain you understood me," he said sharply.

They were almost to the maze entrance; he gripped her elbow and walked briskly toward the hedge, propelling her with him. Momentarily confused, the warning that went off in Abbey's head was as loud as belfry bells but, unfortunately, woefully too late. She tried to pull away from him, but he shoved her toward the narrow entrance cut into the hedge, then crowded in behind her, his frame filling the narrow opening. Once inside, he pushed her forward.

Abbey stumbled, then whirled to face him, walking backward as she stared at him in astonishment. "Mr. Routier, what on earth has come over you? I do not want to explore the maze!"

"But I do," he said casually, advancing on her. Alarm coursed through her veins. Routier's face was cast in stone, and his yellow eyes had hardened so that she suppressed an involuntary shiver. He smiled at her obvious alarm—a thin, faintly snide smile.

"If I have given you cause to believe my friendship was any more than just *friendship,* I am truly sorry. I am a married woman, sir, and not the least bit interested in any assignation." She stepped backward, knocking up against the hedge.

"You are an incomparable beauty, do you know that?" Routier said softly as his eyes languidly perused her, his tongue flicking across his bottom lip.

She quickly brought her arm up, outstretched, in a vain attempt to hold him at bay. "I will thank you to step away, sir. Your advances are most unwelcome," she said bluntly.

Routier's lips curled in a lecherous grin. "Resistance. That's the way I like it, *ma belle.*"

Dear God, he had been her *friend.* How could he possibly intend what she was interpreting? "I *don't.* I think you take my meaning," she insisted.

"I do not think you take mine." He laughed balefully. "Oh, come now, Lady Darfield. Surely you would enjoy a tryst with someone other than Darfield? Really, you should have convinced him to give over your dowry and left that bastard. He's not good enough for you, can't you see that? You don't understand how he cheapens you. He does not know how to love a woman, not like I do," he muttered thickly.

Abbey's entire body reacted violently to his words. Nothing or no one could be more repulsive. She closed her eyes for a brief moment to fight back a spasm of fear and loathing, when she opened them a second later, Routier was upon her. Abbey threw up her hands and hit his chest.

"Pretend if you must, angel, but I know a woman like you appreciates something hard between her thighs," he murmured, breathing heavily.

Abbey's heel came down hard on the soft leather of his shoe. Routier froze, his eyes narrowing to malicious slits. Abbey recoiled, backing farther into the hedge and effectively trapping herself. Dear God, what was happening? Was the entire populace of England insane? She swallowed past a crippling fear that threatened to overwhelm her. She did not move as he coldly studied her face. She barely breathed. She prayed. Fervently.

A grotesque smile that caused Abbey to shudder convulsively snaked across his lips. She had never seen a look quite like it, but she knew what it meant. She could not, would not, let him touch her.

"Darfield will not want you if you are ruined, will he? Is that what is worrying that pretty little head of yours?" He did not wait for an answer. He grabbed her around the waist with one arm and clamped a hand over her mouth. Then he picked her up as if she weighed little more than a feather and hauled her deeper into the maze. Abbey struggled helplessly; Routier merely laughed at her efforts.

"You are right to be concerned, my dear. Darfield will never touch you again if he thinks *I* have had you. And I will have you, every delicious inch of you." He stopped in a small clearing and grinning lecherously, ran his tongue over his lips as he looked down at her. With his hand covering her mouth, Abbey could hardly breathe. "What a wonderful dilemma for the marquis. A pretty little wife, compromised by Malcolm Routier. But he will never be quite certain it wasn't consensual, will he? He does not easily believe you, I think." He chuckled.

Abbey struggled furiously; Routier's hand slipped from her mouth. "Please do not do this," she gasped. Routier answered by grabbing her hair and yanking her head backward. Somehow Abbey managed to wrench free from his grasp and, whirling, started to run. But Routier caught her around the waist and jerked her to his chest so hard that it knocked the air from her lungs.

"Don't fight it, darling. There is no pleasure in fighting," he muttered into her ear. Hysteria mounted swiftly and Abbey screamed. Routier cut it off by clamping a damp hand over her mouth and forced her around to face him.

"Do not scream again, bitch," he said angrily, removing his hand from her mouth, only to replace it with his lips.

His kiss was brutal. When she would not part her lips, he bit her. Her reflexive gasp allowed him entry, and his tongue plunged into her mouth, sickening her. Abbey pushed against his chest, sought his feet with hers in an attempt to strike his instep. Routier only laughed against her mouth and deepened the kiss. She tried to turn away, but he was so much stronger, and with one arm around her waist anchoring her to him, he used the other to force her face to him. He pushed her up against the hedge and trapped her beneath his hard frame, then shoved his hand into the bodice of her gown and maliciously squeezed her breast.

Hysteria pounded in her neck and chest. She continued to struggle, but she knew she was at a great disadvantage, and had never felt more helpless. She could not stop him from assaulting her. When his hand began to claw at the skirt of her gown and drag it upward, Abbey screamed against his mouth.

He would have succeeded in raping her had someone not ripped her from his arms. She was not sure how, but she had the sensation of being shoved aside. The heel of her shoe caught her hem, and she tumbled backward, landing solidly on her rump. Stunned, it took Abbey several moments to focus on the tussle on the grass in front of her. Someone grabbed her roughly by the shoulders and hauled her to her feet.

"God, are you all right?" Lord Southerland was looking down at her with grave concern. She nodded dumbly as her fingers came up and lightly fingered her lip where Routier had bit her. Disgust glanced the duke's features, and he jerked his head to where the two men scuffled.

Abbey dragged her gaze back to the ruckus, her heart skipping several beats. Michael, his face dark with fury, was wrestling with Routier. She stifled a scream when Routier stepped forward and quickly delivered a blow to Michael's jaw that snapped his head backward. Michael stumbled, and Routier advanced on him, swinging. But Michael managed to sidestep him and Routier's fist slammed into the hedge.

Michael leapt through the air and knocked Routier to the earth with a thud, pinning him on his back. He pounded his fist into the man's face and quickly followed it with another blow. Routier tried to get his hands up, but Michael was too intent on killing him. It was Abbey's anguished cry that filtered into his consciousness, and he paused for a split second, but it was enough. Routier leveled an almost lethal blow, knocking him from his perch on his chest.

Before Routier could pounce, Sam grabbed him from behind, locking his arms behind his back. Alex quickly grabbed Michael and likewise locked his arms behind his back.

"Gentlemen," Alex said roughly. "You can settle this at dawn in an *affaire d'honneur.*"

Michael angrily shook Alex off as he brought a hand to his jaw and moved it gingerly from side to side, testing it. "Gladly," he spat out. "Consider this your challenge, Routier, if you are man enough."

Routier laughed. "I can hardly wait. If there was light, I'd suggest we finish this now."

Abbey gaped in horror as she listened to the exchange. A *duel?* "Oh, God, *no!*" She moaned.

Routier looked at Abbey and smiled wickedly. "That's right, Marchioness. I intend to kill him. I should have killed him when I had the chance at Blessing Park, but unfortunately, at that time you seemed to be the better target.''

''Pistols or swords?'' Michael roared as Sam stepped between them.

''Swords,'' Routier shot back. Michael nodded and stepped away from Alex, his eyes riveted on Abbey. Without a word, he marched toward her, removed his coat, and placed it around her shoulders. His dark expression made her shiver. He turned her away from Routier, and for the first time, she saw Galen standing at the entrance to the little clearing, glaring at Routier.

''Sam, will you act as my second?'' Michael asked in a low tone. Sam must have nodded. ''Carrey, get my coach. I'll take her around the side of the house.'' He threw his arm around her shoulders and hauled her closely into his side. He started out of the maze, never looking back.

There was silence in their coach as the vehicle hurtled through the fog-enshrouded night to the Audley Street mansion. Michael dragged his gaze from the window to Abbey, who, with cheeks stained pink, was looking down at her torn bodice. As if feeling her eyes on him, she glanced up. A longing clouded her violet eyes for the briefest of moments, then faded rapidly as she cast her eyes to her lap.

He felt so goddammed responsible. He should have been looking out for her, protecting her. He should have never let her leave the house. It was not as if he had not been warned her life was in danger, a fact driven home quite roundly when Routier had confirmed Abbey had been the target of that shot. But even that was eclipsed by his stupidity for having believed she was part of Carrey's scheme.

When the carriage reached the town house, Michael jumped down, then grabbed Abbey by the waist and wordlessly lifted her down. Neither of them said a word until they reached the foyer.

''Go to bed,'' he said softly, afraid anything more would betray his dark emotion. Abbey did not argue. She ran up the

stairs and disappeared from view. Michael turned on his heel
and marched for the main drawing room. He could not think
of her now. After he killed Routier, then he could decide how
to repair the damage between them.

Sam and Alex joined him to wait for dawn, and despite
their best efforts, he was not able to keep Abbey from his
thoughts. Shortly before the appointed hour, he made his way
to her room and opened the door, his only intent to look at her
before he went to meet Routier. Abbey bolted upright at the
sound. Obviously she had not slept; wearing a silk wrapper,
she was lying on top of the counterpane. Michael stepped
across the threshold, holding his candle high. Abbey swung
her legs over the side of the bed and gripped it on either side
of her knees.

"Is there anything I can say that will keep you from this?"
she whispered hopelessly.

Almost afraid to speak, Michael shook his head and slowly
crossed the room. He gazed down at her, his eyes sweeping
her face, the swell of her breasts, taking in every detail of her.
God, but she was beautiful. With dark hair spilling all around
her, her violet eyes vivid and clear, he realized it was an
image he might carry to his death. His gaze slid to her abdomen and the life she carried there. Her hand—unconsciously,
he thought—slipped protectively across her middle. Michael
went down on his haunches next to her. There was so much to
say, simply too much, and he had no idea where to begin. Did
he say he was sorry? That he was wrong? Did he tell her he
loved her? Time was running out.

"If I don't come back—"

"*No!* Don't say that, please don't say that," she begged,
catching a sob in her throat. Michael reached for her hand and
squeezed it reassuringly.

"Abbey, listen carefully. Sam is the executor of my estate.
Listen to him, do as he says. And promise me . . ." He
broke off, finding it difficult to go on in the face of her silent
tears. "Promise me," he whispered hoarsely, "the child you
carry will bear my name." Abbey's eyes fluttered wide before
she doubled over.

Grief as she had never known swallowed her. "You will come back," she whispered through her sobs. "I know you will. You will!"

Michael did not say anything. His dark gray eyes were red-rimmed; she did not know if it was fatigue or emotion. "Abbey . . ." His voice trailed off. He looked at her for a long moment, his heart in his eyes, and then he pressed his lips to hers. In that brief touch was an eternity of heartache and hope that said everything they could not voice. Then he slowly rose to his feet and turned away. When Abbey heard the door shut behind him, she buried her face in the counterpane and prayed as she had never prayed in her life.

She might have lain there all day, had someone not begun pounding insistently on the door to her chamber. She jumped to her feet and looked at the clock. It was too early; he could not possibly be back. She flew to the door and yanked it open.

A very grim Galen was standing on the other side. "Come on," he said. "Get dressed."

"Galen, what are you—"

"We are going to watch him duel for you. Come on, don't dally! We haven't much time," he snapped. Abbey did not have to think twice. She forgot all pretense of modesty and quickly donned the first dress she could lay her hands on.

The curricle Galen had hired raced through the deserted London streets and over the Thames. As they neared the very private Tarkinton Green on the outskirts of town where Michael would meet Routier, Abbey could see two carriages, a mount, and a group of men gathered. She strained to pick Michael out in the crowd, and brought a hand to her mouth and muffled a cry.

The duel had already begun.

Galen brought the curricle to a screeching halt; Abbey was already leaping from her seat.

"What in the bloody hell are you doing here?" Sam barked at Galen, who purposely ignored him. Alex was also there, with a gentleman carrying a black bag. Another man, unknown to her, was standing off by himself, obviously acting as Routier's second. Beyond this cursory glance, Abbey's eyes were riveted on the sword fighting, and she rushed to the edge of the field.

Michael, stripped down to his shirt, was quite good, but Routier was better. She cringed as the sharp-edged sabers clashed and a deafening clang echoed across the small green. Routier was steadily advancing on Michael, pushing him backward.

But Michael was fighting from an inner strength Routier could not possibly have gauged. He regained his footing and, with a surge, moved forward aggressively. He caught Routier by surprise, he thought, because he stumbled backward a couple of feet before finding his footing again. His yellow eyes narrowed and he picked up the level of his swordplay. Undaunted, Michael continued to make steady progress forward, matching Routier's lightning speed with his own saber. Incredibly, he heard Abbey's voice call to him. He could not believe it; his mind was playing tricks on him.

Neither man could gain ground on the other. It seemed to Michael that they had been fighting for hours; his arm was beginning to burn with the weight of the saber. Sweat poured from his brow, and at times, he had difficulty seeing his foe. Routier seemed just as worn; twice now he had dropped the tip of his sword, and twice Michael had lunged, just barely missing the man's black heart. He believed, given one more opportunity, he could fell him.

The two men had made a mud pit in the ground they covered. With a forward thrust, Routier sent Michael skidding toward the edge of the field. His consciousness registerd the spectators; they were very close. Why in the hell didn't they move? His boot slipped in the mud; he managed to avoid the fall, but Routier definitely had him at an advantage. He thrust again, this time knocking the sword from Michael's hand and sending it flying through the air.

In a desperate bid to live, Michael pitched to the right, found his feet, and lunged for Routier, blinded by his own sweat, as the man thrust his saber one last time. Suddenly he was hit hard in the chest by something blue. He stumbled backward, grabbing the weight thrown at him, and looked up

just in time to see Routier's saber lifted high above his head.
In a fantastic, surreal display, Routier's eyes suddenly went
wide and riveted on Michael. He teetered there, his sword
waving precariously above him, then toppled onto his side.
Galen was standing behind him, his chest heaving, Michael's
bloodied sword in his hand, staring at Routier's body.

Michael looked down at the blue weight that had hit him
and heard an agonizing howl—his own—as he recognized
Abbey, limp in his arms. He struggled with her to the ground
as a line of rapidly spreading blood stretched from below her
breast, across her side and arm. Michael was stunned; she had
thrown herself in front of him and had caught Routier's blade.
She had saved his life.

He scooped her limp body into his arms and clutched her to
his chest. Her head fell back; streams of dark mahogany hair
floated to the ground. She did not appear to be breathing.
*"Oh, God, please no! Please, no!"* He buried his face in her
neck; beneath his lips he could feel her weak pulse. He became aware of Sam forcing his arms apart and lowering Abbey to the ground so the physician could see to her wounds. In
the fog of fear that surrounded him, he heard Alex bark commands to remove Routier's body and for Galen to flee at once.

"It's very deep. She's losing a lot of blood—we have to get
her to town," the physician said.

Michael came immediately to his feet with her limp body
held tightly against his chest, staring into her ashen face.

"Come on, we must go!" Sam barked. Michael nodded
and began stumbling toward his coach. His fear was overwhelming; God forbid, if she did not survive . . . He could
not think that! Lord, how he loved her! How he *needed* her.
"Abbey, sweetheart, you must *fight*," he whispered into her
hair. "I need you, darling. Please *fight!*" He climbed quickly
into the carriage, Sam behind him, and shouted at the driver to
head into town.

# Chapter 20

Blinking rapidly, Abbey grimaced at the pain that shot through her head when she finally awoke after swimming in darkness for what seemed like eternity. It was dim, nothing more than a dull glow in the recesses of the darkness, but it was light. Her tongue darted over her dry, cracked lips as she focused on the light.

*Am I dreaming?* Abbey wondered She had to be; it was the only thing that explained the hazy image of Michael in a chair beside her, his elbows propped on his knees, his face buried in his large hands. Dark curls of his hair fell forward, shielding his face from her. Something was wrong. It had to be a dream. She was freezing. She licked her lips and tried to focus her gaze on the image of Michael.

"Cold," she said, her voice raspy and light.

Michael's head jerked up and he stared at her with blood-shot eyes. *"Abbey?"* he whispered, almost inaudibly.

"I'm cold." The dream heard her then, suddenly disappearing from view, and just as quickly reappearing with a blanket. He gently laid it over her and tucked it securely about her leaden limbs. He knelt beside her.

The dream did not speak but his lips trembled faintly as he gently stroked her hair. His tortured gaze darted across her face and finally settled on her eyes. Abbey blinked, unable to focus clearly, but cognizant of the omnipresent sorrow about him.

"A dream," she managed to state, more to herself than to him.

"No, sweetheart," he said in a voice oddly strained. She frowned a little, wincing at the pain. *What had happened to her?* Why was her dream of Michael so sad?

"Sad?" she tried to ask him.

Michael's eyes watered as he held her gaze for a long moment, then finally choked out, "Not any longer." He tenderly stroked her cheek.

"You are sad," she repeated inanely. He did not answer but buried his face in the bed covers.

Mild surprise drifted through Abbey's fogged mind. Under the added blanket, warmth was seeping through her limbs, carrying her away. Her eyelids grew heavy, and with a last flutter of lashes, she looked at his dark head, the trembling in his broad shoulders, and quietly drifted into unconsciousness again.

After several moments, Michael slowly lifted his head and looked at her. She had slipped away again, but a flood of relief washed over him. With the back of his hand, he wiped his wet eyes, then glanced toward the heavily plastered ceiling. "Thank you, God," he whispered.

He composed himself and pushed himself into the chair that had remained at her bedside for four long days. She was so pale; he could almost see through her skin. She looked so small in the vast bed, so terribly vulnerable. It seemed as if the slightest breeze could carry her away from him.

But her raging fever had broken finally. Dr. Stephens had said she might never waken. He had warned Michael that if her fever did not break soon, the infection from the deep cut could kill her. *She has to fight,* he had said. So Michael had stayed at her bedside, urging her to fight, to live. In the four days the fever had held her captive, he had despaired that she would ever recover. But he had continued to talk to her, to force her to know he was waiting for her. He had read her letters from her family, talked of the places he had seen, and reminisced about their short time together. He had even gone so far as to bring Harry into the sickroom, hoping a friendly lave of her face would rouse her. Nothing had worked, and Dr. Stephens had begun to prepare him for the worst. There were two possibilities, he had said. She would recover completely from the deep wound. Or the infection would ravage her.

And she would die.

*She will not die!* Michael had bellowed like a madman; even Sebastian had cringed. But Michael would not believe she would die. How could he? If she did, there was no point to his life. She was everything to him. She had to live. She had to know how much he loved her. She had to smile again, to play her violin. *She had to live.*

And thank God in heaven, she had awakened, albeit only briefly. A new rash of tears filled his eyes as he sat gazing down at the small bundle under the mound of blankets that was his Abbey. *She had to live.*

Abbey awoke to bright sunlight streaming into the room. She winced when her eyes fluttered open; the light pierced her and sent shooting spasms of pain down her spine. But it paled in comparison to the deep burning in her side.

"Can you hear me, mum?" She recognized Sarah's voice. She could not answer right away; her throat was parched and she swallowed hard.

"Water," she croaked hoarsely. Sarah hastily complied, slipping her arm behind her back and lifting her head so she could drink. The pain was crippling, and she could only take a few sips.

"It hurts," she mumbled.

Sarah's face loomed over hers, frowning. "I know, I know. Dr. Stephens will give you some laudanum after he examines you. It will help ease your pain," Sarah said, her eyes welling. "Oh, mum, you don't know how *relieved* we all are!"

Abbey squinted at her friend and noticed her eyes were wet. Wet like Michael's. She had dreamed he was here.

"What happened?" she rasped.

Sarah looked away. "I'll fetch Dr. Stephens. Lie quietly," she whispered, then was gone.

Abbey strained to see the canopy above her bed and tried to concentrate. She could remember dressing. She remembered thinking how lovely her amethyst earrings would have looked with her gown. The memory inexplicably made her flinch.

"Lady Darfield, how wonderful to see those violet eyes open!" a voice boomed. A pinched face with spectacles and a puckered smile appeared above her, and she recognized Dr. Stephens. "You've given us all quite a scare, madam. Can you see my finger? Ah, very good. Now follow it with your eyes, will you?" He moved his finger to one side. Abbey grimaced; even the smallest movement of her eyes was painful.

"Very good, very good indeed. Don't fret now, you'll be better in time. I'm going to give you some laudanum to help ease the pain." His hands were fluttering down her torso, then pressing against her side. Abbey gasped as his hand ran across the burning and closed her eyes as pain spiraled through her.

"Nasty wound. Quite deep, I'm afraid. It will take some time to heal properly. Happy to say no limbs were broken, but you may notice a headache from the laudanum."

Abbey felt the panic again. "A wound?"

Dr. Stephens puckered smile appeared again and he pushed his spectacles back to the bridge of his nose. "What is your name?"

Surely he remembered her name. "Abbey."

"Do you know where you are?"

Was he addled? "Blessing Park," she muttered weakly.

"Yes, that's right. Do you remember how you were injured?"

Abbey's brows shifted into a confused frown as she thought

about that. She could remember nothing but dressing, and gingerly shook her head.

"You were stabbed with a saber," he announced matter-of-factly.

*Stabbed with a saber?* What was he saying? "I don't think so," she murmured faintly.

"Do you recall anything about that morning?" he asked again.

*What* morning? The last thing she remembered was standing in her dressing room. "I was dressing . . ." She trailed off.

The physician frowned.

"Lady Darfield, you have suffered a rather serious injury that will require some time to heal. You will need plenty of bed rest. Sarah, bring a cup of tea," he boomed.

*Serious injury?* Panic was now racing through her. "What injury?" Abbey struggled to ask, and gasped loudly as his fingers touched the burn beneath her breast.

He glanced up from his ministrations. "You need to rest now." From the corner of her eye, Abbey saw Sarah put the laudanum in the tea, then lean down to help her drink it. Abbey could hardly choke it down, but Dr. Stephens was insistent.

"She's very weak. When she next awakens, get some broth down her," the physician was saying. The laudanum worked quickly, and Abbey suddenly found it difficult to keep her eyes open. Weak was not good for her baby, she thought absently as the tingling warmth spread through her.

*Baby.* Abbey forced her eyes open. "My baby!" she said hoarsely. Sarah exchanged an unmistakable look of pity with the doctor. *"My baby!"* Sarah turned away, her eyes wet, as Dr. Stephens grasped her hand.

"Now, now, don't distress yourself. You weren't very far along after all. You will have ample opportunity to bear other children . . ." Abbey didn't hear anything else; she could barely comprehend what he implied.

She had lost her baby. Hot tears spilled down her cheeks, the pain in her side suddenly matched by a sharp pain in her chest. She struggled to keep her eyes open; she had to know what had happened. But she was no match for the heavy dose of laudanum, and she slipped into oblivion, mourning her unborn child.

Dr. Stephens watched her slip away, then sighed wearily as he turned to Sarah, who was unabashedly wiping tears from her face. "Buck up, now, girl. You've got to make sure she takes some nourishment when she awakens. She's extremely weak." He started toward the door, then glanced back at Abbey.

"I had hoped to keep the unfortunate news from her a bit longer," he said wistfully, then shrugged and walked out the door. He moved rapidly down the hall and winding marble staircase, then silently down the thick blue carpet of the corridor leading to the marquis's study. After rapping sharply, he entered without waiting for an invitation.

Michael was seated behind his desk in a rumpled shirt opened at the neck and pulled from his trousers. His hair was wildly tousled and the dark stubble of a beard shadowed his chin and gaunt cheeks. His features were drawn and haggard; dark circles made his eyes appear sunken. He looked as if he had not slept in several days, and, of course, he had not. He stood when Dr. Stephens entered and came quickly around the desk.

The doctor frowned disapprovingly. "I am not sure which patient is in more need of my services," he said dryly, heading for the sideboard.

"How is she?" Michael demanded.

"She's very weak, but lucid. Her fever has broken for the moment, but I am still quite worried about infection. It appears she recalls nothing of the accident; my guess is that the trauma has blocked her memory."

"*Will* she recall it?" he asked anxiously.

Dr. Stephens very slowly and thoughtfully shook his head. "I don't know. These things are hard to predict, but I'd say there is an even chance she will recall everything. I've given her some laudanum for the pain and to help her sleep. She needs a great deal of bed rest and nourishment. She must take

broth over the next day or so, even if she doesn't want it."
The doctor Stephens paused to sniff his brandy, observing
Michael over the rim of his snifter.

"I must say, I am encouraged. It's rather miraculous that
she isn't suffering more, given the length of her fever and the
severity of her wound. Not to mention the physical trauma of
losing a fetus."

Michael nodded slowly, then sighed and thrust a hand
through his hair.

"If you don't get some sleep soon, you will suffer the
consequence, I can assure you." Michael gave him a very
impatient look. "She's not going anywhere, sir, and her pros-
pects of recovering are vastly improved this morning. She will
need your strength; you are not doing her a bloody bit of good
like this," the doctor scolded. "Should I prescribe laudanum
for you, as well?

"I do not need any of your damned laudanum, Joseph,"
Michael muttered.

"You don't need any more whiskey, either. When was the
last time you ate?" Dr. Stephens demanded.

"Two nights ago," Jones stated from the doorway. His
footfall silent on the Aubusson carpet, he carried a silver tray
and covered plate to Michael's desk.

"I insist you eat whatever is on that plate, Darfield. Then
take a bath and go to bed. She'll sleep through the day and
probably the night. You can renew your vigil in the morning."

"How long, Joseph? Before she fully recovers?" Michael
asked, ignoring the food and Jones.

"She has to get past the threat of infection first. Until she
fully recovers? A month at least, probably longer."

"Will she be able to conceive again?" he asked quietly.

"I think the odds are no worse or no better than before. For
now, the object is to get her strength back."

Dr. Stephens set his snifter down and started toward the
door. "Another thing, Darfield. See to it that she is not unduly
excited. She must remain calm and get plenty of bed rest," he
instructed, "and so should you." He motioned authoritatively

toward the covered dish. "Eat whatever Jones has served you, and get some sleep." He walked to the open door and paused.

"There is one last thing. She knows she lost the babe."

The pain on Michael's face was instantaneous and moving. He quickly glanced away from the doctor and moved woodenly toward the large bank of windows overlooking the gardens below. "I had hoped to tell her," he muttered helplessly.

"I had no choice; she suspected it." With that, Dr. Stephens adjusted his spectacles. "I shall see you in the morning. Send for me if there is any change," he said briskly, and left. Michael remained staring out over the gardens.

Behind him, Jones cleared his throat. "Your dinner, my lord." Resigned, Michael turned and slowly walked to the desk, dropping heavily into the leather chair as Jones uncovered a bowl of beef stew. With the butler hovering directly behind him, Michael felt compelled to taste it, and found after a few bites that he was ravenous. Numb, he ate the entire serving as well as two chunks of bread.

Finally, he pushed the bowl away, feeling exhausted. Dr. Stephens was right; he needed a bath and some sleep. The last four days had been a nightmare for him. From the moment he had lifted her body from the ground, he had been on the verge of shattering. He bitterly recalled how he had rushed Abbey to London, only to be told by the doctor, after stanching the bleeding, that she had lost too much blood and likely would not live. Refusing to believe that dire prognosis, and concerned about the notoriety her injuries might receive in London, he had determined that Dr. Stephens would see to her. He had cradled her limp body in his arms for the two-hour ride to Blessing Park as her blood slowly escaped the bandages and seeped into his clothes. He had prayed fervently and awkwardly that God not take her from him.

Michael had never been a devout man and was at a loss how to ask for the help he needed. He begged, bargained, and promised his own life for hers if God would spare her. In helpless frustration he watched her, lying unconscious in her bed, tossing with fever, and growing paler with each passing day. He had passed each night at her bedside, imagining the worst. At times, a small movement or sound from her made him dare to hope. But most of the time, he saw little change and despaired completely.

So when she had miraculously opened her eyes last night, relief and gratitude had washed over him so strongly that he had wept like a child. Never had he felt such powerful emotions, it was as if he had just escaped the hangman's noose, had been given a second chance at life.

But it was not over yet. Dr. Stephens had warned him of the infection. And there would be more than the physical damage to deal with. Michael could not think of that now. The first task was to get her well, and Dr. Stephens was correct that his lack of sleep and food, coupled with copious quantities of whiskey, was impairing his ability to help her.

Pushing away from the desk, he told Jones to have a bath readied, and began walking wearily to his rooms. At the top of the staircase, he paused outside the door of her sitting room, which he seemed to do every time he was in the corridor. That room had been so full of life before they had gone to London. Bloody hell, *why* had he taken her there? Why had he been so eager to show her to the same society that had once shunned him? This never would have happened if they had remained at Blessing Park as she had wanted. He stared at the door for a long moment, then impulsively opened it and stepped inside.

It was as he remembered. Bright sunshine streamed in the windows. Magazines and books were strewn everywhere, and mounds of needlework were heaped near every seat. He walked slowly through the cheerful room, taking in every detail. Their things had been retrieved from London, and it looked as if she had never left. Near the fireplace, her violin case was propped against the hearth stones. He averted his gaze from the instrument before a deep sense of loss could invade him.

He moved to leave the room when his gaze fell upon the mound of sewing next to an overstuffed armchair. He stooped to pick up a piece of soft linen he vaguely recognized. It was her rendition of Blessing Park—she had told him that, but still, he could not make heads or tails of it. He smiled softly to himself. The memory of her sitting in his study, laboring over that stitchery, made his heart ache. With one last look around the room, he tossed the linen down and quietly left the room.

The first rays of gray morning light were peeking in the windows when Abbey resurfaced. With a moan, she pressed her palm against her forehead; the pain behind her eyes was almost blinding. She struggled against her pillows and finally managed to raise herself an inch or two so she could see the room. On the green silk settee in front of the fireplace, Sarah slept.

"Sarah," she called, noting her voice was stronger. The sleeping figure bolted upright and tossed a blanket aside. It was Michael who strode quickly to her bedside.

He sat gingerly on the side of the bed and leaned over her, his fingers wandering lightly down her cheek and neck. "Are you all right? How do you feel?" he whispered anxiously.

"Michael?" Abbey asked, uncertain why she should be surprised.

"Are you in pain?"

Abbey swallowed and closed her eyes, nodding slightly. 'No laudanum, please," she whispered.

He stroked her face again. "You must take some broth," he murmured, and reached behind her to pull the bell cord.

"What happened?" she asked.

Michael smiled weakly. "It's a long story, sweetheart. It will have to wait until you are stronger."

"You are not supposed to be here," she said uncertainly.

"I'm not?"

"I'm not supposed to be at Blessing Park."

"You belong at Blessing Park," Michael answered curtly, then immediately softened. "I brought you here so Dr. Stephens could attend you," he murmured as he carefully brushed hair from her face.

"I fell, I think," she said as the door opened behind them.

His gaze riveted on her eyes. "Do you remember the accident?" he asked slowly.

"Doctor said I was stabbed," she added, confused.

Michael muttered something over his shoulder, then turned back to her with a gentle smile on his face. "I'm sorry, darling. You were wounded rather badly."

"Did you see?"

His expression darkened. "I saw it, yes," he muttered, sounding almost angry.

Abbey slid her gaze to the windows. Why couldn't she remember? Michael absently stroked her cheek with the back of his knuckles.

"I don't understand." Something was wrong. She could not conceive of being cut, with a saber, no less. How had it happened? *Why* had it happened? And Michael was not supposed to be by her side.

"You should not be here," she tried again.

"Perhaps not. But I am here, and I am not leaving you." She realized he did not deny he should not be there. Something was undeniably and terribly wrong.

"It's not right," she attempted again. Michael's face darkened as the door opened behind him.

Sarah appeared in Abbey's view. "You are looking better all the time," she lied, and set a silver tray on a table.

"How long . . ."

"Almost a week," Michael answered softly.

*A week?* The panic she could not seem to escape was mounting rapidly. "How bad?" she asked, the panic raising the pitch of her voice. Michael said something to Sarah, who immediately brought a bowl over to him.

"You must drink this broth, sweetheart," he said, and forced a spoon between her lips.

Abbey swallowed, but caught his hand before he could force the second spoonful. "Will I recover?" she asked with alarm.

Michael's eyes slipped to her mouth. "Of course you will," he said, and spooned more of the broth down her. He was lying; it was plainly written on his face. Good God, she was going to die! No wonder she could barely move her limbs! She started to struggle. She heard Michael tell Sarah to hold her arms and was aware that he was leaning over her, trapping her with his powerful body, forcing the broth down her throat. *Oh, dear God, please do not let me die! I am not ready to die!* Michael was wiping her mouth with a soft linen towel, saying something to her, but she could not hear him. Whatever had happened, for whatever reason she had been cut by a saber, she had lost everything. Her baby. Her health. *Michael.* She did not know why or how, but she *knew* she had lost him, too.

When Michael pressed the teacup to her lips, she jerked her head away, and the wrenching pain sent her tumbling downward into the black abyss.

After she had been bathed and her linens changed, Michael sat in a chair next to the bed, staring down at his ravaged wife who, for the moment, was resting peacefully. The lines that had appeared the last few days around her eyes were smooth in sleep, and even the dark circles and lack of color in her cheeks weren't as noticeable. She looked angelic.

She also looked very helpless. He knew it would not be long before the dreams would come to her again, tormenting her as they had since they had begun administering the large doses of laudanum. Last night she had tossed and turned, crying out in her sleep and flinching with the pain of her own involuntary movement. He suspected memories were coming back to her in sleep that she had not yet connected with reality. He could only pray that she would regain her strength before she remembered it all.

Several days passed before Abbey was able to sit up in bed. Sarah and Michael took turns at her bedside, forcing broth and, later, some type of mush into her. Most days Harry was allowed to lie at the foot of her bed. His familiar weight against her leg became the subtle assurance that she was going to live. The pain in her head had become less severe, but she was still troubled by a dull ache and periods of darkness. Dr. Stephens seemed quite confident it would disappear altogether, just as he assured her the pain in her side would go away eventually. He prescribed less laudanum for her and pronounced her on the mend, given the circumstances.

Late one afternoon she was propped against the pillows, feeling stronger. Sarah had given in to her demands to have her hair washed, but insisted she sit up until it dried. "Don't want a bad ague on top of everything else," she had cautioned. Dressed in a silk nightrail, Abbey half listened to Sarah and Molly, a chambermaid, as they chatted while cleaning her room. They were oblivious to her; she rarely said anything. She felt so empty, felt such a dull, aching loss she attributed to nothing and everything, that she had begun to believe the laudanum had destroyed her mind and her senses. She felt peculiar, different somehow. As if she had lost not only her baby but a part of herself.

She was preoccupied with her attempt to dredge up fragments of memory from the recesses of her mind. She had reclaimed snatches of it, but the picture was incomplete. She remembered the time she had spent at Blessing Park and was aware that she had felt as whole and complete in that time as she ever had. Yet she was terribly disconcerted that while she loved Michael dearly, she felt oddly disconnected from him, almost fearful. Was that due to the laudanum? Or something else, something she could not remember? On the few occasions she had asked what had happened to her, no one would answer her, leading her to conclude something terrible had indeed happened. She knew she had been in London. She could remember snippets of a ball and dancing with Michael. She remembered hitting him, too, but that was so fantastic that it had to be part of the fiction she was convinced her mind was perpetrating.

"Whatever happened to your cousin Glory? Hadn't she met some fine sailor?" Sarah asked Molly as they folded a freshly laundered bed sheet.

Molly clucked disdainfully. "Rotten one, he was. Promised the moon and the stars. I tell you. And not just to Glory. A serving wench on the west side, too," she said bitterly.

"You don't say? Poor Glory! She was quite smitten with him, wasn't she?"

"Oh, she loved him more than life itself. Crushed her, he did."

"Did he marry the other?" Sarah asked as she took the folded sheet and placed it on a stack of others.

"Marry? Ha! He left town, the coward. Sailed for America, the dirty bounder. Lied to them both," Molly muttered.

"Lied to them both," Abbey mumbled unwittingly. Her eyes widened suddenly. *Galen!* Routier! A flurry of images began to swim in her head. Galen holding a doll. Routier's hands groping her breast in the maze, Galen driving her in a curricle. *A duel.* The memories came in torrents, overloading her senses. The dull ache behind her eyes began to intensify, and her pulse began to pound convulsively in her neck. She heard herself cry out, saw Sarah drop the linens and fly to her bedside.

"Molly! Fetch Lord Darfield! Don't dally, girl, *go!*" Sarah shrieked.

Abbey stared wildly at Sarah. "I remember, I remember, Sarah! Oh, God, I remember!" she rasped hysterically.

Sarah gripped her hands tightly and held them. "It's all over now! It's all over!"

*"Routier!"*

"He's dead!"

"No, no! Galen! Where is my cousin? Where is Galen?"

"It's all over and done!" Sarah pled with her. Abbey shook her head, grimacing in pain as she did. She yanked her hands free of Sarah and began to claw toward the edge of the bed, the pain in her side stabbing her like a hot iron.

"No, no! There is more, much more! Southerland! I want to speak with the duke!" Abbey cried.

"You must stay abed, mum! Molly went to fetch Lord Darfield for you—" Sarah cried as she grabbed Abbey around the waist.

"*No!* I don't want to see him, Sarah!" Abbey sobbed.

"I am already here," Michael said from the doorway. Behind him, Molly's eyes were wide as an owl's. Michael nodded at Sarah, who reluctantly pulled away from Abbey.

"Sarah, don't go!" Abbey begged. Sarah stopped halfway across the room and looked at Michael.

"She'll be quite safe, Sarah. Go on," Michael said softly, and waited for Sarah to skirt around him and shut the door behind her.

Confused and oddly apprehensive, Abbey shrank against the linens as he crossed to the bed. "I want to talk to the duke!" she insisted desperately, pushing herself into the mound of pillows.

"Alex is presently in London. But you can talk to me, sweetheart," he said calmly.

"*No!* Something is not right! *You* are not right!"

Michael squatted next to the bed and reached for her hand, but she pulled it away. "We will make it right, Abbey, you and me."

"I remember! I remember Galen and Routier!"

Michael winced, his jaw clenching. "I know it must be hard for you. It was very traumatic, love. But I'm glad you are remembering—it means you are healing, and I so want you to heal."

"*Glad?* Why? So you can cease pretending to care? I remember, Michael!"

Michael's face fell. He pushed a hand through his hair as his eyes danced across the blanket covering her. "I *do* care, very much, Abbey! You've no idea how much! But unless you remember, we can never rebuild what we had."

Abbey closed her eyes against the pounding in her head. Oh, God, it was so confusing. She wanted to believe him, but she remembered that he despised her. He had refused to believe her, had chosen to believe she had intentionally lied to him. As the memories continued to stream in, she recalled how she had loved him and how he had hurt her, had gone to Lady Davenport. God, how she hated him. How she *loved* him. It was more than she could bear. "Please leave me," she muttered through clenched teeth.

"Abbey, darling, don't send me away! We should talk about this!"

"You didn't want to talk before, Michael. Please go!" she

cried, and rolled away from him, squeezing her eyes tightly against an onslaught of tears.

Michael stood unsteadily. He was not surprised. He instinctively understood that her recovery would not be complete unless it was both physical and emotional. He stood solemnly, his heart aching as sobs racked her emaciated frame. He leaned over and touched her shoulder, but she recoiled from him.

His heart leapt to his throat. He would win her back. Maybe not today, but by God, he would win her back. With a heavy sigh, he turned and walked slowly to the door, fervently hoping she would call him back and closing the door quietly when she did not.

# *Chapter 21*

"She is remarkably well, Darfield. It seems she has completely regained her memory and her wound has healed nicely." Dr. Stephens and Michael stood on the back terrace of Blessing Park overlooking the gardens. Below them, in a circle of rosebushes, Abbey was seated on a wrought-iron bench with Harry at her feet, quietly reading. Her garish gardening hat obscured her view of them.

"I am pleased to see that she's put on some weight," Stephens continued.

"Cook's tarts," Michael replied.

Dr. Stephens chuckled. "Yet she still suffers from melancholy. I would be more encouraged if her spirits were brighter. If it's the miscarriage that has her down, then you should set the matter to rights, Darfield," the doctor said gruffly.

If only he could get close enough to her to set the matter to rights. "I do not think it's that, Joseph." Michael sighed wearily.

Stephens peered over the rim of his spectacles at Michael. "Indeed?" he drawled.

Michael ignored the doctor's pointed question. It was no secret at Blessing Park that the Darfields were estranged, and Michael could hardly defer to her physical condition as the excuse any longer. In truth, Abbey looked very well. Her color was back, and although she was still a little on the thin side, she was well on her way to fully recovering her health.

But her heart had most definitely not healed. In the six weeks since she recalled the accident and the events surrounding it, Michael had tried to talk to her about it. But she avoided him, making feeble excuses. He had done everything he knew to do, including sending armfuls of roses as a peace offering, although it had cost him any hope of peace with Withers. What she thought about them, he never knew. She steadfastly refused to accept his invitation to walk with him, to dine with him, to be with him at all. He had to appreciate the irony; four short months ago, he would have been grateful for her indifference. But that was before he had fallen in love with her, and nothing that had ever happened to him, not war, not his father's betrayal, nothing hurt as badly as her indifference.

He knew instinctively why she was hurting. She believed he had wronged her, had not trusted her when he should have. On one level, he understood it. He should have believed her. But on another level, it angered him, and he could not understand it. He loved her. Yet she had lied to him. For Galen. Even after everything that bastard had done, she still asked Sarah about him, wondering where he was, if he was all right, if he had tried to see her. It angered him and he could not reconcile it, but he was willing to put it behind them. He was willing to do anything to have her back.

Abbey, apparently, was not.

The six weeks of her recovery had been agony for him. He missed her terribly, their conversations, the quiet evenings they had once spent together. He missed the sound of her violin and her light, lilting laugh. He missed her brilliant smile. His need for her was too great; when she was nearby his body turned to marble from sheer longing. During days that seemed endless, he was drawn to wherever she was. He could not stay away from her any more than he could stop torturing himself by gazing at her and thinking of burying himself deep within her.

"Do you think she can withstand the stress of a surprise now?" Michael asked Dr. Stephens.

"Of course. Have a good one in mind, do you?"

"A visit from her family. Sebastian should be returning any day now from America with one aunt and two cousins in tow."

"She should be fine. But do not overtax her, is that clear?"

Michael nodded. He, of course, would not know if she was overtaxed, since he could barely draw more than monosyllabic answers from her about anything. According to Sarah, she was fine. At least on the surface, she seemed alive and well, he thought grimly as he looked down at her from the terrace and swallowed past a lump in his throat. "I'll never be able to thank you enough, Joseph. I was sure I had lost her. If it weren't for you . . ."

"Really, Darfield, it is my duty as a physician," the doctor said self-consciously, his cheeks coloring. "Well, I suppose I had best be on my way. I shall come again next week. Mind you treat her well, old boy," he said, and with a curt nod, turned to leave.

Michael saw the family doctor out and returned to the terrace. Withers had joined Abbey and was relating some animated tale, waving his hamlike fists in the morning sun. Abbey was laughing. God, would she ever bestow that dazzling smile on him again? He settled his hip against the stone wall and watched as Withers motioned toward the hothouse. Abbey placed her book on the bench and walked slowly alongside the gardener, her hips swinging softly beneath the pleats of her skirt as they strolled casually through the garden. As Michael watched her pause to examine some new buds on a rosebush, he decided if he was ever going to have the chance to stroll in the gardens with her again, he had to talk and she had to listen. She could not avoid it any longer.

Neither could he.

*          *          *

Abbey had taken to having her meals in her sitting room, but Michael sent word that he expected her in the dining room at eight-thirty that evening. When she had sent a terse, handwritten note replying she preferred to dine alone, Michael had smiled wryly and penned a note to her saying he would brook no argument. If she was not in the dining room at precisely eight-thirty, he would physically retrieve her.

He prowled the room like a caged animal past two nervous footmen standing at the sideboard. When the mantel clock chimed eight-thirty, Michael looked expectantly at the oak door. She was a fool if she thought he would not carry through on his threat. At eight-thirty-two, she pushed the heavy oak door open and marched into the room, planted her fists on her hips, and glared angrily at him.

"May I ask why I have been summoned?" she snapped.

Michael silently sucked in his breath. She looked ravishing. She had not bothered to dress her hair, and it flowed freely down her back. Her dark-gold gown, free of petticoats, flowed to the floor in gentle folds.

Best of all, her violet eyes were sparkling with complete irritation.

"I want your company, my dear."

"My *company?* That's quite surprising. You have never wanted it before!"

"That is hardly true, Abbey, and you know it. Please be seated. We can argue over supper," he said cheerfully, and pulled out a chair for her. She glanced suspiciously at the chair, then at him. He lifted one dark brow in question. With a sigh of exasperation, she marched over and plopped down without ceremony, giving him almost no time to slide the chair beneath her. He could not help grinning as he took his seat at the head of the table. Abbey glared at the footman when he set a bowl of soup in front of her, causing the poor man practically to sprint back to the sideboard.

Michael was unaffected by her anger. At the moment, he did not care what she did. He was so delighted to have her sitting at his right where she belonged that little else mattered. He stole a glance at her; she stared at her bowl, making no move to eat it. He shrugged indifferently and began to eat.

For several moments, there was no sound but the clink of Michael's spoon against fine china. Abbey abruptly pushed her soup aside. "What do you want?"

"I miss dining with you. Won't you try the soup?"

"I am not the least bit hungry."

"Aren't you indeed? Perhaps you would like a drink?"

"No!" she replied without hesitation.

"What, no ale? We have plenty in stock," he said dryly.

Abbey frowned. "What do you want?" she demanded again.

Michael leaned back, pressing his splayed fingertips together. "I told you. I miss dining with you," he said genuinely. Abbey rolled her eyes and looked away. "You are quite recovered and well enough to begin to take your meals in here, don't you think?"

"My health is not the issue, my lord. I prefer dining alone," she said coldly.

Michael did not intend to let her new habit of addressing him formally or her acerbic tongue deter him. "Nevertheless, I do not prefer to dine alone. Scintillating conversation aids my digestion." The footman set a plate in front of him. "Ah, the veal looks very good this evening," he said casually, and knifed a portion. Abbey ignored her plate. Apparently she preferred to starve than dine with him.

"You should really eat something, Abbey. You're rather thin—"

"I shall be well enough to sail for America in a fortnight or so," she said flippantly.

"Indeed?" Michael asked impassively, then looked to one of the footmen. "My compliments to Cook. This is really quite delicious." He fit another bite into his mouth.

Abbey frowned. "Is there nothing you would say, then?" she demanded.

"I have remarked on the veal. What else is there?"

"That is not what I meant!"

"I beg your pardon. What exactly did you mean?" he asked calmly.

Abbey leaned forward and glared at him. "I *mean*, my lord, is there nothing you would say about my imminent return to America?"

Michael leaned back and turned his gaze to the candelabra above them, pretending to contemplate her declaration. "No, I don't suppose there is," he responded cheerfully after a long moment.

Abbey exhaled loudly. "What did you expect?" he smiled. She picked up a fork and began to push peas around her plate.

"I expected you would be pleased, or angry . . . I don't know! I suppose I thought you would at least acknowledge it!"

"I see no point in acknowledging something that is not about to happen," he remarked.

Abbey's brows snapped together in an angry line. "I should have done it months ago!"

"Ah, it was no more likely then than it is now. What about some pudding?" he asked, nodding to a footman. "At least eat something, sweetheart."

"I don't want any pudding! Stop trying to change the subject."

Michael nodded to the two footmen then and they quietly vacated the room. When the door closed behind them, he poured a small glass of port and held it out in the gesture of a toast.

"Abbey, I hope you will hear me with an open heart and mind," he started. Abbey's swinging foot slowly stopped. Now, *that* was the Abbey he knew and loved. Not one emotion would pass through her that he would not see. She glanced at him from the corner of her eye.

"Hear what?" she asked suspiciously.

"Hear what I have to say about London, about the accident and the events surrounding it."

"You've said quite enough in the past few months, my lord. I am not sure I want to hear any more," she responded quietly. She sounded sadly sincere.

Michael set his port on the table. "I will grant you that I have said quite a lot, but is there no common ground on which we may converse?"

"Common ground?" She laughed. "How rich. We have *never* stood on common ground," she scoffed. "You made that perfectly clear the day I came here."

"We did. Until the day you lied to me about Galen," he said solemnly.

That stopped her cold. Like a dozen afternoon clouds, a range of emotions skirted across her face. Disbelief, anger, hurt; they were all there.

Michael reached for her hand, but she yanked it from his reach. "I am not finding fault, I am stating a fact. I don't blame you, Abbey. I understand why you did it, but at least try to understand my perspective."

"And what perspective would that be? That I would betray you? That I would scheme against you? That everything I ever said to you was a lie? *That* perspective?" she shot back.

Michael sighed. "This is not easy for either of us, darling. But please understand me. I want you back. I love you will all my heart, and I always will."

"*Don't!*" Abbey choked, and flung her hands up in front of her face, shielding herself. "How *dare* you? How dare you say that to me now?" She gasped painfully.

"It's true, Abbey," he said softly, "I love you." Abbey dragged her tortured gaze from him to the candelabra. But at least she was listening.

"When Galen Carrey appeared on our doorstep, I did not believe his claim. I was nonplussed, but I could not believe you would so brazenly betray me or what we shared at Blessing Park. It did not seem possible you could have fabricated the affection or esteem you showed me."

Abbey winced. "Thank you for that much, anyway," she said bitterly.

"But I could not be completely sure," he continued. "You lied to me, Abbey. You did not tell me who he was when I asked you. You had gone to Pemberheath against my express wishes and had seen him there. He had corresponded with you without my knowledge. You gave him *money*. And you had come here under very confusing circumstances, you must admit. What was I to think?''

"I did not *lie* to you, Michael. I just did not tell you everything! I did not tell you he was my cousin. That was my crime.''

"Semantics, love.''

Abbey's eyes flashed angrily. "You didn't tell me everything. You didn't tell me about your suspicions, or the doll. Was that just semantics?''

"I didn't tell you because I wasn't sure of your relationship with Galen.''

"Did you think to *ask*?'' she asked bitterly.

"Of course. Had I asked, would you have told me about the letters and the money?''

Abbey's eyes widened, but she would not look at him. "Had you been here, had you not left me like a dock wench, I might have. But later? I doubt it. You were not even civil to me. I can't believe I could have told you anything you would have believed. You were too busy worrying if I was cuckolding you,'' she said incredulously.

"I was,'' he admitted painfully, "insanely jealous.'' He was still haunted by the image of Routier and Abbey in the maze. He shook his head to clear it.

"Surely you will not try to convince me that the horrid things you said were because you were jealous!'' she gasped.

"I'm not trying to convince you of anything. But the things I said were borne of jealousy. I could not stand to see another man with you, *especially*,'' he muttered angrily, "Routier.''

A long, silent minute passed while Abbey stared at him, slack-jawed. She braced white-knuckled hands against the table to steady herself. "Another man,'' she repeated in a strangled voice.

"Right or wrong, I believed you had lied to me, and when I saw you dancing with other men, then laughing with Routier, of all men, I'm afraid it brought out the worst in me. When I denied his offer for Mariah's hand, he vowed to see me ruined. I saw him attempting to do that through you.'' As painful as it was, Michael was trying his best to be as honest as he knew how.

That startling revelation sent rage spiraling dangerously out of control in Abbey. Was she to understand that Routier was the man who had spread such vile rumors about Michael? Good *God*, why hadn't someone told her? Why hadn't *he* told her? "Let me make sure I understand you," she spoke at last in a voice trembling with fury. "I did not tell you that Galen was my cousin. And because you were absent from Blessing Park, I did not tell you about his letters, or that he borrowed money—*my* money. And from that you concluded that we were lovers and determined to defraud you."

Michael was silent; she did not want a response, she wanted his jugular.

"And then, despite having left me to visit your *lover*, you became jealous when I laughed in the company of *Routier*?" she shrieked. She suddenly pounded her palms on the table and pushed back. The heavy, upholstered oak dining chair toppled behind her.

"Dear God, what an incredible fool I've been! And I thought you didn't believe me, that you thought I had lied about everything I had ever said to you or had *been* with you! How stupid of me! You accused me of cuckolding you because you were *jealous*! By God, Michael, you *told* me to dance with other men!" she cried. "But you *never* told me who Routier was!" She whirled and began marching toward the door. Michael came quickly to his feet and caught her before she could reach it.

"*Unhand me!*" she shouted.

Michael wrapped his arms around her, pinning her arms to her sides. He tightened his grip when she began to struggle. Her soft body was pressed hard against his frame and the familiar scent of sweet lilac wafted over him.

"I know you are angry—"

"What in God's name do you expect?!"

"I am sorry, sweetheart, I was wrong to suspect you. I only want to go back to the way we were. I want to love you, Abbey. And I want you to love me again."

She was not listening; her eyes darted frantically across his chest as thoughts raced through her mind. "And next time I laugh, Michael? Will you think I have betrayed you? When you look death in the face, will you ask me to give my child your name and go to your grave wondering if it is *yours?*" she cried out.

Michael sucked in his breath, realizing she had misconstrued his words the morning of the duel. "I meant if you should remarry, I wanted the child to have my name! Jesus, Abbey, you *lied*! You defended him!" he roared.

Abbey choked on a sob. "Dear God, I can love you with all my heart and *still* have enough for others! It's not all or nothing! But you don't understand that! You choose between your mistress and your wife, all or nothing!"

"Abbey—"

She brought her heel down as hard as she could on the top of his boot. Michael immediately let go and stepped back, wincing with pain. Abbey's hands fisted at her sides, her breath came in angry rasps.

"Did you know," she said hoarsely, unshed tears brimming in her eyes, "that with every doubt, you broke my heart in two?" She angrily hit her chest with her fist. "There is nothing left but *pieces*," she rasped. Michael took a step toward her.

"No!" she shouted angrily. "Don't come near me again! You are an *ass*, Michael Ingram, and I *hate* you," she cried bitterly, and ran from the room.

Stunned, Michael remained standing for some time before returning to his seat and his port. He had lost her. And she was right. He was an ass.

At three in the morning, Abbey had yet to undress. The pounding in her head was almost more than she could bear. She paced about her chamber angrily, heartbroken by what he had told her and furious she had spent so much time feeling guilty, feeling *sorry* for him, believing he was the victim! She had bitterly reconciled herself to the fact that he was faithless and had cast her aside in a heartbeat, and *that* had been more than she thought she could tolerate.

And why, good God in heaven, did he have to say *now* that he loved her, to say the words she had so longed to hear from his lips?

She stared at the door that adjoined their rooms and wondered if he was in there, sleeping peacefully while she was tormented. He had made his little confession and now his confession, his jealousy, was her cross to bear. The very idea infuriated her, and suddenly she could not go another minute without telling him what a heartless scoundrel he was. She wanted to hurt *him*, to see dejected pain in *his* eyes. Ignoring the pounding in her head, she marched to the door and jerked it open, and, passing through the dressing room, shoved forcefully against his door.

The room was swathed in darkness except for the red embers of a dying fire. It was light enough for her to see him sitting on top of the brocade cover of his bed, one leg stretched long in front of him, the other serving as a prop for his arm. He had stripped down to his shirt and trousers, and jerked his head toward her when she marched into the room. Intense fury bubbled to the surface of her consciousness. She flew across the room, intent on inflicting any pain she could. He caught her easily. His strong hold clamped around her as he rolled over, pinning her down beneath him before she realized what had happened. Abbey was speechless as she stared up at his dark face.

"I love you, Abbey, God, I swear I do. I'll spend my life making it up to you."

She caught her breath in her throat; his gray eyes pierced her with a look that made her weak. The realization that one look from him could still send her to her knees and make her body yearn for his touch just added salt to her wounds. Infuriated beyond comprehension, she began to kick wildly. His iron thighs closed around her, and he settled his weight on her, locking her arms with one hand above her head. She was immobilized, and no amount of struggling could free her from his hold.

"I love you," he muttered again, his breath softly fanning her cheek.

"I *hate* you!" she rasped.

"I don't believe you."

"Believe it! How *could* you, Michael? How could you? It's so unfair! I love you so much I would have moved the heavens for you! Why couldn't you just believe it?" she whimpered, closing her eyes against the throbbing in her temples.

"I hope you will find it in that vast heart of yours to forgive me, darling. I will wait as long as it takes," he murmured.

His lips were so close to hers that she could almost feel them. The memory of his lips on hers made her heart pound erratically. Dear God, she was not going to succumb to him now.

But his lips brushed lightly across her forehead, and that tender gesture sent a nerve-shattering pulse down her spine and to the tips of her toes. She closed her eyes against the warring emotions he was evoking. Insane as it was, she desperately needed him to hold her, to soothe her hurt. She felt him lean down until his lips touched hers.

Abbey froze.

His kiss was gentle, carefully molding her lips to his. His tongue darted across her lower lip, then inside. Her own body betrayed her. Desire crashed through her like great waves against the shore. His tongue probed deeply, then retreated, only to return again, sliding slowly past her lips. When he groaned against her mouth, she instinctively responded, meeting him timidly. When he shifted his weight against her, and she felt his swollen manhood pressing against her abdomen, her heart cried out for her to stop.

But her heart was not strong enough. Michael let go of her hands so his own could float to her neck and then her breast. Abbey's own traitorous hands slipped inside his shirt, moving over the soft down, brushing across his nipples. Michael's kiss grew more insistent and deeper. He anchored her to him with one arm while his hand caressed her body. Abbey was dismayed by the stark physical desire and emotional need for him. She had felt so lost the last few weeks, but in his arms, she knew where she was, and as reckless as it was, she needed him. She needed him to hold her, to comfort her, to make love to her.

Somehow, without her help, her gown came off. She was clad in silk chemise, her nipples straining the sheer fabric, and Michael took the peak in his mouth. She lifted beneath him, straining for his touch. His hand floated down her side, found the hem of her chemise, and slipped beneath. She drew her breath, slowly and inaudibly, as his fingers brushed her knee, then the inside of her thigh. When his hand swept the apex of her thighs, she moaned softly in his ear.

"*Abbey,*" he whispered. "*I love you, darling.*" It was the strongest aphrodisiac he could have given her. Tears slipped from her eyes as he began to stroke her seductively, spreading her so he could pleasure her selflessly. He kissed her tears, her lips, her neck. He laved her nipples through the sheer fabric of her chemise while stroking her, exploring her, and bringing her to the edge of fulfillment. And he whispered his love to her, over and over again.

Abbey closed her eyes as tears continued to seep. She was aware when he paused to unsheath his rigid member and, despite her hurt, smiled when he slowly entered her, inch by inch. He continued to stroke her with his fingers while he moved slowly and surely inside of her. Her hands, detached from her body, fluttered over his hard frame, feeling every sinewy muscle, while her tongue painted his lips. She began to teeter on the cusp; his strokes instinctively lengthened.

"*Now, darling.*" He moaned, and as she was swept away by the tide of pleasure that washed over her, she heard him call her name.

She lay there beneath his weight, the path of her tears still wet on her face. He lifted his head from her neck and kissed her cheek.

"Please don't," she whispered through tears of helplessness.

"I'm sorry," he whispered hoarsely again and again. "I'm so so sorry I hurt you. I would that I could take it all back, that we had never left Blessing Park. I would give my life to have those days back, to have you back,'' he said softly, feathering a row of kisses from her cheek to her mouth. Still straddling her, he brought her hand to his mouth, tenderly kissed the palm, then pressed it against his cheek. Abbey's eyes filled, almost blinding her. He sounded so sincere, as if he were in pain, too.

She was so confused! What had she just done?

"Please let me up," she said weakly. He did, reluctantly. She slid off the bed, picked up her gown, and walked away, without a word or a backward glance, through the door adjoining their rooms.

Michael fell onto his back and stared up at the ceiling. Bloody hell, the feel of her in his arms, the sweet, tentative response to him had been his undoing. He had wanted so badly to prove how much he loved her. He had wanted to sink between those soft white thighs and see her eyes pool with desire. He had wanted to hold her close to him, to heal her. But he had not been prepared for the enormity of what just happened. She had come to hurt him, and in her time of need, she had turned to him for comfort, the one person who had hurt her deeply. She had literally clung to him.

Michael moaned and threw his arm over his eyes. She *would* forgive him, if he had to die convincing her. He needed her too badly. He loved her too much. She was more important than the air he breathed, and he'd be damned if he would let her walk out of his life.

Not without a fight.

In all the years Sam had known Michael, he had never seen him so distraught. Not when his sister had been ruined, not when his mother had died, not even the many times his father had disgraced the family name. He watched Michael pacing the library like a caged animal, glaring madly at Galen Carrey, who stood calmly at one end of the room.

He had known there was a risk in bringing Carrey here. But the man had, after all, confessed, had warned Michael about Routier, and, in the end, had killed the bastard. In the weeks since then Sam and Alex had kept him hidden until he could safely leave England, and Sam had softened toward Carrey. He was a young fool, there was no getting around that, and had been led astray, too easily, by Routier. But Sam suspected the young man would pay every day of his life, for the rest of his life, for what he had done. And apologizing to Abbey would not ease that torment, no matter how much Carrey hoped it would.

"She is walking the grounds just now," Sam heard Michael say, and forced his attention back to his friend.

"Thank you, my lord. After I have seen her, I will leave immediately for Portsmouth."

Michael paused in his pacing and eyed Carrey suspiciously. "What are your plans?" he asked slowly.

"I am off to the West Indies. I know a captain of a merchant vessel who might take on an old hand."

"I am sure your cousin will want to hear from you from time to time," Michael muttered.

Carrey arched a brow in surprise. "Then I will oblige her with an occasional letter," he said carefully.

Michael's gaze flicked over him once again, and he turned his back. "Ask Withers. He'll know exactly where she is," he muttered. Carrey shifted a glance to Sam, who nodded, then, without another word, he slipped out through the open doors onto the terrace.

"It was the right thing to do, Michael," Sam offered.

"I doubt it," he muttered. "But it's important to her."

"You might be interested to know I have not heard a single word about the Darfields, other than an outpouring of sympathy for what you must have endured at the hands of Routier," Sam offered.

Michael's gaze slashed across Sam. "You are quite certain?" he asked, a faint tinge of hope evident in his voice.

"Everyone claims to have known that Routier was a scoundrel."

"They knew the truth all along, did they?" Michael muttered sarcastically, and sank into a leather chair. A moment of silence lapsed between them.

"How is Abbey?" Sam asked slowly.

Michael shrugged hopelessly. "Physically? Quite recovered. Emotionally? Terribly distant. Avoids me like death. Seems to think I live by a double standard."

Sam smiled wryly at Michael, who was staring blankly into space. "Be patient awhile longer. I know Abbey loves you, as sure as I stand before you. Just wait for her."

Michael snorted. "Unfortunately, I think I shall wait for the rest of my life."

Just as Withers had said, Abbey was at the ruins. Galen rode to the distant fortress, and when the pile of stones came into view, he could see Abbey standing high atop a mound of rubble that had once been a tower. He reined to a halt at the skirt of the old castle and waved; she did not return his greeting, but peered down at him with a dark frown. A crippled dog, however, roused himself from his nap in the sun and hobbled forward to greet him. Galen slid from his horse and reached down to pet the hound. With a sigh, he straightened, and using a gloved hand to shield the sun, looked up.

"Abbey, it doesn't look quite safe up there!" he called. She responded by turning her back on him. Grumbling, Galen picked his way through rocks that had fallen through the centuries until he stood just below her mound of rubble.

"I know you don't want to speak with me, but I do wish you'd come down from there. If you should fall—"

"So what if I do?" she called down.

"Self-pity does not become you," Galen chided her.

"Do not presume to lecture me, sir," she said icily, but nonetheless began to climb down the mound of rocks. Galen watched as she picked her way down, coming to her side to help her the last few feet. She ignored his outstretched hand and jumped to the ground. She dusted her hands against her black skirt and adjusted her hideous hat before peering up at him.

"How did you get here? I am rather surprised Darfield

would allow it," she said acidly. "Assuming, of course, he knows about it, or are we meeting behind his back again?"

Galen clasped his hands behind his back and gave her a disapproving frown. "I assure you he is very much aware of my presence. I have come to apologize, little one."

"I suppose, like Darfield, you think I should curtsey politely and tell you all is forgiven."

"I do not expect you to do a blasted thing except extend me the common courtesy of at least listening to me," he said.

Abbey shrugged indifferently and began to walk toward what had once been the inner bailey.

Galen fell in beside her. "I know it must be terribly difficult to absorb everything that has happened, but I want you to know I never meant to hurt you."

Abbey laughed disdainfully. "Indeed? You must have thought I would rejoice in your deception when it was all over, seeing that you never meant to hurt me."

"Abbey, I don't expect you to understand, I hardly do myself. But I could not go without telling you how terribly sorry I am that I did this to you. I will never be able to forgive myself."

It was hardly adequate, but it was enough. Abbey sniffed and sat heavily on a pile of rocks that had been a bench at one time. She was not so wounded that she could not see how earnest her cousin was in his apology.

"Oh, Galen." At last she sighed sadly. "I don't pretend to understand, but I bear you no ill will."

Galen sat next to her. "That's exceedingly kind, Abbey, and more than I deserve or could have hoped for. But for some reason, I have the distinct feeling this is not about me," he said softly.

She nodded and cast her gaze to her lap. "You should not have done it. But in the end, it didn't matter what you did, because he never would have believed me. You see, he saw us at the arbor the day you came, and he asked me who you were. I told him you were a deckhand and knew Withers. But I didn't tell him you were my cousin. From that, he assumed I had lied to him about everything."

"I see. That was hardly fair of him."

"It was *horribly* unfair."

"Yes, but what choice did he have?" Galen asked softly.

Confused, Abbey peered at him. "He could have believed me, Galen. I never gave him cause to doubt me."

"You never gave him any cause, but consider it from his viewpoint. What would you think?" A pink stain of embarrassment crept into her cheeks, and she turned away. "You are right, Abbey. He should have believed you. But it is not so unforgivable that he did not, is it? You were not completely truthful. And given the circumstances that followed, he would have been less than human to not at least have questioned."

Abbey's brow wrinkled with thought. "Even if I *did* admit there was some logic to your reasoning, which I have not, the fact of the matter is he did not trust me. And furthermore, he lied to me, too. He didn't tell me he knew the doll you brought was a counterfeit. He accused me of cuckolding him when he had just come from the arms of his lover. I have to ask myself if the affection he professes is true. Or does he say the same thing to *her?*"

Galen chuckled, ignoring Abbey's scowl. He had affection for her, all right. The man was absolutely besotted. Abbey mumbled irritably under her breath.

"My apologies, but the man I just left is so tormented by the thought of losing you that he can barely form a coherent sentence. He paces the library like a panther, glancing frequently out the window to see if you return. I would wager the dark circles under his eyes are from many sleepless nights plagued by thoughts of you."

She rolled her eyes and stood, then walked slowly to what was left of the curtain wall. Galen followed her, closing the distance between them until he was standing directly behind her.

"Lord Hunt told me how he cradled your broken body, stood vigil at your bedside, night after night, praying openly for your health and recovery. I would wager that was not a man who lied about his affections. As for his lover, I think among the *ton*, illicit liaisons are the norm. But I also think the man I saw in the library will never go back to her.''

Abbey's back went rigid. ''How can you be so sure?'' she asked softly.

''Because I have it on good authority that Darfield would have given his own life for yours. He would have infused his own health into you if he could. Sam said 'He would have brought down the moon and doused the sun' if that's what it took to bring you back to life. He was by no means indifferent, Abbey. He was frantic at the thought of losing you. A man who feels that strongly about a woman does not need or want a lover. Little one, men can change. I did, and you can accept that.''

Abbey glanced uneasily over her shoulder at him.

''Forgive him, Abbey. Forgive him as you forgive me. He deserves it far more than I do, and I swear to you, he is more than worthy of your esteem.''

Abbey turned to him then and Galen took her into his arms, hugging her tightly. After a moment, he kissed the top of her head and released her.

''I have said what I came to say. I have permission to write, little one. I am off to the West Indies now, and I'll let you know if I get a post—a *legitimate* post.'' He smiled. With an affectionate chuck for her chin, Galen turned on his heel and left Abbey standing at the old stone wall.

As he swung up on his horse, he was amazed at the tremor in his hands. His crime was far, far worse than he had imagined. He, and he alone, had fundamentally shaken the foundation of trust between two people who truly loved each other. And for that, he would repent until his dying day.

# Chapter 22

Abbey remained at the ruins long after Galen left. It was all so confusing! For the last few weeks, she had been set upon by a sadness she could not quell. Something had died inside her, something she was not sure she wanted to resurrect. Something she was not sure she was capable of resurrecting.

It had been so hard. Michael seemed to be everywhere she was, albeit at a quiet distance. A part of her despised him, but another part loved him deeply. It was impossible not to love him. Try as she might, she was losing the battle to push her feelings for him down to the most remote corner of her soul. He had betrayed her and had refused to trust her when she needed him to trust her most. But on this cloudless day she could not suppress the nagging feeling that Galen was right. Michael had been hurt so many times before, why wouldn't he believe this to be another attempt to defraud or humiliate him?

"Oh, God." She sighed. The truth was that she *did* keep Galen from Michael. Perhaps the time had come for her to take responsibility for her part in what had happened.

\*    \*    \*

Michael was startled by her appearance in the dining room that evening. She was a vision in a velvet and chiffon gown of midnight blue, adorned with small crystal beads that fractured the light when she moved. Her dark mahogany hair was pulled back and hung in great, silken waves down her back. She looked as beautiful as he ever remembered.

"I'm glad you decided to join us. Would you like a drink?" he heard himself say. Abbey smiled demurely, unbalancing him. He did not expect a smile. No, that was about the last thing he expected.

"A vodka, please," she said softly. From across the room, Sam was staring at her over his Madeira and seemed as stunned as Michael felt. Michael inclined his head toward Anderson, who quietly poured the drink and handed it to him. His legs felt like wood as he walked toward her and handed her the glass.

"Thank you," she said shyly. She glanced up at him through her long lashes and blushed slightly. Michael was so unsettled by the change in her mien that he congratulated himself on having handed her the vodka without dropping it.

"Your walk seems to have done you good," he said, for lack of anything else.

She smiled her perfectly brilliant smile and Michael's stomach dropped to his toes. "It was really quite nice, my lord. I believe I have sorted everything out," she answered.

Michael swallowed; he had no idea what to make of that or her sudden serenity.

"I was just telling Michael that the *La Belle* is in port at Brighton. Her maiden voyage was far more successful than we hoped; she made record time to the Mediterranean and back," Sam remarked from across the room. "And another of our newest ships, the *St. Lucie,* is anchored at Portsmouth."

Abbey turned politely toward Sam and glided across the room, sitting daintily on the settee across from him. It was several moments before Michael was able to move to a seat near the hearth.

"I would very much like to see them," she remarked casually.

Michael's brows rose slightly as he looked at Sam. He could not help it; he was immediately suspicious. She wanted to see his ships? Did she want passage to America? To the continent? Anywhere but Blessing Park?

"Planning a voyage?" he asked with more sarcasm than he intended.

She turned a surprised smile to him. "Well, no. I would rather like to see one of the new designs. I have never seen one," she said, then delicately sipped her vodka.

Michael exchanged a wary glance with Sam; he was not convinced that she had not contrived some scheme to escape him, and the thought of it made his heart ache. He had known all along that if she never forgave him, if she despised him as much as it seemed, then naturally he would let her go.

Even if it killed him.

"If you want to go, I will take you," he blurted without thinking. He felt Sam's gaze on him, but he could not take his eyes from Abbey.

Her brows arched above her vivid violet eyes. "Are you planning a voyage?" she asked innocently.

Michael tossed his whiskey down his throat before answering. "Perhaps. I have not as yet decided."

Abbey looked at her drink. "If I were to sail now, I think I should very much like to see the Mediterranean again," she remarked.

Ah, here it was. She had a destination in mind, a destination that would take her far away from him. The Mediterranean was a good choice, he thought wryly. He could not hound her there, as he might be able to do if she chose the continent, or even America.

"What of Harry?" he asked, his mind racing ahead, wondering if she would leave any part of her behind. Abbey exchanged a puzzled look with Sam.

"I doubt the dog is suited for sailing." She smiled. Michael nodded knowingly. It did not surprise him. She did not want anything to remind her of him, not even her dog.

"Is there any other place to which you would like to sail?" he asked. He waited for her to request passage to America, to admit her true desire to leave him, when a commotion in the drive caught their attention.

Sam rose to his feet and went to one of windows that looked out over the long, circular drive. He smiled at Michael.

"Your wayward secretary has returned," he said, and placing his drink on a table, started for the door.

Michael groaned softly. Abbey stood, apparently intending to go after Sam. "Abbey, wait."

She glanced expectantly over her shoulder; Michael rose slowly, his gaze riveted on hers. He knew what she wanted, and he would not hold her against her will. He would even see her home. But she would not go without knowing that it would kill him to let her go, and he would never stop loving her.

"If you want to go to America, I will take you—"

A clamor in the foyer interrupted him. Puzzled, Abbey looked at the door.

"Where is she? Where is my niece?" a woman's voice bellowed. Abbey gasped and swung around, staring at Michael in disbelief.

"Aunt Nan?" she whispered incredibly.

"I believe Miss Victoria Taylor and Virginia, as well," he said with exasperation.

Astonished, Abbey continued to stare at him, then slowly, a brilliant smile spread across her face, wrinkling the corner of her eyes.

"Did you . . . ?"

"I invited them, yes, if that is what you mean."

"But how?"

"Sebastian and the *St. Lucie,*" he said, irritated at their untimely arrival and the fact that *they* could bring such a smile to her face.

"*Where is she?*" Nan bellowed again.

Abbey gleefully clasped her hands together and started for Michael. For a moment, he thought she would fling herself into his arms, but she stopped short of embracing him. The way she was looking at him, the trembling smile on her lips . . .

She moved as if she meant to touch him, and Michael instinctively began to reach for her, but Nan's voice rang through the foyer again.

"Thank you! Oh, Michael, *thank you*!" she cried, and pivoted, quickly leaving the room.

Frustrated and confused, Michael stood unmoving. Had he imagined the look in her eye? Had she wanted to touch him? A gay chorus emanated from the foyer as the Americans greeted Abbey. Shaking his head, Michael reluctantly went to meet his guests.

Bedlam greeted him in the foyer. Looking very drawn, Sebastian was trying to push his way through the bevy of women and servants. The woman Michael presumed to be Aunt Nan was hugging the life from Abbey. Nan, tall, slender, and handsome, her silver hair bound simply at her nape, was prattling about how worried she had been when she had learned of the unfortunate accident. One of the younger women was turning slowly in the middle of the marble-tiled foyer, staring in awe at the walls and ceiling. She was a very pretty young woman with dark hair and green eyes, and her hair was fashioned in the unusual style that Abbey favored. She wore a dark yellow traveling gown that made her skin glow.

The other young woman was as blond as her sister was dark. She, too, was wearing the same unusual hairstyle and a light-blue gown of a fashion like her sister. She was chattering at Sam about her trip. Michael caught Sam's eye and smiled when the young woman reported she had been sick four times, once over the railing in full view of the deckhands. Always the gentleman, Sam stood and listened with a polite smile.

"My lord, I must tell you we encountered the Havershams in Pemberheath. Aunt Nan," Sebastian said with weary sarcasm, "has invited them to dine this evening."

Michael smiled at Sebastian's harried expression. His secretary looked as if he might drop at any moment.

"I will instruct Jones to expect five guests for supper." He looked at his secretary, who, with the dust of the trip from Portsmouth on him, looked as tired as Michael had ever seen him. "I trust your voyage was uneventful?" he asked dryly.

Sebastian rolled his eyes heavenward. "I hope, my lord, that duty never calls me thus again," he said solemnly. "If I may, I would take my leave and find a much-needed bath." Michael nodded and watched Sebastian limp toward the marble staircase, an affliction, he noted, his secretary had not left England with.

"Is that him?" Nan demanded from the door. With an arm around Abbey's shoulder, she marched toward Michael, dragging her niece along. "Lord Darfield, I presume?" she asked, squinting over the rims of her dust-covered spectacles.

"At your service, madam," he said, bowing low.

"Then point me toward a stout ale, sir. Not only has the journey parched me right well, your man drives as if we were being chased by a pack of Indians! My, my, you are a handsome devil, aren't you? Prettier than your sketches, I'd say."

"My sketches?"

"Mama, he doesn't know about the sketches! Uncle had them made and sent to Abbey," the blond girl announced.

"You must be Miss Victoria," Michael said, and bowed again.

"Oh, no." She giggled. "I am *Virginia*."

"The modiste?"

She laughed lightly. "The milliner," she corrected with a pleased grin, and curtsied properly.

"*I* am Victoria," the other one said, and curtsied identically. "Oh, Abbey, he is much more handsome than we thought, isn't he?"

Still locked in her aunt's embrace, Abbey blushed furiously.

"I gather you were quite surprised when you saw my Abbey all grown up, weren't you, young man?" Nan demanded, her head cocked to one side as she appraised him.

"I was, indeed, madam."

"I predicted that you could not possibly have expected her

to turn out as well as she did, and naturally I was right. What about that ale? A woman could die of thirst in Britain!" Nan said, and, following Michael's gesture, began to pull Abbey along with her down the hall.

"Oh, Mama, did you ever imagine such finery? He must be worth *millions*, don't you think?"

"Really, Ginny, how vulgar. We'll ask Abbey later," Victoria chided her, and the two young women fell in behind Abbey and her aunt. For the first time, Michael noticed Jones hovering near the door with a stricken look on his face.

"Chin up, Jones. The Havershams will be along directly," Michael called to his stalwart butler. Jones could hardly nod as he stumbled toward the back of the house.

Sam was all smiles as he strolled to Michael's side. "I believe we have just seen what happens when four women are left to live alone without a man to temper them," he remarked.

"I doubt," Michael said dryly, "that God could temper those women."

The ladies were already in the drawing room, closely examining the furniture and fixtures, all chattering at once. Abbey was trying to explain a portrait, but Virginia was talking over her, swearing that the man in the portrait looked like a drawing of a Swedish prince she had once seen. Nan, with an ale in her hand, peered at a very large and very expensive crystal clock. Anderson was handing Virginia a Madeira, and Victoria announced her preference for a whiskey. At least, Michael thought, Abbey came by her peculiar habit honestly. A footman in the far corner of the room was as white as a ghost.

"All right, girls. There shall be plenty of time to examine the house. I want to hear all about Abbey's new life," Nan announced, and grabbing Abbey's hand, dragged her to the settee and forced her down with a determined push on her shoulder.

Virginia and Victoria immediately took a seat on either side of Abbey. Nan looked expectantly at her niece. "Well, then? Go on, dear."

"I—I hardly know where to start!" Abbey exclaimed.

"With your wedding!" Virginia all but shouted. "Was it a grand affair? How many people attended? Did you wear the gown Tori made?"

"Was it in a large church? You hardly mentioned it in your letters," Victoria added.

Sam joined Michael, who, with one arm propped on the mantel, was observing the scene with surprised amusement.

"Not precisely," Abbey began, obviously uncomfortable.

"I'm afraid I am to blame for a rather small wedding," Michael interjected. Abbey jerked her gaze to him, plainly fearing he would tell the truth. He smiled reassuringly.

"You see, Abbey came later than expected. I was due in Brighton—"

"Brighton? Oh, I've read all about Brighton," Virginia exclaimed, and was about to carry on when Aunt Nan slapped her on the thigh to silence her.

"I was due in Brighton, and I thought it highly improper for Abbey to remain under my roof without proper chaperone, so we married immediately."

Abbey smiled gratefully.

"Oh, how very *romantic*," Victoria sighed.

"You see, Abbey? I told you he'd be waiting for you. I knew he'd rush you right to the altar, didn't I say as much?" Nan said triumphantly.

"Yes, Aunt Nan." Abbey nodded, glancing nervously at Michael with a faint smile on her lips.

"And then?" Virginia asked.

"And then?"

"Your wedding trip! Where did you go, to London?"

Abbey gripped the lap of her gown in a gesture Michael had come to understand was an unconscious display of nerves. "Well, not at first. Why go to London when one has a home as lovely as Blessing Park?"

"Oh, you are quite right. When we came up the drive, I thought I'd died and gone to heaven, it was so grand. I would not want to leave it, either," Victoria declared with an emphatic nod.

"But you went to London, Sebastian said so. Is it marvelous? Ginny bought a magazine in Boston that said all the women in London wear flounced skirts. I made you three new gowns, and not *one* of them has a flounced skirt!" Victoria said with disgust.

"I do not care a thing about flounced skirts, Tori," Abbey assured her.

"Well, I know *you* don't. If left to your own devices, you'd be wearing an old muslin skirt everywhere you went! Trust me, it's all the rage, and no doubt everyone has already noticed your skirts aren't flounced, don't you think, Michael?" Victoria demanded.

Michael tried not to look too taken aback by the girl's outrageous address. "I wouldn't know, really. But I rather like the unique style of her gowns."

Victoria smiled very demurely and inclined her head toward Michael in gracious acceptance of his compliment.

"You are wearing a copy of the silver gown, aren't you?" Nan asked Abbey.

"Abbey made that herself," Michael said proudly. The four women turned startled glances to him before simultaneously shouting their laughter. The three young women fell back against the settee in a fit of hysterics, and Nan all but spilled her ale. Mystified, Michael raised a brow and looked at Sam, who seemed just as puzzled.

"Oh, no, my lord, I didn't make it. *Cook* made the gown." Abbey gasped through her laughter.

The image of Cook making the gown startled him. *"Cook?"*

"Oh, Lord Darfield." Virginia squealed, "You did not honestly think Abbey could sew a straight seam even if her very life depended upon it, did you?" The three young women broke into another gale of hysterical laughter.

"Apparently I was mistaken," he said very gallantly, and signaled for Anderson to pour him a whiskey. He hoped like hell Anderson had enough sense to make it a double.

"Aunt Nan, who is minding the farm while you are away?" Abbey asked when her laughter had subsided.

"Mr. Ramsey," Aunt Nan replied carelessly, and shifted her gaze to the windows.

"Mr. Ramsey? Don't tell me he has renewed his courtship?"

"*Renewed* it? Why, he's all but moved in!" Virginia exclaimed. Abbey's eyes sparkled brilliantly as she turned to her aunt, who, much to Michael's surprise, appeared to be blushing. He would have guessed little could bother that woman.

"Indeed? Why, Aunt Nan, I thought—"

"Whatever you thought, girl, need not be repeated here. Mr. Ramsey is a perfect gentleman, and he very kindly agreed to look after the farm, nothing more," Aunt Nan insisted, then glared at Virginia.

"But what of Mr. Douglas?" Abbey asked.

Virginia giggled gleefully. "Yes, Mama, what *about* Mr. Douglas?"

Michael glanced at Sam, who looked as if he were strangling on his whiskey. This conversation was not one he preferred to hear, and certainly not one proper women should be having in front of gentlemen. Not that it mattered. His perception of impropriety had been drastically altered since Abbey had come into his life. Nonetheless, Sam and the servants looked terribly uncomfortable.

"Ladies, you must want the opportunity to visit before supper. I had promised Lord Hunt a game of billiards, so if you will excuse us . . ." Michael said, and pushed away from the mantel. "We'll leave you to your visit." Sam needed no further encouragement and had almost made it to the door by the time Michael finished with a short, polite bow. The women acknowledged their departure with polite nods. Michael glanced at the two servants who remained behind and shrugged in a gesture of helplessness before closing the door behind him. Almost immediately, the women's laughter pealed in unison. Sam and Michael glanced at each other and, without a word, strode quickly down the hall and to the sanctity of the billiards room.

*    *    *

At nine o'clock the guests were seated for supper. Victoria
and Virginia argued over who would sit next to Abbey, with
Virginia finally winning. Once Victoria realized she was to be
seated next to Sam, her irritation with her sister was forgotten.
Nan sat in the first chair she came to, which happened to be at
the head of the table, where Michael customarily sat, and
remarked on the number of forks. Michael was happy to forgive that gaffe as he found himself seated directly across from
his wife. Lord and Lady Haversham, who had been at Blessing Park for about an hour, both wore silly, happy grins on the
their faces. It never ceased to amaze Michael how easily
amused they could be.

The Taylor women had changed into evening gowns, all
uniquely stunning and obviously designed and made by Victoria. All four women looked terribly appealing, and Michael
noticed that Sam seemed to think so, too. But none of the
Taylor women held a candle to Abbey, who, dressed in the
gown of midnight blue, was smiling and laughing as she had
not in a long time. As always, her light, tingling laughter was
infectious, and as the party settled about the table, they were
laughing gleefully at a remark Victoria had made.

The supper, a five-course meal complete with dressed Cornish game hens, wild barley soup, and marzipan, was a rau-
cous affair. When Virginia and Victoria were not arguing over
insignificant matters, they were peppering Abbey with questions, for which Lady Haversham happily supplied the answers. Nan was pestering Michael with questions about his
status and income, which Lady Haversham also happily answered. Michael and Sam exchanged numerous looks, Michael often rolling his eyes and Sam finding it difficult to
suppress his chuckles at the outrageous remarks that flew
around the table.

"My Abbey was positively beside herself when it was time
to come to England," Nan offered once Lady Haversham had
paused to catch her breath. "She was certain Michael
wouldn't find her suitable, or feared he had given his affec-

tions to another. But I told her he'd be waiting anxiously, and just see if I wasn't right!'' she exclaimed jubilantly to all.

''Oh, my, yes, he was quite taken with her, I'll promise you that. *Everyone* in Pemberheath was quite surprised that he had taken a wife, but one only had to look at his face to know how much he adored her!'' Lady Haversham heartily agreed.

From across the table, Michael caught Abbey's indulgent smile. Her sparkling eyes crinkled in the corners, and she looked at him with an expression that relayed her sympathy. A surge of warmth crept through Michael's limbs and to his face. Her worry was unnecessary. Her happiness was so important to him that he would have willingly endured any humiliation just to see her smile.

''I suppose your long wait did not seem so terribly long after all, did it?'' Nan demanded.

''He was not waiting, Aunt Nan.'' Abbey spoke truthfully.

''That isn't precisely so, Abbey. I wasn't waiting at Blessing Park all those years, true enough. But I never desired another woman as I desire you,'' he responded before she could continue.

Startled, Abbey laughed lightly. ''Please, you hardly recognized me.''

''You must admit, you had changed remarkably in those twelve years.''

''Had I indeed? I thought you quite the same.''

''Not the same at all. Before I had been fool enough to let you go.''

''Oooo, how very *lovely*!'' Virginia gushed. ''How fortunate you are, Abbey!''

A bit of color painted Abbey's cheeks, and she shyly cast her gaze to the Cornish hen on her plate. ''It is *he* who is the fortunate one, if you want my humble opinion,'' Nan said with a firm nod.

''I rather think *I* am the fortunate one, ladies. Where else in all of Britain could I dine with such lovely companions?'' Sam said with gallantry.

''Here, here,'' someone called, and everyone began chattering at once. As Lady Haversham and Aunt Nan exchanged observations, Victoria and Virginia turned their attention to Sam. Lord Haversham became enraptured with his hen, and Abbey and Michael, separated by the wide table, sat quietly, their gazes locked.

After supper, Abbey had to convince her aunt that it was quite proper for the ladies to retire while the men shared cigars and port. Nan declared she had never heard of anything so preposterous, and, disgruntled, complained loudly as she followed Abbey from the dining room. They ensconced themselves in Abbey's sitting room. Twice Michael ventured upstairs to reclaim them, and twice he listened to the excited chatter and laughter when they turned him away. It was not until Lord Haversham insisted that his wife accompany him home that one of the women emerged. Lady Haversham stood at the door of the sitting room extracting a promise that she would be allowed to call first thing in the morning. After Sam and Michael saw Lord Haversham drag Lady Haversham to the door, the two men retired.

Michael could not sleep. He paced his room restlessly after propping his door ajar so he could hear the occasional music coming from the room down the hall. Every so often he would hear Nan's authoritative voice rise above the others, inevitably followed by gales of laughter. In his mind, he ran through a dozen reasons to enter that female sanctuary, but dismissed them all as too contrived. He finally settled himself in front of the fire with a book, admitting to himself that he was not wanted in there. Abbey wanted to be with her aunt and cousins. She wanted to play for *them*. She wanted to laugh with *them*. His eyes scanned the page of the Latin text he was holding, but he comprehended nothing as despair settled over him. Her smiles, her laughter, her gift of music, they were all for her family. They were not for him. The hopefulness he had felt earlier had been just that—hope, nothing more.

*     *     *

He must have fallen asleep, because when he awoke, the hall was dark and no sound came from the sitting room. Stiff from sleeping in the chair, he stood up and stretched before glancing at the clock. It was two in the morning. He walked to the door with the intention of shutting it when he heard the muffled noise of quiet conversation. He ventured out in the hall; a thin shaft of light emanated from a crack in the door of Abbey's sitting room. He moved silently down the corridor. He instantly recognized the soft lilt of Abbey's voice, and the responding, decisive tones of her aunt's low voice. He paused just shy of the door, fully ashamed that he was eavesdropping, and trying to justify it to himself by pretending he intended to warn them of the late hour.

"But you don't understand, Nan. He was *never* waiting for me. He did not even know I existed," Abbey was patiently explaining.

"Posh! He didn't marry in all that time, did he? Think, Abbey. A very eligible man in his third decade, never married? Do you think there were not women enough from which to choose?"

"Of course, but—"

"But nothing. He was waiting for the right woman."

"Nan, a marquis does not wait for the right woman, certainly not one he remembers as a hellion. A marquis marries for gain. And then keeps a mistress."

"He was waiting for you! All right, maybe he didn't know it was you, precisely. Perhaps he truly didn't recall you. But as sure as I am sitting here, that man was waiting for the right woman, and the right woman was you, Abigail Carrington. Don't try and convince yourself otherwise. Whatever has gone between the two of you is past, and you are a fool if you look anywhere but forward. That man loves you, girl, and I'll tell you right now, he most definitely is *not* keeping a mistress on the side!"

"I don't know . . ."

"Do you love him?" Nan demanded.

Michael drew in his breath and closed his eyes when she

did not answer right away. "I have *always* loved him, Aunt. I always will."

Michael swallowed hard. Had he heard her right? Did she truly love him?

"There you have it," Nan was saying. "Now, I don't want to hear another word about returning to America, or how he didn't trust you, or any of that nonsense. He had good reason for what he did, and, besides, he loves you very much, and you love him. It's time to stop dwelling on the past."

There was another very long pause, broken by Abbey's light giggle. "By the by, in Britain it is considered quite rude to address a marquis by his given name."

"Indeed? Pray tell, how would the Redcoats have me address my dearest niece's husband?" Nan sniffed.

"His lordship. My lord. Lord Darfield." Abbey giggled again.

"Well. If I should ever have occasion to address Mr. High and Mighty Marquis in front of the King of England, then perhaps I shall consider it. Until then, he is family and his name is Michael!"

Michael heard nothing more than Abbey's light laugh as he turned and made his way back to his chambers. He could only pray Abbey had the good sense to listen to her aunt, whom he had just determined was a *very* wise woman.

# Chapter 23

In preparation for a walk the next morning, Victoria, Virginia, and Abbey appeared on the large circular drive, each wearing a simple skirt and blouse, and each sporting a ridiculous straw hat overburdened with silk flowers. Observing from the shadows of the entry, Sebastian glanced at Jones.

"I thought spring had come and gone," he remarked dryly.

Jones's expression did not change. "Apparently spring has descended anew and with a vengeance," he responded without moving his gaze from the three women.

"Here there! You!" A woman's voice, one that was becoming particularly familiar to the two men, rang from behind. Exchanging wary glances, the two loyal servants turned to see Nan standing in the middle of the tiled foyer with her feet spread apart and her fists stacked resolutely on her hips. She wore a similar hat to the girls and a healthy scowl.

"Madam?" Jones asked smoothly.

"Who is responsible for the menu here?"

" 'Tis I, madam," Jones said, bowing gallantly.

"Was it your idea of a jest?" she asked as she came toward him, squinting at him over the rims of her spectacles.

"I beg your pardon?"

"That . . . that *fish* you served for breakfast! Good God, man, who can break their fast with that?! We don't need any fancy foreign dishes in the morning, my good fellow. A caddie of toast, some fruit, and an egg or two will be quite sufficient!" she boomed.

Jones was expressionless. "As you wish, madam," he said, and stepped aside to let her pass.

"Scared us out of our wits, it did," she muttered as she brushed by them. Sebastian looked questioningly at Jones.

"Kippers," Jones said evenly.

"What of them?" Michael asked. Michael and Sam entered the foyer, pausing to accept their hats and gloves from two footmen standing there.

"Madam Nan does not care for kippers," Jones responded.

Michael chuckled. "Somehow, I am not surprised. Send a boy for our mounts, would you? We're to Pemberheath." Michael and Sam both accepted a riding crop from a footman and moved forward. The men stopped simultaneously at the door.

"Good God," Sam whispered.

"I do not believe it," Michael said softly at the exact same time as they stared out at the sea of hats.

"The milliner has struck with fury," Sam remarked.

"Pray she does not fashion men's hats," Michael agreed before stepping outside. "G'day ladies!" he called brightly.

The sound of his voice sent a shiver of delight up Abbey's spine, and she whirled about, smiling brightly. She was puzzled by the curious look on his face until she remembered the godawful hat she wore. The warmth of embarrassment crept into her cheeks as he approached her, and she shyly looked at the ground. Why, oh why, did Ginny have to bring her a new hat?

"Where are you going?" Victoria demanded, more of Sam than Michael.

"Pemberheath. We have some business to attend to," Sam replied. Abbey glanced up covertly. Michael was studying her hat, all right, with his head cocked to one side. His warm gaze slid from the contraption atop her head to her eyes.

"New hat?" he asked calmly, a smile playing at the corner of his eyes.

"Ginny," she said simply.

"I gathered as much," he said, then winked at her.

Abbey blushed furiously, mortified that his nearness was causing such a heat to build within her. He was standing so close that she could smell the spicy scent of his cologne. She stared at his broad chest, impeccably covered by the white lawn shirt and ruby-red waistcoat trimmed in gold. His black hair brushed the top of his collar, and a black neckcloth, the same shade as his hair, contrasted sharply with the white collar. She thought, rather giddily, that he looked quite tanned and healthy.

She was so engrossed with her husband and the slow warmth of desire spreading through her that she did not notice the horses being brought around. When Samson snorted directly behind her, she jumped and let out a little shriek that jerked every head toward her. She tried to get away from the horse, stumbling into Michael. He caught her by the arm, holding her close to his chest. With a look of bafflement, he glanced down at her, then to the horse. A light dawned in his eyes, and he pulled her back a few steps, away from the horse.

"What on earth is the matter?" Nan all but shouted.

"N-nothing. The horse startled me, that's all."

Nan's eyes narrowed skeptically, then she shrugged and turned back to Sam, who was now surrounded by a sea of silk flowers, bobbing excitedly about him like little boats.

"If there is anything you need while I am away, you need only ask Sebastian," Michael was saying to her as Abbey tried to calm the tremor in her hand.

"We shall be fine, thank you," she murmured.

"We should return by nightfall," he continued.

"We are to dine with the Havershams tonight," she said, moving to put him between her and the huge horse. "Lord Haversham is away and Lady Haversham is having a ladies' evening. I hope you don't mind."

"Not at all. Whatever you want, whatever makes you happy, Abbey, I want you to have," he said softly.

She dragged her gaze from the horse to him. His gray eyes were sparkling as they slowly perused her face, lingering on her lips. Abbey's blush only intensified, and she nervously stepped backward.

"What would make me happy," she whispered softly, "is a different hat." Michael grinned broadly, his teeth glistening against his lips. Good God, her knees were growing weak as they always did when he looked at her like that. She could not tear her eyes away from him while a million questions popped into mind. Was it possible that the emptiness she had felt could be filled again? Could she *really* leave him and return to America? Could she somehow put the horrid events of London behind her?

"Abbey!" Victoria said emphatically. She jerked her head around to her cousin who had managed to come stand at her elbow without Abbey's noticing. "Didn't you hear me? Sam said he would teach us to ride!"

"Splendid," Abbey murmured, unable to keep her gaze from slipping to Michael again, who was still smiling at her, melting her with the intensity of his gaze.

"Not today, as they are to Pemberheath. But on the morrow. He says there is a fine gray mare, Desdemona is her name, and he will teach us all to ride . . ."

Victoria stopped and frowned at Abbey when she began to laugh. Giddiness suddenly came bubbling forth at the mere mention of Desdemona, and Abbey could not stop her laughter. Michael watched her with a gleam in his eye, chuckling low along with her. The more she laughed, the more she found it impossible to stop.

"Aye, Desdemona is a *fine* horse, indeed! How terribly thoughtful of you, Sam!" she managed, then fell into another fit of laughter.

Sam smiled and tipped his hat while the cousins looked at each other in confusion. "I thought you'd approve. Darfield, if we are to make it Pemberheath before nightfall—"

"Yes, yes, I'm coming." He surprised Abbey by grasping

her hand and bringing it to his mouth. His lips barely brushed her skin, but the effect on her senses was explosive. The laughter abruptly died as a furious blush heated Abbey's face. He swung easily on to his horse and looked down at her as if he wanted to say something. Finally he spurred his horse forward, but not before bestowing a look on her that made her pulse race madly.

Getting the Taylor women dressed for the evening was an affair in and of itself. Abbey thought Sarah looked exhausted, and Molly completely frazzled. Tori and Ginny each tried on several gowns before deciding what they would wear. Abbey's spacious bedchamber was strewn with brightly colored gowns and petticoats. Even Nan insisted on having her hair dressed. It was painfully obvious that it was a rare occurrence for her, because she wailed at every stroke of the brush on her hair and complained that the pins stabbed her scalp.

Abbey dressed herself. Sarah and Molly were too preoccupied with the demands of her house guests, which was fine by her. She had never cared much for the assistance of a maid, but for the months she had been in England, it seemed impossible to escape that single protocol.

She was sitting on the settee leafing through a magazine Ginny had brought from Boston when she heard the rap on the door. She rose, motioning Sarah to continue what she was doing, and giggled at the dozen hair pins Sarah held in her mouth as she fought Ginny's thick blond tresses.

A servant bowed deeply when Abbey swung the door open. "The master requests an audience in the formal study, milady."

Abbey's pulse immediately began to race. "When?"

"At once, if you please, milady."

"Tell Lord Darfield I shall be there directly." Abbey shut the door and looked back at the expectant faces.

"You look startled! Is something wrong?" Nan demanded.

"Oh, no, of course not," Abbey said hurriedly, and quickly

moved to the far side of the room. "I must fetch my slippers," she called, and slipped into the closet.

"What did that man say?" Nan called.

"Nothing, Aunt. I am wanted in the study, that's all," she called back.

In truth, his summons made her anxious. Could he be displeased with her? She shook her head as she searched for slippers. How ridiculous; what on earth should he have to be displeased about? Just because the last few times he had summoned her had been to accuse her of wrongdoing or to explain his own was no reason to overreact. Her family had been on their best behavior. Galen was gone. Abbey found the light-blue slippers she was looking for and pulled them on her feet. She was being absurd. He probably wanted to tell her he was leaving on business, or that they were temporarily out of ale, or some such nonsense. It was no more than that.

She smiled as she exited the closet and told the women she would meet them in the foyer when they were ready. Before Nan could say anything, Abbey was out the door.

When she reached the door of the study, she rapped lightly and heard him bid her enter. Very gingerly she opened the door and peeked around it. Michael was leaning against his booted foot propped upon a window seat. He looked as if he had just returned from Pemberheath; he had discarded the formal dress and wore his shirt opened halfway to his waist. His tousled hair fell artlessly across his open collar. He looked wonderfully virile.

"You wanted to see me?" she asked timidly.

"I did. Please come in."

Abbey tentatively crossed the threshold. Why in God's name was she so nervous? "Is something wrong?"

Michael lifted a brow. "Wrong? No."

Abbey clasped her hands behind her back and stood, feeling terribly self-conscious under his searching gaze. She noticed she was rocking back and forth on her feet and made herself stop.

"How was your day?" Michael asked casually, dropping his foot to the floor.

"Very well, my lord."

Michael crossed slowly to the sideboard and poured a glass of water. "Won't you have a seat?"

Abbey's eyes flicked about the room, expecting to discover the reason for his invitation lying in the open somewhere.

"Would you prefer to stand?" he asked again, and she realized she had not moved.

"You sent for me?" she said again, suddenly desperate to know what he wanted.

"You seem preoccupied," he remarked. Abbey's hands shifted to the front of her gown, where she clasped them tightly in dreaded anticipation.

"I apologize. It's just that Aunt Nan and the girls . . ."

"I see. Your mind is on your guests."

What did he mean by that? "Yes, I suppose it is."

His gray eyes slid from the water in his hand to her, and he seemed to hesitate for a moment. "I had not meant to detain you from your guests," he said coolly. Abbey did not respond. He seemed mildly irritated when she did not. "I suppose there is no need to ask if you would like a drink," he remarked. "Naturally," he added sardonically when Abbey shook her head. He set his glass down and took several steps until he stood in the middle of the room. The late-afternoon sun coming in the windows behind him framed him in a soft light. With his weight on one hip and his arms folded across his chest, he frowned at Abbey. She thought he looked quite imposing.

He thought she was acting peculiar.

"I intended only to inquire as to your day, Abbey. Nothing more," he said in a clipped tone.

Abbey took an involuntary step backward. "It was uneventful, my lord," she said softly. Why in heaven was she acting so reticent? She almost seemed afraid of him.

"My name," he said with more irritation than he would have liked, "is Michael. Stop addressing me as your lord." He immediately held up his hand in regret. "I apologize. I hope your evening with the Havershams is entertaining." He turned away from her. Obviously he had been foolishly encouraged by her demeanor last night and this morning. Her feelings for him had not changed, and the disappointment was overwhelming.

"Thank you," Abbey said behind him, and reached for the door. She opened it but could not resist a look over her shoulder. He had moved to the windows and was staring straight ahead, intent on something beyond her view.

Abbey slipped quietly from the room and hurried down the corridor. What in the bloody hell was the matter with her? He had called her to politely inquire as to her day! So why did she feel so nervous? What was she so afraid of? Disgusted with herself, she flew up the marble stairs and into her private study. Shutting the door behind her, she paced in front of the hearth.

She knew very well why she was afraid—she had thought of little else that day. She was afraid of being hurt again. She had somehow reconciled the hideous events of London, but she could not overcome the fear of something like that happening again. The only way to protect herself was to keep a respectable distance. Her fear translated into trepidation at the thought of being alone with him. She knew instinctively she would not be able to resist and would be helpless to stop from falling madly in love with him all over again. And what would happen if he rejected her again? She could not be able to bear it a second time, she was certain of that.


Supper with Lady Haversham was a delight to the Taylor women, who regaled each other with increasingly outlandish stories. Abbey picked at her food amid the feminine mayhem and forced herself to laugh or respond at appropriate moments. All evening she had been haunted by an image of Michael, standing at the window of the study, looking out over the garden. The more she had thought of him, the more she had realized how foolish she had been these last several weeks. What an idiot she could be at times. And unforgiving. And petulant. She loved him dearly, had always loved him, would forever love him. And he loved her. She could *feel* it.

The evening with Lady Haversham was interminable. When at last they called for the coach, Abbey was the first one inside, settling against the squabs and willing the coach to go faster. Her cousins chattered incessantly during the half-hour ride home, but Abbey was oblivious. So was Nan. She stared at Abbey the whole way, with a very somber look on her face.

Her cousins and aunt must have sensed her anxiety, for all three insisted on retiring the moment they reached Blessing Park. Abbey was grateful when her aunt ushered the girls up the stairs and down the guest corridor. Before she left, she leaned over and whispered in Abbey's ear. *"Go forward and do not look back."* Abbey gave her a baffled look, but she knew very well what her aunt meant by that.

She watched the women climb the stairs and disappear around a corner. She then walked down the long corridor of the ground floor looking for any sign of life. Except for the footman who greeted them on their return, the house was dark and quiet.

Surely Michael had long since retired. She would have to wait until the morrow to see him, and even then, what would she say? She wanted to beg him to forget the past. She wanted to tell him she loved him and had always loved him. She wanted to feel his arms around her, his lips against her skin, his weight on her in bed. Without realizing it, she found herself standing outside Michael's room. A thin ray of light spilled into the corridor from his door, which was slightly ajar.

She stopped, staring at the door. Was he awake? Should she knock? What would she say? Maybe he had fallen asleep without realizing the door was open. Maybe Damon was in there with him. She could not stop herself from moving silently toward the door, the only sound being the faint rustle of her skirts. She grasped the brass door knob and looked down at her white knuckles. *Knock, you idiot!* she commanded herself, but her hand, reacting to some other set of commands, slowly pushed the door open.

A fire was crackling at the hearth. A book lay open on a leather chair pulled directly in front of the fire. There was no sign that anyone was about. She breathed a sigh of relief; Michael was not even inside. With the tip of her toe, she nudged the door a little farther. Her curiosity and her desire to be near him were causing her to be outrageously nosy. She shoved herself in behind the partially opened door. This room, she thought longingly, craning her neck to see past the door. How many blissful nights had she spent here? How many nights had she drifted off to sleep with his arms wrapped protectively around her? How many mornings had she watched him shave, and how many times had he come to stand beside the bed and smile down at her?

Her toe nudged the door a little farther, and it creaked softly on its hinges. She stopped and waited but did not hear a sound.

He was not within.

Abbey boldly pushed the door open and stepped inside, smiling as she looked up at the green ceiling with its medallions and ornate moldings. Her eyes fell to the Aubusson carpet, and she impulsively kicked off her slippers. She crossed slowly to his wardrobe and ran her fingers across the smooth mahogany. She pulled one door open and reached for a handful of dozens of neckcloths that hung there. She brought them to her face, relishing the feel of the cloth against her skin and inhaling his masculine scent. After a long moment, she dropped them and watched them swing gently against the peg before closing the door.

She moved to the basin and lightly fingered his brush and comb, then picked up his razor and ran a finger down the cold blade. She could picture him now, bare to the waist, his face lathered as he scraped at his beard, the muscles in his chest and stomach moving softly with his breath. She smiled as she put the razor down and walked toward the bed. She ran her hand along the rich damask bed hangings as she glided to the foot of the bed and grasped one of the tall, mahogany posts.

Her soft shriek startled her more than him. Michael stood next to the velvet drapes in the dark recess of the window, wearing a black velvet dressing gown. In the dimly lit room, he was barely distinguishable from the draperies. His bare feet were braced apart, his hands clasped behind his back, and he was watching her intently.

"Dear God! What are you doing?" Abbey gasped, more mortified than frightened by the unexpected sight of him.

He did not answer for a long moment. "Waiting for you," he said hoarsely.

Abbey's hand immediately flew to her throat. "I'm . . . I'm sorry, I didn't realize you were expecting us—"

"No. Waiting for *you*, Abbey. Waiting every night for you to come through that door."

"Waiting?" she echoed breathlessly.

He nodded, taking a step toward her, his hands swinging down to his sides. "Waiting."

"For me?" she whispered weakly, mesmerized by the passion smoldering in his gray eyes.

"Every minute, every hour." He took another step; he was standing directly before her, his hands clenched at his sides as if he sought to restrain himself. "Waiting for you to understand how much I love you," he whispered, then cautiously reached up and stroked her burning cheek with his knuckles.

"Michael, you must know—"

"I must know that you love me, too."

Abbey's breath caught in her throat as his hand moved to her neck and gently pulled her forward. His other hand swept across her waist and to the small of her back. "Do you love me, Abbey?" he whispered as his mouth descended to hers.

Desire unfolded within her, and she hungrily accepted his probing kiss. Her arms slipped around his neck, pulling him toward her.

He lifted his head. "Do you love me?" he whispered again. A powerful rush of emotion came over her.

"I have always loved you"—she gasped—"and I always will. But I'm afraid . . ."

"No," he said hoarsely. "No, darling, don't be afraid. I will never hurt you again, I swear it on my life. I love you, Abbey, no other but you. There will never be another woman for me, no mistress, no one. Only you. Only my darling Abbey."

She gasped softly. There was such emotion in his voice, and God, how she wanted to believe it. He pulled her to him, pressing his hard body against every inch of hers, and claimed her mouth again. His hands slid down her back, releasing the tiny buttons as they moved. The draft of air on her back suddenly awakened her senses, and she pushed back.

"Michael, listen to me . . ." she whispered against his chest.

He moaned very low in his throat and pulled a pin from her hair. A long, thick tress floated down between them. He pulled another pin free.

"You must listen. I want to put it all behind us, truly I do. I want to look forward . . ." He began to nuzzle her neck, muttering his agreement against her flushed skin. She closed her eyes and willed herself to speak.

"But I am afraid, so afraid it will happen again," she insisted.

He slowly dragged himself away from her neck. "Abbey. I love you. I need you. I do not ever want you from my side. I do not ever want to be from your side. I promise you I will be faithful, in all respects. There is nothing that will ever change that." His voice was as intent as his expression. Abbey's heart climbed to her throat.

"I love you, darling," he said again, his sweet breath brushing her face.

Unbelieving, Abbey slowly lifted her eyes. He was smiling down at her with such adoration that tears welled in her eyes. She did not deserve this.

"What about the baby?" she said, barely above a whisper.

"It was an unfortunate, terrible tragedy. But it wasn't your fault," he said tenderly as he pulled another pin from her hair and caught the falling tress.

"What if—"

"I don't care," he said, anticipating her question. "It's you I want, don't you understand that?" He cupped her face and tilted it upward. "If we are blessed with children, then so be it, and I will cherish each one of them as I cherish you. If we are not, it matters little, because I will still have you. *You* are what's important. *You* are what makes me happy. *You* are the air that I breathe," he whispered, and pressed his lips to her forehead.

Abbey was not aware that she gripped the lapels of his dressing gown, or that she buried her face against the soft down of his chest. She was only aware that hot tears stung her eyes as the depth of his love settled around her. He said again in a voice thick with emotion, "I love you, Abbey, more than life. God, I need you so."

"Oh, Michael!" she breathed against his chest.

He swung her up in his arms, marched to the door and slammed it shut with his foot, then turned and strode to his bed. He set her on her feet and pulled the gown from her shoulders, heatedly caressing her as he did. He stroked her breasts through the thin cotton chemise she wore, rubbing the pads of his thumbs across her nipples, which rose instantly to his touch.

"I have missed you so," she whispered as he cupped her breast.

He smiled as his hands found the straps of her chemise and pushed it to her waist. It slid from there to the floor, pooling at her feet. "I've missed you, too, sweetheart. God, how I have missed you," he said thickly, and lowered her onto the bed. He removed her stockings then stood back to admire her naked body for a moment before stripping off his dressing gown. His manhood, pulsing with desire, sprang forward as he lowered himself onto her.

"Promise me you will never leave me," he demanded. His hands had started their exploration of her, fluttering quickly between her thighs.

"Never," she whispered.

"Never," he echoed, then crushed his mouth to hers.

His kiss was intoxicating; everything ceased to exist except his taste, his scent, the feel of his body straining against hers. Abbey moaned as his fingers slipped inside her. His mouth slanted over hers, his tongue delving into every crevice. Her hands flitted across the soft down that lightly covered his chest and found his nipples. He groaned; his kiss became more urgent. When he lowered his head to her breasts, Abbey arched, bringing herself closer to him. He suckled one, then the other, and, with his tongue, began to paint a moist path down her belly. He paused to kiss the scar she bore, which was slowly beginning to fade, and then moved to the dark curls at the apex of her thighs.

*"Michael,"* she breathed. She heard his low chuckle before his tongue darted between her warm, soft folds. She lifted up off the bed; the pleasure he evoked was excruciating, and she writhed uncontrollably beneath him. He cupped her buttocks in his strong hands and laved her slowly, tantalizing her with each stroke. Abbey was lost on a sea of passion. Her body screamed for release; her hands curled in the dark mane on his head, urging him, pleading with him to end the torture. Michael was unrelenting in his exploration of her body, and when he felt her begin to tighten with anticipation of release, the stroking of his tongue intensified, bringing her to the brink.

Abbey imploded and was carried away by pure ecstasy. Wave after wave of sweet convulsion coursed through her. She arched her back, giving into it, rejoicing in it. He lifted her and entered her with a savage thrust, and Abbey gasped in complete exhilaration.

"My God . . . Abbey, my love . . ." he whispered as he braced himself above her and began to move inside her. Her hands found his back, her legs wrapped around his hips. She pressed herself against him, letting her head fall backward, exposing the creamy white skin of her throat to him. As his strokes intensified, she felt warm tears trace a path from the corner of her eyes to her ears.

"I love you, Michael," she whispered intently as his strokes lengthened. A deep, low groan emanated from somewhere above her, and, with a final, powerful thrust, she felt his seed spill deep within her. Michael shuddered violently with release before sinking on top of her and burying his face in her neck.

"Good God, how I have longed for you," he whispered, kissing her neck and the path of her tears.

Abbey choked on a sob. Moved by the intensity of their lovemaking and the beating of his heart against hers, the emptiness she had felt for so many weeks was gone. That place in her was suddenly filled and overflowing with love and desire for her husband.

"Don't cry, sweetheart," Michael whispered, coming up on an elbow and gently wiped the tears from her cheeks.

"I'm so . . . sorry, I'm so very sorry!"

"No, darling, I am the one who is sorry." Michael began to pull away from her.

"No! No, no, please stay," she whispered.

He smiled down on her, then wrapped his arms around her and rolled to his side. "I was foolish, sweetheart . . . I should never have put you in the situation I did. You did nothing wrong, nothing at all."

"But I did, Michael! You were right. I wasn't completely truthful in the beginning . . ."

"Hush . . . It's all history now. It's over. What's important is I have you here with me now and your solemn promise you'll never leave me, isn't that so?"

Abbey nodded slowly. He was too good to her, better than she deserved. The tears would not stop.

"Don't brood on the past. What do you say? We shall live at Blessing Park and take periodic voyages to America, so your cousins can see our children and make outlandish hats for them. We shall grow old together, watching our children mature and have children of their own. *That's* what you shall brood upon, all right?"

Abbey wrapped a lock of his hair around her finger. "And if there are no children?" she whispered.

"Then we shall grow old together, delighting in each other, and, of course, the Havershams. Your cousin will make new hats for you, and I will compliment each and every one. And we will take voyages around the world, and you, my sweet, will play for me at night. You don't know how I've missed your music."

Abbey pushed closer into his chest, truly healed by his

powerful embrace and tender words. "I would ask one thing," she whispered.

He made a sound in his throat as her tongue darted across the hardened nub of his nipple; she felt his member lurch inside her.

"Anything, my love," he said, very softly.

"I shall play for you at night, but then you must promise to play for me, too."

He chuckled, pulling her bottom lip between his teeth as her hand found the juncture of their bodies. "As God is my witness, you will never want for love," he said as he rolled onto his back. She straddled him now and began to move slowly, seductively. He cupped her breasts.

"Indeed? What if I am heavy with child? Fat?" She giggled.

"I don't care, I shall wait until you have borne your children."

"If I smell of dogs and sheep? Shall you wait for me then?" she teased.

Michael did not answer immediately as his attention was with her seductive movement. Above him, Abbey giggled. Michael looked up. She was radiant. *His wife.* His beautiful wife was back where she belonged. He pressed the palm of his hand against her cheek, and she leaned into it, her soft violet eyes glowing with love.

"I shall always wait for you, my love," he whispered.

Abbey sighed contentedly and lowered herself to her husband.

# Epilogue

## TWELVE YEARS LATER

Michael scrawled his signature across a bank draft Sebastian handed him. A sudden silence caused him to lift his head; the quill pen stilled on the paper. The music had stopped. He handed a sheaf of papers to Sebastian and turned to greet the young boy who burst through the French doors and onto the terrace.

"Papa, Papa!" the boy cried as he threw himself into his father's waiting arms.

"Aidan, how is my boy?" Michael asked cheerfully as he tousled the boy's hair and hugged him tightly before putting him on his feet. "Have you finished your music lesson?"

The boy nodded vigorously. "Mama said I may play with an orchestra someday!" he announced proudly. Michael doubted his young son knew what an orchestra was.

"That you will, son." In truth, all three of his children showed the promise of rare talent. He no longer had to imagine an orchestra when Abbey played. With Alaina on the pianoforte and Alexa on the violin, the three women of his family played sweet trios. Aidan, his youngest child, was showing even more promise than his sisters on the strings. Michael sat down and gathered the boy on his lap.

"Aunt Tori and Uncle Sam are coming for supper, did you know?" he asked. The little boy frowned.

"She has a *baby,* Papa, and it cries all the time. Mama said that's what babies do, but I don't remember *ever* crying like that!" he averred, and folded his arms across his chest and nodded for emphasis.

Michael and Sebastian laughed.

"I assure you, my little prince, you also cried," Michael told him.

Aidan wrinkled his nose and tilted his head as he looked up at his father. "I did?" he asked incredulously.

"You did indeed," Michael said again, then leaned forward and whispered, "But not as often as Alexa, and certainly not as loudly as Alaina."

"No one could *ever* cry as loud as Alaina," the boy said, rolling his eyes.

As if on cue, two young girls came bounding through the French doors.

"Papa!" they cried in unison. Michael smiled warmly at his two young daughters. Alexa, with her hair the color of coal and crystal-blue eyes, resembled him. Alaina had her mother's mahogany hair and violet eyes. Aidan, the youngest, was a peculiar mix of them both, with his father's black hair and his mother's violet eyes. Michael thought the three were the most handsome children he had ever seen and thought himself rather objective in his assessment. Of course, when he had mentioned that to Sam, his good friend had differed, and pointed to his own son and new daughter as proof that he and Tori had produced the more handsome offspring.

"What are you doing, Papa?" Alaina asked as she poked through some papers he had left on the wrought-iron table.

"I am waiting for your mother, my love. Kindly keep your hands to yourself."

The girl immediately pulled back and turned her lovely face to him. "Where is she?" she asked.

"She has gone to Pemberheath, pet."

"You are *forever* waiting on Mama! Every time she goes away, you say the same thing," Alexa declared, fingering his neckcloth.

"Yes, Papa, why don't you make her stay? Then you won't have to wait so terribly long!" Alaina added. The three children turned expectant faces up to him.

"Because, my dear ones, if your mama never left, I would never wait for her."

"But why do you want to wait for her all the time?" Alexa demanded.

Michael smiled and caressed his daughter's cheek. "If I don't wait, sweetheart, I may well forget *why* I wait for her."

"Why do you wait, Papa?" Aidan asked.

"Because I love your mama very much. Now go and find your nanny. Your aunt and uncle shall be here soon." The three children scampered off, knocking into one another as they tried to crowd through the door at the same time.

Sebastian rose. "I think I should assess the damage to the study," he remarked dryly, and followed the children inside. Michael turned back to retrieve some papers he had forgotten, and caught a glimpse of Abbey walking with Withers through the garden. Obviously, the old gardener had waylaid her as she came in the drive to have her look at his newest accomplishment. Abbey, now thirty-four years of age, was more beautiful than ever. He was beginning to see a few gray hairs in her mahogany tresses, and the crinkles around her eyes were a bit more pronounced, but she had grown lovelier with each passing year. With the birth of their first child, Alexa, she had gained an appealing maturity.

Abbey saw him standing on the terrace and waved, her brilliant smile still capable of sending a quiet shiver down his spine. Lord, how his life had been blessed. He wished he could say he had earned it through years of waiting or some good deed. But in truth, it had all fallen on him unexpectedly, like the old stones of the ruins that tumbled to the earth. One cold day, when he was not really looking, she had tumbled into his life and into his heart.

Abbey was climbing the stairs now, and when she reached

the terrace, she walked straight into his open arms, and kissed him lightly. "What are you doing out here?" she asked.

"Waiting for you, sweetheart."

Abbey laughed, her violet eyes sparkling, and linked her arm through his. "Wait no more, darling. I am here."

## About the Author

JULIA LONDON is the *New York Times* and *USA Today* bestselling author of more than a dozen historical romance novels, including the acclaimed Desperate Debutantes series, the Lockhart Family Highland trilogy (for which she was twice the finalist for the prestigious RITA award for excellence in romantic fiction), and The Rogues of Regent Street series, including *The Dangerous Gentleman, The Ruthless Charmer, The Beautiful Stranger,* and *The Secret Lover*. You may write Julia at P.O. Box 228, Georgetown, Texas, 78627, or at julia@julialondon.com. For news and updates, please visit her website at www.julialondon.com.